Highly Unsuitable Girl

Also by Carolyn McCrae

The Iniquities Trilogy:
The Last Dance
(Winner 2007 David St Thomas Prize for Fiction)
Walking Alone
Runaways

All published by Troubador Publishing Ltd.

Highly Unsuitable Girl

Carolyn McCrae

Copyright © 2012 Carolyn McCrae

The moral right of the author has been asserted.

Apart from any fair dealing for the purposes of research or private study, or criticism or review, as permitted under the Copyright, Designs and Patents Act 1988, this publication may only be reproduced, stored or transmitted, in any form or by any means, with the prior permission in writing of the publishers, or in the case of reprographic reproduction in accordance with the terms of licences issued by the Copyright Licensing Agency. Enquiries concerning reproduction outside those terms should be sent to the publishers.

Matador
9 Priory Business Park,
Wistow Road, Kibworth Beauchamp,
Leicestershire. LE8 0RX
Tel: (+44) 116 279 2299
Fax: (+44) 116 279 2277
Email: books@troubador.co.uk
Web: www.troubador.co.uk/matador

ISBN 978 1780880 662

British Library Cataloguing in Publication Data.
A catalogue record for this book is available from the British Library.

Typeset in 11pt Minion Pro by Troubador Publishing Ltd, Leicester, UK
Printed and bound in the UK by TJ International, Padstow, Cornwall

Matador is an imprint of Troubador Publishing Ltd

For my husband Colin.
Yet again he has spent months living with different people he does not yet know.
Their lives would have been very different without his insights.

Also for our good friend, The Lodger, because it would be unfair to leave him out.

Thanks are due to Mrs Cath Hedley of The Bradford Arms Hotel, Llanymynech for finding the time to read and encourage.

Chapter 1: Adolescence

Merseyside, August 1968

Anya stared at the pattern of dark circles forming on the pale blue quilt that had been her bedcover for as long as she could remember.

The steady flow of teardrops was slowing and her mind was beginning to focus on the interlocking patterns of damp dark blue. When she cried, which was often, she made no sound, she didn't sob to get attention or sympathy or to be consoled. She had known from a very young age that that would be a waste of energy as her mother was rarely in the house to hear and even if she had been around she wouldn't have cared less. In her eighteen years Anya had never cried to gain sympathy or attention.

As she lay sobbing on her bed she tried not to hear the noises coming from her mother's bedroom. She was used to the men. Sometimes they stayed for only a few hours, sometimes a few weeks, but sooner or later they would leave and there would be a few days of quiet before another arrived. Some never spoke to Anya but others were kind, helping her with the washing up or, when she was younger, slipping her a few pennies to spend on sweets. She may not have known their names but she knew what they did with her mother as the walls of the two-up two-down terraced house were very thin.

Before she had given in to those tears that had given her no comfort, Anya had taken the key from the chain around her neck and unlocked the tin trunk that she kept under her bed. It was half filled with her multi-coloured diaries, exercise books acquired over several years from the school stationery cupboard all carefully labelled and stored in strict chronological order.

Almost every day since she was 10 years old Anya would sit up in her bed, her radio tuned to Radio Luxembourg or, more recently, Radio Caroline, to write in her diary. Sometimes she just described, without comment, what she had done hour by hour through the day, but frequently she would try to explain what she was feeling. For the last two years she had had a thesaurus by her bed so she could find the right words. Instead of repeating 'lonely' she tried 'forlorn', 'friendless' 'abandoned' 'isolated' 'desolate'. She found it helped to locate exactly the right word.

There were times when she found some consolation in knowing she was clever. She hoped that in thinking intelligent thoughts she could separate herself from her mother and one day have a different life.

If anyone had known she kept the diaries, and had asked her why she kept them so assiduously, she would have said that she had no one else to talk to but herself. Had she had any friends they might have told her that much of what she was feeling was perfectly normal for a girl of her age. Had she had a mother who cared she might have been told that she would grow out of it and that, in time, she might even look back on her childhood as the happiest years of her life.

As she gazed at the fading blotches on the quilt she knew the black feeling would sweep over her and the tears would come again. But they were gone for now so she wiped her eyes fiercely with the back of her hand and returned to her diaries.

Picking out the next empty page of the most recent volume she wrote, slowly and neatly, *Relief.* She thought that perhaps there was an element of that now she had received her exam results, they had been far better than she had expected. It had seemed important to get better results than all those girls, like Henrietta Hodge, who thought they had more right to be at that school than she had; those girls who had clustered together in classes and in the playground, ignoring her. For seven years they had thought they were better than she was and she had beaten them all. She wondered whether she should write *Satisfaction* but she decided against it and instead wrote *Fear.*

She hated the life she led but at least it was familiar. Now her schooldays were over she would have to cope with new places, new people and new routines. She knew she couldn't face it with the same confidence and self-assurance as Henrietta who had a mother who cared and, most importantly, a father.

Confusion was the next word Anya wrote. For as long as she could remember there had been two Anya Caves and she would soon have to make some kind of decision as to which one she was going to be. She bit the end of her pen before adding the word *Loneliness*. She looked at the words she had written trying to make some sense of her feelings.

As she wiped her eyes she knew anyone seeing her tears would have had little sympathy for her. They would have said that she had no reason to feel so sorry for herself. They would have said that, ten days after her 18th birthday, Anya had her whole life ahead of her; she had prospects as good as many and better than most and they would have concluded that the little madam should think herself lucky. Anya would have stuck two fingers in their direction and said 'What the fuck do you know?'

She began to write the questions that she couldn't answer. *Who was my dad? What happened to him? Why don't I have any family other than Mum?* It was several minutes before she closed the book, placing it carefully back in its correct order.

Picking another out at random she opened it in the middle pages and read her thoughts of two years before.

> *Tuesday 17th May, 1966*
>
> *Bloody O Levels seem to go on for ever. I wonder why I bother. I suppose so I'll do better than that spiteful cow bloody Henrietta bloody Hodge. That'd really tear her up, she thinks she's so bloody superior all the time. She's done her best to show me up ever since that first day. Everyone has to know what bloody Henrietta thinks about everything and how much she knows about everything and what her mummy and daddy are buying her for her birthday. WHO BLOODY CARES? Mum doesn't even know I've got exams never mind what sort and*

> how many and what subjects. I can't remember when she last said anything to me other than 'be a good kid and piss off' or 'here, take this and go buy me some cigs' or 'get your effing face out of that book and make the effing tea' and 'why isn't there any effing food in the house' and and and... Fuck her. I've got to find a way out of here, somehow, anyhow. I've been trying SO hard to get caught out. If I got pregnant I'd get married or I could get a place in a hostel, I might even get somewhere of my own and I could always have the baby adopted or fostered or something if it didn't work out. But it would get me away from HER.

Anya, from the distance of two years, grimaced at her words. How naïve she had been. No, she corrected herself, she hadn't been naïve, she had been stupid.

Putting *1966 Volume* 2 back in its place Anya closed her eyes, drew circles with her finger in the air above the trunk and let it drop. She checked the date of the diary chosen, *1961 Volume 2*. She paused before picking it out, she had hated 1961, that had been the worst year of her life.

She made herself open the book near the beginning and stared at the childish writing of her 11 year old self. She studied it objectively, noting the carefully dotted i's and crossed t's. She hadn't written like that for years.

> Monday, May 22nd 1961
> Mum got the letter today. I've passed the 11 plus AND I got a scholarship. I thought she'd be proud of me but she said she'd rather have a daughter who fitted in than a clever one. She said what use was it to a girl to be clever. She said no one would want to be friends with someone like me and I'd hate it at the grammar.

Never without a man in tow, though never with the same one for long, her mum had had a particularly demanding boyfriend that

Spring. Anya scanned the pages of the diary to see if she had written his name anywhere but could not find it, perhaps she had never known it. While he, whatever his name was, was around she had had to be out of the house so she had tagged along on the fringes of the gang that hung around the pub at the bottom of the next street. At first they had ignored her but, after she offered them a packet of ciggies she had nicked from her mother's bag, they began to talk to her. She knew she looked a lot older than 11, maybe she could pass for 14 or even 15. It wasn't long before each evening one of the boys would put his arm casually around her shoulder and lead her off to have a snog in the bus shelter or to go further lying down in one of the clumps of bushes in the park. She knew the gang were using her, but, if that was the price of having friends, she was willing to pay it. It didn't mean she had to enjoy any of it.

With her hand tight in a fist Anya angrily wiped away the tears that gathered in her eyes at the memories. It all seemed so vivid and it hadn't been fair. She shouldn't have been allowed to do those things. She should have had parents who stopped her from being so stupid. It wasn't fair that her mum didn't give a shit. It wasn't fair that she didn't have a dad.

She picked out the next diary and found the entry for her first day at the school she had left for the last time that afternoon.

> *Tuesday, 5th September 1961*
>
> *I HATE IT. How am I going to put up with five years of this? Maybe Mum was right! NO I didn't say that!!! Mum is NEVER. EVER. RIGHT. I tried not to speak to anyone but there was this big fat girl called Henrietta Hodge. She kept going on at me so I turned my back on her and walked away. How did she know I'm a scholarship girl from Tennyson Street? I called her worse names back, words that she probably didn't know the meaning of but she did try to hit me and pull my hair when I called her a fucking toffee nosed slag.*
>
> *It was just like the day I started at the primary and they asked me what my Dad did for a living and I said I didn't have*

a Dad. Everyone laughed, even the teacher and said I must have a Dad, everybody had a Dad. It was probably that afternoon I went home and asked Mum why I didn't have one. All I learned was that Mum could smack really hard when she was angry. After that whenever anyone at school asked about my family I made something up but the stories were never the same so they all laughed at me and called me a liar and never asked me to be their friend. I don't think I'm going to have any more friends now than I did then.

'I was right,' she thought wryly, 'that was nearly seven years ago and in all that time I've never had what I could call a friend.' With pursed lips and a grim determination to relive bad times she turned to the back of the book.

>Sunday 31st December 1961
>The last day of a horrid year. I asked Mum if any of the men I saw in the mornings was my dad. She slapped me so hard. I kept going on about Dad. Who was he? I asked why I had no grand-parents? No family at all? Only her? She really lost her temper. She kept hitting me and the more she hit out the more questions I asked. I don't think she has the first idea who my dad was. I don't think she's ever been married and all she's ever done is lie to me every day of every week about every single bloody thing.

Anya closed the book and put it carefully back in the box. 1961 was best forgotten.

She sat on the bed looking at the volumes of her diary feeling sorry for the girl who had written them. All the times she had recorded school work and exam results the handwriting was neat and precise. But there were many barely legible entries scribbled in haste when she was drunk on sex and cheap cider.

Carefully she chose *Anya Cave 1964 Volume 2*.

Saturday 23rd May, 1964 actually written on Sunday 24th

I lifted some stuff from Lewis's. I wondered if I'd get caught but decided it didn't really matter. Put them on in the dressing room and just walked out. It was so easy. It was worth the risk when a boy in the lift nodded towards me and said 'nice tits' to his mate. He must have meant me to hear. I looked over my shoulder as I walked out of the shop and they were following me. I wiggled a bit and kept checking and they kept following. Just as I was reaching the station they caught up with me and asked if I wanted a coffee or something. I said I'd prefer 'something' in a really grown up voice. They looked at each other the way boys do and I went with them.

I've been pretty close lots of times but it was great to find out what it was really like. It hurt a bit and at first I wondered what all the fuss was about but one of the boys was gentler than the other and just as they were finishing I began to enjoy it.

After a bit I said I'd better be getting home and they said I didn't really want to go did I? They'd go out and get some fish and chips and some beer and we could make a night of it. I didn't think Mum would miss me. When I got back she was still in her room with whatever-his-name-is-this-time. She didn't even know I'd been out all night. So at 13 years 9 months 2 weeks I'm not a virgin any more. It wasn't so bad after all.

Anya held the book open wondering how she could have been so stupid.

One by one she took other diaries out of the box and read pages at random, picking out the ones written carelessly in an almost undecipherable scrawl. It was masochistic of her, she knew, but the pain suited her mood. But then the girl who had written all this wasn't really her was it? She really didn't want it to be her.

She flicked through page after page which she knew described evenings spent hanging around The Anchor. The entries most days ended with an initial and a score out of ten. The most frequent initial in her diary was R. Anya remembered Ray, the youngest Longton boy. He had been her favourite because he was always gentle and usually thanked her afterwards. She wondered what had happened to him, she hoped he wasn't in borstal somewhere, or jail. She didn't think he would do well in jail. She hadn't seen the Longton boys for a couple of years but there had been a time when every night of the week she had gone off with one of them.

It was the Longton boys who had taught her how to steal from shops and from cars. She had got quite good at it but she didn't go with them when they broke into houses because she felt that was wrong.

Page after page of her diaries repeated the stories of nights occupied with drink, sex and petty vandalism but always, mixed in with the badly written scrawl, there were short, neat entries recording the days when she had only school work, essays and exam results to report.

> Monday 9th May 1966
> Exams started today. UGH. Still I should be all right. I've worked hard and Maths this morning seemed OK. Haven't been out for a couple of weeks, I wonder if they've missed me, I doubt they've even noticed I'm not there. In a way I wish it wasn't like this. I wish I could be different. I know I'm becoming as bad as Mum but it's the only way to get away from here. I know people say unmarried mothers are the lowest of the low, just slags, and their families chuck them out but I wouldn't mind that, what could possibly be worse than staying here? But I can't believe I've not got caught yet. I must have done it a couple of hundred times now (though who's counting) and nothing. Not one month missed or even late. It's not fair.

Anya knew better now, but that didn't make the reading any easier. Determined to feel as much humiliation as she could inflict on herself she flicked through the pages to the entry for the day that had really changed her life.

> Wednesday 22nd June 1966
> It's been SUCH a WEIRD day.
> I was sitting in the library at lunchtime. Exams are over and

I was reading just for the sake of it when Miss Hill came up to me. I put my head down in the book but it didn't work as she tapped me on the shoulder and gestured for me to follow her. I followed her up the staircase we're never supposed to use to her office. She shut the door behind us and told me to sit down in one of the comfortable armchairs and started to chat! Chat! It was WEIRD.

She wanted to know what I was going to do now O's are finished. Did I want to stay on to do A's? I just said I hadn't thought. She was really nice. She said I had a chance of going to University! University! Me! I had to point out that money wasn't exactly flowing out of my ears. I'd have to leave school, earn some money, my Mum was expecting me to get a job.

She just changed the subject and told me her brother was a doctor whose surgery was on the other side of the park from our street. She said that when she visited him she'd seen me hanging around with the boys outside The Anchor. She said she wants to make sure I'm doing what I'm doing with my eyes open. Miss Hill said her brother knew everything that went on in and around the park because he'd had to clear up the mess for girls like me more than once. I didn't need to ask her what she meant, it was pretty obvious.

She said I could do so well in life as long as I didn't think leaving home would be the answer to all my problems. How could she possibly know I was trying to do that! She said I'd never stand on my own two feet unless I got qualifications and O levels would never be enough. She asked what I wanted to do with my life. Did I want to work in a shop or worse, have to find some man to keep me whether I loved him or not. I couldn't think of anything to say so I said nothing. She said 'Please don't throw your life away.' She really seemed to care.

She didn't tell me off, she didn't threaten anything, she just said how disappointed she would be in me if I gave up now. She said I was an intelligent girl and should know better and I should understand that what I was doing was stupid. Stupid that was the word she used. not indecent or promiscuous or immoral. And then she stood up and told me to go with her, there was someone she wanted me to meet.

It didn't take long to work out we were heading for one of the blocks of flats by the docks. The lift was out of order so I followed her up three flights of stairs and along a stinking corridor before we stopped. A girl, my age or a little older, answered the door with a toddler on her hip. Miss Hill introduced us rather formally, she was Marion Whitehead. 'You're the really bright one?' Marion said 'You're here to see what a mess you can get yourself into if you're not careful?'

She'd thought she couldn't fall pregnant the first time. She'd just thought she was late and then she forgot she was late and then it was too late to get rid of it. As soon as they saw what was happening her parents had thrown her out of their house. They didn't care what happened to her, she was no daughter of theirs. It had never occurred to me that a girl with proper parents would be chucked out because she'd made a mistake. I looked at Marion and wondered how she could have coped with learning her mum and dad cared more for their good name than for her. 'They chucked you out?' I asked her 'Just like that?' She hadn't heard from them since. 'Why didn't the bloke marry you? Couldn't you have got rid of it?' He'd said it was nothing to do with him and a woman who did that sort of thing said it was too late. 'What would she have done?' I had to ask. 'Made me sit in really really hot water, drink something foul and if nothing else worked something to do with knitting needles.' Marion's voice tailed off. Perhaps she was grateful she had left it too late. I asked her if she wished she was back living with her parents, going to school, taking exams. Then I realised, as she tightened her t-shirt over her stomach that she was pregnant again. She said there'd been no reason not to have another one and the money came in handy. It took me a while to realise what she'd meant.

Miss Hill talked to me as if Marion wasn't there. 'You must

recognise what you've been flirting with. There is a real stigma in being an unmarried mother, it's less than it was but it is still insurmountable. One day there may be a more enlightened view about abortion as back street operations are so very dangerous, but that day is not here yet. Not long ago men took responsibility for their actions but they don't anymore, they will always leave you to cope with the consequences, and it is so very difficult to get any financial support as a lone mother.' And I'd always thought getting pregnant was the way out.

So I'm going to stay on at school. I'll just have to work out how to tell Mum that I won't be earning for a couple more years.

Anya glanced quickly through the entries for 1966 and 1967. They were all short, just neat litanies of work, and, as she read them from the distance of a year or more, they seemed very boring. She still found staying at home difficult, even when her mother had no man hanging around there was always too much noise from the television for her to be able to concentrate. But instead of heading to The Anchor every evening she walked in the opposite direction to the local library. Perhaps she hadn't needed to work so hard but Anya soon realised she was enjoying herself; it had really been quite a happy time, not having friends somehow seemed less important than it had ever done.

But Anya was not in the mood for thinking of happy times; she wanted to wallow in hard memories and self-pity. She turned back to her current diary.

Wednesday 19th June 1968

Exams over. It's almost like she's been watching me from a distance these past two years, never saying anything, just watching, waiting.

As I walked out of the exam hall, well the gym, for the last time, the final A level exam finished, I felt an arm around my shoulders. 'Well done my dear.' Miss Hill spoke with her usual quiet voice, the one that makes you listen to what she's saying. I was being summoned to her office again for another chat. We'd hardly spoken in two years. I asked how Marion was doing and heard the disappointment in her voice when she said that she hadn't had a chance to take any exams as she was pregnant again, the third. Then she asked me if I was still having regular unprotected sex. I was tempted to suggest she asks her brother but she was trying to be kind so I said not nearly as often as before but yes, I still did it now and again. If she was going to talk about sex so would I, we'd see who got more embarrassed first. I couldn't help wondering what this middle aged spinster was aiming at. Then she asked if I'd ever been pregnant. My reply 'just lucky I guess' must have seemed a bit flippant as I got one of her put down stares 'I think it may be a little more than luck.'

She then told me she was worried about me because she didn't want my talent to go to waste as Marion's had. She said she had admired how I had put up with so much from Miss Henrietta Hodge (she actually called her Miss Henrietta Hodge) and she said she'd admired the way I'd handled myself throughout my school years 'coming from where you do it can't have been easy'. The most surprising thing was she said she saw a bit of herself in me.

She started talking about her own life. 'I was your age when war broke out' I did a quick calculation, 18 in 1939 makes her 47 now, somehow I'd always assumed she'd be much older than that. She told me how her brother and his friends had joined up as soon as war broke out, mostly into the Air Force. They all knew life would be short so they set out to make what time they had as much fun as possible, her words. She said that the young men she had been with had died, sooner or later, mostly sooner. I couldn't help thinking how awful it must have been, how frightening not to know whether or not you were going to be alive the next day. I couldn't begin to understand what that must have been like. It didn't seem like I was talking to my headmistress, especially when she said she hadn't got pregnant even when she'd tried. She sounded so sad. 'I was in love with one of those young men and I so wanted his child. But it wasn't to be.' I didn't have to ask whether he had survived. 'Yes he died. Only one of the boys in our set survived and that was my brother. He became a doctor after the war.'

I wondered why she was telling me all this. 'After Michael I had lots more boyfriends, things were very different during the war, behaviour was acceptable then that wasn't as soon as the war ended. But despite all that I never got caught as so many girls did. 'It was my brother who persuaded me to get checked out.' I asked her what she meant by 'checked out'. She said to see if she had just been lucky or whether there was a reason she hadn't 'got caught out'. She said they'd found that she was barren, her word, barren. She could never have a child. That's why she became a teacher and why she never married. She said she believed the only reason to marry was to raise children. She said it was very important not to trap a man into marriage with false hopes of a family. She thinks I should be checked out to find out if I'm barren. She thinks I need to know the truth so I can lead my life in the best possible way. For me and for any man I fall in love with. Somehow I feel years older than I did this morning.

Anya looked down at the fading dark marks on the blue satin bedspread. She had agreed to the tests, the appointment had been made and two weeks later Dr Hill had given her the news. She could remember his face as he had told her the chances of her conceiving were nil. He hadn't told her why, she hadn't asked. It hadn't seemed important to know.

Monday 1st July, 1968
So that's it. I can never have children. No need for the pill or Durex, no need to say no. I can have as much sex as I like and I'll never have to face the consequences. I can't ever have a baby. Never. I want to talk to someone about it but Mum is still locked in her room with the bloke she picked up on Saturday. Shit.

Well, since she's not around I'll have to talk to myself. I suppose I can enjoy as much sex as I like. I can do what all men can do, have sex without worrying about anything. I know I'm good at it. Will I ever think this is a bad thing? I doubt it. Who'd want to bring a baby into this stupid world? We'll all be blown up before long anyway.

Anya picked up her pen, turned the pages to the words she had written an hour earlier *Relief Fear Confusion Loneliness*. In her neatest handwriting she wrote the last entry she was to make in her diaries for some years.

Monday 19th August, 1968
Went in to school to get results today. I should feel so proud of myself so why do I feel so depressed? Why does it seem like the end of everything? It should feel like a beginning. I should be excited not so overwhelmingly miserable. I've got into Liverpool and I can go there for three years, get a degree, open up a whole world but somehow that feels all wrong. How will I fit in? I don't think I'll be able to for one moment. I suppose I could just say fuck it all and get a job on the checkouts in the new supermarket. I'd probably be more suited to that. I have absolutely no idea what I really want to do.

When I got home I told Mum how well I'd done but she was staring at the mirror on the hall wall finishing her make up. All she said was sorry honeybun, gotta run, catch up in the morning. She didn't give a shit. She's never given a shit.

It shouldn't have been an argument. I didn't want an argument. I said I didn't owe her anything, that I'd done it all on my own, that no one in my class had done as well as I had and they all had mothers and fathers to help them. She went to give me a slap but I moved and she missed. I was surprised how quiet she was. She didn't scream and yell she just said what I did was none of her business now, I was 18 and as far as she was concerned I could do what I liked. I told her I'd been doing what

I liked for years. She said as long as I kept my grubby little paws off her men I was free to fuck whoever I wanted. Fucking is all she ever thinks about. I shouldn't have let her get to me. As soon as she'd gone I got dressed up and headed down to the ferry over to Liverpool and the Adelphi. Sitting in the bar it was easy to make a pick up. He wasn't that old but he wasn't worth the effort. He ended up kneeling on the floor by the bed crying. He tried to give me twenty quid. Pathetic.

But as I headed home I've realised that it's me that's pathetic.

Who are you Anya Cave?

Are you that attractive, intelligent girl who will go to university and find how to be make a real success of your life or are you that promiscuous little tart who'll end up throwing everything away?

I wish I knew.

Chapter 2: Independence

Kent, August 1968

"Liverpool?" Kathleen's tone was one of melodramatic incredulity. 'Liverpool? You want to go to Liverpool?'

"I am going to Liverpool." Geoff's knew there was going to be an argument, at least he hoped there would be one, he had been trying to bring everything out into the open for months. Four years at university would allow him to escape the cloying over-security of his home.

"I don't think so." There was a familiar finality in his mother's voice.

"Why not? What's wrong with Liverpool?" He had known for years that one day he would have to fight and win if he was ever going to leave home.

"Now where can I start with listing all the things that are wrong with Liverpool?" Kathleen frequently resorted to sarcasm. "Let me think. Perhaps the fact that it's 200 miles from home?"

"That's actually a real plus point."

Kathleen was fighting too, to keep her son at home and under her control. She arched an eyebrow and looked at him as if he had no idea what he was talking about.

"I don't want to stay living here at home and I don't want to join all those idiots commuting into town every day, I want to get away. That's what university is all about Mother, it's about leaving the nest, spreading wings, growing up."

"How wrong I must have been all this time! Here have I been thinking that going to university was about learning and getting a good degree from a respected institution. I must also be mistaken that a degree from a university in London is worth more than one from Liverpool."

"Yes Mother, you are wrong. The course in computing in Liverpool is the best in the country."

"But, darling, computing and in Liverpool!" Kathleen Philips spoke as if the city were beyond the pale. "Surely you don't want to spend three years…"

"Four." Geoff corrected his mother so quietly she may not even have heard.

"… in that God-forsaken city."

"But Mum…"

"I've told you so many times Geoffrey." she interrupted wearily. "Do not call me Mum."

He called her Mum because she called him Geoffrey. He was Geoff to everyone he knew, even his sister called him Geoff, at least when their mother was not around.

"But Mother," he put unnecessary emphasis on the formal title, "I don't want to stay at home, I want to go somewhere new, meet new people, do new things."

Frequently in the two weeks since he had first told his mother that he had accepted the offer at Liverpool University they had touched on the issue but there had never been what Geoff always wanted, a no-holds-barred, out-and-out argument, that would resolve the issue in his favour. "But Mum… Mother, I'm 18. I'm not your little boy in grey shorts and knee length socks any more. I don't want jelly for tea and a cuddle at bedtime, at least not from you." He avoided his mother's eye knowing the outraged look she would be giving him. "I want friends of my own whose families you don't know and haven't known since before I was born. It would be really nice to have a few minutes in every day when you don't know where I am and who I'm with and I want to do things you don't find out about through the spy network you call your friends."

"That's enough Geoffrey."

"And that's another thing Mum. Please call me Geoff. One single syllable. Geoff." He knew that however many times he asked her she would never agree.

"It was your father's wish that you be called Geoffrey. It was one of the last things he ever said to me. That is your name and that is what I shall call you."

Geoff knew that any hope of further discussion was lost when his mother mentioned his father, as she invariably did when she decided one of their disagreements should come to an end. He watched unsympathetically as his mother ran through a familiar routine. The tone of her voice changed, her eyes filled with unnecessary tears which she dabbed exaggeratedly with the corner of the handkerchief she always kept handy for whenever she Remembered Her Loss. He always thought of it with capital letters. 18 years was a long time to be a widow but, as she made clear when it suited her, double that time would still be insufficient to soften the pain. Geoff knew the act was designed to make him feel guilt for upsetting his mother who had Suffered So Much. He insolently, silently mouthed the words as she spoke. 'You were christened Geoffrey, as your father wished, and that is your name.' He knew what she was going to say. It was what she always said.

Kathleen was heavily pregnant and the last thing she wanted to do was sit on the cramped back seat of a sports car with five year old Margaret and be driven, uncomfortably fast, the 50 miles to the coast. She tried to persuade him that she didn't feel well enough, but her husband had, as was usual, had his way. "It'll be my last opportunity before Geoffrey Junior arrives" he said over the breakfast table as if that were the end of any discussion on the matter, which, of course, it was.

"It might be another girl." Kathleen rubbed her enormous bump praying silently that it would be a boy. She really didn't want to have to go through the whole process again. The standard of living her husband provided was nice but it really wasn't worth all that trouble.

From the first evening they had met, at a tea dance in the summer of 1943, Kathleen had known Geoffrey Philips' advantageous financial position. Perhaps it was that which had made the man who many warned her was an arrogant bully, so attractive. Even after they had married in the Spring of 1944, she had never asked him where his money came from. When she had asked why he wasn't in the forces he had tapped his nose conspiratorially and said that he was more use on the Home Front. She was aware that there were many lines of work in wartime about which it was best not to know too much. Kathleen was happy to be securely married, to have a comfortable home and, within a few weeks of marriage, to be enjoying the attention her first pregnancy brought. When Margaret was born in January 1945 Geoffrey's disappointment at not having a son was acute. It was her fault, Geoffrey said, that he only had a daughter and a plain daughter at that. He blamed Kathleen for not giving him the son who would carry on his name and join him in the business, a daughter could do neither.

"If it's another bloody girl then you'll just have to have another until you give me the son I need and you'll have to do it a bit quicker." Geoffrey chose to forget the three miscarriages that had intervened between pregnancies. "We'll leave in an hour, Kathleen." He wiped his mouth on the linen napkin, folded it precisely and placed it on the table next to his empty plate.

Twenty years younger than her husband, Kathleen had never been an equal partner in their relationship. The money was his, the house was his, every decision, whether it was about a holiday destination or the purchase of a car, was made by him. Nothing was shared, nothing was hers. As she watched him walk from the room she wondered in a rather disinterested way whether she had ever loved him at all. She was certain he had never loved her, she was in his life only to give him a son.

She gathered all the paraphernalia that was required for a day out with a five year old, all the time thinking that this was the last thing in the world she wanted to do. She knew that for the two hours it would take them to reach the coast Margaret would not stop fidgeting or crying. She would be car sick and the combination of the noise and the smell would make the trip almost unbearable. She dreaded what the day would bring but knew there was no point in arguing with

Geoffrey, if he wanted to take his daughter for a sail that was what he would do. Geoffrey was used to doing as he wished. It never occurred to him that others were worthy of consideration, not even his wife.

The journey felt as long as Kathleen had expected it would. Margaret acted up all the way, wriggling and chattering incessantly, excited that she was to be going out in her beloved Daddy's yacht *Guillemot* for the first time. Kathleen had tried to persuade him not to say anything until they had reached the yacht club, she knew how difficult an excited Margaret would be to control on the journey but she hadn't been at all surprised when he had ignored her and told Margaret as they loaded the car.

By the time Geoffrey turned the Jaguar into the Yacht Club car park he was barely able to control his impatience. The journey had taken far longer than he had planned as he had had to pull into lay-bys three times to allow his daughter to be sick. He would be lucky to catch the tide.

"Why couldn't you calm her down?" He asked impatiently, as they unloaded the car. "She's been behaving like a baby."

"You didn't help making her so excited." Kathleen replied, defensively.

"I hope you bring up Geoffrey Junior to be better behaved. The girl is uncontrollable."

Margaret stood holding her father's hand staring with undisguised idolatry up at his face. Kathleen hoped she had not realised what her father was saying about her.

"Have a lovely time Margaret. Be a good girl, do everything your Daddy tells you to do." Margaret, tugging impatiently at her father's hand, didn't answer.

Kathleen was about to tell her husband to remember his promise to keep close to the shore but he was already turning away from her so she didn't bother. She watched them walk away, Geoffrey striding out quickly with Margaret almost running to keep up.

She found a seat on the clubhouse balcony and took out her knitting, exchanging brief pleasantries with the other wives occupying themselves as their men enjoyed their freedom on the water. She looked up occasionally from her knitting trying to catch a glimpse of *Guillemot* amongst the irregular flotilla of yachts tacking backwards and forwards.

Geoffrey hadn't stayed close to shore, but then she hadn't really expected he would. He only did as he promised when that was what he had always intended.

Whenever she thought of her father Margaret remembered that short time, no more than an hour, that they had spent together on *Guillemot*. She had only moved when her Daddy told her to and she obeyed immediately every one of his instructions. She had never known her adored Daddy to have so much time for her. He always left for his office before she was allowed downstairs in the mornings and he always worked so late that he had never spent more than a few minutes with her before she had to go upstairs to bed. For the remaining eighty years of her life she could close her eyes and picture her father's strong arms, tanned even though it was so early in the year, the dark waves of his hair, the way it had blown across his eyes, and his long brown fingers as he held on to the tiller and pulled on ropes. Then she would see the brown of his eyes, terrified, as they sank below the water.

She was in the water too, she didn't know how, but her Daddy was with her. She had floated, her head back, looking at the seagulls flying in the sky. Then he wasn't with her. She heard him calling her name but she couldn't see him. She heard him telling her to keep her head above the water. Still she couldn't see him. She heard him tell her not to worry, they would be fine, help would be on its way. Then the water turned her and she saw him and for a lifetime she wished she hadn't. He kept disappearing then she could see him no more. Brown straight wet hair, brown eyes, brown arms, brown fingers. Gone. She resolutely kept her head back as he had told her to, not knowing what else she should do.

Kathleen was sitting on the Yacht Club veranda trying to control the ball of wool in the breeze as she worried about the journey home. She became aware of shouting, but she didn't think it unusual, there would always have been noise as the estuary was crowded on the first sunny, breezy, bank holiday of the year.

She looked up from her knitting to see the railings were crowded with people and realised there was a problem. 'Is the child safe?' she heard someone cry. One woman was pointing out to the estuary, another had her hands over her face as if she didn't want to see horror unfold. 'What is it?' Kathleen had asked one of the women who, she realised, had tears running down her cheeks. The response 'Oh my God', accompanied by a look of horror, didn't seem to serve as an adequate answer. She realised that the women who were not crowded on the balcony railings were looking at her.

Ten minutes later she was seated in the Commodore's office trying to take in what the kindly man was telling her. The few words she heard seemed disjointed, completely out of context and made no sense. 'Capsize' 'no life jacket' 'water still very cold at this time of year' 'tried to swim to shore' 'drowned' 'sad'.

Geoffrey was a strong swimmer she tried to tell him. He couldn't have drowned. He could swim for miles. But then she had remembered the fall he had had while out riding the previous week. He had hurt his shoulder. At the time he had laughed at her worry, saying it was nothing. But 'nothing' had killed him.

"He's drowned?" She asked as if she didn't quite understand what the word meant. 'Dead?'

The commodore nodded then had seemed to cheer up as he spoke about Margaret. "Your daughter is safe though. She was wearing a life jacket. The ambulance men are checking her over but she seems none the worse for her adventure." Belatedly he caught the look of horror on Kathleen's face.

Kathleen replied with icy calm. "Adventure? You think this is an adventure? My husband is dead, my daughter's father is dead, and you call it an adventure? Where is she? I must go to her. She will need me."

Kathleen struggled to stand up. She knew she must find Margaret. Margaret would be frightened, she would need her mother. But as Kathleen tried to stand her legs collapsed and she fell to the floor.

"The baby." She screamed, not caring that she was losing all remnants of respectability and control. "Help me! The bloody baby's coming. Now!"

Geoffrey's son had come into the world within an hour of his father's leaving of it. It was her husband's tragedy he never knew he had a son, and it was his son's tragedy that he was never allowed to forget it.

Kathleen was freed by her husband's death in a way she could never have anticipated. For the first time in her life she was able to do exactly as she pleased. She never went so far as to acknowledge that she was happy Geoffrey had drowned, it just wasn't the disaster it might have been had their relationship been different.

Geoffrey's will had been read after the funeral by the family solicitor who seemed embarrassed as he detailed the scale of the wealth involved. Geoffrey had been convinced his child would be a son and had re-written his will only a few weeks before on that basis leaving his widow and her daughter very well provided for but ensuring, when the son reached his majority, everything would be his. It would be up to the boy what provision should be made for his mother and his sister. All the financial arrangements that Kathleen had never cared to know about were placed in the hands of a board of trustees of which she would not be a member. She had access to a great deal of money but it was not hers. In twenty-one years everything would be his and she could have nothing.

Determined to make the most of those years she hired a live-in nanny and a housekeeper and she used the freedom they gave her to spend weekends shopping in London and countless afternoons drinking tea and gossiping with her friends, the wives of the men who controlled her son's fortune. She played the dignified widow to perfection implying to all that her grief was something she would only allow to overcome her in the privacy of her own home.

To these friends and acquaintances Kathleen always talked of her son as her 'little man' and 'the man of the house' but Geoff knew from a very young age that he could be nothing of the sort. His father's memory ruled the family. Every disagreement between mother and son ended in Kathleen's tears and recriminations that his father would be so disappointed in him. His birthday, 10th April, was dedicated to the memory of his father so throughout his childhood the day was spent listening to his mother and sister talk of the man he had never known. His birthday parties were always held, cards and presents given and received, on the 11th as Kathleen, with increasing resentment, counted down the years to his twenty-first when she would no longer be in control.

"I really don't think Liverpool is a good idea Geoffrey."
"Tough, Mum, I'm going."
It was one of the very few times in his life that he stood up to his mother and won.
She never forgave him.

Chapter 3: Realities

Merseyside, August 1970

Anya had to get a holiday job. She had enjoyed her first term at university but she knew she would have enjoyed it more if she could leave home and live in a hall of residence but that was out of the question when she had no money but her grant. The book shop turned her down because of her accent, the post office would only be up to Christmas so she ended up folding sheets in the local laundry. If she worked every holiday and saved every penny she would be able to afford hall in her final year. Then, at last, she could make friends.

She was just as lonely as she had ever been. She didn't have the confidence, or the cash, to join any of the noisy groups which, at the end of each day, headed for the union bar or the buses back to halls as she turned in the opposite direction to the ferry and home. She was enjoying her course but every evening, as she walked round the ferry's deck as it crossed the Mersey, she knew she was missing out. Exceeding her tutor's expectations was no compensation for having no social life.

There were advantages to the job in the laundry; it was close to home and the money was good, it had to be because it was hard work. At six o'clock every evening her feet ached from standing all day, her head ached from the clanking machinery and her back ached from the incessant bending and straightening the job required but at the end of each week, when she picked up her small brown pay packet, she knew it would all be worth it.

Every morning at 8 o'clock she would take her place at the conveyor belt that fed flat ironed bed sheets one every 30 seconds. Moments later the motors cranked into action and for the next two hours she folded crisply starched sheets, 120 times an hour. The radio played pop music all day every day but it was almost impossible to hear with the noise of the machinery.

At the end of the first week in January she went in to the office to pick up her wages and say goodbye with some regret. 'You'll be back at Easter?' Mr Lupton, the owner, asked nonchalantly. She could have kissed him. 'Oh yes please! I've really enjoyed it.' 'Not many people say that.' He had replied with a smile.

In the Christmas vacation of 1969 she got to talking in her breaks with a good looking student who was working in the office. Martin was there again in the summer vacation of 1970 when she found out more about him, he was at Newcastle University, he lived a few miles out of town and came to work every day on his powerful Norton motor bike. They discussed politics, arguing over America's involvement in Vietnam. She knew he liked her and she wondered what it would take to make him ask her out. Anya spent the long, monotonous days imagining a holiday romance with Martin. He was different from the other boys she had known, he had good manners and spoke with a slightly posh accent. From October, when she would be living in hall, she would meet lots of interesting, intelligent, good-looking, middle-class boys like Martin.

When, at the end of a particularly hot day in early August Anya opened her front door she had known immediately that something was wrong. There was no sound. The television was always on when she got home but that evening the house was silent. Anya looked in the kitchen which seemed unnaturally tidy and called upstairs. 'Mum? Are you here?' When there was no reply she climbed the stairs. She knocked tentatively on her mother's bedroom door and pushed it open. If her mum had a boyfriend she would never have dared, but there hadn't been a man around for months.

Anya saw her mother lying on her bed and knew immediately she was dead.

She had never seen anyone dead and for a few long seconds she looked at her mother's face thinking with a strange detachment how pretty she could have been, before turning away and closing the door quietly behind her. She could call 999 later, just for a few minutes more she wanted things to be normal. She walked back down the stairs and boiled the kettle and then sat on the settee staring at the grey screen of the silent television as the mug of tea cooled in her hands. She couldn't call 999, she didn't know how she could say 'my mum's dead.' She had hated her mother and their life for so many reasons but it had had the advantage of familiarity and she needed a few minutes of that old life before everything would change.

It was getting dark when she eventually walked out of the front door and down the street to The Anchor. She walked up to the bar and asked for a brandy. She drank it before realising she had no money with her. She tried to explain to the barman that she only lived up the street, she'd go and get her purse, she wouldn't be a minute, but he didn't believe her. She looked around in muted panic.

"I'll pay for that." A voice she felt was familiar seemed to take control.

"Are you sure doctor?" she heard the barman say.

Dr Hill was standing next to her. "Anya. Anya Cave isn't it?"

She nodded.

"You look like you've had a shock. What's happened?"

"It's my mum."

With those three words it was out of her hands. She didn't have to call 999, she didn't have to explain anything to anyone.

It was very late when Dr Hill finally left. He had called the police and the ambulance and dealt with them all as Anya sat in the front room answering the very basic questions 'who' and 'when'. She would leave the 'how' and the 'why' for another day. Left alone in the empty house she didn't want to go to sleep, she didn't want to have to wake up the next morning only to realise that her life had changed, anyway, she told herself, there were things to do. She sat down at the desk in her bedroom and wrote a note to Mr Lupton explaining that she could not return to work. She wrote that she hated to let them down when they had all been so good to her for more than two years, but a sudden family bereavement meant she was needed at home.

Dawn was breaking as she walked the familiar route and dropped the envelope through the office letter box. She walked away quickly as she knew the boiler men started work very early and she didn't want anyone to see her. Reluctant to go back to the empty house she walked to the park and sat down shivering until she began to feel the warmth of the sun.

Should she have realised her mum was so ill? There hadn't been a boyfriend for quite a while but there hadn't been anything other than that out of the ordinary, they had bickered about anything and everything just as they always did. Maybe her mum had lost some weight and not used as much makeup as usual, perhaps she hadn't been down the market to buy new clothes for months, maybe she hadn't been out of the house at all for a while. Should she have realised something was very wrong? Should she have been more aware of what was going on? If she had been just a little less focussed on her own life would she have seen something? She sat alone on the park bench watching children play and mothers push prams.

It was nearly lunchtime when hunger made her pluck up the courage to go home. As she turned the corner into Tennyson Street she saw Dr Hill and his sister at the front door. She invited them in and they all sat down, rather formally, in the uncannily quiet and tidy front room.

"Did your mother have difficulty sleeping?" Miss Hill asked kindly.

"I don't know."

"Did she go to a doctor?"

"She never came to see me, or anyone at the practice." Dr Hill volunteered

"I don't know."

She didn't know the answer to anything they asked her about her mother and she saw Miss Hill and her brother exchange glances that she couldn't interpret.

"We didn't really talk much." Anya said in self-defence, feeling they were critical of her lack of closeness with her mother.

"She didn't tell you she was ill?"

"Ill? No. She didn't say anything. Was she?"

Neither answered her.

"Was she depressed at all?"

"No. Not really. Why?"

"Well your mother swallowed a lot of tablets. That's why she died."

"She committed suicide?"

"There will have to be a proper post mortem but I would say everything points to that."

"Why would she do that?"

"Didn't she tell you she had cancer?"

"No. She didn't. Not a word." They had had so many secrets from each other but why couldn't her mother have trusted her with something so important?

"But that's not what killed her, though it would have done eventually and rather painfully." Dr Hill had never believed in shielding people from necessary truths.

"She probably just didn't want to wait until it did."

"She probably wanted to spare you that." Miss Hill added.

"She wouldn't have had much longer, maybe a no more than a few months."

"Months?" For a moment Anya imagined what that time would have been like, looking after her dying mother when she should have been concentrating on her finals. She had hated life with her mother and done what she could to leave her but she had never imagined a life without her. "I don't know what I'm going to do."

The Hills spent time with Anya every day of the ten between her mother's death and the funeral. They helped her with the administrative paperwork of death, drove her to Registrars and Undertakers, but she was still alone for most of every day and every night. She spent her 20th birthday reading her diaries and trying to think of good times, perhaps the past hadn't been as bad as she thought.

Anya with Miss Hill and her brother were the only ones at the short service. Now was the time she should have seen her father, whoever he had been, her grandparents, they must exist, she thought there should have been some family. But there was no one, only her, to mourn. They drove back in silence, Dr Hill pulling up outside the house as the neighbours' front doors shut too quickly.

"Do you want to come in?"

There was an envelope on the mat which Anya picked up as she opened the door into the empty house. She sat with it on her lap as Miss Hill put the kettle on. She knew it was not going to be good news so she handed it to Dr Hill who, as soon as his sister had appeared with the tea, opened the envelope and skimmed over the content. Without comment but with a warning glance at his sister, he began to read aloud.

"Dear Miss Cave, Please accept our condolences on the recent death of your mother Miss Melanie Cave."

"Miss. She always said she'd been married. Miss is very definite isn't it?" Anya was not surprised, she had thought for years that her mother calling herself 'Mrs Cave' had been a lie.

"It does look like that." Miss Hill patted Anya's hand consolingly.

"Miss Cave has been a good tenant..."

Anya interrupted again, suppressing rising panic. "Tenant? This is mum's house. It's always been hers."

"I'm afraid the word 'tenant' is unambiguous my dear." Miss Hill held on to Anya's hand.

"She let me think it was ours." Anya said to herself. "I never knew she paid rent."

Dr Hill continued quickly, nothing in the letter was going to be easy for Anya.

"... of the property 16 Tennyson Street, Birkenhead for nearly 21 years but in view of the fact that we understand you have not yet attained your majority..."

"How pompous! They could simply have said since you are under age. Full of their own self-importance that's their trouble."

Dr Hill was aware that the worst news was yet to come and was somewhat irritated by his sister's interruption. He continued firmly without comment.

"...*the property must be left vacant and clean by Friday 11th September.*"

"I've got to leave? In a month?" Anya did not want to believe what Dr Hill had said and grabbed the letter from his hand. "Where am I supposed to go? What can I do with all my things, all Mum's things? What do they think I'm going to do?" For two years she had been trying to leave but that had only been for term time. She had never imagined she wouldn't have a home to return to when she needed one.

"They really are being rather petty." Miss Hill added to her brother. "Clean! They didn't have to be so deliberately insulting."

Anya hadn't cried, even at the funeral, and she wasn't going to cry now so she rubbed her eyes fiercely with her fists. "It doesn't get any better. Listen. '*We will attend the property on Monday 17th August to determine damage and defects which require rectification.*' How am I supposed to pay for anything that needs doing? They'll probably pick at everything and want windows done and painted and everything!"

"Don't worry my dear, we'll be here to make sure they are fair. You've been in this house for over 20 years and they've probably not spent a penny on it in all that time so you mustn't worry." Miss Hill's practicality calmed Anya.

"It's signed D & M Hodge, Landlords." Anya recognised the name and hoped that these Hodges were nothing to do with the Henrietta Hodge who had made her schooldays so miserable. Anya caught Miss Hill's eye and realised there was a connection.

"Yes, my dear, Henrietta's father Donald and her uncle Michael."

"You knew and you never told me!" Anya felt betrayed. Had Miss Hill known, and never told her, that the father of the girl who had bullied her for years owned the house she had lived in all her life?

"No Anya. I know them, of course, and I know they have something of a rental empire but I had no idea that your home was one of those properties."

"But Henrietta would have done."

Miss Hill nodded her head ruefully, "Yes, my dear, she probably would." They sat drinking tea until she broke the silence. "Let us be practical. You say you have a provisional place in hall for next year?"

Anya nodded.

"I have contacts and I'm sure they will be understanding. We'll make sure you can go there as soon as you like. You'll have plenty of time to sort out what to do more permanently when you graduate, things will be a little less raw then. And we will be happy to store any bits and pieces you want to keep until you have a home of your own."

"And I'll be here on Monday to argue your case." Her brother added, nodding assent to all that his sister had promised. We will help you in any way we can."

"But you must find for yourself the strength to cope with all that life is throwing at you." Miss Hill's words reminded Anya of school assemblies but her tone softened as she added "We'll leave you on your own now, you have a lot to think about and you don't need us interfering. But we'll be back on Monday morning and if you need anything in the meantime you will phone won't you?"

Anya shut the door behind them and leant back against it. The house already felt as if it was not her home. She had three days until Monday morning and in those three days she would clear the house and when the Hodges came they could leave with the key. She wasn't going to stay a day longer. The next morning she would ring Miss Hill and ask her to get a hall place for Monday. If there was a problem she would hitch around the country until she could move in; nothing would persuade her to stay in the house one single day after Monday.

She walked down to the corner shop and begged for some boxes. All day Saturday she cleaned and cleared and the piles of rubbish in the back yard waiting for the bin men grew. She kept very little. There seemed to be little worth keeping.

She left her mother's room until last. The bed had been stripped, she wondered who had done that, but the dressing table had not been touched. She swept the brushes and combs and bottles of makeup and cheap scent into a box before tentatively opening a drawer. It was empty. There were no stockings or crumpled underwear as she had expected. She opened the other drawers, they were all empty. She turned to the wardrobe and there were no wire hangers crammed with blouses and skirts. There was just one pink satin hanger and one dress.

But that dress was beautiful. Anya stripped off all her clothes and slipped the pale cream chiffon over her head. Her back was bare, without thinking she straightened it, standing tall, she held her head high and let the folds of the elegant cowl neck fall. She couldn't remember having ever seen her mother wearing it. It was far too sexy to be a wedding dress even if her mother had ever been married. It was a dress for seduction. She wondered why it was the only thing her mother had left her.

She slipped out of the dress and as she climbed into her own clothes she saw how cheap they were. She sat down on the bed with understanding flooding through her. Martin hadn't asked her out, she had made no friends at school or at university, because she really wasn't 'one of them'. When they looked at her they saw a cheap working class girl dressed in badly made, cheap, market-stall clothes, on the occasions when they had spoken to her she had replied in her lazy scouse accent.

She looked at the dress hanging on its pink satin hanger and determined to change. 'That's what you meant about not fitting in wasn't it Mum? You wanted me to but didn't know how to help me?'

It was only when she was closing the door that she noticed the metal trunk under the bed, it was identical to the one she kept her own diaries in. 'Perhaps, Mum, we were more alike than I thought.' Anya spoke aloud for no reason other than that it felt right.

She didn't have to worry about how she could open the box as the key was in the lock. The contents weren't as well organised as hers but the contents were far more varied. In amongst the jumble of bundles of envelopes of different sizes and colours she saw a small box wrapped in brown paper, tied with string and addressed, in a barely literate scrawl in pencil to *Mel Cave, 16 Tennyson Street, Birkenhead, Cheshire, England.* As she picked it up and turned it over in her hands

Anya saw that the parcel had never been opened. The stamps had been ripped off, Anya wondered why, but she could make out parts of a blurred postmark. *11 ARBA 1955.* She pulled at the knot in the string and eventually unpicked it. As she prised off the lid and pulled at the crimpled tissue paper to see what the parcel contained she wondered why her mother had never been sufficiently curious to find out what someone had sent her from '*ARBA*'.

The ring was beautiful. Set in gold the blue stone, which looked like a sapphire, was surrounded by twelve white stones that looked like diamonds. Even if the stones were paste it was beautiful and Anya went to place it on the fourth finger of her left hand. She hesitated and put it instead on her right hand. It fitted perfectly. She held her hand out and admired it. Her mum had never opened the parcel and had never worn the ring, she had never known that she had something that might be valuable and could have been pawned or sold for enough money to have made her life easier or at least bought some luxury that would have made it more bearable.

In the box, folded so small that she nearly missed it, was a piece of paper.

"*Dear Mel, I cant send money but this should be worth a bit so sell it or keep it I dont mind which. Sorry Im not there to help. You know why I had to go. Your 21 now. Grown up. I think of you all the time, your loving brother, Vince.*"

'So I have an Uncle Vince.' Anya thought. 'Why didn't Mum ever mention him?' Maybe she did have some family after all, maybe Vince was still alive, maybe so were her grandmother and grandfather. Maybe she wasn't alone. She put the ring back in the box where it had been for 15 years, she would decide what to do with it another time.

Anya turned her attention back to the box and picked out a bundle of envelopes held together with rubber bands. Anya hadn't thought her mother was the type to have kept love letters but when she looked more closely she realised they had never been posted and were all addressed to '*Mr Vincent Cave*' at a Post Office Box number in Bridgetown Barbados. So that was where *ARBA* was.

With some trepidation Anya opened the first envelope and unfolded the letter. The nearest thing to a date was the word 'Monday' written in the top right hand corner of the single sheet of cheap lined note paper. The letter was signed 'Mel'. She looked back at 'Monday' trying to work out what she could understand from the fact that there was no date. She decided it meant that Mel wrote to her brother Vince very often. Maybe she had even posted some.

> "Vince, it's a girl. I've called it Anya because it's got to have a name and the woman in the bed next to me was reading a book by someone called Anya something. Perhaps it's too pretty a name for something that should never have existed. I should have got rid of it like you said. But you'd left and I was too scared to do it on my own. I will never forgive you for leaving. Now what can I do? Just put up with everything I suppose. It was alright for you, you could leave. I couldn't."

Thoughtfully Anya put the letter back with the others in the rubber band. She wondered why her mother had never posted all these letters, perhaps they were her diaries.

Anya thought of Marion in her flat in the block near the docks. Her mother, Mel, had been in the same position but things would have been a lot worse in 1950. How had she managed? Why hadn't she ever said anything about it? She had so many questions but it was too late for answers. No wonder her mum had resented her.

There was a bundle of cheaper envelopes with the addresses written in the same handwriting that had been on the small parcel wrapped in brown paper.

> "Mel. Im sorry. I just ran when I found out. I didnt know what else to do. It was me nicked the rent box there wasnt much in it but it got me here. Write to me. Tell me how your getting on. Sorry for leaving you when you needed me. Your loving brother, Vincent A Cave."

"Why couldn't you have told me the truth Mum?" Anya spoke aloud to the empty house. "What was the problem? Was Vince my Dad? Was your brother my father?" Anya remembered a girl in her form who found out just before her exams that the woman she thought was her mother was really her grandmother because her eldest sister was her mother.

Anya realised she knew nothing about herself and, worse, she had no one to help her find answers. She took the ring out of the box and put it on her finger again. It was the only connection she had with anyone else in the world so she turned it round on her finger and promised herself that one day she would find out what it all meant.

She turned back to the box and pulled out a long narrow brown envelope. She tipped it over and two pieces of folded paper fell out.

She unfolded one and saw it was her birth certificate. She read the carefully written words in 'Column 1 When and Where Born' *Ninth August 1950, Clatterbridge Hospital*. That much she knew. In 'Column 2 Name if any' was written '*Anya*'. So far so good. But her eye was drawn to Column 4 Name and Surname of Father. Underneath was written the one stark, stigmatic word '*Unknown*'. 'Why did she say unknown?' thought Anya, 'Whoever it had been she must have known. Then she read 'Column 5 Name and Maiden Surname of Mother'. There was only one name '*Melanie Elizabeth Cave*' There was no maiden name. There was just a black dash in 'Column 6 Rank or Profession of Father'. Here was the proof that her mother had never been married, she didn't have only the Hodges' letter to tell her she was illegitimate. Somehow seeing this in black and white made it worse and the bubble of her fantasy that she had a father, somewhere, who would come back to care for her burst.

She turned to the other certificate, her mother's. The date of birth '*The 24th day of January 1934*'. She would have been just 16 when her daughter was born.

She looked across at the names of her mother's parents on her mother's birth certificate, both were there. Father was named as

Albert Edward Cave and mother was *Elizabeth Ena Cave formerly Goodwin*.

'So these are my grandparents.' Anya looked at the old fashioned names. Her grandmother had a maiden name so at least they had been married. Why had her mum had nothing to do with them? She knew nothing about Albert and Elizabeth Cave other than their names. They might be alive somewhere. They must have abandoned their pregnant daughter, thrown her out of their house just as Marion's parents had done. Anya guiltily thought back to those years when she had thought that getting pregnant was the answer to all her problems. How little she had known.

After several minutes staring at the pieces of official paper she had in her hands Anya thought she had the answer. Melanie's brother made her pregnant. Why else would he have run away? Their parents threw them both out. Melanie, not yet 16, found somewhere to live but Vincent ran away to Barbados leaving his sister to fend for herself. Five years later, filled with guilt, he sent her a ring in a parcel she never opened because she knew who had sent it. These things, Anya knew, happened in families.

She recognised there were gaps in her explanation. How her mother found a home? How had she paid the rent for twenty years? Why did she have that beautiful dress? But her theory answered so many other questions. Why there had never been a father around, why her mother hated her, why there was no family at all in their lives.

Since there was no one to tell her that her presumptions were wrong, this was what she believed about herself for many years.

Anya turned to an envelope marked '*Clatterbridge 1958*'. She remembered that week in hospital when she had had her appendix out. She had enjoyed herself though it had hurt a lot. She had been in a ward with lots of older women and they had looked after her well, giving her their ice cream. There were half a dozen forms inside which all seemed to be consent forms. Only one seemed to be saying what the consent was required for. '*Sterilisation*'

She couldn't decipher much of what was written in very poor handwriting in the notes section but she could pick out the words *'rape'* and *'incestuous impregnation'*. She was right. Vincent had raped his sister and run away to Barbados. "Oh shit." She spoke aloud. "Oh Mum." As she sat with the contents of the silver trunk surrounding her Anya forgave her mother so many things.

It was dark when Anya let herself think about the practical problems that faced her. If she was to leave the house on Monday she would need help and the only person she could think of was Mr Lupton. He had the use of vans and she knew he had connections with various charities from all the notices on the canteen wall. She had to get in touch with him but he wouldn't be at the laundry late on a Saturday night. She leafed through the phone book thankful that he had an unusual name. He was very sympathetic and said that he would be very happy to collect all the furniture the next day.

She was ready early, standing at the window waiting for the pale blue laundry van to pull up outside. Mr Lupton had said 5 o'clock and he was exactly on time. When she opened the door she was embarrassed when he gave her a fatherly hug and was surprised to see Martin standing by the van.

"How are you Anya? We've all been worried about you."

"I'm fine." Anya didn't want to talk. But then she didn't want to be rude either. "Thanks."

"I've brought my son to help, no doubt there's a lot of lifting to do."

'So' Anya thought, 'Martin was Mr Lupton's son, no wonder he had spoken so little about himself and had never asked me out. It wouldn't be appropriate for him to screw one of the laundry girls.'

"You want this all to go?" Mr Lupton asked appraising whether he had brought a big enough van.

"Everything. And everything upstairs except the stuff in the bathroom. I'm keeping all that."

"We will find a good home for as much as possible." Martin said,

"There are so many families that need furniture. We'll have to burn some stuff as we can't distribute anything soiled." He nodded towards a pile in which Anya noticed, with some embarrassment, was the pale blue of her bed cover.

Anya thought again of Marion in her flat in the tower block. Perhaps her furniture had come from a house being cleared under circumstances such as these.

It took Martin and his father less than an hour to load the van. From the twitching of her neighbours' curtains she knew she was not the only one watching as they removed her bed and wardrobe, her mother's bed, the front room carpet. Everything she was familiar with, the backdrop of her life, became interlocking geometrical shapes in the back of a van.

When all was done the three of them sat on the bare boards of the front room sipping at the mugs of tea she had made to give herself something to do.

"I'm glad you called my father Anya, I'm glad we have been able to help." Anya tried to identify the qualities in Martin's voice. There was pity, condescension and what she recognised as an intrinsic superiority.

As they were leaving Mr Lupton handed her a brown envelope which she looked at but made no attempt to open. "We had a collection." He explained. "There's two hundred and fifty pounds."

"Two hundred and fifty pounds?" She repeated involuntarily, it was an unimaginably large amount of money.

"Everyone wanted to contribute, and then there was the three day's pay you didn't collect." She thanked him too briefly and too hurriedly shut the door. The tears came unwanted but unstoppable as she curled up on the bare floor. There was no blue quilt, as there had been all her life, to comfort her and it was a long time before she pulled herself together and remembered her other comfort when she was alone and afraid, her diary.

Sunday 16th August 1970
Tomorrow is the beginning of my new life. I'm saying

goodbye to being the illegitimate daughter of the cheap tart (that's the only way she could have earned any money) who lived at 16 Tennyson Street. I'm saying goodbye to not being good enough for the stuck up son of a man whose only success in life is to own a laundry. I'm saying goodbye to everything and everyone I've been in my life.

I've changed in the last two years, I've become a bit of a snob. I like men with manners and clean finger nails, I like people who speak well and use words properly. So from now on I'm going to be like that, I'm going to get some decent clothes, lose my accent, become one of those people who take advantage of others not one who is taken advantage of.

Resolutions: 1) justify Miss H's faith in me, 2) never let myself be looked down on by anyone 3) find out what the ring and the dress mean 4) one day find Vincent A Cave.

Anya looked at her writing in the diary, barely making out the words she had written in the gloom. It was nearly dark but she was damned if she was going to put any more money in the meter. It was too dark to do anything but she had nothing comfortable to sleep on so she carried on making resolutions for the future and writing some of those thoughts in her diary.

Can you make life into what you want it to be? I might like men who speak well and have clean finger nails but they won't like me will they? I'll just be someone they sleep with before going back to their posh, rich, fecund girlfriends. I might get a good degree but if I'm going to be one of them I've really got to be someone completely different. Martin liked me but he wouldn't ask me out because I wasn't good enough for him. It'll be the same with everyone else. If they know the truth about me no one will think I'm good enough for them so I'll be very careful who knows what and where I've come from. I'll be very careful who knows I'm sterile. And why.

She looked around the room which was brightening as the full moon rose above the roofs of the houses on the opposite side of the road. She would never spend another day in this house. She pictured what it had been a few weeks before with her mother sitting on the settee and the television in the corner.

> *I wish the house could talk. It could answer some of my questions like am I right? Is Vince my dad? Did he ever stand in this room? It'll never be able to tell me other things though. Is he still alive? Is he looking at this full moon now? Are Albert and Elizabeth still alive? Maybe they live round the corner and have kept an eye on their daughter all these years. Perhaps they've heard she killed herself and that her daughter is homeless? Would they even care? If the shame was too much for them when their daughter needed them it still would be now. When I leave here tomorrow no-one will be able to trace me even if they wanted to. Only the Hills know where I'll be and no-one knows about them. After I leave here tomorrow only one person will be able to help Anya Cave make the life she wants and that's Anya Cave.*

Dr Hill and the agent for the Hodge brothers arrived at exactly 9.30 the next morning. They walked through the empty rooms that had been her home but she had already moved on and they now meant nothing. A small sum was agreed to cover the replacement of several cracked window panes and Anya paid with cash from the laundry collection. She was surprised at how quickly it was all over and by noon they had arrived at the Hall of Residence that would be her home for a year.

"Are you sure that's all you want us to keep for you?"

Anya had asked him to store her silver trunk of diaries and a small case into which she had packed the contents of her mother's box and the dress. She was taking only the clothes she wore, her files of notes and textbooks.

"You won't lose touch will you? Dot, that is my sister, is rather fond of you, you know."

"I'll try not to let her down."

"I'm sure you couldn't."

Anya found it remarkably easy to say goodbye to the man who was one of her only two friends in the world as she began her new life in the Hall of Residence she had dreamed of for two years. She was shown the refectory, the common room and finally her corridor and the room, F10, that would be her home. As she put her books and files on the shelves of the small desk she tried not to focus on how much her world had shrunk.

16 Tennyson Street had only been a two-up-two-down terraced cottage but as well as her bedroom she had a kitchen, a bathroom and the front room. She hadn't always had the house to herself but she could usually have a bath when she wanted, make a mug of coffee or eat when it suited her and, when her mum wasn't around, she could watch what television programme she wanted. Those freedoms now seemed like luxury. F10 was a very small room. There was only the bed or the uncomfortable desk chair to sit on. If she wanted to watch television she would have to go to the common room and watch the channel others had chosen. She sat on her bed and wondered why she had thought this was a good idea.

She soon pulled herself together and sat at the desk, pulled out her notebook and listed what she would achieve in the seven weeks before the term began.

Buy:	*Colour co-ordinated kitchen stuff, good quality Poster (Van Gogh Starry Night) calendar. Clothes good quality, blue and white. Red shoes.*
Work:	*Read papers and set books. Plan Dissertation.*
Me:	*Get a tan, sort nails and hair, slim! Accent! Voice!*

Monday 5th October was the day she would dress in her skin tight denims, prize on her high heeled red sandals and wriggle into her skimpy white t-shirt. That was the day Anya Cave would join the world of the people who took advantage.

Chapter 4: Beginnings

Liverpool, September 1970

"Who is that girl?" Geoff nudged his neighbour in the queue for supper in the Hall's refectory.

"Where?" Mark looked up from his feet to where Geoff was pointing.

"You have to ask? Look over there."

"Wow!" Mark was never one to use two words when one would do.

Geoff had been standing in the queue wondering whether this would be his third and final year in Liverpool or whether he would go for a fourth. In six months he would be 21 and he would have control of his money so the decision was his. He was pleased to be back after the long summer vacation, free to be himself again away from his mother and sister and their ever more blatant encouragement of his relationship with Fiona. He tried not to think of Fiona and his failure to get her to go all the way with him. He didn't love her; he simply hated losing a challenge.

"I haven't seen her before." Geoff was interested in the girl with the long brown hair and the faraway look in her eyes.

"We'd remember." Mark's thick Glaswegian accent seemed to emphasise his admiration.

"Yes, I think I might." said Geoff thoughtfully.

He watched the girl as she threaded her way between the tables. He hadn't wasted his two years in Liverpool experimenting with drugs as others had done. He had spent his time with girls and believed he could judge, at first sight, how far they would go and whether the effort would be worthwhile. This one was tall, slim and confident, walking as though she knew many eyes were on her. Her tight t-shirt emphasised her breasts, the clean white cotton showed off her tan and the shine in her long dark hair, the tight jeans displayed her every movement as she walked.

"Go and bag two seats next to her." Geoff instructed his friend. "We don't want anyone else getting there first and there's at least fifteen ahead of us in this sodding queue."

"OK." Mark always did as Geoff said. He threaded his way between the tables and just managed to reach his target before a group of five giggling girls.

"OK to sit here?" He asked Anya politely.

"Sure." She was disappointed at the sandy haired, freckled boy but hoped her voice wouldn't discourage him. It was either him or the girls and she couldn't stand giggly girls.

"Hi I'm Mark."

"Anya."

"Are you a fresher?" Mark thought he had better try to be friendly but chat up lines had never been his strong point.

"No. Final year."

"Haven't seen you before."

"My first in Hall."

"Yeah?" Mark was doing his best to elicit information for Geoff. He knew this girl was out of his league.

"I live, used to live, only a few miles away you see. There seemed no point in paying for hall when I could live at home."

"Oh." Then he thought of a good question. "What are you doing?"

"History."

"Oh."

"You?"

"Maths and Computer Studies."

"Ah."

There was an embarrassing silence as all topics of conversation appeared to have been exhausted. Anya began eating and Mark sat there, hoping desperately that Geoff wouldn't be much longer.

"Don't you eat?" Anya asked looking pointedly at the empty table in front of Mark.

"Geoff, that's my friend over there, he's getting my food."

"You can't get it yourself?"

There was no way Mark could avoid admitting their motives. "He wanted to sit with you and he thought the table would be filled by the time we got our food. So…"

"So he sent you over to do the embarrassing bit." She smiled, relieved that perhaps Mark's friend Geoff would be less awkward, he certainly seemed to be the leader of the two. "That's good of you, you must be good friends."

"We are." Geoff answered her as he arrived with two trays which he just managed to get flat on the table before he dropped them. "Hi." He said looking at Anya, ignoring Mark. "I'm Geoff."

"This is Anya." Mark said. "She's in her final year doing History but this is her first year in Hall as she lived within commuting distance." He thought he had done well in acquiring so much information.

"Hi Anya."

If it wasn't love at first sight it was certainly lust.

Geoff had already decided that he would sleep with this girl, probably more than once, and it would definitely be worth any effort that might be needed. He bet himself ten pounds he would get off with her that evening.

Anya looked at the man sitting next to her. Whereas Mark had been a boy, a bit awkward and gangling, Geoff had already grown into his body. Even sitting down she could see he was tall and the shirt sleeves rolled up above his elbows showed he was muscular. She imagined those arms around her and his body on hers. It had been a long time. She wanted a man and this Geoff, who spoke with a rather posh southern accent and had perfectly clean fingernails, would do quite nicely.

They didn't talk much as they left the refectory together but as soon as they were out of the building and Mark had tactfully disappeared Geoff pushed Anya against the wall and kissed her, pushing his tongue far into her mouth to see if she resisted. She pushed herself against him, encouraging him, teasing him, loving the feeling of control, loving the anticipation of pleasure. No one seemed to take any notice as they weren't the only couple groping each other in the dark garden. Within minutes they were in Geoff's room which Anya had time to notice was a lot bigger than hers. He locked the door behind him.

"OK?" He asked.

"OK." She agreed.

They had both known from the moment they had first seen each other what was going to happen sooner or later and both wanted it to be sooner.

Two days before Geoff had thought he was finally going to get Fiona to go all the way. They had been lying on a blanket in the wood at the bottom of his garden his hands kneading her small breasts as he half lay across her. His left hand moved to push her skirt higher and she had not resisted. He felt awkward and uncomfortable, a bracken stalk was pushing into his shoulder, but anticipation of success kept him from shifting his position. As he grew more excited he had forgotten he was with Fiona, thinking of the girls he had been with in Liverpool. 'No, Geoff, no don't. Stop it!' She had pushed him off her and stood up, straightening her blouse and skirt before walking towards the house without a backward glance. 'Fucking prick teaser' he muttered under his breath. If his mother hadn't been old friends with her parents he wouldn't have given up so easily. He didn't follow her, staying to work himself to a climax in seconds.

His summer of forced abstinence came to a spectacular end as Anya stroked, licked and bit, then let him do exactly what he wanted.

Throughout that Autumn Geoff made no mention of Anya in his regular phone calls home. He told himself he was just waiting for the right time to tell his mother that she should forget any hopes she may have that he and Fiona would get together. He had no way of describing Anya to his mother. She was his girlfriend, lover, co-conspirator, room-mate, friend, sounding-board. In a short time they were inseparable.

Despite strict rules in the first mixed hall at the university, she wasn't the only girl who spent every night on that corridor in the men's hall, so they woke up together, they went into the university together where they separated for the days studies and then met up every evening in the Union bar. University life was exactly as the old Anya had hoped it would be. They spent the evenings together, shut up in his room or working or watching television curled up together on one of the uncomfortable chairs in the gloom at the back of the common room. Mark didn't resent Anya's taking over of Geoff; he knew he could never compete with her for Geoff's attention. He doubted anyone could.

In the first week of December, however, Mark saw much more of his friend because Geoff and Anya had first argument.

"Are you looking forward to Christmas?" Geoff had asked innocently enough as they waited in the rain for the morning bus into the campus.

She didn't answer immediately. She had been worrying about the holidays and desperately wanted Geoff to ask her to go home with him but didn't know how to get him to suggest it.

"Not sure. I haven't really thought about it." She answered, thinking that would give Geoff the opportunity to invite her.

"I'm off home next week."

"Oh." It hadn't occurred to her that he would be leaving so soon, most people were staying at least another week, some weren't leaving until the week after that, some weren't going home at all.

"Won't you be going home?"

In the months they had been together they hadn't talked much about their home life. Anya knew that Geoff lived in Kent and had a sort of girlfriend there, Fiona, who he didn't like very much. He knew no more about her than he had learned that first night. She had said nothing about her family or her home. He had never asked.

"I haven't got one."

It took a few moments for that to sink in.

"You haven't got a home?"

"No, and no family. Both my parents are dead." Surely he would invite her to go home with him for Christmas when he knew that.

"I'm sorry."

"No need to be, it's not your fault."

"What happened?"

But she wasn't going to be side tracked, if he wasn't going to ask her she'd have to ask him.

"Can I go home with you?"

She wasn't prepared for his anger. "God no Anya! You can't possibly do that!"

"Why the fuck not?" She could be angry too.

"Don't even think about it."

There was something about his tone of voice that made her lose control. She almost shouted her response. "You're ashamed of me! I'm not good enough for you! I'm good enough to screw but not to meet your precious bloody mother!"

"Shut up Anya, people are looking at us."

"I won't shut up."

Geoff took her arm and steered her away from the bus-stop. If they were going to argue they would do it in the privacy of the park.

"You cannot come home with me Anya."

"Why not?"

Geoff resorted to all the phrases his mother used.

"Christmas is a time for families, Anya. I'm sorry you don't have one but I do and I have to spend Christmas with them."

"Don't you want me to be with you?"

"Not at Christmas. "My father is dead too, I'm the man of the family and have responsibilities at Christmas."

"I can't believe you said that." Her tone changed, she used the ugly sneering voice she had often used when arguing with her mother. "You're the sodding man of the family are you you pompous fucking little twat?"

"You're not very attractive when you swear."

"You fucking like it when I tell you to keep fucking me, that's fucking swearing."

"I'm not inviting you home for Christmas Anya, that's final."

"So you don't give a fuck what I'm doing."

"No. You can fuck with whoever you want, as often as you like, you're not coming home with me."

She had stormed off, missing lectures for the day and for the next three nights she had slept in her own room. It was the first time since the day they had met and she hated it. She drank coffee in the mug she hadn't used since the summer and lived on baked beans on toast. She didn't want to go out, she didn't want anyone to see her without Geoff.

On the Friday evening, three days after their argument, she heard a light knock on her door and Geoff walked in.

"Fuck off."

"I'm sorry."

"Sorry?"

"Sorry we argued. Honestly I'm not ashamed of you or anything…"

"I know I speak with a scouse accent. I don't have the right clothes for your family. I wouldn't know how to behave properly. I wouldn't know which knife and fork to use and I'd speak with my mouth full and slouch and put my elbows on the table. I should never have thought I could visit your family. You've got every reason to be ashamed of me."

Geoff had not expected her to be so defensive, so self-deprecating.

"I'm not ashamed of you it's just that things are difficult at home. I couldn't take anyone home. I shouldn't have lost my temper, I just panicked. You see mother is a bit, well difficult, she's a bit possessive. I just panicked when you mentioned it. I wasn't expecting it. I'm sorry."

She had never seen Geoff so tongue tied.

"You're going to be away for ages."

"Just over three weeks."

"That's ages."

"You won't be alone, there'll be others staying in hall over

Christmas. You might even have some fun."

"I'll miss you." She didn't say any more as Geoff had locked the door behind him and his arms were already around her and his mouth on hers.

Nearly an hour later they lay together on the bed, Geoff gently stroking Anya's hair and pulling it out of her face, tucking it gently behind her ears.

"You never said anything about having no family."

"I don't suppose we have had a lot of talking time."

"Tell me now."

What Anya told him then was all Geoff ever knew of Anya's background for far too many years.

"My father died when I was very young, I don't know anything about him really. We didn't have any money so things were a bit tough then Mum died last summer of cancer."

"No brothers or sisters?"

"No. Just me."

"No grand-parents, uncles or aunts or cousins?"

"I've got an uncle but he lives abroad. I've never met him. Uncle Vincent."

"My poor Anya."

"And you? What about you? You said your Dad's dead?"

"He died on the day I was born."

"That must have been tough on your Mum."

"She's never lets us forget it."

"Us? You've got brothers? Sisters?"

"One sister, Margaret, 5 years older than me. That's it. You see I have to be there for them, at Christmas. I'm sorry I made you think you weren't good enough. If anything you're too good for them."

"Geoff?"

"Yes?"

"Nothing."

She wanted to know whether he loved her enough to cope with all her problems, whether they were going to have a long term relationship or just pack it in at the end of the year and go their separate ways; she wanted to know if he cared for her enough to stay with her when he knew she couldn't have children and the reason why not. She had wanted to know, if they did stay together, whether he would be on her side whatever life threw at them. But the opportunity was lost. She didn't ask, she just lay back as he began to work on her again.

Years later Anya remembered that evening and wished that so much more had been said, so many more secrets had been aired. It would have saved so much heartache.

Anya was surprised at how lonely she felt when Geoff said goodbye. She was going to be on her own for a far shorter time than through the previous summer and there were still lectures and seminars to attend and essays to write but the time went very slowly. Everything she did that had been their normal routine made her miss Geoff more. Back in her own room again she found the list of things she had planned to do over the summer to become the New Anya.

Me: *Get a tan, sort nails and hair, slim! Accent! Voice!*

Despite listening to the BBC rather than pirate radio she had not lost her accent. She would focus on that while Geoff was away. She allowed herself to be chatted up by Harold, a well-spoken postgraduate from the English department. The first morning they lay in his bed together she asked him if he would help her lose all traces of her accent and teach her all the things about manners and knives and forks that all middle class girls would know. He agreed with certain conditions about what she would have to do in return to which she agreed readily. Harold chose passages for her to read and she found herself enjoying the sonnets of John Donne, extracts from Shakespeare's plays and chapters of Jane Austen. He listened abstractly as she read, speaking only to correct her pronunciation, his fingers exploring her as she tried to ignore him. She allowed it only because it was her part of their bargain.

'Are you ashamed of who you are?' he had asked suddenly one evening in the middle of explaining the use of various pieces of cutlery Anya had never imagined existed. She hadn't been sure how to answer so she said nothing. 'The only difference between you and me is that I have the confidence to be who and what I am whether other people like me or not. It is the confidence of breeding. You have no such confidence as you have no breeding but I must give you credit for learning fast. Hold yourself well, speak quietly and clearly, don't say *y'know* at the end of every sentence, be polite to everyone whoever they are, say nothing if you have nothing to say, these are the best pieces of advice I can give you.' There were times she thought she was paying too great a price as she lay back and let him do what he wanted but on the whole she thought it was time well spent. By the day before New Year's Eve she had had enough of Harold's dingy bedroom that, for all his 'breeding' stank of sweat and sheets that needed washing, and went back to her room in hall to practice on her own until Geoff returned.

Geoff's Christmas was as frustrating as he had expected it to be.

He did his duty, organising the traditional Philips family Christmas, negotiating with a local farmer for the turkey, discussing the wines with the vintner who had served his family for years. Frantic Christmas preparations helped take his mind off Anya. He couldn't avoid seeing Fiona as her family were invited to the same parties as the Philips family but he did his best not to be alone with her. Geoff looked at the older and younger generations mixing and, with all the men in Dinner Jackets and the women in what he now thought of in Anya's words as 'posh frocks', he could identify no differences. Margaret and Fiona looked just the same age, and more importantly acted the same age, as their mothers. How many noses would Anya put out of joint if only she were here. He was surprised by how much he thought about her. None of his other Liverpool girls had affected him like this.

At the golf club New Year's Eve ball he was surprised when Fiona took his hand and led him outside, away from the lights and noise to her father's car. She arranged herself awkwardly on the back seat where she would allow some necking as long as it didn't mark her dress. She was shocked when Geoff, without saying a word, lay almost on top of her and tried to push her dress up with one hand. Fiona's outraged 'Geoff! No! What do you think you are doing?' made him realise where he was and who he was with.

"I was going to make love to you, you stupid woman." He spoke quickly and without thinking.

"You were what?"

"I thought it was what you wanted."

"Of course it wasn't. What on earth made you think I wanted you to do that to me?"

"You brought me up here. What else was I supposed to think?"

"I thought if we were alone together, well, you're graduating this year, I thought we'd talk about, well, what you were going to do, what we…"

Geoff had to stifle his laughter when he realised she had led him away from the crowds of the New Year's Ball so he could propose to her. Fiona was working with their mothers to trap him. They probably already had the wedding planned.

Fiona's attitude changed from one of wheedling regret to anger. "You've been having it off with someone else haven't you? I know you have. How could you? I thought we were waiting for each other."

Geoff returned anger with anger. "What the fuck do you expect? A Virgin? I'm nearly 21 for fucks sake."

She switched off her anger and began to cry. "Oh Geoff. I thought you loved me. I thought…"

"Well you know what thought did don't you? Is this why you've been leading me on? Letting me have a little bit more of you every time. Well it hasn't worked. One day, Fiona, you'll realise you can't lead men on. One day the man you're with won't stop when you say so."

"There will never be another man."

"No." He spoke quietly but firmly. "It's my turn to say no. I am not going to be drawn along like some bloody fish on a hook. I have a proper girlfriend in Liverpool. She's a real woman, not some inexperienced, immature little prick-teaser who looks like a clone of her mother. If ever you succeed in wheedling me into a quiet room or the back of a car I will not stop, I'll take you whether you like it or not. You know what? I think if push came to shove you'd enjoy it."

The next morning at breakfast he told his mother he had to go back to Liverpool early.

"You can't darling, we've been so busy with Christmas and the New Year we haven't had a chance to discuss your 21st birthday."

"I didn't think there was much to discuss."

"You'll be on your Easter vacation so we'll be able to have a real family party."

"But it won't be on my birthday will it? It'll be the day before or the week after. My birthday doesn't really matter does it? Not even my 21st."

"I don't think that's very fair Geoffrey. You know why it's such a difficult day for me."

"I do think it's fair, very fair. This is my 21st. It's the most important birthday of my life, the least you could do is celebrate it on the right day."

His mother, as she always did when she suspected she might not win, changed the subject. "You aren't the same boy you were. You used to be so understanding and now you're just self-centred, it's as if your family and your life here mean nothing to you."

"Oh for God's sake Mother don't do this. I'm nearly 21. This silly attempt at manipulation won't work anymore. Anyway I've got to go. I'm meeting Eric Atherton, yes I know it's New Year's Day but he's said he's happy to meet me at the beginning of such an important year for me, then I'm driving straight back to Liverpool."

"We're meeting Eric? What time? I must get ready."

"No mother. I am meeting Eric, not us. Me. On my own."

Kathleen was shocked to hear her son called their elderly solicitor by his first name. She shivered, filled with the fear that the moment she had dreaded for twenty-one years had arrived. Kathleen had known since the reading of her husband's will that when Geoffrey took control of his inheritance her life would change immeasurably but over the years she had persuaded herself she could control that change. As she listened to the determination in her son's voice she knew that her attempts at control of her son had been self-defeating.

His mother's silence told Geoff that at last he held the reins of his life in his own hands and he was not kind. "It's a big year for me. I have to decide what to do with my life, I have to decide how to provide for you and Margaret. But these are my decisions. Eric has told me that my father's firm belief was not to weaken the inheritance by dividing it. He insisted that the wealth be kept in one set of hands, and those hands were to be mine and there is absolutely nothing you can do about it."

Kathleen could not keep the bitterness out of her voice. "What is there to talk to Eric about? We all know everything is yours, Margaret gets nothing, I get nothing. We don't even have a right to live in our own home."

"Oh for God's sake why do you have to over-dramatise everything? Do you think I'm going to throw you and Margaret out? As to money the estate will give you an allowance."

Nothing could have made Kathleen more aware of her imminent change of status than his using the word 'allowance'.

"And you have to give me an allowance! An allowance! You, my 21 year old son, have to give me an allowance!"

"The sum Eric has suggested is extremely generous. You won't want for much."

"You've actually discussed a sum? Without me?" Kathleen's humiliation seemed complete. "And what about your sister?"

"Apparently my father didn't think that would be his problem. He would have expected her to be married before now, she's 26, almost middle aged as far as he and anyone in the 1950s would have been concerned."

Kathleen had difficulty holding back her tears of frustration. "How can you be so horrid? I don't know why she isn't married yet. Tim will come up to scratch it's just that he's taking longer than we expected."

"Poor old Tim He's got no chance has he! Margaret will get an allowance since she seems unable to earn decent money, but that can't go on indefinitely. She can't expect me to subsidise her for longer than a year or so. When she gets married I'll buy her a house as a sort of dowry. She won't be penniless."

"How very magnanimous of you." Ever since the week after he had died Kathleen had understood the depths of the contempt her husband had felt for women in general and for her in particular. "I suppose my job is to get Margaret and Tim married as soon as possible."

"If he's the only option."

"Margaret and Tim are very well suited." Kathleen tried to speak with dignity as she discussed her daughter's future.

"But they don't love each other."

"What's love got to do with a successful marriage?"

"Is that what you really think?" Geoff was shocked but wasn't going to show it.

"Perhaps I'm old fashioned."

"I think you are, and they don't even seem to like each other very much and I think that that should be the very minimum requirement. Is there no one else on the cards? No one else whose mother you've known since time began and who will have an excellent and lucrative professional career or who will inherit loads of cash, or both?"

"Don't be so offensive! Who Margaret marries is no business of yours."

"I'm afraid it is. Even though she's over 21 my consent is required if she is to benefit in any way from our father's will." Geoff wished, not for the first time, that he had met his father. He would have liked to understand the man who could leave a son that hadn't been born such power over his wife and daughter. Despite never having met him Geoff knew exactly what his father had intended. "He really didn't think much of women did he?"

"Will you take up the business interests?" Kathleen asked in a resigned voice that made Geoff think perhaps he had gone too far.

"I will learn what I can at board meetings but I'll probably let it carry on running itself. I'll learn what I can but I can't see myself being hands on for a good few years. I'm still a student and," he looked at his watch, "I've got to go. It'll be a long day what with meeting Eric then the drive up north." He kissed his mother briefly on the cheek and left. "Forget about any 21st party it'll be far too much trouble, it's Easter weekend anyway and close to my finals so I'll probably stay up in Liverpool until graduation."

"But that's June!"

"Only six months."

He picked up his bag and his briefcase and escaped.

"Do you ever worry I'll get pregnant?" Anya asked him as they lay together on his bed twelve hours later.

"Shit! Aren't you on the pill or something?" Geoff hadn't thought about it. He had assumed she had got it all under control.

"No I'm not on the pill or anything."

"A coil?" He had no idea what one was but he knew it was some form of birth control. "You've never asked me to use a Durex."

"I hate the things. Ruin everything. No feeling."

"We've been having sex with no protection at all?" With his mind full of money and inheritance it crossed his mind that Anya might be trapping him into marriage far more effectively than Fiona.

"I've never used contraception not once in the, how long is it, seven years since I started having sex."

"Seven years! You could only have been what? 14?"

"It was 23rd May 1964 so I was 13 years 9 months and 17 days old. Five thousand and thirty six days to be precise. I've worked it out."

"That's pretty young. Under age, statutory rape as the Americans would say."

"So?"

"How many boys, men, have you been with?"

"Don't ask Geoff. Hundreds. It's not important."

"Isn't it?"

"Absolutely not. Practice, as they say, makes perfect. And I'm pretty good at it wouldn't you say? I wouldn't be so practised if I'd only done it once or twice now would I?" She ran her fingers up and down his body, lingering in the places she knew were the most sensitive but Geoff was not to be distracted.

"What about VD or whatever?"

"Nothing to worry about there. My best friend is a doctor and he's made sure that I get checked out. I'm OK. Clean as they say. No problems."

"Stop it Anya. This is serious. You've had sex…"

"…hundreds of times. And no, I've not been pregnant once. I can't." She wasn't sure he understood what she meant as she distracted him by wriggling down underneath him, tempting him to make it one more time.

After, as they lay with their heads touching on the pillow, each was thinking very different thoughts.

Anya was glad Geoff wasn't pushing her to explain more. She was persuading herself it wasn't necessary to tell him. They would probably go their separate ways at the end of the year and he would never have needed to know. It was too hurtful, too personal, too demeaning to tell anyone until she really had to. So she would keep quiet.

Geoff was wondering vaguely why Anya seemed different. They had been apart for three weeks yet she was more composed, more in control and then he realised she had lost her accent.

"You sound different. Have you been taking elocution lessons?"

"Sort of."

He lay back thinking perhaps he was in love with her. She was clever, she was beautiful, she satisfied all his needs. They had been together for months with only that one argument when she had wanted to go south with him at Christmas. He decided he wouldn't make that mistake again. Next time he went back to Kent Anya would go with him.

His mother would absolutely hate her.

Chapter 5: Introductions

Kent, July 1971

Geoff and Anya moved out of the hall of residence and into the third floor flat in a Victorian semi-detached villa overlooking Sefton Park the day before Geoff left for Kent.

They had had something of an argument when Anya discovered his plan to leave her alone for a week but he insisted he had things to do and people to see.

They'd had several arguments since Geoff decided to spend a fourth year in Liverpool. They had argued first about what she should do after graduation. If she had had the courage to do what she really wanted she would have left Liverpool to travel around Europe, to see all the places she had studied but Geoff pointed out all the arguments against that plan and pushed her to stay with him for another year. So belatedly she applied for, and was accepted on, a year's BPhil course. The second bone of contention had been the flat. Geoff had paid the deposit and several month's advance rent before Anya had even seen it. That was a manufactured argument on her part as she liked the light, airy flat with its large rooms and lovely view through the trees. Then they had argued about the cost, it was far more than Anya could afford but Geoff had said that if she insisted on sharing the rent she could contribute her half in other ways. Then they had disagreed about what to do during the long summer vacation. Anya suggested hitching round Europe, but Geoff had said that he would buy a car and they could drive anywhere they wanted to go. Anya began to worry that whenever she and Geoff disagreed it was his view that prevailed.

By far the longest running disagreement had been about the

week Geoff wanted with his family before Anya joined him in Kent. When he had told her about his sister's engagement party any pleasure she had had from apparently being accepted into his other life was crushed when he told her he would travel south alone and she would join him a week later, travelling by train, and stay for just two days. 'You'll find two days of my mother and sister will be quite enough.' When she had changed the subject asking him what she should wear for the party he had said unhelpfully 'something beautiful'. They had argued again when he had reached for his wallet and Anya had said coldly that there was no need for him to buy her anything, she had just the dress.

When she stood on the doorstep watching as he threw his bag into his new car and climbed into the driving seat she was resigned, but still angry that he had not understood her feelings. "Remember, you're meeting Tim underneath the clock in Charing Cross Station at 6 o'clock on Thursday night."

"Why can't you meet me in London?"

"I'll probably be running around doing all sorts of things. Anyway Tim works in London, it'll be much simpler if you meet him at the station. Don't worry, everything will be fine."

She walked back up the three flights of stairs and let herself into the empty flat and sat at the unfamiliar table. "Everything will be fine he says. He hasn't the first idea what this is like for me." She spoke out loud addressing the flat that was to be her home for a year. The furniture was basic; a square wooden table with four chairs that didn't match; a worn settee and two arm chairs that were threadbare, a modern looking but rickety side table with a green phone. She thought it was worse furniture than Tennyson Street and it reminded her of the week she had spent with Harold the English student. She supposed landlords didn't spend any more than they had to. "Pull yourself together girl." She told herself in her best BBC accent. "There are so many things you can do in a week."

After clearing away the breakfast things she phoned the Hills, she hadn't spoken to them for far too long and now she had a home she should get back the things they had stored for her.

"Anya, my dear, how wonderful to hear from you, my brother and I were wondering how you were getting on."

"I'm so sorry I haven't been in touch."

"I suppose you've been busy, though we did appreciate your Christmas Card."

"I should have done more."

"Of course you shouldn't you silly girl! You've had a lot of work to do and no doubt a wonderful social life."

"But I should have invited you to graduation." Geoff hadn't wanted his mother and sister there so they had invited no-one, standing together, away from the crowd of fellow graduates and their families taking photographs on that sunny afternoon at the end of June. She should have overruled Geoff and invited them, they would have appreciated it.

"Don't you worry about that. Now, when are we going to see you?"

The misery that had threatened to overwhelm Anya disappeared.

"This afternoon?"

The journey back to Birkenhead was a familiar one. As she walked around the deck she thought of the changes in her life in the year since she had last taken the ferry. Then she had been heading home, to Tennyson Street, to her mother, to a long summer holiday working in the laundry. So many changes, such a different life, such different prospects, she felt she was a different person.

"You look so well Anya dear." Miss Hill welcomed her with a hug.

Anya couldn't say the same about her old headmistress. Anya was relieved not to have to reply as Dr Hill appeared behind his sister and ushered them into the small front room, crowded with photographs.

"We believe congratulations are in order."

"Thanks, I got my First. And it's only because of you, both of you."

"We are so proud of you."

"You knew about the First?"

"Of course we did. I haven't been a headmistress for ten years without having some contacts who will always let me know how my girls have got on. Fifteen of my girls graduated this year, three from Liverpool."

"I'm sorry, I didn't mean I was special."

"But you are special Anya, you were the only one who got a First."

"And the only one who had such difficult circumstances to deal with." Dr Hill added as he turned opened a drawer in the sideboard and took out a blue box.

"I know I shouldn't say this but you'll possibly be quite pleased to know that Henrietta Hodge scraped a 2.2. You two were always so competitive I remember." Miss Hill seemed anxious, almost nervous as her brother handed the box to Anya who carefully opened it.

"It's absolutely beautiful." She stared at the gold locket on a chain.

"Isn't it?" Miss Hill agreed. "It was given to me by a young man but I never wore it."

Anya remembered the conversation when she had learned that generations weren't so very different. She thought of a young man, soon to die in a burning plane giving the locket to the girl who would have been younger than she was now. It had been a promise for a future that would never happen.

"I want you to wear it but you must be very careful whose picture you put inside, that person must be with you for life. You will wear it won't you?" Miss Hill's enquiry seemed urgent.

"Of course I'll wear it, but are you sure you want me to have it? Are you sure you want to give it away?"

"I'm absolutely certain my dear. Wear it to remind you of so many things."

"Always remember the courage of the lady who gave it to you." Dr Hill looked at his sister with deep affection. "In your life you will have difficult decisions to make, hold onto the locket and think what Dot would have advised you to do. It will remind you always to meet Dot's standards."

"Yes, you must think of me as Dot. There's no need for 'Miss Hill' now."

"You must explain to that boyfriend of yours who has given you this so he doesn't think you have another man in tow."

"What boyfriend?" Anya had asked the question but then she realised that, of course, Dot would have had reports of her activities through the year.

"A mathematician and computer scientist I believe."

"Is there no way of keeping a secret from you?" Anya smiled. "His name's Geoff. He's from Kent and we do see rather a lot of each other. In fact we've just got a flat together. Just for a year. He's doing a fourth while I do a BPhil."

"Having a steady boyfriend can do you no harm at all. I should probably tell you not to rush things but instead I'll tell you that if he's right for you and he makes you happy then grab him and don't let him go."

"I don't know about that but I am going to meet his mother next week." It sounded so respectable.

"Conforming at last?"

"Oh no! I'll be completely unsuitable! Geoff said that his mother will absolutely hate me."

"Well just don't be too outrageous dear girl, I'm sure Geoff's mother loves him dearly and you wouldn't want to hurt her, or anyone else, unnecessarily would you?"

"I can't promise that. From what Geoff says she a bit of a cow but I'll take her as I see her. If she's nice to me I'll be nice to her but if she isn't, then we'll see."

"She can't say fairer than that can she?" Dr Hill asked his sister with a wink.

"I'll be in touch in when I get back. I'll tell you how it all goes."

The afternoon went quickly as they had tea and Anya collected her boxes. Dr Hill insisted on driving her back to Liverpool. Months later Anya wondered why he hadn't taken the opportunity to tell her Dot was ill but had simply used the time to warn her. "Be careful, your Geoff may be sound enough but don't throw your lot in with him until you're sure he can cope with your situation." He was obviously choosing his words carefully. "By the way, we love your new accent but don't change yourself too much, just for a man."

The following Friday Anya stood on the platform watching the train wind laboriously into the station and grind noisily to a halt. She tried to feel less nervous, she had never been on a train where she had to open the carriage door and wasn't sure whether to close it behind her or leave it open for other passengers. She found a seat near the buffet and placed her canvas bag on the rack above. She worried whether she had packed the right things, her bag containing her sponge bag, two bra and pants sets carefully chosen on her shopping trip the day before, a pair of high heeled sandals and her mother's dress, carefully folded in tissue paper, seemed inadequate. Too late she realised she should have bought something to read but took too long to decide whether or not she had time to get to the kiosk and back, in the end deciding she should stay put.

For the hours of the journey she had only the view from the window to take her mind off the weekend to come. She worried that she wouldn't know anyone to talk to at the party and that if she did speak to anyone she would let Geoff down. Nervously she put her hand many times to the locket around her neck trying to absorb Dot's confidence in her. Frequently she looked down at her mother's ring wondering what her mother would make of her life now. She had decided to wear the ring all weekend as she wanted Mrs Philips to notice it and hoped she would think that Geoff had given it to her. 'Let her think her son is really serious about me.'

As the miles passed the world began to look different, there were more cars in the station car parks, more houses and fewer fields along the route. As they reached the suburbs of London she stared out of the window at the seemingly never ending walls and blocks of flats and thought of Marion. She should have asked Dot about Marion.

By the time the train finally stopped at Euston it seemed to Anya that London had already gone on forever and she was only just reached the northern part of it. She steeled herself for the trip across the capital and the meeting with Tim.

Geoff had given her clear instructions. First she had to get a taxi to Charing Cross Station. He had told her it would be easy but she had to find the queue and then wait for twenty minutes as black cab after black cab came and went and the queue very slowly grew shorter. As she drew nearer the front of the queue she watched other people climbing in the taxis to see what they did and decided she would tell the cabbie her destination then open the door to get in. It seemed an important thing to get right. When it was her turn she found the window to the cabbie shut so all her planning had been wasted. The journey to Charing Cross took longer than she had expected, though there was no shortage of things to look at. She recognised the British Library, she loved the narrow streets of Covent Garden but was disappointed not to see more well-known sights such as Trafalgar Square or Buckingham Palace. The cabbie pulled into the courtyard of the station and she handed over the exact money for the fare, smiling into the disdainful face of the cabbie.

Her second instruction from Geoff had been to buy her ticket and be under the clock in the main concourse at exactly six o'clock. As she turned away from the ticket office it wasn't yet five-thirty. At first she stood, looking around at the endless stream of people who all seemed to know exactly what they were doing and where they were going. She looked up at the clock again and there were still over 20 minutes to go so she hitched her bag over her shoulder and walked out of the station. Looking in the shop windows as she walked along the street she knew to be the Strand she was disappointed to see they were exactly the same as the shop windows in Liverpool, the only ones that were different were the tourist traps filled with tacky souvenirs. She reached the Savoy and stood staring down the access road wondering what went on behind those revolving doors. She turned back towards the station and found heading in the same direction as the crowds made the walk a lot easier. As she re-entered the concourse she glanced at the clock, she was still a few minutes early so she followed the signs to the Ladies where she checked her make-up. Staring at her reflection she remembered Harold's words at Christmas *'have the confidence to be who and what you are whether other people like it or not'* She held her head high as she climbed the stairs and headed for the clock.

Tim was standing in the bar watching the concourse. He was on his second pint, as were Dave and John. Every evening they met in the station bar to have a drink or two, to wind down from the day's work and wait for the trains to be less crowded. They shared a flat and spent all their leisure time together playing golf and cricket, they even commuted on the same trains. The only thing that separated them was work, Tim was an accountant, Dave on the road to being a solicitor and John was a management consultant earning more than the other two put together.

"Bet that's her." Tim felt a nudge and looked in the direction John was indicating with a jerk of his head. "You reckoned Geoff couldn't pull anything smart so I bet that's her." The girl they laughed at was overweight and badly dressed, the remains of an ice cream staining her mouth.

"What do you know about the girl?" David asked before draining his glass.

"She's called Anya."

"We know that." David showed his impatience at Tim's deliberate unhelpfulness by speaking slowly, as if to a particularly ignorant client. "What I mean is how do we recognise her?"

"She's 21 years old."

"Obviously old chap, she's just graduated." John was pleased at his deduction.

"She could have been a mature student; you know some 30 year old spinster who gave up finding a man and took to academia." Tim nudged Dave "Like that one." Their eyes followed another dowdy woman in late middle age as she dragged a shopping basket on wheels across the station forecourt and their laughter was the laughter of men utterly confident of their positions in life.

"Geoff said she got a First."

"So she can't be thick."

"He seemed impressed."

"But it was only Liverpool." Tim shared the views of his future mother-in-law regarding provincial universities.

"But how are you going to recognise her if there's more than one female under the clock at six?"

"Introduce myself to the best looking one of course."

"On the basis it will be the other but you'll have enjoyed chatting up the looker."

"Good plan."

"What about that?" Dave pointed out a tall, slender girl with a bag slung over her shoulder, walking with her head held high, her dark hair almost reaching the small of her back, drawing attention to the neat bottom in tight jeans. They all looked at her but only Tim spoke. "Nice arse. Wouldn't say no."

"Hold on Tim, you're getting engaged this weekend. Remember?"

"That's never going to stop me looking."

"Or more if it suits you?"

"Back in a bit, got to make room for more beer." Tim made his excuses but didn't go in the direction of the Gents.

He had noticed the girl walking out of the station and he had to follow her. As he walked up the Strand a discreet few yards behind the girl Tim wondered what the hell he was doing getting engaged to Margaret. It seemed to him that he had known her forever and that, between the two families, it had always been a matter of when, not if, they would get engaged. He watched the girl's bottom in the tight jeans as she walked and found the contrast with his future wife's figure obscene. Margaret had her good points, she was sensible, she would make a good home and she would be perfectly acceptable to all his future colleagues, but she was not in any way physically attractive. As the girl he was following was. One day he would have his own practice and then he would need a wife to look after his comforts and, when he could afford it without inconveniencing his quality of life, she would present him with the two children, a boy then a girl, to complete the aura of respectability. For all that Margaret would be eminently more suitable than this girl whose hair shone as it swished from side to side as she walked. He thought it rather a shame that he was going to marry someone who he didn't like very much. He had never pretended his marriage to Margaret was to be anything other than one of convenience arranged as it had been by their mothers. He had every intention of finding his entertainment elsewhere, with girls like this one. He knew, if they ever met, he would like her very much.

He just stopped in time to prevent bumping into her as she stood looking towards the Savoy. He looked down quickly to check his watch, she couldn't be Anya as Anya would be under the clock nervously awaiting his arrival. He turned and headed back to the station, there would just be time for Dave to get in another round before six.

"There's that girl again."

Tim was back in the bar with Dave and John as Anya walked across the forecourt and stopped under the clock.

"Christ! It can't be her. Surely not?"

They all stared at the girl, taking in the tan, the curves under the t-shirt, the shape of her body and length of her legs clearly emphasised by the tight jeans.

"High heels and jeans! That's unusual."

"And such tight jeans."

"Such very, very tight jeans."

"Such a white t-shirt. Don't you think that white t-shirts are far better than dark coloured ones…"

"for emphasising curves…"

"And what curves."

When she headed towards the Ladies they looked at each other and laughed. "Of course it's not her." Tim failed to hide his disappointment from his friends as they sat drinking, staring at the space under the clock.

"Bloody hell Tim. Look." John indicated the girl leaving the Ladies and heading for the clock.

"No!"

"Coincidence."

"She'll be moving on before then. There is absolutely no way Geoffers could pull that one." Tim liked Geoff about as much as he liked his sister. They finished their pints and still the girl hadn't moved from under the clock. She was looking round her as if expecting someone.

"It must be her. Come on Tim."

"Stay here." For no reason he could have explained meeting this girl was very important to Tim and he didn't want his friends to mess everything up. "She's meeting me not the three of us."

"She'll have to meet us all sooner or later."

Anya, standing directly under the clock, couldn't see the time but she was fairly sure it was after six. She was beginning to plan what she could do if Tim didn't turn up when she was approached by three men.

"Are you, by any wonderful chance, called Anya?"

"Tim?"

"No I'm John." He gave a slight bow, hamming up chivalry.

She turned away to a shorter man. "Tim?"

"No I'm Dave, but still delighted to make your acquaintance."

"So you must be Tim."

"Absolutely. That's me."

Anya looked up at the bluest of blue, almost violet, eyes. Tim was tall, even in her high heels he stood at least four inches above her. He was taller even than Geoff. Those eyes were set in a tanned face which was framed with a mess of curly blond hair. His fingers, hooked around the tag of his suit jacket which was slung over his shoulder in a pose of studied nonchalance, were long and tapered, the nails perfectly manicured.

"I'm Anya."

They held their look, each appraising the other, for more than a fraction too long.

"Come on at this rate we'll miss the train." David brought the moment to an end but only after catching John's eye and raising a quizzical eyebrow.

Anya was in her element, she knew she had their attention and she held it. By the time the train pulled into Tunbridge Wells station she had three admirers, at least one of whom was determined to get to know her extremely well before the end of the weekend.

"Goodbye Dave, John." She carefully looked at each of them in turn as she said goodbye. "It's been a fun journey."

"We'll see you at the party."

"Oh good. I'm glad I'll know someone there."

"You know Geoff!"

"Of course. Geoff." As the train had hurtled through the Kent countryside she had almost forgotten she was about to see Geoff for the first time in more than week.

"Come on Anya, let me take your bag." Tim flung it over his shoulder, glaring at John and Dave. "We'll be expected up at the house. See you at the pub later." He was smiling broadly as he watched Dave and John heading up the hill while he led Anya in the opposite direction.

"They're nice guys." Anya started the conversation, easily keeping up with Tim as they walked across the common despite her high heeled sandals.

"Known them for years, since we were all kids really. And Geoff, though he's a lot younger of course."

"Not a lot surely?"

"Five years."

"What's Geoff's mum like?" Anya knew that in the next few minutes she would be under the strict evaluation of Geoff's mother and sister and they would be a lot more difficult to win round than the three young men.

"To be honest…"

"Please."

"She's a snobbish, possessive old bat. For years she's made Margaret and Geoff do exactly what she wants them to do. Geoff was really brave to escape to Liverpool, that really pissed her off."

"Are Margaret and Geoff close? He never speaks of her."

"No. Not at all. Geoff has always been his mother's favourite that's why Margaret's getting engaged to me."

"It's funny that. I mean you're 'getting engaged' as an event. Surely you 'got engaged' when you asked her to marry you and she said yes?"

"It doesn't work like that. I never actually asked her. I suppose it's just been assumed we'd get engaged one day."

"Assumed?" Anya laughed and she noticed the look Tim gave her, at once speculative, enquiring and admiring.

"Our families have known each other for years, we're the right age for each other. You know."

"No I don't! I think that's perfectly idiotic. And another thing, you don't talk about getting married, just about getting engaged. When are you going to actually 'get married'?"

"I don't have any say in that either." He tried to make a joke of it but as he spoke he realised the truth in the words. "Margaret and her mother and my mother will get together and set the date."

"I know I've only known you half an hour but I hadn't put you down as such a drip."

He had no time to defend himself. Instead he attacked.

"That ring? Is it from Geoff?"

"Oh God no! It's…" Her voice changed, becoming suddenly serious, "It was my mother's. She's dead. She didn't leave me much but she left me this." She didn't know Tim well enough to explain, she hadn't even explained it to Geoff. But then Geoff had never asked.

"I'm sorry." Tim was thinking fast. Half formed thoughts raced through his mind. Well spoken, though with the slightest hint of a Merseyside lilt, no family, a casually worn ring worth at least five hundred pounds. She was obviously not after Geoff's money.

"Here we are, the Philips family residence."

Anya had a good first look at the house that would eventually mean so much to her. It was detached and large and set well back from the road, surrounded by trees. She had had no idea Geoff was this well off. She had assumed he lived in a three bed-roomed semi-detached house like everyone who was middle class, even Henrietta, did. This was a really big house, a rich family's house.

As they reached the front door and Tim rang the doorbell Anya wondered why they hadn't gone round to the back door, after all he was about to marry into the family. As they waited for the door to open he handed her her bag and she rewarded him with a kiss on his lips to which he responded far too enthusiastically for a man about to become engaged. He only stepped back when they heard the door opening. She wondered why it had taken so long for the bell to be answered, Geoff must have known what time they would be arriving.

Anya had no experience of families but had an uncomfortable feeling that she would not get on well with this one.

"Is everything ready?" Kathleen Philips looked critically around the large living room and strode out through the French windows to the garden.

"Yes Mother, you've thought of everything." Margaret, walking slightly behind her mother, tried to catch her up.

"Really, that girl!" They both looked across the lawn at Anya who was carefully snipping a rose from one of the bushes and putting it in Geoff's button hole.

"She doesn't know any better Mother."

"I really don't know what he sees in her."

"Yes you do mother."

"She's not suitable at all."

"It's just a university thing."

"He's brought her down for your party when everyone will be here."

"But he's not going to get engaged to her or anything."

"Maybe not but have you seen the ring she's wearing? How could she have got hold of a ring like that if Geoffrey hadn't given it to her?"

"Can you just leave worrying about my little brother until tomorrow? Tonight is supposed to be about me and Tim."

"Of course darling, of course. You look very nice."

Margaret knew the compliment was an afterthought, and a lie as she felt frumpish and old fashioned. The green evening dress made her feel awkward, its boned bodice emphasised her lack of figure and the colour reflected on her shiny face and made her look nauseous.

She had wanted to look good for Tim, he always looked so distinguished in his dinner jacket and she had wanted to look as attractive as Anya, but she had failed. Whatever she wore she would never look as good as Anya.

"Just be yourself darling. Tim loves you as you are." Kathleen tried to be encouraging but was unconvincing.

As she watched Anya in the garden she tried to make an objective comparison between her daughter and her son's girlfriend. Anya had the advantage of being tall and having a very good figure whereas Margaret was short of average height and was the typical English shape with breasts too small and hips too large. Anya's hair was long straight and shone with a slight copper tinge as it hung down the length of her bare tanned back. Margaret's short, light brown, wavy hair never stayed in place for long and the hairdresser had not done a good job, forcing every hair into place with far too much hairspray. Anya's dress, Kathleen had to admit, made her look simultaneously innocent and sophisticated, whereas Margaret's dress had undoubtedly been a mistake. She wondered what it was that Anya saw in Geoffrey, a man like Tim would be far more her type. It had, undoubtedly, to be his money.

"I don't think he loves me at all. I have no idea why he wants to get engaged. He's only doing it because you and Esme have had it planned since I was born." Margaret sounded on the verge of tears and Kathleen turned her attention back to her daughter. "That is not true, darling. Esme loves her son as much as I love you. We would never want anything for either of you that would bring unhappiness."

"But it is what you both wanted."

"Of course it is darling. You should have no doubts at all, it is such a suitable alliance. Tim will make you very happy." She kissed her daughter on the cheek. "You look lovely when you smile. Now Geoffrey. Here please." She turned her attention to ensuring the smooth running of the evening.

"There's Tim." Margaret smiled as her mother left her. She walked uncertainly towards her future husband. She was really going to try.

Tim gave Margaret a hug and kissed her briefly on the cheek. He never liked to show affection in public even when he felt it. As he did his duty by Margaret he watched as Dave and John headed straight for Anya who was standing alone now Geoff had been cajoled by his mother into arranging the closest members of the two families into a formal welcoming line for the arrival of the guests.

Tim took every opportunity to look at Anya, something not lost on his future mother-in-law. Her dress was sheer, so slim fitting that he decided she could be wearing no underwear at all. If she had been there would have been lines in the outline of the dress, and there weren't. He began to feel inappropriate arousal.

To calm himself down he turned back to Margaret in the green dress. It looked like it was a shell around her, protecting her from any contact with any man. He took his future wife by the arm and, as he led her towards her mother, he was put in mind of the aristocrats in the French Revolution being led towards the guillotine. He listened dutifully to Mrs Philips as she instructed him on his role in the receiving line. He smiled, playing the part of the soon-to-be-son-in-law. He'd had a lot of practice at playing roles while his mind was somewhere else entirely.

Anya looked at the receiving line as she talked to Dave and John.

"Why are they doing that?" she asked "It's so, I don't know, so old fashioned."

"That's Mrs Philips's way."

"I thought that sort of thing went out before the war."

"It probably did."

"But try telling Mrs Philips that!"

Anya was pleased she had these two to talk to.

"Did I say how lovely you look tonight?" Dave spoke tentatively.

"That's a nice pre-war thing to say."

"No I mean it. You look…" Dave tried to find the right word and gave up.

John completed his sentence for him. "Stunning. Absolutely beautiful."

"Why thank you kind sirs." Anya smiled and did a small curtsey that only served to show Dave and John more of her cleavage beneath the flattering folds of the cowl neck.

"It's such a silly idea that reception line," Anya said, this time with some seriousness, "just look at them."

Kathleen stood nearest the door, the first to welcome her guests. Geoff stood next to her, with what, he told her later, was a mixture of embarrassment and pride at taking his father's place. Margaret stood next to him then Tim with his mother on his right.

"Doesn't Tim have a father either?" She asked.

"They divorced when Tim was 18. There was an enormous scandal. Sex obviously." Dave explained.

"He was thrown out of the Golf Club and the Rugby Club and everything." John spoke as if that was the worst thing that could possibly happen to anyone. "But then he died and all was forgiven when it was too late."

Looking at Tim and Margaret together Anya knew that any relationship, let alone a marriage, was doomed. There was no spark between them, they seemed barely to be talking to each other on what should be the happiest occasion. Anya watched and understood that Margaret would never be able to handle Tim, he was a taker never a giver, whose appetites would always rule his actions. He reminded her of so many of her mother's men. Anya didn't feel in the least sorry for Margaret, if she didn't have the brains to rebel against what her mother was doing to her then that was no-one's fault but her own.

She turned her attention to Geoff. He talked a short time to everyone who shook his hand, engaging them with his intelligent brown eyes. She had seen the photographs in the living room and had, at first, thought them to be of Geoff but once she recognised the woman to be a young, attractive, slim version of Kathleen she realised the man had to be Geoff's father. Geoff really was very like him, even to their identical prematurely receding hairlines. She watched Geoff for some minutes but he never once looked towards her. He must have realised she knew no one and she would have thought, hoped, that he would be concerned about her but he had been absorbed into the role of son, brother and father replacement. In a slight lull in arrivals Mrs Philips looked up at her son and smiled. Anya was chilled by the look they gave each other. This was a Geoff she did not know, did not recognise and didn't like very much.

"Dave?" she asked, unsure whether she should go this far. "Have you ever wondered if Mrs Philips is just a wee bit too possessive?"

"You've noticed that?"

"It's pretty bloody obvious."

"She's always been like that. It's because Mr Philips died, you know, on the day Geoff was born."

"Yes I knew that but that was years ago. Has she always been like that?"

"Always. Nothing will change her."

"We'll see." Anya spoke deliberately.

Dave looked at John, the look said 'this isn't going to have a happy ending'.

"Immovable object."

"Irresistible force."

"Mountain."

"Mohammed."

"Pardon?"

"Nothing Anya, just man stuff."

Tim extracted himself from the reception line, an action he felt excusable since most of the guests had arrived, and walked straight towards Anya.

"Can I get you another drink?"

She had no chance to answer as he put his hand firmly under her elbow and propelled her towards the kitchen. She wondered fleetingly if Geoff had noticed.

"You are just too gorgeous to leave with those two."

"I like them. They're fun."

"So am I."

"You're about to get engaged."

"Come outside anyway, just for a minute."

"A minute? That's all you think it'll take?" She asked

provocatively, but she allowed him to lead her through the kitchen door and into the dark part of the garden. He walked quickly for the time. When he finally stopped, he turned and put his arms around her.

"I'm about to give you what you've been asking for."

"I've been asking for? How do you make that out?"

"Your dress. The fact that you are wearing nothing underneath."

"How do you know that?"

"I can tell." Tim ran his hand slowly from the nape of her neck down her back, past her waist, and rested on her buttocks. "No bra, no pants, nothing."

She placed her index finger gently on his lips and ran it down, over his chin, down his neck and his chest, past his waist and onto his trousers which were bulging.

"And you are ..."

"Come on." His voice was low and urgent.

He took her hand and led her further into the trees, she thought they must be a hundred yards from the house by now and he seemed to know exactly where he was going. He stopped at a slight clearing where a rug was on the ground.

"Prepared?" She asked.

"Absolutely. Someone would be willing, even if it had only been Margaret."

"Hardly a flattering thing to say about your fiancée."

"She isn't my fiancée yet."

"Or me for that matter."

"Would flattery make any difference?"

"No."

While they sparred Tim had taken off his jacket and folded it carefully inside out before placing it on the ground, then he became more urgent, pushing Anya down with one hand and pushing her dress up with the other. She parted her legs and accepted him willingly.

He came quickly and she was not at all satisfied but she was exultant. He had taken her on the night of his engagement, she decided he would on the day of his wedding, and perhaps on a few occasions before and after. Sex was as important to Tim as it was to her and to Geoff. Thoughts of Geoff didn't worry her, in the past months neither had expected the other to be faithful, and their having sex with others had added to their excitement of their own relationship.

"What are you doing tomorrow?" He asked, in a perfectly normal voice as he pushed his shirt down inside his trousers and sorted out the ridiculous maroon cummerbund he had been forced by his mother to wear.

"Heading back up north I suppose." Anya answered nonchalantly, determined that Tim should realise he was nothing special.

"But is that it?" she asked, "That's all you've got to offer?"

He leant down and kissed her properly for the first time. After just the right amount of time she let his tongue into her mouth and alternately bit and licked it gently, it was a kiss like none Tim had ever experienced. He pulled away, aroused and admiring. "Again?" They reversed the process of dressing and this time he lasted longer and Anya was nearly satisfied.

"Won't they be wondering where we are?"

"I shouldn't think so."

"Your future mother-in-law will be keeping her eagle eyes on you every minute she can for the rest of her life."

"I think you're right. Again?"

"Take a little longer this time please." She asked, showing him she was totally in control of herself, and of him.

Anya was beginning to be impressed with Tim's stamina. She approved, three times in fifteen minutes was good going and each time he was giving her more pleasure.

"Come on. Sort yourself out."

Tim stood up and sorted his clothes out again. "How do I look?"

"Reasonable considering you've been fucking the shit out of me."

Tim looked at her fiercely disapprovingly. "Do you normally talk like that?"

"What? Saying you've been fucking me? It's what you've been doing."

"Is that what Geoff does?"

Was he asking whether he was better than Geoff? She'd go along with the game. "Does Geoff fuck me? Of course he does, though usually he lasts a little longer." She noticed him frown slightly.

"But how often?"

"Oh usually every day, sometimes twice, sometimes three times."

"Never four?"

Anya thought how stupid men were to be so competitive and how inevitably Tim was rising to the bait. "I can't possibly say."

He pushed her back and ripped her dress as he forced himself down into her one more time and proved to himself, if not to Anya, that he was a better lover than Geoff.

"That's enough Tim, we must get back to the party."

"Well you can't go with that dress. Look, it's torn and filthy."

She had worn it for a little under two hours but somehow she thought her mother would approve.

Ten minutes later she was back in the party, wearing jeans, white t-shirt and high red heels.

"Anne, dear." She heard Mrs Philips's voice and turned around. "I see you've changed, what happened to your lovely dress?"

Anya spoke very clearly with no trace of any accent other than refined middle class. "Anya, my name is Anya, and I'm afraid I spilt some wine which made it rather see-through. I'm afraid these are the only other clothes I have to change into. I do apologise to be so inappropriately dressed but it's not what people wear but the way they behave that matters, don't you agree?" She was delighted with the ambiguity of her words.

"Such a shame." Mrs Philips didn't believe a word of the story about wine. If ever she had seen a girl who had been lying on her back for a man this was it. She looked around for Geoff and saw him doing his duty talking to Fiona, Esme and some cousins of Tim. The other candidate, in Kathleen's mind, was Tim and she found him laughing with Dave and John. His tie didn't look quite as neatly tied as it had an hour before, and he looked very relaxed. Her suspicions were furthered by the fact he was not with Margaret. She tapped a small silver swizzle stick against her champagne glasses to bring everyone's attention to her. It didn't take long. Everyone had been waiting for the speeches to be over with so they could get on with the party.

"Ladies. Gentlemen." She spoke quietly having long ago realised that that was the way to get people to listen. "I think my son has an announcement to make."

There was a small, self-conscious meeting of hands in something approaching applause.

"I have my speech here. Just a moment." Dramatically he took what looked like a sheet of paper from his pocket. It was computer paper, sheet after sheet with perforated joins and sprocket holes at each side dropped down to the floor. Everyone laughed on cue. "Only joking." Everyone stopped laughing, again right on cue. "I think we all know what the announcement is, after all the invitations did say 'to celebrate the engagement of Margaret with, what is his name?" Again people laughed self-consciously at the weak joke. "Ah yes. Tim. Well come on Tim? Margaret? Where are they? Have they sneaked off somewhere to practise for their wedding night?" Dave and John started to laugh but stopped quickly as theirs was the only laughter. "Ah here they are." Tim and Margaret walked from different parts of the room to stand by Geoff. "I'll hand over to Tim."

Anya had to admire Tim's ability to step into character. No one would have guessed what he had been saying and doing minutes before as he charmed his family and guests with a smoothly prepared speech.

"I just want to say that when Margaret's pregnant mum and mine, slightly more pregnant, got together about 27 years ago they decided one would have a girl and one would have a boy and that in 27 years' time they would get engaged. The first part of their plan came to fruition. I was born and then, four months later Margaret came into the world and, as you can see, she is most definitely a girl!" Everyone muttered the required agreement at the clever compliment.

"The second part of their plan took rather longer. Margaret and I had to grow up which, I think, we have almost done. Then, of course, we had to fall in love with each other. I can't remember a time when I didn't have Margaret to love. I can't remember a time when she was not a part of my life and I can't imagine a time when she would not be." Tim paused and took Margaret's hand. "Margaret Olivia Philips. Would you do me the great honour of becoming my wife?" Margaret blushed and made a mock curtsey. "I will." He pulled her up and kissed her lightly on the mouth. He was aware that she tensed slightly in a barely perceptible flinch as his lips met hers.

Geoffrey raised his glass. "A toast, ladies and gentlemen. Margaret and Timothy." Mutterings of 'Margaret and Timothy' were followed by the clink of glasses and a short round of applause with calls for more champagne.

Anya had watched all this carefully, as if learning a part in a play. It was so contrived, so outside anything she had ever experienced. She admired Tim's careful choice of words. She, perhaps alone in the room apart from Margaret, had realised that Tim had never actually said he loved his fiancée.

Margaret had, up to the moment that Tim had leant down to kiss her, been happy. But as he had lent down to kiss her she had noticed lipstick on his collar, just a trace, but enough, and of a recognisable shade. Anya's. Anya had kissed Tim low down on the neck. Not somewhere where you would lay a social kiss, even if Anya were the sort to do social kissing. No. Tim and Anya had been snogging. At the very least. Tim had been off with that tart tonight, her night. She knew it as clearly as if she had been watching. She was hurt, and she was angry.

Without fuss, and unnoticed by all but her mother, Margaret took her fiancé's hand and led him out of the room. Kathleen didn't mind, they were engaged now, she didn't care what they got up to.

Tim followed Margaret up the stairs to her room anticipating a session of Margaret's wet open mouthed kisses. Instead, as he closed her bedroom door behind them, he received a sharp, painful, slap on his face.

"You shit, you absolute shit. You've been with her haven't you?"
He had to strain to hear her, she spoke so quietly.
"What?"
"You and that, that Liverpudlian slut." She spat the words out, as if squeezing the words between her teeth. "Her lipstick is on your collar. Low down. And why did she have to change! I bet she didn't spill wine on her dress. She ruined it lying on the ground her legs spread for you didn't she." It wasn't a question so he said nothing, waiting for her to fall quiet. "You bastard, you absolute bloody bastard." And she pummelled her fists against his chest, careless that her tears were destroying her makeup, unable to put her jealousy and pain into words.

"Margaret, Maggie, my Moppet. Calm down." Tim was soothing her, holding her tight to him so she couldn't hit him anymore. It took a few minutes but eventually he felt her body relax. "Nothing happened, Moppet, honestly nothing. She tried it on but I said no. Geoff is welcome to her. Honestly nothing happened. Here." He handed her his handkerchief so she could wipe her tears and clean her face.

Without a word she reached behind her back and unzipped her dress. She let it fall to the ground and as she stepped out of it he tried not to look at the white flesh between the patches of unattractive underwear. He looked at her face, it seemed the safest thing to do, but her eyes never left the floor as she let him lead her to the bed.

His passion sated by Anya, without fuss, recrimination or any enjoyment on either side, Tim took his future wife's virginity.

Breakfast the next morning was always going to be difficult.

As Kathleen laid the table her mind was on the events of the night before. The party had undoubtedly been a success. She believed all the guests had had a good time, the last of them leaving well after one o'clock in the morning. There was very little food left indicating, to Kathleen, that she had supplied exactly the correct amount and there had been more than enough wine and champagne for everyone. Perhaps the most satisfying part of the evening was that Geoffrey had performed his role magnificently. She carefully straightened the cutlery that Geoffrey would be using when he came down to breakfast, he really was a very good boy. She just had to make him realise that Anya was completely unsuitable for anything other than being a vessel into which he could sow his youthful wild oats. She would soon make him understand that Fiona was the wife for him. She decided to have a word with Fiona, she must give Geoff some encouragement, otherwise she would lose him. They would both lose him.

"Good morning Darling."

"Yeah. Mum."

"Don't call me…"

"I know. 'don't call me Mum'. I don't care really. You know Anya screwed Tim last night. Four times apparently. Not bad going really." He spoke conversationally, as he poured cornflakes into a bowl and sprinkled it with sugar, as if what he said was the most normal conversation at breakfast.

She had to impose her authority. "Don't talk like that."

"Well they did." He poured some milk on the cereal and went to sit down. "Are you absolutely sure you want Margaret to marry him? He's obviously not going to change. I can't see him being a particularly faithful husband."

Kathleen knew that he was right but wasn't sure it was a conversation they should be having as she didn't expect husbands to be faithful. She had always felt it best to ignore her Geoffrey's indiscretions, and since they were never mentioned it was as if they never happened. She had always thought that the best approach. It would, however, never have occurred to her to be unfaithful, as it was a woman's duty to support her man. She turned the question back to her son. "Don't you mind? Surely you can't like to see your girlfriend being used so by another man." She tried to sound concerned and caring but, having decided she had to drive a wedge between them continued relentlessly. "Are you sure it was only Tim last night. I mean, John and David, well, she seemed to spend a lot of time with them."

"I'm not sure what you're getting at but she's free to do what she likes." He paused, wondering whether or not to shock his mother and decided he would. "You know why? She likes sex. She's good at it, very good. She's got a man's attitude to it, if someone offers she takes them up on it. Tim must have offered and Anya would not have said no and if the others did, so what? At the end of the evening she came back to me. She always does."

"She came back to you?"

"Of course we slept together last night. We do every night. She said Tim was very good at …"

"You've changed Geoffrey." Kathleen interrupted. She had no intention of knowing what Tim was very good at.

"I've grown up? Escaped your apron strings? Started making my own decisions about what I want to do and who I want in my life? You can't manipulate me as you have manipulated Margaret."

"Let's not argue, darling, I just want you to be happy. Your father…"

"Don't, and I mean don't, do that mother. I am not my father, I will never be. I could never live up to the idealised memory you have of him, even he probably wouldn't have been able to live up to that."

Kathleen was too shocked that her tactic, reliable for so many years, had failed.

"But she hardly knew them." She tried to have the last word.

"I hardly knew her. In fact it took me less than an hour to get her into bed, it took Tim over 24."

Kathleen had one last attempt at resurrecting her plan. "What about Fiona? She's such a…"

"… boring girl, a boring little virgin who will always remain so. I wouldn't be surprised if she's a lesbian. Just accept my world has changed I'm with Anya now and I will not give her up. You must understand it really doesn't matter that she fucks with other men. It doesn't matter, as long as she comes back to me, which she has done and which she will always do."

Kathleen was appalled. It all sounded so, she fumbled in her mind for the right words and after firmly rejecting 'permanent' found 'long term'.

"Did you buy her that ring?" Kathleen could not resist asking any longer and she could not keep the hostility from her voice.

"What ring?"

"The ring on Anya's finger."

"I haven't bought her a ring. Yet. If she's wearing a ring it'll be her mother's. You know her mother died last year don't you? Of course you don't because you've never asked anything about her. You know nothing about her but you've made up your mind and you are so wrong."

Kathleen was stunned by the cold hostility in her son's voice as he stood up to her. It was a tone so like the one his father had used when he was telling her how much he despised her and how he wished they had never married, how incompetent she had been, how incapable of the simplest task for a woman, the task of giving her husband a son. She could not stop the genuine tears that welled in her eyes.

Geoff made no sign he had noticed. "We're going back to Liverpool. We've got a flat together I'll let you know the address so you can send us a 'Happiness in your New Home' card."

The argument with his mother was over, the uneasy silence broken only by the sound of a religious service on the radio when Margaret joined them.

"You look dreadful."

"Thanks brother of mine."

"Well you do."

"You've been crying darling." Kathleen tried to sound consoling.

"So?"

"Did you have an argument with Tim?"

"Why would I have had an argument with him? We're engaged. We're going to get married."

"You could look happier about it." Geoff's voice was without humour.

Kathleen hoped that Tim had done the business and tied her to him, she had never understood her daughter's desire to be a virgin on her wedding day. Surely he had done the decent thing and taken her gently, his urges reduced by his earlier adventure. Kathleen hoped that Margaret's quietness this morning was due to a feeling of guilt rather than of disappointment in her fiancé's performance.

"Where's that girl?" Margaret couldn't bring herself to use Anya's name.

"She's gone."

"She's waiting for me at the station. I'm meeting her there in a few minutes. I didn't want her to have to face you this morning. She's tired…"

"And we all know why!" Margaret sounded childish and petulant.

"And she knows that you don't like her." Geoff carried on through his sister's interruption "She wanted to leave. I don't see why she should put up with your hostility. And before you say how bad her manners are she asked me to say 'thank you for having her'."

"Surely that should be addressed to Tim."

Geoff ignored Margaret's rare attempt at wit. "We'll both be back for the wedding. Just let me know when Mum and Esme finally set the date."

Chapter 6: Disillusionment

Liverpool, Summer 1971

In the three days Anya had been away she had seen a different side of Geoff, one she did not like and, as she followed him up the stairs to their new flat, she regretted moving in with him.

Geoff had made no comment on the changes to the flat made in the week he had left Anya there alone. He said nothing to indicate he had noticed the bright posters, cushions and rugs that made the place more like a home. Instead he turned the television on and sat down and asked what was for supper. Anya made excuses for him, it had been a tiring weekend and a long drive.

"How should I know? Beans on toast?"

"I don't think so." He half turned away from her and she felt she had somehow let herself down by not having prepared something before she had left for the south.

"Well what do you want?"

"If we haven't got any food in then I've no idea."

Anya tried to work out why Geoff was being so pompous and decided it must be because he had been with his mother for ten days. She wondered if this was how he acted there, or maybe there was always a hot meal at night, complete with meat and two veg.

She bit back caustic remarks about not being his mother. "Do you fancy a chinky?"

"What, when it's at home, is a chinky?" He sounded unimpressed.

"You mean you've been in Liverpool for three years and haven't learned about chinkies?" She was incredulous.

"I thought you were the dangerously left leaning liberal who tried to ignore people's class or race or sex?"

She tried to keep her voice level and spoke very precisely. "Haven't you realised that most chippies, sorry 'chip shops', in Liverpool are run by people of Chinese heritage and therefore known to all and sundry, except obviously stuck up pricks from Kent, as a Chinky."

"The finer details of the ownership of Liverpudlian chip shops have obviously passed me by."

Perhaps they were both tired, and what chip shops were called was hardly a good reason to argue but Anya felt herself slipping inexorably into another quarrel.

"Since you seem to expect me to wait on you hand and foot I'd better go and fetch something."

"Fine, here's a fiver."

"I don't need your fucking money."

If Geoff was surprised he didn't show it.

When she returned, after having had to queue for more than ten minutes to be served, Anya was ready to become more irritated by Geoff's attitude. He said nothing as she laid the table, heated the plates and put the containers out.

"Your dinner is served, sir." She hoped he would catch her eye, smile, apologise for being an idiot and eat the meal with a smile. But he ate in silence and as soon as he had finished he returned to his chair and his television programme leaving the plates on the table. Silently she cleared the table, washed up and tidied the kitchen wondering how she had got herself into this situation.

That morning she had been getting dressed, looking forward to continuing her verbal sparring with Geoff's mother and sister when he had said it would be better if she left quietly and waited for him in the station café. He said he'd be half an hour behind her and then they would have all day to drive back. She had been on her third coffee and had finished reading all she wanted to read in the Sunday Times before she saw his car turn into the station forecourt. She wondered how saying goodbye to his mother and sister could have taken more than two hours.

Once they had settled in the car she sat back to watch the miles pass, putting distance between her and a world she hadn't enjoyed and never wanted to be part of. Geoff had been quiet but she put that down to having to concentrate on his driving so she was surprised at the edge in his voice when he finally spoke.

"Was he worth it?"

"Who?" Anya's mind had been miles away and she had no idea what he was talking about.

"Tim."

"Was he worth what?"

"It really upset Margaret you know, you screwing Tim."

"What?" Anya couldn't believe Geoff was taking Margaret's side, if indeed there were sides to take.

"She was really upset this morning. You ruined the day for her."

"I can't believe you're saying this! You don't even like your sister."

"Well was he?"

"Was he what?"

"Worth all the agro. If you'd needed a fuck that badly I would have been available. It didn't have to be Tim."

"I did not 'need a fuck' and you're jealous!"

"I am not jealous. I'd hardly be with you if I was the jealous type would I? You'd screw the dustman if you felt like it."

She didn't pursue the jealousy angle as another thought occurred to her. "You're worried in case he was better at it than you."

His answer, an indignant "I am not" served only to tell Anya she had been right.

"You men are all so petty. Tim wanted to know if he was better than you."

"Well? Was he?"

"Oh shut up and drive." She would never give an answer to that particular question.

The brakes slammed on and the car came to a rapid halt, horns hooted around their car and she felt a moment's relief that nothing hit them.

"I will not shut up. Are you going to give me an answer?"

"OK." She had leant over and squeezed his leg, "you are the best."

"Really?"

"You are an insecure little shit aren't you?" She spoke gently.

He smiled. "Probably." The argument seemed forgotten but it was lurking, waiting to be revived when the first thing had gone wrong, when there had been nothing to eat in the flat.

Anya stood in the kitchen door, waiting for Geoff to ask whether there was anything she wanted to watch or whether she was tired and wanted an early night, waiting for him to acknowledge in some way that he knew she was there. When he made no move at all she went to the room that was her study and unlocked the silver trunk that contained all her diaries.

As she carefully wrote '*Anya Cave 1971*' on the outer cover of a pale green third year Latin exercise book, one of several she had taken in her last raid of the stationery cupboard, she wondered where she would be and who she would be with when she looked back at this book as her history.

> *Sunday 1st August 1971: The Flat, Liverpool*
> *Summary of what happened since last proper diary.*
> *August 1968 to August 1971:*

She sat writing for a long time, there was so much to say even though the minutiae of detail was missing. After a couple of hours she was aware Geoff was standing in the doorway looking at her. She wondered how long he had been there.

"Hi. You OK?" She asked, wondering whether he was still in his mood.

"I'm just going to bed. Sorry about earlier, I suppose I'm just tired. I hate it when I'm supposed to be Dad, I suppose something of him rubs off on me." She knew that as far as Geoff was concerned that counted as an apology.

"OK, I'll carry on here for a while, you go to bed."

She turned back to her writing.

Yesterday
Engagement party. Preparation all day but no amount of work would make Margaret anything but a frump. Obvious from first moment G different person when at home almost boring he didn't want me to sleep in his bed at first but I persuaded him. Lucky there was Tim or there would have been no fun. At the time I thought G was fine about it, in fact he was so fine about it I thought he'd probably arranged it. He could easily have told me to get a certain train and he could have met me at the station. But it was his idea for me to meet Tim at Charing Cross and I bet he knew exactly what that would lead to. But on the drive up he was so jealous and competitive about it all. I thought he'd think it a big laugh but he didn't. I wanted to talk about us. I have no idea where this relationship is heading. We've got a year (if we last that long) then what? I can't see him worrying about me having a career. He'll want to go back south in a year but after last weekend I know I don't want to do that. I know what I don't want to do but I'm no nearer knowing what I do want to do than I was three years ago.

She absent-mindedly fiddled with the locket she had worn around her neck since it had been put there by Dr Hill just ten days earlier. There was no photo inside it yet. She wondered about asking Geoff for a photo but decided against it. The person she put in the locket was to be the one man in her life. And she wasn't sure that that man was going to be Geoff.

The next morning she phoned Dot. She was surprised to hear her on the phone so soon after her last visit.

"How did it go?" She asked, "The visitation to your young man's mother?"

"As well as either of us expected I suppose."

"That good?"

"Worse." She then gave a highly edited version of the events of the past weekend. "Before I go, do you know what happened to Marion? You know, the girl…"

"… in the tower block. That was five years ago. What made you think of her now?"

"It was the blocks of flats along the railway line into London."

"It's so very sad. She had the little boy when you saw her didn't she?"

"And she was having another."

"She had another boy and then a little girl."

"So no exams then?" Anya didn't mean to sound as judgmental as she did.

"Three months ago there was an accident. She was waiting at a bus stop with the baby in the pushchair and the two toddlers standing next to her when they were hit by a car."

"Oh my God! Were they badly hurt?"

"The boys were killed outright and the baby died in hospital the next day."

"Oh my God! How awful? What about Marion?"

"She was not badly hurt in the accident but gassed herself the day after the little ones' funeral."

Anya could think of nothing appropriate to say. "Why didn't you tell me last week?"

"We didn't know if you'd remember her and if you did we didn't want to upset you on such a happy day."

"I owe Marion so much. It was that visit that turned my life into something approaching sensible."

"I know dear."

"It's so sad. She had such a tough time."

"Yes, so very sad. Just remember, my dear, life can be shorter than you think. Don't waste a moment of it. Treat every day as the precious gift it is."

Anya grabbed the gold locket, given to a young woman, now middle aged, by a young man, long dead. She began to think she should take life a little more seriously but decided she wasn't quite ready.

Thursday 9th September 1971
Took G to tea at Dot and Dr Hill They seemed to like him, he adored them. Asked me why I'd kept them so quiet. Went to see 16 Tennyson. They've knocked it down. They're even knocking down the laundry building a supermarket or something. All my old life disappearing. Is Anya Cave disappearing too?

When, in late December, Dr Hill rang her Anya knew something was seriously wrong.

"Dot's in Clatterbridge. Can you visit her? She wants to see you."

"Dot's in hospital?"

"I'm afraid so. She's not been well for a while."

"But she seemed fine when we saw her in September." Anya was more upset than she had ever been at the thought of losing Dot.

"She won't leave hospital again and she wants to see you."

"Of course."

"Please wear her locket."

"I never take it off."

Geoff stayed outside as Anya went into the ward and found Dot's bed. As she had walked up the steps and along the echoing corridor Anya remembered that Dot had been born in 1921. She was only 50 years old. Perhaps that was what she had meant when she had said that life was too short.

Dot held out her hand and Anya took it. Was this the first time they had ever touched? She couldn't remember.

"Thank you for coming." Dot's voice was surprisingly strong.

"I had to."

"I wanted to say thank you."

"But that was what I wanted to say."

"Thank you Anya for not letting me down. You haven't so far and you won't in the future will you?"

"I'll try not to."

"But you must have fun. Take life seriously, my dear, but never lose sight of the fun. Life isn't just about work and a career and life isn't only about having children. Remember that. There are other important things to do, but always balance work with pleasure. I never did that."

"Can I ask you a question?"

Dot nodded.

"Why do you have such faith in me?"

"You remind me so much of me when I was young. You were at the start of everything but you were throwing it all away. I couldn't let you do that, I had to do what I could to make you see that not having children is not the end of the world it can sometimes seem." She lay back, tired out by her thoughts and her words.

"You've made such a difference to my life. I won't let you down. I promise."

"Don't forget." The voice was different, the eyes were shut and a nurse came and hustled Anya away.

> *Tuesday 11th January 1972*
>
> *We went to Dot's funeral today. The crematorium was packed. I recognised a few people, teachers (it's only three and a bit years since I left) and pupils, but loads of people I didn't. No one said anything to me. It was a strange service, no religion at all. It hadn't occurred to me that she didn't believe in God after all those school assemblies she'd taken. We didn't go back to the wake. I wanted to help Dr Hill, he looked 10 years older, but I couldn't think of anything to say. I should have done Psychology and a treatise on the nature of relationships between brothers and sisters. The devoted, Dr Hill and Dot, and the literally unspeakable... I came home and cried. She was only my headmistress but it seems like there's only Dr Hill left of my old life. Everything and everyone else is gone. All I have is Geoff and I'm not sure that he's enough anymore.*

"We need to talk."

Anya had been planning the conversation for weeks. Perhaps it was the funeral, perhaps it was Dot's voice in her head telling her not to forget how precious life was that gave her the courage.

"I'm not sure I like the way my life is going."

"What?" Geoff looked up from his book, taking a while to focus his mind back into the real world.

"I'm getting a bit fed up with things."

"Fed up?" Geoff wasn't particularly worried, Anya had been moodier than normal the past few days but nothing seemed to have changed between them, she still tantalised and satisfied him when it mattered.

"Haven't you noticed how since we've been in this flat things haven't been the same?"

"How do you mean?" Geoff genuinely did not understand.

"We've both working hard aren't we?"

"Yes, of course we are."

"We've both got projects we're working on that take up a lot of time and mental and physical energy?"

"Yes, of course we have. What are you getting at?"

"Then why is it me that does all the shopping and the cooking and the clearing up and take the washing down to the laundrette and the ironing and tidying up?"

"That's what women do isn't it?"

"That is the wrong answer!"

It hadn't occurred to him that she wouldn't do all those things. Perhaps it was having had a doting mother and an elder sister but he had never done anything around the house.

"Did your mother do everything for you?"

"No we had Eileen…"

"What did you do in hall?"

"There wasn't much to do."

"No. Food was cooked, there was no washing up other than the odd mug and, if I remember rightly, you didn't bother to do that very often."

It had never occurred to him that those were jobs he should allow time for.

"I went to the laundrette." Geoff wasn't sure why he felt he had to justify his actions.

"How many times?"

"A couple."

"What have you done since we moved in here? It's nearly six months and I can't think of anything you've done unless it's a special occasion."

"This isn't fair."

"No. It isn't fair." Anya was finding it difficult to keep control of her anger. Geoff just didn't seem to think he was doing anything wrong. "It's not fair that you get home and eat and work and watch the box but I have to do all the sodding housework before I can decide whether to do some reading or relax a bit or go to bed or do some work because I'm so bloody tired! It isn't bloody fair Geoff. You've got to start doing your share, I'm not your wife, I'm not your skivvie and I'm not your bloody mother's Eileen."

She looked at him waiting for him to say something, but he stayed quiet.

"I know I don't pay rent or anything but I would if you'd let me. Do you think doing all the chores is my way of paying my share of the rent? Am I just your home help or am I just a prostitute, your kept woman who has all expenses paid as long as I fuck you every night and twice on Saturdays. I want to work hard but I also want to have some fun."

"Fun?" Geoff didn't seem to understand what she was talking about and picked out the easiest point to respond to. He didn't feel up to discussing the role of women and liberation and equality. "You have fun with just about every man you meet."

"That's not fun, that's sex."

"Why do you screw around so much?"

"I don't."

Geoff started ticking off on his fingers. "The English student who lives next door, the dentist in the pub last week I was talking to about rugby, the barman at The Phil, the guy on that train when we went to Manchester, that Portuguese chap visiting your department…"

"University is supposed to be the most fun time of your life isn't it? Well for the first two years I was at home every night when I bet you were screwing yourself silly with all and sundry. Then there was the year in Hall when all I did in the evenings was be with you and now all I do is work and housework. If I only had sex with you I'd be so fucking bored."

"I get the picture."

"No you fucking don't! I have as much right to enjoy myself as you do! All you want to be is the nice little man being looked after by the nice little woman but the nice little woman is pissed off."

"You mean it's my fault you go out, find complete strangers and screw them."

"I'd do it more if you weren't around. Why shouldn't I?"

"Why shouldn't you? You have to ask?" Geoff was beginning to realise the depth of Anya's anger even if he had no idea what was causing it.

"And what a fucking mistake this flat was! You do sod all around the place. I need to work just as much as you but I do all the housework because it's not as important for me to do well is it? Of course not! My course is just to keep me occupied for a year until you're ready to move on with your life and drag me along too. What a pity I can't get pregnant then I'd have to give up all those silly ideas about having a career wouldn't I? You'd be the centre of everyone's attention. The house would revolve around you, just what your bloody mother made you believe for your whole life. Well I'm not going to do the same.

"I thought..." Geoff tried to find an answer but was quickly interrupted.

"Why are we living like a sodding middle aged bloody married couple? And another thing. I'm sick to death of having to ask you for money all the time. This is your flat, you paid the rent before I had a chance to contribute. I have sex with you and you give me money to keep this bloody place going. What does that remind you of? You think you bloody own me! Well you fucking well don't. Stuff it. I'm off."

"Is that 'off' as in 'going out' or as in 'going for good'?"

"Which do you want?"

"I thought we were happy."

"Well you know what fucking thought did don't you!" She knew she wasn't making any sense.

"We have some good times?" She didn't answer. "I really thought you were happy." He repeated, more quietly and with some sadness.

"No. I. Am. Not. Happy." And she burst into tears.

Geoff put his books carefully on the floor and got up from the settee, walking over to put his arms around her.

"OK I'll do more. Honestly I will. I'll do more."

"No you won't. You'll never do more. I'm only your bit of rough, housekeeping for you while you finish your degree then you'll fuck off south to your precious Fiona and your precious fucking middle class family. I've never been good enough have I? OK for a shag, OK to do the housework but I'll never be good enough for you. I heard your mother '*not suitable*' she said, I heard her telling some pompous old git, '*that tart isn't a suitable friend for my Geoffrey*.'"

"Ignore my mother, you probably didn't hear her right anyway. We're good together, why do we need to be with other people? Aren't I enough for you?"

"Listen to yourself! We're 21 years old. We should be out at clubs or discos or parties or anything when we're not working. We can be like this for years if we want to but not yet, not now. We shouldn't be like this now."

"I love you Anya. I don't want to go with anyone else. I thought you loved me?" It was the first time he had mentioned love. He sounded pathetic and he knew it. Anya didn't answer, she just stared at him.

"I'm going."

"Will you…"

Anya turned her back and he listened as drawers opened and shut and he could picture her throwing things into her duffle bag before the sharp crack of the front door being shut rather too forcefully told him she had left.

"… be coming back?" Geoff asked the empty flat.

Geoff kept the silence in the flat at bay by having the radio or television on at all times but they couldn't stop him thinking. He wasn't used to questioning his own actions but he recognised that he had been rather domesticated, it suited him that way. He liked having Anya around, she made him feel comfortable and he tried to understand why it was different for her.

On her second evening away he sought out people they both knew to ask them nonchalantly whether anyone had seen her. When no one had he began to worry about where she might have gone and who she might have fallen in with. Whenever he returned to the flat he hoped to see the lights on and Anya back. He had never been on his own like this and he didn't like it.

On the third day he sat on the bed and promised the absent Anya that things would be different, he would be different, when she got back, if she came back. He stared out of the window willing the next person to walk round the corner to be Anya. When it wasn't he said she would be tenth person to round the corner. When she still hadn't come after twenty people had walked along that stretch of pavement he turned away from the window. He made himself consider how he might change, perhaps if he made the right decisions she would come home.

As it grew dark he stood in the kitchen waiting for the kettle to boil wondering what she had thought about when she had been on that spot. He stared around him at the fridge and the well-stocked shelves and thought they were really very lucky; most post-grad students had to scrimp and save to afford the steak meals that they ate regularly. It slowly dawned on him why she was so resentful. She had chosen none of these things, not the flat, nor the mugs and plates. He had bought everything, not because she didn't want to, or couldn't, but because he had not given her the chance. Her grant was not overgenerous but it would be enough to do the normal things in life. He had never let her be herself. He had overwhelmed her. He thought about the posters she had put up in that first week, when, he realised, he had left her alone in the flat they had only been in for one day. He had taken them down, replacing them with some prints which he thought looked better but he had never said her posters had been nice or asked her which she preferred. He had just gone ahead and done it. As he ticked off thoughtless action after thoughtless action he wondered why she had stayed with him so long.

In a few months they would have to make decisions that would set the course for their lives. She would be determined to be independent. Perhaps she would want a career that would take her away from him. She would listen to Women's Libbers and think she could make it through life on her own. Somehow, if, when, she came back, he had to find a way of making her want to stay with him.

He knew her well enough to realise independence meant money of her own. And somehow they would have to have more of what she insisted on calling 'fun'. He remembered Fiona telling him in great, and at the time immensely boring, detail how it was necessary to let the more headstrong puppies and ponies have the longest leads when they were being trained. Anya was a wonderful, spirited, stubborn animal but she was not yet ready to be trained. He would have to let Anya have her head in the short term if he wanted her with him for the long. He looked down at the now cold cup of coffee and realised how important it was to him to have her with him. He just had to find a way.

As he walked in the park on the Thursday afternoon when Anya had been away four days he found what he thought would be the perfect answer. He sat on a bench by the pond for an hour trying to think through the consequences if Anya agreed. There were risks and he would have to swallow his pride and control his possessiveness more than he had ever had to before, but he thought it might work. Anya would have her 'fun', he could make sure she had money of her own yet he would still be in control. As he watched the ducks dabbling in the shallow water he felt snowflakes landing on his hands. More and more snow fell and it began to turn the grey path and the dirty looking grass white. More than anything he wanted to share the park's transformation with Anya, he couldn't enjoy it without her.

He was at the front gate when he looked up and saw the lights on in the flat. She was back. He closed the gate quietly and in the few strides it took to get to the front door he had time to tell himself that he must be patient, he must listen to what she had to say. Then they'd go to bed and he'd show her how much he had missed her.

Anya had lit the fire and was sitting cross legged on the hearth rug staring at the flames as he came in.

"You're home then."

He had to stop himself asking questions, he made himself wait until she was ready to talk. He sat down next to her and was relieved when she laid her head on his shoulder and took his hand in hers.

"Yes I'm home."

They sat together watching the fire for what seemed to Geoff to be a long time. He had to break the silence.

"Things will be different. I promise."

She took a few moments to reply and then it was a dull monosyllable full of doubt. "How?"

"I'll start by doing more around the flat." She turned and looked at him, her expression one of scepticism. "Honestly Anya, I will, and I'll start by cooking supper tonight. And I'll do the washing up." He was rewarded by her head returning to its position on his shoulder and a slight pressure from her hand on his. They sat together until the fire needed more coal and his getting up broke the spell. He left her by the fire as he busied himself in the kitchen. Every few minutes he looked round the door but she hadn't moved. He began to worry what had happened to her. Her stillness was so unusual.

"Only egg on toast with beans." He said putting the plates on the table.

She unwrapped her long legs and stood, stretching for a few moments before turning to the table. "Fine. Thanks." Both were remembering their argument of five months before about chinkies.

They ate in silence, Geoff glancing up occasionally but he never managed to catch her eye. She seemed to be miles away.

He gathered up the plates and washed them up, drawing out the process by carefully drying and putting away the plates, the pans and the cutlery. He wanted to put off the moment he knew was coming.

She was going to tell him she was leaving him.

"Coffee?" he asked trying to hide the panic in his voice.

"Please."

She was sitting in front of the fire again and didn't move when he came in so he put her mug on the hearth in front of her and sat down next to her, cradling his mug in his hands. Never, he told himself, had he felt so awkward. He had no idea when to break the silence or what words to use. They sat, not touching, until the fire had almost died again.

When she spoke it was as if she was reading from a script and had over-rehearsed the words.

"I'm back, Geoff, but I can't stay more than a day unless things change. You have to let me be me. I know I'm not someone you always like or respect but I'm me. I have to drink with and screw with whoever I want. It's never anything serious, it's my way of sticking two fingers up at the world. Two fingers at the world, Geoff, not at you. I'm not ready to be tied down but if I was, when I am, I can't think of a kinder, more generous, nicer man to be tied down with. So you can take me or leave me Geoff. Cope with my ways or don't. It's up to you."

"You do want to stay then?" He asked tentatively.

"Only if things change."

"They will."

"Promise?" She held out her hand and he squeezed it.

"I promise. Anya, you mean so much to me. I don't think you know how much."

"Perhaps you should have shown me a bit more, taken me a little less for granted?"

"I'm so sorry."

"So you should be. You should have shown me a little bit more respect."

He tried to see the old Anya in her words. Was she teasing him? Was she playing with him?

"Shown you respect? How?"

She reached over and touched his face. Then she leant forward and kissed his mouth in a way he remembered from their early days together. He moved his tongue to hold hers, she moved hers away, tantalising, teasing. He had had enough of her playing and pushed her to the floor.

"Anya." He said more firmly than he meant to. "If you don't want me to do this tell me. Just say no and I'll let you go."

Anya didn't say a word.

They lay together on the rug in front of the burned out fire.

"Changes, Anya, there will be changes."

She didn't reply so he continued.

"From now on we'll take it in turns to make bets."

"Bets?"

"Yeah. Say I bet you that you can't screw so and so on a particular day."

"And?" Anya was intrigued.

"I'll be there to check."

"You'll watch?"

"Sometimes, yes, I'd have to check you're actually winning the bet."

"If I don't?"

"You lose the bet and pay me."

"Could be fun." Anya lay back with the warm feeling of satisfying sex filling her. She wondered if the feeling she had for Geoff was love. She felt comfortable, relaxed, warm and complete.

"Geoff?"

"Yes?"

"Do you understand why I hate myself so much?"

It had never occurred to him that someone could hate themselves. "Do you?"

"I've always hated myself. I hate myself for being different from everyone else."

"You're not. You're brilliant and beautiful. How can you hate yourself?"

"I'll tell you some day."

"When you're ready." He leant over and kissed her.

"Geoff?" She asked as he moved himself ready to take her again.
"Yes?"
"Are you pleased I'm back?"
"Pleased? Just you feel how pleased I am."
They lay back together on the mat in front of the long dead fire. Geoff folded his arms around Anya keeping her warm against the chill of the night.
"Come to bed."
Another opportunity was missed for Anya and Geoff to talk about things that mattered. Instead they made love and the moment for explanations that would have saved so much pain passed.

The next morning they lay together as if there had never been a problem.
"You know those bets you were talking about last night?" Anya asked nonchalantly.
"Yes?"
"Who starts?"
"Me."
"OK what and how much?"
"To start you off, and this is the one and only time I'm involved directly, I bet you twenty pounds…"
"I haven't got twenty to spare."
"… twenty pounds that I won't have made love to you in half an hour."
"That's too easy."
"Well what's your suggestion?"
"You know that barman at the Phil?"
"You've been with him before."
"Is that against the rules?"
"Yes." Geoff sounded less doubtful than he felt, he hadn't thought about rules. "There's this guy on my course. He'll be more of a test."

Friday 21st January 1972 Back in Liverpool
Four days in London was far too long and despite having

great time (in some ways) I was surprised how much I missed G. I even worried about him worrying about me. Why did I go?

The problems are easy: 1. Domesticity 2. No money 3. Dependence on G. Such simple problems. I certainly didn't find any solutions in London. When I got home G had this silly idea to make me earn money by gambling. He'll bet me I can't screw people or do other stuff and he'll pay me. I'll get my own money (well almost my own) from the bets. I'll go along with it because at least he's trying. The first bet is a weird chap on his course, he always wears a knitted woollen hat of many colours I get £20 if he fucks me by next Friday. G reckons he's a virgin. I asked how he'd know I'd done it. He said he'd know because Arthur (really!) wouldn't be able not to tell everybody. Is this just another sort of perverted prostitution? Another Psychology treatise: 'Is sex for money always prostitution?' What about all those young blondes who marry old men exchanging sex for a couple of years for their vast fortune when they die? Is what we're doing prostitution? I've thought about and I don't think so. Not really anyway.

G is doing more around the flat. So far cooked steak last night, did the washing up (eventually), tidied his clothes away even put his dirty pants in the laundry bag (!!) and he didn't complain that he had no clean t-shirt. He is being quite sweet really but we'll see how long it lasts.

A quarter of a century later, lying on a beach in Barbados and reflecting on her many failures and few successes in life, Anya thought back to those final six months of her university career and decided it had been the happiest time of her life.

Geoff had been true to his word and, from the day of Anya's return from London, he had shared the chores of living. As they had shared more than sex their relationship had grown. They had learned about each other; their strengths and weaknesses, their likes and dislikes, and their moods. They had helped each other with their revision and research learning greater respect for the other's intelligence and knowledge. Two or three times a week they had gone to a music club, a bar or a pub to take it in turns to choose her target for the evening. But, Anya reflected as she let the white sand run through her tanned hands, they had never talked about the issues that drove her behaviour. He never asked her why she couldn't have children. He had never asked her why she hated herself and whether she still did.

Monday 10th April 1972 Happy Birthday Birthday Boy. 22 today.

What a great day! We headed for the Union in celebration and to define the arrangements for the night. Sex in public his first bet today. £50. A shop doorway before it got dark was a challenge but Arthur obliged. Such a nice boy he seemed to enjoy it more this time. Then my bet was Geoff to have sex with some tart from 1st year social studies. He said she just talked and talked so much he gave up. He was quite miffed but seemed to have enjoyed the chase a tad more than I was happy with but then sauce for the gander is sauce for the goose. His next bet was us on a bar stool. The room was crowded and it was dark and he didn't last long. Afterwards he said he really loved me, he didn't care what anyone thought, he just wanted me to know how much he cared.

Tomorrow we buy a new car I've earned so much I'm paying half so I can choose the colour (red) and he's promised to teach me to drive.

A year ago we didn't really celebrate his 21st, he kept telling me it was important but we hadn't done anything different from usual. He talked about it as we walked home tonight, a year too late. He told me that he has responsibility for his father's money, lots of it. He explained how he helped run his family's money affairs, even his Mum's. That's why he gets so many letters in brown envelopes and stays at home some days instead of going into lectures. I had no idea he had been doing that all year. He never discussed it with me. He said he will now. What does that mean?

On the day of Geoff's last exam they were sitting in the bath together celebrating with a bottle of champagne.

"What now?" Anya asked.

Geoff took that as an invitation and put his glass on the ledge behind him and manoeuvring his toes between Anya's legs in a way he had done many times before. He was surprised when she pushed him away.

"No seriously. What are we going to do now? All this, the flat, everything's got to change hasn't it?"

"We don't have to worry for a bit. There's lots of…"

"… I know, there's lots of money in the bank. But what was the last four years about if it wasn't to have a career? Wouldn't we get bored with nothing to do? And what would I do if we broke up? University couples rarely stay together."

"So many questions! I thought we'd maybe take a year off, travel a bit, there's lots of time before we have to make decisions like that."

"I was thinking of trying my hand at writing."

"What? A book?"

"Possibly, eventually, but first journalism, articles, that sort of thing."

"What's to stop you?"

"You think it's a good idea?"

"I think it's terrific, you could do that anywhere couldn't you?"

"And I've got a date for my driving test."

In their different ways they both realised that decisions about their future were making themselves.

Thursday 20th July 1972

Driving test- passed! I've got enough in the bet account to buy a mini or something if sharing the car doesn't work out. Geoff's been great about it, taking me out for practice, encouraging me. I thought he'd be a bit reluctant, he does have a tendency to be a little possessive (!). We've decided to stay up here for a few months while we work out what we're going to do.

I think we want to stay together but I think he wants to go home and I'm SO anti going south. I don't know what I'd do without him if we go different ways but if I have to start on my own I will. Maybe it won't come down to a battle between his career (and family) and mine.

"We're off to Kent next week." Geoff handed Anya the card he had taken out of the envelope in the drawer by his side of the bed.

"How long have you had this?"

"A few weeks."

"*Mrs Geoffrey Philips* ... Mrs Geoffrey? How does she do that?"

"It's correct etiquette, she's a widow so she keeps her husband's name. She always does it when she wants to make a point."

"*...requests the pleasure of your company.* Pleasure! I doubt she gets any pleasure inviting us."

"She hasn't." Geoff spoke deliberately. "Look at the top of the card." Anya did and saw the one single name *Geoffrey* written in blue ink.

Anya ignored the deliberate insult, she knew she would be going whether invited or not. "Why send you an invitation anyway? Surely you're giving the bride away?"

"Oh yes, I'll be pretending to be my father again. God knows why she sent it."

"She did it to specifically exclude me."

"You're coming aren't you?"

"Keep me away."

"It won't be as bad as last year."

"It had better not be! Springing all those awful people on me was so unfair."

"You didn't seem to mind one awful person springing on you!"

"I'll screw with him again you know." Anya warned Geoff, her voice suddenly serious.

"Only on condition I finally get Fiona. I can't let her win that battle."

"We have a few bets to work out." Anya thought for a minute, "I bet you £100 that I get Tim on his stag night. And £100 you don't get Fiona."

"That's a lot of money. Are they really worth twice anyone else?"

"Absolutely, and I'll bet you a further £100." She didn't say what for immediately, preferring to tease him. Geoff was easy to tease.

"What for?"

"He'll break his marriage vows during the reception."

"That's ridiculous!" Geoff's laugh was forced, he didn't know exactly why but he knew of all the men Anya had sex with Tim was the one who threatened him the most. "The stag do is fair game but not the reception."

"Well what about any others on the stag night then?"

"John and Dave?"

"Yeah. Right." She didn't sound as enthusiastic.

"It'll be OK won't it?" Geoff had hoped that Anya's appetite for sex would wear itself out. It didn't matter in Liverpool but he worried she wouldn't change when she moved with him to Kent, as he was determined she would.

"Of course it will." Anya tried to be convincing but she was thinking she had lived the last two years as if reality had been suspended. Whatever she had done had nothing to do with the real world but now her real world, whatever that was going to be, had to be faced and she wasn't sure she wanted to face it in middle class respectability in Kent.

Chapter 7: Manipulations

Kent, July 1972

"I'm looking forward to this."

"What? The driving or the wedding?"

"Well both really, the drive should be fun and your mother really won't want me anywhere near the wedding so it'll be fun winding her up." Anya piled the last of her things into the boot of their car.

"I'm glad we've rented a house for the week."

"At least we won't be in your family's pocket all the time."

"Though," Geoff spoke a little sheepishly, "I'll have to leave you to your own devices for quite a bit of the time." He had reassured himself that Tim would be too busy and have far too many commitments to spend much time with Anya.

"Fair enough, as long as I don't have to spend a night in that house. I hate it, it's so cold and tidy."

The inconsequential chatter of DJs and familiar pop music kept them company as Anya drove carefully out of Liverpool and through the green fields of Cheshire. Geoff was content to be a passenger as they headed south on Anya's first drive of any distance since she had passed her test.

"Shall we stop for something to eat? There's a transport café."

Anya drove into the deeply rutted car park and pulled up, satisfied she had done a good job.

"Well done that girl."

"That was fun but you can take over the driving for the final motorway bit and London. I don't really fancy that yet."

"Any idea which county we're in?" Geoff asked as they walked into the ramshackle looking café.

"Warwickshire, I think. Does it matter?"

"Not really."

"Must have been a popular place this." He nodded at the signed photographs of pop stars that covered the walls as they sat at one of the many empty tables. "Adam Faith and Cliff Richard, this goes back a bit. "Look! The Shadows and Lonnie Donegan. Everyone seems to have stopped here sometime."

"Half way between London and the north I suppose."

"But now the motorways will be taking all their trade away."

She watched him as he walked to the counter and chatted to the server. She saw him as others would see him, tall, smart and confident; she was proud to be his girl.

"I've been meaning to ask you." Geoff started tentatively as he put the plates of sausage, beans and chips on the table.

"Yes?" She held her breath.

"You know when you went missing in January?"

"Yes?" She breathed a sigh of relief, she had been afraid he was going to propose.

"Where did you go?"

Anya twirled the chips and beans around her plate. She had always known he would ask one day. She wasn't the most honest of people but she had always found it difficult to tell a lie to a direct question. "You really want to know?"

"If you don't want to tell me don't but I would like to know. I nearly went to see Dr Hill, you were in such a state after her funeral."

"Well that was only the week before. But you didn't worry him did you?"

Geoff shook his head. "Where did you go? Will you tell me?"

Perhaps, after all he had done since January to make their lives better, he deserved an honest answer.

"I went to London."

"Where?" It was not the answer Geoff had expected.

"I went to London." Anya repeated.

"To Tim?"

"Not exactly. I didn't go with the idea of meeting him but I thought they'd probably be at Charing Cross so I went. They were quite surprised to see me."

"I bet they were." Geoff tried to keep the cold jealousy from his voice.

"But they seemed quite pleased."

"I bet they did." Anya told herself if Geoff didn't know her by now he never would and he should realise he couldn't take her for granted. "What did you do?"

She shrugged her shoulders. "What do you think we did?"

"You probably fetched off to some hotel in an awful part of town and screwed them all silly." Geoff tried to laugh but it didn't quite come out the way he intended, sounding more like a splutter. In some ways he was relieved that she had been with people she knew, he had imagined her being with strangers who might have hurt her. But why had she gone to Tim?

"Actually we stayed in a nice hotel in Covent Garden."

"Did you have fun?"

"Yeah. It was great."

Geoff tried to ignore his jealousy. "What did you tell them about why you were there?" He didn't want her to have told them she'd run away from him.

"I said I'd temporarily escaped the ties of academia and domesticity."

"Temporarily? You always meant to come back?"

"Of course I did. After three days they saw me onto the train at Euston and told me not to so silly again."

"They didn't."

"No, you're right, they didn't but they did tell me off for not getting in touch with you. They said you'd be worried."

"I was."

"In the end I realised I was missing you too much."

"You missed me?"

"Yes. I was rather surprised to realise how much."

Geoff leant across the table and kissed her. It was beginning to be a problem that he needed her far more than she needed him.

"What's the plot?" Anya asked as they settled into the second half of their drive south.

"We'll stay at the house tonight, then tomorrow morning I'll go and see Mum and Margaret. You don't have to if you don't want to."

"I'll come for a few minutes. They need to know I'm around and that they can't ignore my existence then I'll leave you to it and go shopping or something."

"Something?" Geoff left the question hanging in the air for a minute.

"Shopping." She said firmly but with a smile in her voice as she knew what he was thinking. "We still haven't bought them a wedding present."

"Then I've got the stag night."

"I won't be invited to the hen night so do you want a chauffeur?"

"Good idea. Lots of opportunity for those bets."

"I hadn't thought of that!"

"Of course you had." Their laughter was relaxed, friendly, free of any issues. Perhaps, Geoff thought, everything would be all right after all.

Geoff and Anya joined his mother and sister in the kitchen. He poured their coffee and they sat around the table, to all appearances a happy family anticipating a wedding.

"Good evening Anya."

"Good evening Mrs Philips." Anya set out to be perfectly polite.

"I gather you have done well?" Perhaps she was making an effort to be nice.

"Yes, thank you, I did. So did Geoff, you must be very proud of him." Anya knew that would be difficult to argue against and she could afford to be generous. Because neither Kathleen nor Margaret replied Anya continued with less generosity. "We worked very hard you know, helping each other. Geoffrey is a very clever man, you know that don't you? You have to be exceptional to get a first."

"But, my dear," Kathleen spoke as slowly and condescendingly as she was able, "it was, after all, only Liverpool. It's not as if my son got his degree at a good university."

Anya answered before Geoff could say a word, her resolutions to behave sorely tried. "Liverpool is very well respected."

"But only red brick." Kathleen spoke as though the university had been built of dung.

"The first and original red brick. It's quite interesting …"

"You are a bitch." Margaret interrupted. She hadn't been listening to the conversation and had been winding herself up to an argument with Anya.

"Undoubtedly."

"You don't mind me calling you that? You don't mind me calling you a bitch?" Margaret repeated.

Anya kept her response calm and measured though she gave up her hopes of behaving well. "Not at all. You're absolutely right, I am a bitch. I screwed your fiancé on the night of his engagement and… Anya ignored Geoff's kick under the table. "… back in January we met up in London for a few days. Didn't he tell you?" She ignored the shock on Margaret's face and the warning in Geoff's. "We spent three days together in a very expensive hotel in Covent Garden." Anya enjoyed every moment of the effect her words had on Margaret and Kathleen. "He didn't tell you? But then he wouldn't have done would he?" Anya was now enjoying herself. "We went to some lovely restaurants and then, of course, we spent a great deal of time in bed. He really is quite good at that side of things."

"You should know." Margaret's voice was so low no one but Geoff heard her.

"Tim is good but he was nowhere near as good as your brother, he is really good."

"You will not talk like this!" Kathleen was horrified.

"Tim doesn't have to tell me what he does." Margaret said quietly but neither her mother nor Anya was listening.

"Oh yes I can and I will." Anya spoke quietly to Kathleen, ignoring Margaret. "Your daughter may be marrying Tim tomorrow, but she should understand what kind of man he is."

Geoff sat silently, part of him enjoying the battle between his mother and the girl he was increasingly determined would one day be his wife and the other part wracked with jealousy at the thought of Tim and Anya together. As Anya warmed to her theme he sat with smile gradually relaxing and widening, agreeing with everything she said.

"He will never be faithful to her, he will screw around. He is a weak man, you only have to look at his chin and how close his eyes are together. He is weak, gullible and led by what he's got in his pants."

"You think I don't know what he's like?" Margaret finally made herself be heard. "Does it matter what he's like? He'll be my husband and that's all that matters in the real world."

"You've grown cynical." Geoff spoke directly to his sister for the first time.

"I've had to. I've been engaged to Tim for a year and I know he's been all the way with at least three of my friends and God knows how many others. Not to mention her." She glared across the table at Anya, then she turned that same look at him. "You were the chosen one Geoff, Dad left you all his money and so you can do whatever you want with your life. He left me nothing, no money, nothing. The only thing I can possibly do is get a husband. You think marrying Tim is an option. It is not. It is a necessity if I am to have any sort of standard of living. I'm marrying Tim, whether it's a good idea or not."

"Do you love him?"

"What's love got to do with anything?"

Anya noticed the bitter resignation in Margaret's voice and for a few seconds felt sorry for having been so cruel. But that brief sympathy was rapidly replaced by a feeling of something approaching anger. Margaret was not academically gifted but neither was she stupid. She could have set her sights higher. She could get qualifications, forge a career for herself. Her life and livelihood didn't have to be dependent on any man, let alone Tim.

Anya looked across at Kathleen and understood. From their

earliest years she had brought up both her children to believe that men were the breadwinners and women the supporters. In the past two years Anya had taught Geoff that that was wrong but no one had made Margaret understand that there were other roles she could play in life. When she spoke to break the heavy silence Anya spoke directly to Kathleen.

"I had no family to leave me money. I have always known that if I'm going to get anywhere in life I have to do it by myself so I've worked hard and now what I do is my choice. Whatever my mother may have been she made me understand that what I make of my life is down to me. I have never felt that my only option is to be a parasite on a man." Without pausing Anya turned to Margaret. "It's not your father who's put you in the position you think you are in, it's your mother. She's made you think that all you can do is to get a man to look after you. And she didn't even let you find your own man. She's arranged everything with an arrogant, philandering, egotistical shit called Tim. It's not your father who's the source of all your problems it's your mother."

Neither Kathleen nor Margaret ever forgave her.

"Pile on in there!" Anya instructed the twelve men who made up the stag party. "All aboard for… where is it? The Chequers?"

In the back of the van Geoff, Tim, John and Dave sat with eight men she did not know. She had been told who they were but within minutes she had forgotten their names, they weren't important.

At The Chequers, the first pub stop of many, she stayed in the van studying the map Tim had given her of their route for the night. She was on her own for half an hour and wondered when someone was going to take the opportunity to spend time with her.

They had been at the second pub for ten minutes when she was relieved to see John walking out of the pub, two glasses in his hands "Sorry Anya, it's only orange juice since you're driving."

"That's really nice of you John."

"Can I?"

"Of course." She welcomed him into the van where he sat down on the cushions that were all the seating available.

"That week in London was the best." He took her hand awkwardly.

"No need for all that." Anya interrupted. "Do you want to repeat the experience or not?" She was already stripping off her t-shirt and reaching to unhook her bra.

"Christ Anya. Geoff's inside."

"So what?"

John had been alone at the station bar when he had seen a girl who reminded him of Anya crossing the station forecourt. Dave and Tim were later than usual and the station was crowded since many trains were cancelled due to the bad weather. When he realised it really was Anya he looked around for Geoff thinking that surely she wouldn't be in London on her own.

"Hi John." She dropped her bag at his feet and gave him a strong hug, kissing him full on his lips. "The others not here yet?"

"Anya! Where's Geoff?"

"We're not tied by an umbilical cord you know. I'm here on my own for a few days so I thought I'd look up some old friends."

"Who?"

"You three of course." She hugged him again.

"Why are you here?" John could never accept anything on its face value, there was always a reason, an alternative motive, for people acting out of character.

"An old friend of mine died, Geoff and I had some arguments and I needed to get away for a bit."

John realised that was all she was going to say. He noticed the way she was turning the locket around her neck around her finger and imagined the scenario. Old friend, old boyfriend, the one who had given her the locket had died. He would have been young so it had probably been an accident. Geoff hadn't understood her grief, had been jealous and had picked an argument, Anya, quite justifiably, walked away for a break. It all seemed perfectly reasonable. "Geoff knows where you are?"

She was saved from answering as Dave arrived, pushing his way through the crowd towards them.

"Where's Geoff?"

John answered for her. "In Liverpool, Anya's having a break for a few days and we're going to look after her."

"Yes? How? Have you seen all the trains are cancelled because of the snow. We're stuck up here."

"Hi guys. Have you seen the…" Tim was pushing through the crowd looking very pleased with himself when he spotted Anya. "Anya. What a wonderful surprise. Where's Geoff?"

Anya smiled and John answered for her a second time. "He's in Liverpool, Anya has thrown herself on our tender mercy for two or three days."

"Really?"

Anya wondered if Tim practised his leer in front of a mirror.

"Well we're not going to get back to the flat tonight. I heard the news about the trains before I left the office so I booked a hotel room, lucky that because I reckon if we were trying now we wouldn't have a hope in heaven. Have you seen how many people there are trying to find a place other than their office floors to sleep the night?"

"But there's four of us?" John had said.

"I knew there'd be three so I got a suite, anyway it was the last they had. Two double beds. That'll be just about right."

Anya knew what he meant, he would share one with her and Dave and John would double up on the other or one of them would have the, no doubt comfortable, settee.

"I'm laying down a few ground rules." She spoke with a confidence that had been lacking recently. "If I sleep with one of you I sleep with all three." She noticed the look on their faces and continued with a smile "One at a time. No-one is to be left out and no one is to have more favours that the others." She was pleased to see that Tim didn't seem too happy about the deal.

"OK. Agreed?" He looked at Dave and John but didn't wait for an answer. "Follow me."

The fraught receptionist in the hotel was dealing single handed with the unexpected rush of guests and checked in 'Mr and Mrs Tim Cross' and their two stranded friends without question.

As the door shut behind the porter Tim pulled three matches out of a box on the mantelpiece and, with the penknife he had on his keyring, carefully sawed a few millimetres off one. "Whoever gets the short straw goes first." It was John. "Now who's second?" He threw one of the long matches into the fire. "Short straw goes last." He seemed to be making the rules up as he went along. Dave drew the long match from Tim's clenched fist. "Dave, you're second. Then me."

Anya watched Tim as he organised everything. "Don't I have any say in this?"

"No. You don't. Come on Dave. We'll go to the bar and leave John to it for, how long?" Now he did turn to Anya for an answer.

"An hour each."

"OK Dave will be here at," he looked at his watch, "eight o'clock, and I'll be here at nine. Won't you be wanting anything to eat?"

"We'll all go out at ten." She said firmly, knowing that Tim, being last, had hoped for longer than his allotted hour.

She had been kind, encouraging, gentle, teasing, and had made John enjoy the experience that he had worried would lead him to come third in any ranking. As he relaxed he had gained in confidence and her hour with him passed more pleasurably than she had expected.

Anya lay back on the cushions in the van and let John show her how much he remembered of what he had learned in January. It was barely ten minutes before John rolled off her and leant over to pick up his glass and finished his pint.

"Go back and send out Dave. But before you go, I've got an idea…"

A few minutes later Dave was in the van. "Jesus Anya are you working through us all?"

"Only re-visiting January."

Again Anya made the running and Dave was amazed at himself as he managed to delay his climax to give Anya more pleasure than he had managed six months before. He had thought then that she was a really nice, interesting girl and he wished she was around more, he wanted to know her better. He wondered if he was the only one who thought there was so much more to Anya than just sex.

"Anya?"

"Yes?"

"Do you make everyone you bonk feel this good?"

"Bonk! What a lovely word. I hope so. Before you go, Dave, I've got an idea…"

Twenty minutes later Tim was on the floor of the van. He was far more experienced and far more skilful than either John or Dave. He manipulated her as though he wanted her to enjoy sex with him. He took her near to climax and then away, he took her near again, and then away, finally he took her there and stayed there, for what seemed like hours. He stayed on her, in her, with her, longer than he needed to. With John and Dave she had been the leader, it was she who had directed the action, but Tim was the director, leading her to do what he wanted, when he wanted. She realised she rather enjoyed that.

"Shit."

"Was I that bad?"

"You know what I mean."

"Good then?"

"Christ Tim. What were we doing back then?"

"I think I was shagging you."

"I know that but there was something different."

"I'm marrying Margaret tomorrow but one day, Anya, one day you and I will be together. We're like one person you and I, two sides of the same coin."

"Hi there you two." Geoff opened the door of the van unsurprised at seeing Tim with Anya. "How much do I owe you?" He was business-like as he turned his back allowing his soon to be brother-in-law some privacy as put his clothes back on.

"I'm a bet?" Tim asked weakly.

"Of course you are. One hundred a go."

Tim was not going to admit that his pride was dented. "Come on

Geoff, let's get our own back on this little lady of yours."

"No Tim, you go back to the bar, it's my turn."

Anya was surprised at how bright she felt when she woke in the uncomfortable bed in the unfamiliar bedroom half an hour before the alarm was due to go off. She watched Geoff as he slept, his breathing even, his mouth slightly open. The light caught his face and showed the dark stubble around his cheeks. It was a gentle face, trustworthy, calm and kind. But did she love him? She thought perhaps she might.

Tim and Margaret would be waking up in their separate beds on the day of their mockery of a wedding. It was a wedding for show, an arranged marriage between the families. 'So suitable' Kathleen had said. Yet Anya was certain there was no love involved. It was only a ceremony; nothing would change for either of them. Tim would continue his bachelor lifestyle of work, drinks with the boys, golf and cricket at the weekends with an occasional screw and probably a longer term mistress, his secretary perhaps. Margaret would play house until she had a baby or two and then she would be a bored wife and maybe even have an affair of her own. How long before they were divorced? How long before the lives of those two children, inevitably a boy and a girl, would be messed up by their parents' divorce? Then the children would marry too young, have children of their own and then divorce or even they might be brave and not marry, just have the children anyway. So whichever way they went they would muck up another generation. And so the downward spiral would continue.

The whole thing, Anya thought, was so depressing.

She turned over to stare at the hands of the clock waiting for them to work round to the time for her to make the tea. Was Margaret lying awake, wondering whether she really had no option other than to marry Tim. Was she having last minute doubts? She should be, Tim was a shit. Surely she knew that she was letting herself in for a life of excuses, late meetings and cancelled trains. Anya almost felt sorry for the bride. Almost.

She wondered what it was that made people want to tie themselves to one person for life. Was it money? Security? She thought of unmarried Marion, with three babies by the time she was twenty-one, all dead, all gone, with so little left to prove she had ever existed. She thought of Dot, unmarried because of her memories of the young man she had loved and who had died. Perhaps, had they married, they would have grown bored with each other; perhaps reality could never have matched the life imagined in the excitement of the war years.

As she looked across to Geoff she wondered whether she would say 'yes' if he proposed. If she did she would be stepping onto a conveyor belt that would take her where she really did not want to go but would she have the strength to say no, to leave him and start a new life on her own? If she did take that easy way out could their marriage possibly last? Geoff was fun, kind, gentle and generous but he was his mother's son. Under her influence he would soon forget his Liverpool Resolutions and come to expect his wife to do nothing with her life other than be his wife. In time, inevitably, his mother would encourage him to have a family and that was the one thing she could never give him. If they married they would, sooner or later, divorce, however much love might be involved.

Dispirited, she got up and made the tea.

By eight o'clock Anya had dropped Geoff at his mother's and had driven the van back to Tim's house.

"Good morning." He seemed none the worse for his stag night experiences but looked serious. "I'm afraid we've got a bit of a problem. I don't suppose you can help?" Nothing in his voice would have betrayed their very different relationship a few hours before. He was, Anya thought, cold, distant and incredibly pompous.

This was the Tim who was going to do what was expected of him, this Tim would spend a few hours of his life playing the game. Anya went along with it. "What is it? I'll help if I can."

"Mother has ordered the cake from somewhere miles in the country and the woman's car has broken down. Could you pick it up then deliver it to the Golf Club. You take my car and I'll take the van back."

"Sure, just tell me where. I'm getting to know the roads round here."

Half an hour later Anya arrived at the Golf Club and entered a world she had never guessed existed.

There were signs *'Men Only', 'Members Only', 'No women except Weekdays before 6pm.'* Anya walked confidently to a door that said *'Members Only'* and was stopped by a man in a white jacket with white gloves.

"And where might you be going young lady?"

"I have the cake for the Philips-Cross wedding reception." Tim had told her what to say.

"Ah yes. In here Miss." The attitude of the attendant changed. "Can I help at all? Where is the cake?"

"In the boot of my car, there're five boxes I think. It'll need reconstructing."

"That's alright Miss I'll show you to the housekeeper. In the meantime can I get you a coffee? Sorry." He stopped her walking through the open French windows. "Ladies aren't allowed on the terrace on Saturday."

"I'll help you get the cake then and thanks, no coffee."

"Mr Cross. He's a real gentleman." The attendant spoke conversationally as they crossed the car park to Tim's car. She had enjoyed driving it that morning and had parked it neatly between two Jags. "But you shouldn't have parked there you know, 'Members only.'" He was not telling her off, simply commenting and they shared a mischievous glance. "But what the heck. No harm done is there?"

"And in any case Mr Cross is a member." She added innocently.

"And it is his car." He agreed.

Anya thought for a moment whether she could arrange a retrospective bet with Geoff '£30 each for golf club staff' but decided she didn't have the time.

They carried the boxes carefully to the kitchen and Anya kissed the young man lightly, but provocatively, on the cheek. "Thanks for all your help. I've got to get back now." She knew he would be looking at her bottom as she walked back to the car so she didn't disappoint him, walking with rather more movement than was necessary in her tight jeans.

Instead of the organised calm she had expected when she arrived back at Tim's house she found Esme Cross standing in tears in the middle of the living room. "How could they do this? They've let us all down!"

"Now now mother." Tim was doing his best to calm his mother. He threw Anya a look of desperation as she walked in. "Everything will be fine Mother. Don't worry. We'll get it all sorted out. Trust me."

"But Kathleen…" Esme gulped "Kathleen will expect everything to be… perfect. Oh dear. What can we do?"

"It will be fine mother. Don't worry. Sit down. Let me get you a gin."

"It's only half past nine."

"But this is my wedding day Mother, you could say that's a special occasion."

"All right then." Esme allowed herself to be led to the comfortable settee where she sat down, rather inelegantly, as Tim handed her a large glass filled with clear liquid.

"What's up?"

"John. He was going to be best man."

"And?"

"He's disappeared."

"Disappeared?"

"Gone. He's got the ring and everything. He's my best man for Christ's sake."

A small voice said 'Don't blaspheme darling,' but they ignored it.

"What about Dave?"

"He's gone too. I phoned the flat. There's no reply. I went round. There's no one there."

Anya began to laugh.

"What's so bloody funny?"

"Nothing Tim. Silly really. It's just that last night we talked about the wedding and we all thought you were making a dreadful mistake so they decided the only way to stop you was to run away with the ring. I thought it was just the drink talking, I didn't for one moment think they were serious."

"There's nothing for it Anya, you'll have to be my best man."

Anya raised an eyebrow and checking to see that they were out of Esme's sight asked provocatively 'best what?'

"Not now." Tim turned away and she realised she had made a mistake, he was in 'getting married to the right person' mode. Instantly she switched her mood to match his, becoming business like and efficient. "Tell me which jeweller you got the rings from, I assume you're having one too, and I'll go round. You can pay me back later. What else do you need?"

Anya was surprised at how much there was to do on the morning of a wedding. For the rest of the morning Anya sorted out the things that Dave and John had left undone. She bought new rings, she collected Tim's suit from the dress hire shop, she calmed Esme, who had no idea who she was but kept calling her 'my dear child'. With all her jobs done she returned to the Cross household just after twelve thirty. "I think that's everything!" she laughed as she collapsed on a chair next to Esme.

"You have been so very helpful, my dear child, but I still have no idea who you are."

"I'm Geoff's girlfriend. Anya."

"Ah yes, the girl at the party." Esme looked guiltily at Anya. "I'm so sorry my dear it's just that after the engagement party Kathleen was, well, she wasn't very complimentary about you."

"Don't you think that's natural? Her only son's girlfriend? She's bound to be a little suspicious."

"I'm not at all suspicious about Tim's dear Margaret."

"That's different, you've known each other for years. I'm a new kid on the block."

"Well 'new kid on the block', whatever that might mean, I really don't know what we would have done without you this morning. Tim!" She called to her son. "Tim I insist you take this delightful young lady to lunch. You have plenty of time and she has been such a help. Take her for a nice drink. I can't imagine what has happened to David and John, they are normally so reliable. Just make sure you're back in time to be ready to be at the church on time. Dear child, dear child." She took another sip of her gin.

As Tim stepped aside to let Anya out of the door Esme wondered, rather vaguely, whether she and Kathleen were doing the right thing by their children. Perhaps Tim was a little unreliable for Margaret, perhaps Margaret a little on the unattractive side to be able to keep a man like Tim faithful to her. She and Tim's father had been divorced years before because she wasn't attractive enough to stop him straying. It had all been dressed up in other words but she knew that that was the fact of the matter. Perhaps someone like Anya would have suited Tim better. Perhaps it was all a mistake. 'Too late for that, they'll all have to sort it out for themselves after the wedding.'

"Will you have enough time to change?" Tim was being polite.

"Half an hour should do it. Everything's ready back at the house."

They sat, awkwardly sipping their drinks in the crowded pub.

"Your mother isn't really so bad is she? I thought, last year, well, she wasn't very friendly." Anya tried to break down the barrier that Tim had put between them. "It must be nice for her, seeing her plans come to fruition, her only son getting married, settling down." Only after she had spoken did she realise that that was probably the wrong thing to have said.

"I am not, repeat not, settling down. My life won't change in any way at all other than I go home to a wife rather than a flat filled with my currently mysteriously absent friends. You know more about Dave and John going missing than you've let on don't you?"

"How could I possibly know where they are?" Anya sounded genuinely surprised.

"It seemed like a very nice plot to spend time with me."

"That is the most extraordinarily arrogant thing I've ever heard."

"Well whatever your plan it hasn't worked has it? Was this another of your silly bets with Geoff? Screw me on my wedding day too?"

"It was not! You really aren't that irresistible."

"There was no plot then?"

"Not that I know anything about."

"Honestly?"

"Cross my heart and hope to die." Anya licked her finger and marked a cross over her left breast, running the finger rather too suggestively round her nipple.

He ignored the provocation. "So there's really no bet with Geoff?"

"No bet." She was very convincing.

"You were doing all this running around out of the goodness of your heart."

"And because it needed to be done and there was no one else to do it."

"I bet there's a bet." As he spoke she realised there was some humour in his voice.

She laughed. "Of course there's a bet but it's for this afternoon, after you're married. That's what makes it fun. This morning wasn't part of that, honestly, this morning I just wanted to help."

"How much?"

"A lot, I really wanted to help."

"No silly girl, how much was the bet for?"

"Five hundredish depending on, well, depending on a few other things."

"That's a lot."

"It was worth it to him to prove how stupid his mother and his sister are."

"It'll be the easiest money you'll ever make."

"Yeah?"

"Yeah. After the speeches Margaret will go and change. I'll find you then."

"Well that went rather well don't you think?" Kathleen was standing with Esme and Geoff as they waved the newly-married, if not entirely happy, couple off on their honeymoon.

"A triumph my dear." Esme was always keen to agree with her old friend.

"I can't think of anything that went wrong." Kathleen was never slow to congratulate herself. "And everyone seems to have enjoyed themselves."

"Some of them quite a lot." Geoff added under his breath.

Kathleen was right about the wedding, it had gone off without a hitch. The church flowers were perfection, Margaret looked as pretty as she ever could, as did the bridesmaids, even Fiona looked less like one of her horses than usual. Everyone knew the hymns, deliberately chosen for their familiarity and the homily was short, the vicar restricting himself to encouraging the bride and groom to ignore any faults and always look for the best in one another. The sun shone as they all left the church and the photographer seemed to know his business, though Kathleen considered him considerably under-dressed in faded denims and a light linen jacket.

'He came highly recommended.' Kathleen had said to Esme in unnecessary self-justification. 'I'm sure he will do an excellent job. We will have a perfect record of this perfect day'.

Geoffrey, Kathleen thought, had played the part of father of the bride with panache and confidence. Looking at her son she thought, not for the first time, what a good job she had made of raising him. She had thought she might miss the presence of a husband on her daughter's wedding day but she had not. The only blot on Geoffrey's copybook was his ignoring her unmistakeable hint that Anya should not be present, but she took comfort in the knowledge that he had seemed to have spent no time at all with the girl all afternoon.

"We have Anya to thank for so much." Esme didn't understand the look of hostility that was flashed towards her from her old friend.

"In what possible way could that girl have contributed towards the success of the day?" Kathleen's tone was harsh. The triumph was hers and she was not about to share it.

Esme looked at her old friend but said nothing, she didn't want to upset the happy atmosphere of the day. The uncomfortable silence was broken when Geoff answered for her. "As I understand it Anya was running around all morning acting as Tim's best men. John only turned up at the church five minutes before Margaret. I think I agree with Esme, Anya was extraordinarily helpful."

Kathleen didn't deign to answer, she was wondering what Anya's motives had been. Anya was not the unselfishly helpful sort.

"Come my dear, you must sit down." Esme, trying to relax the atmosphere, put her arm on Kathleen's and guided her back in to the club. "I'll get someone to get you a fresh glass of champagne or would you prefer something a little stronger?"

Geoff followed them back into the throng of guests who seemed determined not to leave until the free drink had dried up. He walked over to Anya. "Well they're off."

"How long do you give it?"

"What, until the divorce? Three years. Tops." He hoped his mother, who was walking back into the clubhouse with Esme heard him.

"I didn't think you could get a divorce sooner than that." Anya said doubtfully.

"Three years is the current minimum sentence. How much do I owe you?"

"I suppose we're equal with one Tim minus one Fiona. I assume you managed it at long last?"

"Yes." She was surprised at how downbeat Geoff seemed.

"Was she worth it?"

"She wasn't terribly happy but I told her I'd had enough of her prick-teasing and if she wanted the tiniest chance of being with me she would have to let me go all the way. I left the final decision up to her."

"And she did want the tiniest chance?"

"She did."

"Was she a virgin?"

"She's ridden horses since she was about eight years old how the hell was I supposed to know?"

Anya was shocked at the sharpness, almost regret, in Geoff's voice. "That's a dreadful thing to say."

"I think she was, she seemed very upset afterwards and she didn't enjoy it one bit, she just lay back and let me get on with it. And she wouldn't stop crying."

"I thought you'd been gone longer than strictly necessary, I wondered if you hadn't got involved with one of the other bridesmaids as well."

"It was all over with Fiona in a couple of minutes but I stayed to talk to her, calm her down a bit. She said she'd never forgive me. She said she had always known men were horrid but she hadn't realised just how disgusting they were. Disgusting, that was the word she used. She said that one day she'd make me feel as humiliated and defeated and used as she did."

"Poor little madam." Anya had no sympathy.

She wasn't prepared for his look of guilt. "It meant so little to me and so much to her. I shouldn't have done it."

"She'll get over it."

It was not the Geoff she knew who replied. "I don't think she will. She took it really badly. I really wish I hadn't done it." It was the first time she had heard him regret a conquest. And that conquest had had to be Fiona.

Chapter 8: Deceptions

Kent, Christmas 1972

Kathleen's voice down the phone was barely audible. "I will not invite that girl. She cannot come. Not for Christmas."

"That girl, mother, is my wife and she will be there."

Two weeks after they had returned from his sister's wedding Geoff had asked Anya to marry him, it was the only way he could think of to be sure she wouldn't leave him. He knew he wasn't being fair as there were so many things, important things, she didn't yet know. He hadn't told her that for two of the afternoons in the week after the wedding when he had said he was with his mother, he had actually been attending job interviews, interviews, he knew, that had gone rather well. He didn't tell her that the day he went to London with the brief explanation that it was 'stuff to do with the estate' had been in fact to go through the vetting procedure required by the government department. He hadn't told her that the official looking letter he received two days after their trip had been the job offer. He had discussed nothing with her as he made decisions for them both. He had told her nothing of his decision that his four years in Liverpool had been enough; his years of rebellion were over; now he was ready to go back to Kent and settle down.

Anya had been surprised when Geoff had suggested they drive up to the Lake District for the weekend but had been happy to go. She was surprised at the hotel he had chosen, standing high above Lake Ullswater, it seemed expensive even by his standards. At first she was uncomfortable in the surroundings and wondered why he hadn't realised that she would be. He had given her a gold band to wear on her ring finger 'it's the sort of place that expects us to be married' he had explained. They checked in as 'Mr and Mrs Philips'. The atmosphere was rather more relaxed than she had expected and she began to enjoy herself, especially when she noticed that they were not the most casually dressed guests at dinner.

"Happy?" Geoff had asked gently as they lay in bed the following morning watching the sun on the hills on the other side of the lake.

"Mmm."

"Do you like being Mrs Philips?"

"Mmm."

"Would you like to be Mrs Philips?"

She said no at first. She said no over breakfast, served on an oversized trolley in the big bay window of their room. She said no as they showered together and dressed. She said no as they undressed each other and made love but she finally said yes as a shaft of sunlight fed through the window onto the blue bed covering that made her think of sadness and of tears and of loneliness. "I suppose that will be the end of the bets then."

The wedding had been easily organised. There was no guest list, there were only the two of them and witnesses supplied by the Register Office. There was no reception, they had lunch at the first restaurant they came to. He rang his mother that evening to tell her. It had been a very short conversation.

Three months later phone calls between mother and son were no easier.

"I won't have that girl ruining our Christmas."

"Why would she ruin it?"

Kathleen didn't answer the question directly. "Christmas should be spent with people one likes."

"Then most Christmases would be spent alone."

"Your marriage," She spoke the word as if it were in inverted commas, "will not last. Not now she has got what she wants."

"And what would that be?"

"Your name and your money, but not necessarily in that order."

"You know nothing about her."

"I neither want nor need to."

The silence on the line was broken when Geoff presented his ultimatum. "It's either both of us or neither Mother."

"I will not have her in my house."

Geoff paused for a fraction of a second too long. They each knew what the other was thinking. The house was not hers, it was his and had been since the day he had turned 21. He spoke firmly and coldly. "Then we'll go elsewhere."

His mother made no reply faced as she was with the impossible idea that she should, after nearly thirty years, change Christmas. Every one she had had with Geoffrey had been the same and it had been a matter of honour to maintain that standard after his death. Champagne and buttered toast for breakfast, smart dress for the walk to church, drinks and conversation while the food was prepared, the Queen's speech as the turkey rested at the table, Christmas pudding set light after being doused in a ladle-full of brandy then, and only then, the gathering under the Christmas Tree for the giving and receiving of presents.

Geoff knew what the traditions meant to his mother and many of his early memories were bound up with the ceremonies that went with the day. When he was eight he was given the task of warming the brandy, though he was ten before he was allowed to pour it over the pudding and set it alight. When he was thirteen he was surprised to see his mother moving his knives and forks from his place on her right to the end of the table. He clearly remembered her words and could almost hear the familiar, theatrical, catch in her voice. 'You are the head of the family now, your place is at the head of the table.'

"For years you've said 'I'm head of the family and I don't think you've meant it even for a moment. Well now, as head of the family, I have made a decision. We'll go to Tim and Margaret, she'll probably jump at the chance to cook for us all."

Before she had a chance to reply he put the phone down, picked it up again and dialled Margaret's number. On hearing the ring tone he realised he had beaten his mother to it.

"Christmas? You want everyone to come to us for Christmas?" She had sounded doubtful, Geoff thought she sounded as if she had been crying.

"Forget all about the old routines. Do it your way."

"Why not?" She sounded less doubtful.

Geoff was surprised she said nothing about 'family tradition' and didn't ask if he had 'checked with Mummy'.

"Will Tim be OK about it?"

"He'll be fine. We were only talking about Christmas this afternoon."

"We're going south." Geoff had thought carefully about how he was going to tell Anya and he couldn't put it off any longer. "We're going south for the weekend."

"Any particular reason?" Anya was sitting at the table typing and was concentrating on an article she was writing. She was finding it hard going and didn't really want to be interrupted.

"We need to start looking for a house."

He had her attention.

"A house? What would we want to look for a house for?"

"Come here, sit next to me and I'll explain."

Reluctantly she joined him, not really wanting to hear what he was going to say. She sat down and listened as he explained how it had all started.

"An interview? Back in August?"

She listened as he talked on, not really hearing what he was saying. She interrupted him again. "You knew this when we went up to the Lakes?"

He nodded.

"You knew this when you asked me to marry you?"

He nodded again, waiting for the storm he knew would follow. It didn't come. Anya was calm and cold as she questioned him.

"You didn't think to ask me what I wanted to do?" He had no answer to the coolness in her voice. "You've been planning this move for months and you never bothered to talk to me about it?"

"I couldn't risk you not coming."

"That's it is it? I've got no say in it? My life, my career, what I want to do means nothing? Everything I want is second to your career and what you want to do?" She was still speaking calmly. Geoff could find nothing to say. He had expected an argument, not this coldness.

She stood up and walked back to the table, her typewriter and the article that seemed even more important than ever. Nothing more was said as Geoff read the evening paper against the soundtrack of the clattering keys. After a while he made two mugs of tea, placing one carefully on the table next to Anya.

"Thanks." Anya was hardly encouraging.

"Look Anya, I never meant things to go so long without talking to you."

She looked up and stared at him over the top of her glasses, saying nothing.

"I know I should have talked it all over with you but the chance of the interview came up when we were down for the wedding, then the right moment never came. The further in I got and the more I had to talk to you the harder it became." He knew he sounded very weak.

"I thought we were being honest with each other now." He would rather have had her anger than this sadness.

"I'm sorry. Really. I'm sorry."

"But you won't turn the offer down will you? You may be sorry you didn't tell me but it's what you want to do isn't it?"

"But not without you."

"Is that why you married me?"

He couldn't say 'yes' but he pursed his lips together and shrugged.

"You didn't think I'd go with you unless I had to?"

Again he shrugged.

"When are you supposed to start?"

"Not until the new year. The first week in January."

"So that gives us six weeks…"

"Seven weeks today."

"OK seven weeks to find a house and move. At least we don't have to bother about a mortgage." He tried to ignore the bitterness in her voice.

"It's OK then?"

"No it's not OK, but I suppose I'll have to make the best of it." He had won but he couldn't help thinking it was a Pyrrhic victory.

Margaret had never had high expectations of her marriage to Tim but a week into her honeymoon she had begun to think that Anya had been right and she should have tried harder to find another way.

She had been 13 when her mother had told her that she would inherit nothing of her father's estate that she would have to marry to retain her standard of living and social status after her brother's 21st birthday. She had grown up knowing that her mother and Esme expected that she and Tim would make a match of it. Those were the words Tim had used when he had suggested they might as well do as their mothers expected. She had never loved Tim but she had been in love with the idea of the wedding day itself, of the status of being married, of the freedom of setting up her own home.

She sat by the pool in their honeymoon hotel and looked down at the simple gold ring on her finger. She calculated quite cold-bloodedly, as she watched him flirt with a middle aged woman in a bikini that was too young for her, that she would have a baby as soon as possible. She knew he wanted to put off starting a family for as long as possible but once she had a child he could not leave her. She would let him do what he liked and she would not make a fuss as long as he was discreet and caused her no embarrassment. As long as she had her home and a baby he could do what he liked and she would be content.

Happiness, Margaret thought as she watched Tim walk into the hotel with his conquest, his arm draped casually over the older woman's shoulder, his hand too close to her breast, was an impossible ambition and probably much over-rated.

On their return from honeymoon to the house that Kathleen had chosen, a large 1930s detached house in a desirable cul-de-sac on the edge of the town, they soon settled into a routine. Weekdays were always the same. After breakfast, when she had kissed her husband on the cheek and waved him off on his short walk to the station, Margaret would clean and tidy, dust and polish, vacuum and sweep. She seemed determined it would be the best kept house in the crescent even though very few people saw inside. Every day she changed something about the house, moving a piece of furniture, re-hanging a picture, re-arranging an ornament to make the house feel more hers. At lunchtime she would read through magazines, newspapers and cook-books to decide on what to cook for Tim that evening. In the afternoon she would walk to the shops, sometimes treating herself to tea and cakes before heading home. Dinner was always ready for Tim's return from the city punctually at seven-thirty. Through that autumn of 1972 he was rarely late home and he always ate his dinner with suitable appreciation before kissing her briefly on the cheek and escaping to the rugby club. Tim spent his weekends playing golf or rugby and spending time in the bars afterwards. Every Sunday they would have lunch with Kathleen. It was never an easy afternoon as Tim rarely hid the fact that he wanted to be somewhere else.

Leaving Kathleen's one Sunday in late November conversation between them was as strained as usual.

"How was the golf?"

"OK. I won 3 and 2 but I didn't play particularly well, not as well as I'd expect."

"Was there anyone there I'd know?"

"Not really."

"Christmas is only a month away and Mummy's worried what to do about, you know, Geoff."

"Simple. Anya and Geoff are married, she's part of the family, she comes to Christmas."

"Not simple. Mother hates the very idea of Anya. She's going to tell Geoff to come alone."

"You are joking! She can't be that stupid!"

"She isn't stupid. She just doesn't want her in her house at Christmas. It's our first Christmas together and she wants it to be special for us."

"Why would having Anya around make it not special for us?"

"Perhaps she thinks you still fancy Anya."

"I never fancied Anya. I just fucked her."

Perhaps it was Tim's insensitivity, perhaps it was that she felt tired and drained with the strain of her secret. She hadn't meant to tell him here, in the car, she had meant to break the news to him gently.

"You fucked me too and I'm pregnant."

She spoke quietly and Tim wasn't sure he'd heard her right, she never used bad language.

"You're what?"

"Pregnant, having a baby." She repeated, explaining unnecessarily.

The bus stop was convenient as Tim slammed on the brakes and the car swerved sharply to the left. As it came to a halt he turned and stared at her.

"I know we said we'd leave it a year or so. I know we agreed."

"Yes. We did agree didn't we? We agreed we'd leave it until my career is established. We agreed Margaret, you agreed with me. We would wait."

They both stared out of the window, the view quickly being obliterated by the rain that was falling heavily.

"How long have you known?" He asked the question as dispassionately as he could.

"A few days."

"And you told your mother already?"

"No! Of course I haven't! I wouldn't! I had to tell you first!"

"So this has got something to do with me after all." Tim said angrily thinking his mood was as dark as the world outside the car as dusk descended and the rain fell more and more heavily. "Don't you think you could have mentioned your plan just a little bit earlier?"

He rested his arms on the steering wheel and put his hands up to his forehead. He had married Margaret because she would make an excellent partner's wife or lady to the captain of the golf club and that had been his mistake. In the months of their marriage he had longed for someone like Anya, someone exciting, unconventional and attractive. He knew it wasn't just 'someone like Anya' he wanted so desperately, it was Anya herself and on the day he heard she had married Geoff he decided he had to leave Margaret and he had to do that before they had children. He wouldn't be able to leave a child, as his father had left him. Margaret had agreed to wait and he had thought he had a year or more. But she was pregnant now. She had trapped him. And he didn't know what to do.

Margaret was crying, sobbing, getting into a state and he hated seeing her like that. She was so different when she cried, so unattractive. So like her mother.

"Calm down Moppet." He used the endearment deliberately. "We'll be OK. I'll get used to it. It's just a bit of a shock."

They sat facing each other in the gloom of the car. Tim switched on the ignition and the lights, preparing to drive home, realising that nothing would ever be the same again.

They had only been in the house a few minutes, just time to close the curtains and switch on the lights, when the phone rang. Margaret answered it, it gave her something else to do other than face Tim.

"Hello Margaret? It's Geoff. Have you thought about Christmas?"

Geoff was preoccupied as he drove south on the day before Christmas Eve. The hired van was filled with their belongings and Anya followed in their car. They had done this journey several times in the preceding weeks and this was to be the last time.

Once she realised that the move was inevitable Anya had travelled south with Geoff to do the rounds of the estate agents and had been partially won over by the fourth house they had seen. It was unprepossessing, built over a hundred years before but it was in the country, surrounded only by fields and its rooms were large and with high ceilings. She wondered, as she walked round it with the sycophantic estate agent, what her mother would have thought. The best thing about the house as far as Geoff was concerned was that it was empty and if they wanted to, they could move in before Christmas.

It was dark when the convoy of two pulled up outside their new home. Geoff jumped down from the van but Anya stayed in the car, as if reluctant to begin her new life, until he opened her door.

"Tired?"

She nodded and slowly swung her legs onto the tarmacked drive and allowed Geoff to put his arms around her.

"Here we are then." He spoke gently.

"Yes. Here we are." Geoff was sure she had been crying.

"Look Anya, it's too late to do much now and we're both pretty tired. Shall we just get some stuff inside and then go to The Oak for a meal? Maybe get a room if they've got one?"

"I know you Geoff Philips, you've already booked the table and the room." She sounded resigned at the prospect.

"Of course I have. Hang on a minute, we've got to do this properly." He stopped Anya as she was opening the front door and lifted her up and over the threshold. He was worried when she didn't laugh, she just let herself be picked up and put down on the shiny parquet floor of the large hall. "Welcome to your new home Mrs Philips."

Still she didn't smile.

"We don't have to go out if you don't want to." He said as she turned and walked towards the lounge, already furnished with the three piece suite and tables they had ordered on their last trip south.

"We'll have to move some of this furniture, they haven't put it in very good positions."

"Do you want a bath first? Or shall we change at The Oak?"

"I'm not sure this dining table was the right choice." Anya spoke in a detached tone, "I thought the black ash would be nice but it doesn't really go with the house."

"I'm sure they'll take it back and you can choose something you like better. Now what do you want to do?"

Anya was already half way up the stairs. "This carpet is right though, it's just the right colour, not too light and not too dark." Geoff followed her.

"This is a nice room isn't it?" He spoke, giving up on finding out what she wanted to do for the evening.

She didn't answer him, she just went to the window, looked out over the garden, and closed the curtains.

He followed her as she went from room to room, finally sitting down on the bed next to her. He resisted his impulse to put his arms round her, push her down on the bed and make love to her, instead he put his hands on hers. "We will be happy here."

She let his hands stay where they were but looked up at him. "I hope so Geoff but I wonder if I can ever be happy anywhere."

An hour later they had checked into their room at The Oak and it seemed to Geoff that Anya was a little more relaxed. Perhaps she had only been tired, the last few weeks had been very stressful. There had been all the journeys south to find the house and even packing up the flat had been difficult, he had had so much more than Anya. Neither had said anything but they were both aware that what little Anya had was all that Anya had.

"I think Margaret and Tim are meeting us downstairs." He had said as Anya lay in the bath full of bubbles, her long hair pinned loosely on top of her head.

"You don't think Geoff, you know, because you organised it."

"I thought it might be best, you know to break the ice before tomorrow."

"Is it going to be so difficult?"

"Well Mother will be on her worst behaviour, moaning at everything being 'different' and she'll complain at everyone else's manners without realising how bad hers are."

"When will you tell them you're moving back?"

"When conversation flags I suppose, when Mother is being particularly awful."

"Will Margaret cope?"

"She'll be fine. Apparently she's become quite a good cook since she got married. I've always meant to ask you." He asked trying to be nonchalant. "Who gave you this?"

"What's this? I can't see."

"This ring."

She had left her sapphire ring on the dressing table so many times before. She wondered why he was asking about it now.

"I told you ages ago. My mother left it to me."

"But where do you think she got it. I mean it's really nice, really valuable."

"Don't be such a shit Geoff. Just because we were poor doesn't mean she couldn't have had something really beautiful."

"Why? Who could have given her something so, so…"

"Expensive?"

"Well it's obviously very valuable, it should be insured."

"You've never mentioned it before."

"Where did it come from?"

"I've told you. It was my mother's. Her brother gave it to her."

"OK don't answer if you don't want to."

"Why won't you believe me? I suppose you want to know whose photo is in my locket as well?"

"Well? Whose?"

"No one's, it's empty."

"Not even me?"

"No. Not even you. You haven't earned it yet."

They finished dressing in uncomfortable silence and a few minutes later they walked down the stairs into the bar together to find Tim sitting alone at a table.

"No Margaret?" Geoff asked without any preliminary greeting.

"She makes her excuses, says she'll see you tomorrow but she's still got loads of stuff to do. She's making so many lists. I keep telling her it's only a meal but she gives me one of her stares and says if I really believe that then I must be completely stupid."

Anya leant down and kissed Tim lightly on the cheek. "What relation are we now Tim?"

"Brother and sister-in-law?"

"Probably not." Geoff had an idea where the conversation was going. He had braced himself for it and thought he was prepared as he watched Anya and Tim dance around each other.

"Would that be incest?"

"Probably not."

Geoff had decided days before that the best way to appear not to mind was to arrange the liaison. Letting Anya and Tim spend time together, encouraging them to get any unresolved sexual tension out of the way before Christmas, had seemed like a good idea but it didn't make it any easier as he watched them disappear up the stairs together. He sat alone in the strangely empty lounge, regretting the argument about the ring. He had no real reason not to believe her, he had just been uptight about what he knew was now going on in the room two floors above. It was over an hour before they joined him.

"What would have happened if Margaret had come with me?" Geoff thought Tim seemed very relaxed when he had just spent an hour screwing his wife.

"We'd have had a happy evening's drinking and catching up."

"Well I'm glad she didn't, that was one of the best Christmas presents I've ever had."

"How are things with Margaret?" Anya asked the question that no man would ever ask. No answer was necessary as Tim's face explained everything.

"She's fine. We're fine." He finally acknowledged the question.

"No you're not." Anya persevered.

"We've only been married five months. Of course we're fine." Tim was still unconvincing. "Margaret's fine. She hasn't said she isn't."

"I should think Mum's making your life an absolute misery." Geoff was beginning to agree with Anya.

"Well yes."

"Is she sticking her oar in where it's not wanted?"

"Of course she is." Anya felt no need to be polite. "I bet she's over every week, tweaking the cushions and criticising everything."

"We go over to her for Sunday lunch every week but she still finds excuses to come over."

"Tim. Why do you let her? You're a big boy now, just say no."

"There is no way, absolutely no way, of stopping her. I keep out of the way as much as I can. Golf you know, rugby, then there'll be cricket next spring, at least that lasts all day. Sometimes I manage to miss her visits entirely."

"Leaving Margaret to put up with her mother, that's hardly fair is it? I mean shouldn't you be sharing the burden that is our mother-in-law?"

"She hasn't said anything."

"Well of course she hasn't. She wouldn't be that disloyal. But you should understand your wife a bit better and realise she wants to be free of Kathleen as much as you do." Anya spoke with the authority of the outsider.

"Do you think so? You might have a point. But what do I do? She just says it's always been a family thing, Sunday lunch,"

"If we ever lived down here," Anya was careful not to give away that they already did live 'down here', "we'd change that. Kathleen would never invite me to anything and she couldn't invite Margaret and you and not Geoff and me could she?"

"She'd just invite Geoff on his own."

"Well Geoff wouldn't go. Would you?" She turned sharply to look at her husband.

Geoff took just a fraction too long to deny that he would go anywhere his wife wasn't welcome. Anya ignored the prescient twinge of worry that second of silence caused. "We would change the pattern." She said firmly.

"How?" Geoff and Tim spoke as one.

"Somehow."

Tim smiled, managing to avoid Geoff's eyes and turned towards the bar. "Bottle of Veuve Cliquot, ice cold please, and three glasses. Somehow it's the only champagne I drink. The widow you know, in honour of our mother-in-law."

Tim, Geoff realised with some jealousy, was speaking only to Anya.

The next morning Anya and Geoff arrived, apparently relaxed with each other, more than two hours before Kathleen was due. Tim showed them into the kitchen and sat down pouring coffee into a mug. "Help yourselves, it's all very informal here." Geoff smiled at the contrast with what would have been happening had Christmas been at his mother's. "Margaret?" he asked as he hunted for two clean mugs.

"She's not feeling very well. She seems to have a bit of food poisoning, can't keep anything down."

"On Christmas Day? Unheard of!"

"Stress probably." Anya added with dry sympathy "It must be awful having to cope with the whole dysfunctional lot of us."

"Perhaps she's coming down with something." Geoff was determined not to be anything but considerate to his sister.

"Perhaps she's pregnant." Anya suggested, keeping the cold shaft of jealousy out of her voice as she watched Tim's face carefully. "She is!"

"God Tim, you don't hang about."

"It wasn't meant to happen this soon."

"She's just so fucking fertile." Anya could not hide her resentment.

There was an uncomfortable silence as Anya pulled herself together. "Sorry. I shouldn't have said that. Congratulations. Well done. When's it due?" Her voice was lifeless, but at least, Geoff thought, she was trying.

"Don't for God's sake tell her you know. Please. I shouldn't have said anything. Not today."

"You didn't want it to happen did you?" Anya looked at Tim sharply. He didn't answer and Anya took that as confirmation that Margaret and her mother had conspired to set the trap.

"Are you going to tell Mum?" Geoff wasn't as perceptive as his wife.

"Absolutely not. Kathleen really must not know. It's early days yet and so much can go wrong." Only Anya heard the slight hint of hope in Tim's voice as he continued. "So many pregnancies go wrong in the first three months or so. So I'm told anyway."

"How far gone is she?" Anya tried to be practical.

"A couple of months I think. She's only known definitely for a month or so. Please don't let on you know. You mustn't say a word." Anya noticed how subtly Tim was disassociating himself from the pregnancy, 'she' not 'we'.

"OK." Anya thought she spoke for her husband as well as herself. "Not a word, not an inkling."

"OK" agreed Geoff. "But how are we going to get through today? Mum will be here in half an hour."

"No problem. Tim, tell Margaret everything is under control." Anya walked around the units in the kitchen opening and closing cupboard doors, checking the contents of the fridge and the prominent notice board. "Eureka!" she cried triumphantly waving a piece of paper in her hand. "You said Margaret had made loads of lists, everything's here, what time to put stuff in and what time to take it out. I've never used one of these things." She stroked the cream enamel of the Aga as if it were a pet she was slightly unsure of.

"Really?" Tim asked tentatively. "It's a lot to take on. Margaret's been planning this for days."

"I'll be fine. Everything will be fine. Tell her not to worry."

Geoff watched his wife as she moved around the kitchen. 'My wife. My *wife*. *My* wife.' He was proud of her as she opened drawers and cupboards to check where things were. He noticed Tim's look as he stared at Anya as she bent to check a low cupboard. Geoff tried to read what was in Tim's look; admiration, lust, anticipation, possession. 'But that beautiful body is mine. She is my wife, my *wife*, *my* wife.' He repeated in his head, changing the emphasis from word to word.

They had tried to put the night before behind them. They had both been tired from the journey, unsettled by the sight of their new home, anxious about spending Christmas with his family, but, he had recognised too late, he had made a mistake in arranging for Anya and Tim to spend that time together. He had been disappointed when she didn't want to make love, and surprised when she didn't even kiss him goodnight, or touch feet, before turning over to sleep in the unfamiliar room. The morning had been a rush as they had had to leave the hotel, go home, change; nothing was settled, neither was comfortable. And he still didn't understand why Anya hadn't made a joke or teased him about the previous night's arrangement as she had always done with the other objects of bets. He had to assume Tim meant more to her than any of the others.

When the doorbell rang Geoff answered it and kissed his mother on both cheeks. "Happy Christmas Mum."

"Happy Christmas Geoffrey." She detached herself from her son "And to you Tim." She added as she turned, waiting for one of them to slip her fur coat off her shoulders. Geoff did the honours.

"Margaret?" Kathleen asked, surprised that her daughter was not at the door to welcome her. "In the kitchen I suppose. Well Christmas Dinner is such a difficult meal to prepare. It takes years of practice to get it absolutely right."

Tim ignored the implied anticipation of failure. "I'm afraid she's not very well, she's eaten something that disagrees with her and can't leave the bathroom for long."

"I don't think we need to know all the details Timothy. I'll go up to see her."

"No, Kathleen, please leave her alone. You know how upset she gets when people see her looking, well not looking her best."

"I think I've seen her looking far from her best."

"Well anyway, don't go up." She responded to the authority in Tim's voice and turned reluctantly from the stairs.

"Who, then, dear boy, is doing the cooking?"

"Anya's doing her best."

"I'd better see what she's getting up to. She can't possibly know what she's doing." Kathleen pushed past the men into the kitchen.

Anya was sitting at the kitchen table, the bottom half of a large glass of wine in her hand, watching television. It was the first time she had seen Anya since she had become her daughter-in-law but she said nothing, she was not going to recognise the marriage because it would soon end and Geoff would be free to marry Fiona. That had always been the arrangement she wanted. She had been talking to Fiona's mother about the possibility of encouraging their children to make a go of it when she had had the call from Geoff to say he had married Anya. It had been a disappointment but she took it as only a temporary setback. She had little doubt Geoffrey would see sense and the marriage would be over before too long and then she would bring Geoffrey and Fiona together.

"Happy Christmas mother-in-law." Anya was relaxed and unembarrassed by the situation. "Everything's under control. Geoff, darling, get your mum a drink. I'll be with you in a minute. Just got to…" She paused as she sipped the last contents of the glass, "… check the bird one more time. I've never cooked a goose before. Go on you two, I'll be there in a minute."

Kathleen, appalled at the informality of it all, followed her son out of the kitchen with Anya's voice unavoidable as she sang along with Fred Astaire *'I'm putting on my top hat, tying up my white tie, brushing off my tails di dum da didi da da dum di didi da da polishing my nails'*.

Tim led them into the living room hoping that the decorations Margaret had worked on for a fortnight would distract Kathleen. She made no mention of them, simply sitting in what she knew to be Tim's chair by the fire.

"I wouldn't dream of watching a film on Christmas morning." She spoke with disapproval dripping from every word. "It is not suitable behaviour for Christmas. I suppose it was her idea to have the television in the kitchen, I've never heard of anything like it. It wasn't there last week."

"I think my wife's doing really well." Geoff spoke pointedly, "And what's wrong with a drink while you're slaving over a hot stove. She's never used an Aga before," he continued conversationally, "I think that's rather brave of her."

"And Christmas dinner! That's really brave, cooking for her mother-in-law for the first time, in an unfamiliar kitchen." Tim added, handing Kathleen a glass of sherry and his brother-in-law a large scotch. "And you suppose wrong, I bought that television for Margaret as a Christmas present so she could do just what Anya is doing, watch while she slaves over preparing Christmas dinner."

Kathleen changed the subject as she usually did when the conversation was not going her way. "Will Margaret be well enough to come to church?"

"I shouldn't think so but I'll go up and check." Tim left Geoff to look after his mother.

"Anya doesn't do church." Geoff said, before Kathleen had a chance to make any comment.

"If I am not very much mistaken she attended your sister's wedding. That was in a church I believe."

"Weddings are different. No, she won't be going to church besides it'll let her get on with cooking dinner."

"That is why Christmas Dinner should always be in the late afternoon. I have no idea what time she thinks she's going to serve up but there should always be time for church."

"Anya's doing exactly what Margaret planned to do. All the instructions were written down so everything is exactly as it would have been." Geoff knew his mother would now change the subject.

"Will you be joining me at church? You're hardly dressed for it."

"I don't suppose God will mind jeans and polo necked sweater, they're all perfectly clean. Even my pants and socks are freshly ironed."

As they had left home this morning Anya had tried to be conciliatory. 'I will be good today Geoff, but please don't let your mother take you over, I'm really going to need you to be on my side.' He had known his mother would make her dislike of Anya and his marriage very obvious so he had promised his wife that he would show he was on her side by not doing everything his mother expected of him. 'I won't even go to church' he had promised, but in the face of his mother's determination he gave in.

"I'm coming with you, Mother, of course I am." He excused his weakness with the thought that this was as difficult a day for his mother as it was for every member of the new, extended family. An argument would simply ruin the meal Anya was working so hard to make perfect. They sat in a silence broken only by Anya's singing along with the film. The sound, not unpleasant to Geoff, was as irritating as a chair pushed back on a stone floor to Kathleen.

"Why did you marry her Geoffrey?" Kathleen asked loudly, hoping Anya would hear. "Did you have to marry her? Is she expecting?"

"No mother, she is not expecting. And even if she were we wouldn't have needed that as an excuse to get married."

"But why marry? Don't people of your generation simply live together?"

"We have lived together, for the best part of two years, as you well know. We got married because that's what people do when they love each other and they love being together and there's no reason not to."

"Whose idea was it?"

"What do you mean?"

"She knew you have money."

"It wasn't like that."

"Well what was it like?"

"I love her, we love each other. I asked her to marry me because I love her. She said no at first."

"I bet she did." Geoff just heard his mother's cynical comment.

"She said no for most of the morning. She didn't like the idea of marriage, she believed it could only bring pain because of her, well the fact that she can't have children…"

"She can't what?" Kathleen interrupted speaking very slowly and deliberately. Geoff realised his mistake. If only he could take back the words. She would have to have known some time, but not yet. Anya would be horrified. "You married her even though she can't have your children? There'll be nobody to carry on your father's name. You cannot have forgotten that any sons of Margaret do not count. I had never put you down as stupid, headstrong yes, but not so stupid as to marry someone who is barren. I can't imagine what you thought you were thinking."

Deceptions

Geoff wished his mother would speak more quietly, Anya must not hear their argument. "She didn't want to marry me because of that, she knew how you would feel."

"I doubt that."

"She did. She had an old friend who warned her that marriage when she couldn't have children could be a marriage under false pretences as all men want children. But I don't. I never will. I married her because I love her, the children thing really doesn't matter."

"The children thing, as you put it, does indeed matter, it is of considerable importance. It may not matter to you now but it will as you grow older. And you have been immensely selfish, you must have realised you are not the only one involved in such decisions. You have responsibilities to me and to Margaret and to the memory of your dear father."

"Oh Mother do shut up. I have responsibilities to myself to be happy and to Anya to make her happy too. That is it."

They listened through the silence that followed, picking out any noise to break the tension. Anya was clattering pans in the kitchen, they could just hear the sound of the film, there were whisperings in the room above but neither could make out what was being said. Geoff poured his mother another sherry just for something to do.

"Sherry. On Christmas Day. Whatever happened to a bottle of Champagne?"

Geoff heard the dramatic sigh and was trying to find a suitable answer when Tim finally joined them. "Margaret won't be going to church."

"Well I'll just pop upstairs to see her before we go." Kathleen held out her glass of sherry for someone to take so she could get out of the comfortable chair.

"No, don't. She doesn't want to see anyone."

"But..."

"She was just dropping off to sleep, you'd only disturb her. Whatever it was she ate is really taking it out of her. I'm only going because of meeting Mum there." Kathleen must not suspect the true reason for Margaret's inability to go to church on Christmas Day for the first time in her life.

An hour later Geoff sat only half involved with the familiar service. He was worrying about the many hostages to fortune that were hanging over the family. Kathleen didn't know of her daughter's pregnancy, a pregnancy Tim obviously did not want. But she did know that he and Anya could never be in the same position, something Anya must not realise. No one knew that he and Anya had left Liverpool for good and that it hadn't been altogether a joint decision. And no one knew how afraid he was that his wife was regretting marrying him and would rather be with Tim.

When the family returned with Esme, everything in the house was calm and prepared. The house was in silence, Geoff had a moment of irrational panic that Anya had left.

"Everything OK?" Geoff called from the hall as he took his mother's coat.

"Fine." Relieved to hear his wife's voice he walked through to the kitchen. She was sitting quietly at the kitchen table, her eyes shut.

"I've never done this before. I think I've thought of everything but I never had family Christmases to help me know how things should be done."

Geoff remembered each of the two Christmases since he and Anya had been together. The first when he had abandoned her in hall, the second when he had left her alone in the flat. He realised how selfish he had been and regretted that his family Christmases had always been more important than her happiness.

"Not really." A range of images came to mind, her mother in bed all day with someone she had picked up in the pub the night before, a Bird's Eye Chicken pie with frozen peas with a piece of holly stuck on it, never any celebration or anything to say it was a special family day, certainly no presents.

Geoff had no time to give his wife the encouragement she needed when Tim summoned them to join the others. "Come on you two, time for champagne." He put his arm possessively across her shoulders as he led her out of the kitchen.

Tim was taking control. "I'd better tell you all what's planned for today. We're going to have drinks now and do those presents that haven't been exchanged yet and then eat. If we're still eating when The Queen is on then we can bring a television into the dining room if there is anyone who wants to watch it.

He saw out of the corner of his eye Kathleen going to interrupt. "But…" was as far as she got as Tim and Geoff each opened a bottle of champagne with all the signs of having done it many times before, and expertly filled five glasses.

"What about Margaret?" Kathleen was determined no one would forget her daughter. "You haven't been to see how she is. I'd better…"

"She's best left alone." Tim's voice was firm as he handed his mother-in-law her glass. "A toast everyone." Our extended family." Only Esme's voice was heard confidently repeating her son's words.

"Now it's time for presents. Everyone into the hall" Tim did his best not to catch Kathleen's eye, instead concentrating rather too obviously on helping his mother.

"Mum, Kathleen, let me have any presents you've brought with you and I'll put them under the tree then I'll find one present in turn for everyone. If we run out for someone I will get one of the presents from the tree itself." It was what the Cross family had done every year, it was a familiar tradition for them, but totally alien to Kathleen and she did little to hide her discomfort. None of this Christmas felt right to her, especially with Margaret mysteriously ill upstairs.

"Kathleen, you first." Tim handed her a well wrapped present which she opened without enthusiasm.

"Thank you Esme. What a well-judged gift. I shall enjoy reading that." They all suspected the book, on Victorian country houses, would be placed on a shelf and never opened.

Anya was surprised to receive, as her first present, a small unwrapped box from Kathleen. As she opened it she realised it contained a ring. She looked at Kathleen questioningly.

"It was Geoffrey's great-grandmother's. It is passed to the first

Mrs Philips of each generation and since there is no doubt that that is what you are then it is yours." She spoke with a precision and lack of feeling that belied the generosity of the gift.

Anya looked at the emerald and diamond ring. "It's beautiful. Thank you so much." Geoff walked over and put it on the fourth finger of his wife's left hand and kissed her. He wished she'd tell him the truth about where her other ring had come from, he didn't believed what she had said about her mother. No one who lived the way the Caves had lived would have had a ring like that.

Geoff walked over to his mother and kissed her cheek. "Thank you Mother, that was really nice of you."

"It is your wife's by right, Geoffrey, whoever that might be. And as long as she is your wife she has a right to wear it." She turned to look severely at Anya. "But it is not hers, should she cease to be Mrs Philips she will return it to the family." Anya returned Kathleen's look with one of utter indifference, she then turned to Geoff and frowned, warning him that he shouldn't grace his mother's rudeness with any response. Geoff bent down, picked up a parcel from beneath the tree and handed it gracelessly to his mother. "From Anya and me."

Anya had taken a great deal of care in choosing the sweater she and Geoff had bought for his mother. It was fine cashmere and a delicate colour that would suit Kathleen's pale skin and grey hair. She knew that battle lines were drawn with her mother-in-law as she watched Kathleen open the carefully wrapped parcel, take one look at the sweater and place it, with no word of thanks, on the table behind her.

Other presents were given and received with varying amounts of enthusiasm. Geoff watched Anya sitting quietly as few of the presents were for her. Again he thought the words over and over, the emphasis on different words. 'My wife. *My* wife. My *wife*." He realised with a certainty that shocked him that he loved her and that he wanted her to love him, only him. In a moment that he couldn't tie down, almost without the words forming in his consciousness, he understood the mistakes he had made. He should not have persuaded Anya to marry him when they could easily have lived together. He should have discussed his plans with her about taking the job. He should never have thought going back to his home town, so close to his family, was a good idea. He should never have thought that his love for her was enough to overcome every problem they would face. He also understood that he had no idea how to make things right.

The meal started well. There were enough meat and vegetables for Geoff and Tim to eat as much they wanted and even Kathleen could find little other than the slight firmness of the sprouts to criticise. Tim kept their glasses topped up with wine and there was little need for conversation.

"That was brilliant." Geoff sat back after clearing his plate. "I had no idea I'd married such a good cook."

"Margaret was so well organised, all I had to do was follow instructions and I'm quite good at that." Anya sounded tired, hardly surprising, thought Geoff, after yesterday's leaving of Liverpool, the long journey followed by the evening at the Oak. He shuddered involuntarily at the thought of the events at The Oak. Why had he thought it a good idea to push them together?

"Well I think you picked up the reins beautifully, my dear." Esme smiled as she spoke. "We all know what a lovely cook Margaret is, you have done her proud. Tim I think it's time for some toasts."

Kathleen looked surprised. Toasts were for the evening, never before the Queen's speech and never before the pudding. That was how it had been at every Philips family Christmas.

"Of course Mum. OK people." Tim smiled as he saw Kathleen's look of horror. "Make sure your glasses are full, we have a good few toasts to get through."

Geoff walked round the table filling glasses.

"First. To our mothers…" Tim raised his glass in turn to Esme and to Kathleen. Geoffrey responded with "Our hosts, Tim and Margaret", then regretted including Margaret because it reminded everyone of her absence. Tim responded, with a glance in Anya's direction, with "Our cook and her husband. Geoff and Anya."

Glasses were drained and refilled.

"Absent friends." Geoff, relaxed after the good meal and the free-flowing alcohol, raised his glass, it seemed an obscure toast so he elaborated "Our fathers, Geoffrey and Marcus. We miss them today as we do every Christmas."

"And also to Anya's parents." Esme added, unsettled by the reference to her ex-husband. Geoff was unprepared for the look of pain on Anya's face. She rarely mentioned her mother and never spoke of her father. He began to realise there was so much he hadn't begun to know or understand about her.

"Generations gone and generations to come." Geoff spoke without thinking. He had meant to take attention from Anya's pain but understood immediately he had served only to add to it. She looked as though she wouldn't be able to hold back her tears much longer. Thoughts came quickly and instinctively. He had to protect Anya. He could not lose her. Tim was a threat. If everyone knew the truth Tim could never be with Anya. Then it was clear to him what he had to do. He didn't look at his wife or at Tim as he spoke firmly. "To Margaret and the baby."

The silence was broken by Kathleen's overly polite enquiry. "To whom?"

"Margaret's expecting?" Esme asked excitedly. "Oh that's wonderful news."

Anya pushed her chair back, leaving for the refuge of the kitchen. No one would miss her and she could busy herself with the Christmas pudding. She couldn't listen to the family congratulating itself. She should never have married Geoff. He would never escape his family and she hated every self-satisfied, self-righteous, smug one of them.

In the dining room, trying to ignore Anya's departure, Tim bowed to the inevitable and, with a poisonous look at Geoff, he spoke to the newly expectant grandmothers. "It's very early days. She's not having an easy time and she didn't want to get people's hopes up in case anything went wrong. A third of all pregnancies do in the early month so please don't get too excited yet."

"There's no reason why she should have any problem. Unlike

other women we could mention, there's nothing at all wrong with Margaret." Kathleen's defence of her daughter was strident.

"Perhaps I shouldn't have said anything." Geoff didn't sound as if he was regretting his words.

"No you bloody shouldn't." Tim was angry.

"I must go up to her." Kathleen had put aside her napkin and was standing up.

"You will not." Tim was adamant. "She doesn't want you. Don't you dare go up there."

"But she's my daughter. I must go up to her."

"You will not." Tim was standing in the doorway.

"This is farcical." Geoff stood up and stood between the two, facing his mother. "Sit down mother. Anya has worked hard today to cook Christmas dinner and you will eat the pudding. We will all eat the pudding. Sit down. Everyone." Esme watched, bemused at emotions she did not understand. "We'll sort out all this stuff after we've finished lunch but finish lunch we will." And he walked through to the kitchen where Anya was sitting, hunched over, her eyes closed, tears running in a line down each cheek.

"Is the pudding ready? They're ready for the pudding." He tried to sound cheerful.

"It's ready." The sparkle of presenting a wonderful meal, all the better for challenging their expectations, was gone. She dropped her voice to ask "Why did you say anything? You knew that they wanted it kept secret."

Geoff defended himself, almost whispering. "I don't know, honestly. I don't know why I said it."

"I do."

"Tell me then."

"You're jealous. You want Tim to be tied to Margaret because of me."

"Let's finish this lunch."

"Listen to me." Anya spoke softly, she didn't want anyone to overhear. "Last night we didn't do anything."

"You didn't do anything?"

"No. We just talked."

"Then what was all that about 'best Christmas Present ever'?"

"He had found someone on his side, that he could talk to about how he felt about Margaret and Kathleen. No one else could possibly understand."

"You didn't do anything?" Geoff repeated.

"No and we aren't going to. So let's get this lunch over with so we can go home and start again."

Geoff carefully carried the ladle filled with brandy into the dining room and with false jollity called for lights to be turned off. Anya had been really proud of the pudding but now she just wanted to throw it down and run away.

The conversation had calmed down as if the five people around the table had wordlessly decided to call a truce. As they finished the meal Geoff told Anya to stay where she was, he and Tim would do the clearing away and the washing up. Kathleen and Esme were quietly gossiping about something that didn't seem important even to them leaving Anya to her thoughts. Every family occasion would be a strain. As Margaret and Tim's family grew, as it would, those occasions would become unbearable. However much she and Geoff may love each other their marriage didn't have a hope of lasting for the single, simple reason that she could not give him what he didn't yet know he needed.

Children.

Chapter 9: Miscalculations

Kent, January 1976

Anya pulled the silver trunk out of the cupboard in the room that she called her study and Geoff called the spare room. She unlocked it and looked at the volumes, carefully choosing one from almost exactly three years before.

> *Tuesday 9th January 1973*
> *Well here we go then. G's off to his second day at work and I'm alone for the day. It's been two weeks since we said goodbye to the flat, goodbye to Liverpool, goodbye to Anya Cave. I must learn to be Anya Philips somehow. The house was ready to move into when we came down but it's just a house not a home and that has to be my job. But I will not be just a housewife. Unless I can make a life for myself I will grow to resent G so much for tricking me into this position. I will not be a Stepford wife. I will make a life for myself.*
> *Christmas Eve at the Oak T and I talked. It was good to talk. I was probably so tired after the drive I gave too much away I told him we'd moved down. He talked about his problems I talked about mine. He said although he fancied the pants off me (his words) we couldn't do the sex thing (his words again). But he said I wasn't to worry about being alone. He understood how difficult it would be for me and he'd always be there to talk to, so I'd always have someone on my side. Did he think already that G wouldn't be?*
> *I think about Dr Hill a lot. He really was a friend. I went to see him before we left, just to say goodbye. I said I'd come and*

see him whenever I could but we both knew we'd never meet again. How melodramatic is that. I promised I would never forget what Dot had said and never forget what they had done for me. I think he realised what I had already realised, that it was a mistake to have married G. We should have just lived together, and then I could have upped sticks and escaped at any time. Marrying G has meant I've lost control of my life.

Anya looked up from the diary and stared out of the window at the garden, her garden.

It was Sunday and Geoff had gone to his mother's for lunch. As had been usual for most of the previous three years, she stayed at home. She had joined him on Sundays for the first few months despite it being obvious she was not welcome. She had listened politely to the conversation, answering the few questions that were directed her way, usually by Geoff, and trying to be part of the family. Despite his promises to be her ally, Tim seemed to do his best to ignore her. Irrationally, she had felt betrayed. The visit that was to be her last was spent discussing plans for the increasingly imminent birth of Margaret's baby. Kathleen had commented 'of course that's something Geoffrey will never have to worry about unless he comes to his senses and divorces the woman.' Anya had looked towards Geoff expecting him to remonstrate with his mother but he kept quiet and avoided meeting her eyes. The next week she cooked Sunday lunch expecting that they would both stay at home but his mother's hold on him was too strong.

She looked back at her diaries and flipped through *Anya Philips 1974*.

Sunday, no need to date it, it's just the same as every other bloody Sunday

Woke up half an hour before the alarm. Lay in bed waiting for G to wake up. Sex, excellent, as ever. Breakfast always the same on a Sunday scrambled eggs, orange juice, freshly ground coffee. Second coffee no later than 10 while reading papers. 11.30 G leaves for T & M or K (alternating weeks). Why does he keep going without me? He said his mother said I wasn't to darken her door any more. I said he should tell her it was his fucking door. And when it's at T & M's why doesn't T make them include me? He said he would be my friend and he's done nothing. But still G goes off every Sunday for lunch with the family and muggins here stays at home. Why do I put up with it? No idea. G gets back 5ish. Always awkward for a bit as he tells me how awful it was, what M said, what T did, what the children got up to. Doesn't he realise? He just doesn't think. He wouldn't do it if he knew how much it hurts. Rest of the weeks are OK. But Sundays I can do without.

She put *Anya Philips 1974* back in the box and pulled out *Anya Philips 1975*. She held it unopened in her hands as she stared out of the window. The garden looked lovely as the sun melted the frost from the lawn. She watched as the area of white slowly receded as the sun rose higher on the clear January morning. The flower beds were empty apart from carefully located perennial shrubs which gave some colour and she noticed the first signs of bulbs sprouting signalling that spring would inevitably arrive. Discouraged from finding a career, Anya had found she had a talent for gardening and enjoyed writing irregular articles for the local newspapers. She would miss the garden when the farce that was her marriage was finally brought to an end. She knew she had to leave Geoff but she still loved him and just looking at him when he was unaware of her scrutiny always softened her resolve. She knew that, had they not moved to this house, in this area, they would have been happy. But they had and they weren't.

She wanted to understand why he was letting his mother change him into a man she knew he didn't really want to be. She wanted to understand so she could forgive him. But she could do neither.

She wrote *Anya Philips née Cave 1976* on the cover of a new volume. It was only eight years since she had left school with a briefcase full of exercise books from the stationery cupboard for her diary. It felt so much longer than that.

She looked at the empty page and decided to write a letter which, like her mother's, would never be posted.

> Sunday 11th January 1976
> Darling Geoff,
> Tomorrow I go to a solicitor and get our divorce under way. While you're with your mother I'm spending the afternoon preparing to end our time together.
> Geoff I love you so much. We started this marriage wrong, you really should have told me what you were planning, but I did try to make the best of it. It would have helped so much if you could have been more on my side. Whenever there was a choice to be made between 'them' and me 'they' always won. You and I were happy before we were married, but we were fooling ourselves weren't we? As soon as we moved down here your mother got her talons into you. I did see it coming that first Christmas. Family. Tradition. It was so important to you all and I could never be part of that. I should have known that, sooner or later, Family would be more important to you than I could ever be. I should have realised that it would become important to you that we couldn't have children. You could have children, but you couldn't if you stayed married to me. Your mother was right after all.
> Why did you tell her about me? When? How? I wish we could talk about the things that matter. But we have never done that have we? You've never believed that the ring was my Mum's but you never talk about it. Your resentment just festers. You probably think the locket has some sordid explanation but I've never told you where it came from because you never asked. You've certainly never been brave enough to ask me why I can't have children.
> We never talk about anything that matters in our lives. We can't speak about your so important, hush hush work at the

Ministry of Defence and you've never told me anything about your father's business and all those meetings you go to, all the papers you read, you never tell me anything. You never encouraged me to do anything other than look after you and the house. When I found an agent who believed in me and had begun to get some of my stuff published you didn't once say you were proud of me. You didn't once give me any encouragement. I'm as clever, as quick witted, as intelligent, as bright as you but you go to work and I stay at home doing the bloody gardening. Why don't you understand how miserable that makes me? It's as if you don't trust me out in the big wide world. At least it seems like that.

I've never been accepted into your family, not really. Not at all really. Every Christmas, every Easter, every family birthday was celebrated and every celebration seemed to have the sole function of making me feel inadequate. Children, the next generation, the Family, it was so important to you all and I couldn't contribute anything. I always wanted to tell you about my mother, where I came from, why at times I hate being me so much, but you never asked. Not once. If you had I'd have told you all my fears and worries. Maybe you tried. You must have tried. Probably, if I'm honest, a lot of that was my fault.

Could we have made it with perseverance? Or luck? I doubt it, not with the persistence and the sheer bloody-mindedness of your mother.

If I don't leave now it'll be too late for us both. I'm sure you don't want a divorce. But it's inevitable now isn't it? How am I going to explain to a stranger how difficult the past three years have been and how impossible it is to continue like this when I can't even make you understand? You don't see there's a problem do you?

I think you're as scared of change as I am.

I think I'll never love anyone else as I've loved, and still love, you.

She turned back to the window and watched the lengthening shadows as she waited for Geoff to get home.

"Now, Mrs Philips, you say you want to discuss a divorce from your husband. Have you any idea of the grounds?"

Anya sat in Stuart Benthall's office trying to overcome the feeling that this boy was far too young to be a solicitor and wondering whether she was making an awful mistake.

"Oh yes. Adultery."

"Your husband has been unfaithful to you?"

"Of course, but I have no names or any idea who they were. But I've been unfaithful to him. I've got the details of that. Can't we use that?"

"I'm not entirely sure that it works that way round Mrs Philips. You'd have to get him to divorce you."

"I don't think he wants to divorce me, at least he's never mentioned it."

"So we'll have to find other grounds."

"I'm quite happy to be the guilty party."

"But then your husband would have to start the proceedings."

"I can't see him doing that."

"So," the young solicitor repeated slowly and with laboured patience, "as I said, we'll have to work out other grounds. Let me take some details."

Anya gave him the details he requested, her name and address, the date of their marriage. "Have you any children?"

"No. There are no children." Her tone told the young man that that was not a subject for discussion.

"Do you still live together, in the same house?"

"Oh yes."

"Are you still, um, do you still, um …" He was obviously so embarrassed she interrupted.

"You mean do we still sleep together? Oh yes."

"So the marriage is, shall we say, on-going?"

"On that front yes."

"May I ask why you want a divorce then?"

"Several reasons." Anya answered defiantly. "I can't stand always having to ask him for money, his family hate me and I really want a fresh start while I'm still young enough."

"In my understanding of the law I'm not sure those points are sufficient grounds for divorce." He replaced his glasses and peered at the paper in front of him. "You married quite young I see?"

"I was 22, is that young?"

"Quite. Can you give me some background? How you met, that sort of thing?"

"We met at university, we got on well together. I had no family. It seemed like a good idea at the time." She blurted out not sure whether it was explanation, reason or excuse. Realising that she should perhaps show Geoff up in a less positive light she added "He tricked me into saying yes when he proposed."

Seeing a look something like relief on the young solicitor's face she elaborated. "I come from Liverpool, we lived there and I wanted to stay there but he'd already got a job down here when he asked me and he hadn't told me." She watched as he wrote careful notes.

"That's not much to go on Mrs Philips. You came south and you live in a nice house in a nice area. Many would say you were lucky indeed to have such a secure financial life in these recessionary times. I gather your husband has supported you financially throughout the marriage?"

"I always wanted to work, I'm well qualified, but all I've been allowed to do is some freelance writing. That's brought in a little money but Geoff says I should keep it for myself. Geoff's inheritance from his father was enormous so we never had to worry about that sort of thing."

"But your husband has a career as well as his family money?"

"Oh yes. He works with computers and he's done really well. He's very clever you know."

"So what has been your contribution to the marriage?"

"That's a funny question. I look after the house, look after him. What else is a wife who isn't allowed to have a job supposed to do?"

"You say you haven't any children?" The solicitor left the question open.

"I can't. I was sterilised as a child."

Stuart hid his feelings well. "And your husband knew this?"

"Geoff has known since the beginning though he doesn't know why. He didn't just accept it, he thought it was great because we didn't have to worry about contraception or anything. He's never asked why."

"So," He paused and looked carefully through the notes he had taken. "So, you had an intimate relationship before you were married and your husband was fully understanding of your, shall we say, circumstances, yet he married you anyway?"

"Yes." There seemed little else to say.

"That's unfortunate. Had he not known, had it been new information so to speak, it could have been an acceptable reason for him to bring an action against you."

"But I'm sure he won't. He doesn't want to divorce me."

"We must find something he has done wrong, nothing you have done, or have not been able to do, will help."

Anya became more challenging. "I could cite his unreasonable behaviour with his mother. He meets her at least twice a week and I'm never invited to join them. He goes on holiday with her, for Christ's sake, making sure I don't go with them. It's perverted."

Stuart was somewhat taken aback by Anya's sudden vehemence but he was determined to stay professional. "When they go on holiday do you have any indication of…" he paused to find the right words, "any indication of intimacy between them. Such a relationship between mother and son is not unknown but we would need some proof."

"Oh no! They don't sleep together!" Anya grimaced at the thought.

"But you said they were very close."

"Too close for comfort but not in that way." Stuart was obviously relieved that he didn't have a case of incest to deal with and concentrated hard on his notes as Anya gave him some background.

"Geoff's father died in an accident the day he was born and ever since that day I think she has been very confused about things. She gave her son the same name as her dead husband. That was really weird. I think, as Geoff has got older, and he does look very like his dad, I think she wishes…" Anya couldn't finish the sentence. "Anyway she hates me. She has done from the beginning. She always considered me unsuitable for her son. Mind you, no one could ever be good enough for her Geoffrey."

"It must have been difficult." Stuart began to have more sympathy for his client. Up until that point he had put her down as a spoilt rich girl who was bored with her husband and wanted to explore pastures new.

"It has been."

"But you have found… comfort … elsewhere?"

"Oh yes." Anya agreed enthusiastically. "Geoff has always encouraged me to have sex with other men. In the early days it turned him on. When we were first married we had a year or so when we were faithful to each other but since then we've had a very open marriage. Sex really isn't that important is it? It's just for fun, at least it should be."

The young solicitor tried to hide his shock, not so much at the promiscuity she spoke of, but of her willingness to admit to it. "How many partners would you say you have had then?"

"I have absolutely no idea. Everyone slept around then. Everyone did in the 60s, we just carried on into the 70s." She felt that was explanation enough.

"What about your husband? Has he had many partners?"

"I really don't know. When we were in Liverpool he was pretty wild but now he doesn't tell me when or who he's been with. I never ask."

"To divorce him you'd have to name a particular person who has destroyed your marriage. More than a one night stand you understand?"

"Other than with his mother?" She asked with half a smile.

"Obviously." He nearly grinned back.

"I don't think there's been one more important than any other. I leave him to it. As I said, the act of sex isn't important. It's a biological thing, nothing to do with how good a relationship is. Why does the law think otherwise?"

"I really don't know Mrs Philips."

Stuart again checked through his notes. Anya looked around the old fashioned office, the bare floor boards were wide and highly polished, the bookshelves were filled with volumes which all looked the same but had different years on the binding. She had chosen this firm because it was the first in the list in the phone book. The receptionist had said that 'Mr Benthall is our divorce specialist. We don't get much call for divorce so he's not too busy.' Anya couldn't help thinking that that wasn't the sort of information the receptionist should have been giving out.

"You seem to have had a very free, open and modern marriage Mrs Philips."

"I suppose it looks like that, sexually at any rate, but in every other way it has been horribly traditional. Husband goes to work leaving wife at home to do all the housework, plan the meals etcetera. In any time that is left she is allowed to develop her career, but that is not encouraged. Husband comes home in the evening expecting his meal, his slippers warmed and his marital comforts. Wife is dependent for all things on her husband. It's really very traditional. Have you seen the film Stepford Wives, read the book perhaps? No? Never mind."

"I'm not sure I understand what you want me to do. Do you want to divorce your husband using his many extra marital relationships as reason for the irretrievable breakdown? If that is the case I think our main problem is the openness and freeness of your marriage. You say he doesn't want a divorce in which case he could argue that you agreed, with no pressure whatsoever from him, to have had this openness in your relationship, even before your marriage. I think that might be tricky. You wouldn't consider leaving him and then suing for divorce on the grounds that you have lived apart for five years?"

"I'm 26 soon. I need to start my new life now, not when I'm over 30."

"Well how do you think you might persuade your husband to divorce you? You're obviously happy to admit adultery."

"I don't think he will, he really doesn't seem to think there's a problem. Why would he want anything to change? Life's great for him he's got everything he wants or needs. Perhaps he's still fighting his mother. She never wanted him to marry me in the first place, perhaps he would think she had won the battle between them if he divorced me. I've often wondered why he's never mentioned it, I'm sure his mother does every week, though maybe she's torn between wanting to get rid of me and the social stigma of a divorce in the family."

"I'm afraid divorce is not the stigma it was a few years ago, Mrs Philips."

"But still, in her circles, at the Golf Club, it is probably something not to be taken lightly and she is a dreadful snob."

"I think I have understood that from what you have been saying, but divorce is something to be taken as seriously as marriage."

"I'm not taking it lightly, Mr Benthall. I just see it as the best option for both of us, the only option really."

"If it's really what you want to do…"

"It is."

"Then I'm afraid we'll have to get proof of a serious adulterous relationship, one that is far beyond what you have always seen as acceptable, and then sue him for divorce on those grounds. I'm afraid nothing else is likely to succeed, though he'll be advised to counter the charge and, I should warn you, it could get very messy."

"I'll face that if I have to."

"Can you think of anyone who would stand out from the usual casual affaires you both seem to have had and accepted in your marriage?"

"There's only Fiona. They go back a long way, she was his girlfriend before we met. Their families have known each other since time began."

"Ah, there we may have something." Stuart sat back in his chair and made an arch with his long fingers.

Ten minutes later they had their strategy. Anya would issue divorce papers naming Fiona Shepherd. Geoff would undoubtedly object on the grounds that it was untrue and prepare to fight but Kathleen would throw their hands up in horror at the scandal. After some discussion Anya would reluctantly agree to be the guilty party to save Fiona's good name. Knowing it would never happen, she would provocatively suggest they name Tim. That would serve them all right for treating her so badly for three years.

That afternoon Anya sat and wrote her diary, spending more time thinking about what she was to write than actually writing.

> *Monday 12th January 1976*
> *Solicitors today. So many things I didn't say, couldn't say. He asked why Geoff and I married. I couldn't say. If I could go back to that morning in the Lakes I would say No and No and No again. I knew it was the wrong thing to do, especially when he told me he had a job, and wanted a house so he could be near his mother. I should have known I could never win in a straight fight between the mountain and Mohammed.*
>
> *I couldn't tell the solicitor why I keep going with other men. I'm annoyed with Geoff. I'm annoyed with me. I'm annoyed with Tim. I really thought Tim & I would get together a lot but we haven't since his wedding day. He gave up far too easily in the face of Margaret's obvious trap, she knew exactly what she was doing. Tim, the father, would never play away, let alone leave her. He said he would be my friend, my ally, but he hasn't been. He just left me to fight them all on my own.*
>
> *When I was 16, even when I first went with Geoff, fucking around had seemed so rebellious, so adventurous, so modern, but now all it seems is rather sad and sordid. In the past four years Tim and Margaret had Matthew two years after Maggie. Dave had a boy five months after his wedding and then John's*

twins came two months later. All of them. But not me. Geoff never understood what that felt like. If he did he never bothered to make me feel any better about it. But then perhaps I should try to understand a bit more about what he feels about it now, but it's so difficult to talk. I say he has never asked me why I can't be like every other bloody woman in the world but then I suppose I've never sat him down and made him listen. Well divorce will be the best thing for both of us and then he can get married 'suitably' and join the rest of them breeding the next generation of the toffee-nosed middle classes.

"Do you ever see anything of Fiona?" She asked innocently enough at breakfast the next morning.

Geoff looked up from his paper. "Fiona? Whatever's made you think of her?"

"I thought I saw her in the town last week and wondered what she was up to. Has she ever forgiven you for stealing her virginity?"

"Probably not." Geoff made a show of concentrating on his paper.

"Has she ever forgiven you for dumping her?"

"I did not dump her. There is, was, nothing to dump."

Anya knew when Geoff was hiding something. He was a very bad liar. Perhaps she had accidentally hit on something that was actually going on. "Is, was?" She asked suspiciously.

"Anya what's all this about? You haven't thought about Fiona for years. Why bring up the subject now. Anyway I've got to go." He folded his paper, stood up, and left without kissing her goodbye.

"Guilty as charged me lud." Anya said to his departing back. She thought of all those days he said he was with his mother, that week in the Spring when he had said he had gone to Germany with her. She knew with utter certainty what was going on. Kathleen was throwing them together and he was going through the motions because he could not tell his mother he loved his wife. How naïve she had been.

She went upstairs to her study, opened her steel box and took out a new exercise book. She wrote *Fiona Shepherd, January 1976* on the cover. She was going to follow Fiona and log everything she did for the week, a month, for as long as it took.

It wasn't difficult for Anya to find out the bare bones of Fiona's life. Looking through their Christmas cards, so recently taken down, she found the one signed *Bonnie, Richard and Fiona* with their address printed ostentatiously in gold italics underneath the traditional seasonal greetings. Fiona was 26 years old yet was unmarried and still lived with her parents. Feeling like a character in a television police drama Anya filled a thermos flask with coffee and, collecting a rug to keep her warm and her notebook to record everything she saw, she set out to follow Fiona.

She spent every day that week sitting in her car outside the Shepherd's house or following the red mini through the lanes to the stables where Fiona kept her horses. When Fiona set off to ride around the bridleways and through the woods there was nothing Anya could do but wait in her car. Anya was frustrated as she could have no idea what Fiona was up to on her rides, or who she might be meeting.

After a week Anya realised there was a pattern to Fiona's day. Whatever time she left her home she would always set off for her ride within five or ten minutes of 12 o'clock and she always returned to the stables between 2 and 2:30. In Anya's suspicious mind that meant she was meeting someone for lunch but she had no way of knowing who that someone might be and where an assignation might take place.

Anya spent one of her day's vigils looking at the Ordnance Survey map. She wished she knew more about horses and how far one might travel in, say, half an hour. Thinking it couldn't be much more than two or three miles from the stable she decided not to follow Fiona but to spend Friday lunchtime parked outside a pub that was less than two miles from Fiona's stables and also happened to be close to Geoff's work.

She wrote her report as soon as she got home.

> *Friday 16th January, 1976*
> *Sat in car park at The Chequers wondering why I was*

wasting my time when three cars arrived. None were Geoff's but he was a passenger in one. I hadn't seen him that relaxed and carefree for months. There were eight or nine of them, obviously going for their Friday lunchtime beer. I would like to have had a job where we all went out to the pub on a Friday lunchtime. I didn't recognise anyone. He had always kept his life at work completely separate. I wondered what he would say if I joined him in the pub. Would he be embarrassed or angry? I felt stupid spying on him so I was about to start the car and leave him to his friends when I saw the horse. Fiona. I left it a few minutes before going into the bar. It was a small country pub and it was packed, the Friday lunchtime crowd was noisy so I stood near the door wondering whether I hoped he would see me or not. Fiona was standing next to Geoff, she seemed to know the others as they were all laughing and talking at the same time. She was a regular part of this separate life of his. I left.

I know that this was exactly what I had wished for, what I thought was the best for both of us. Well, what do they say? Be careful what you wish for in case it comes true. The bastard. The absolute fucking miserable toe-rag of a bastard.

Anya sat staring out of the window. She had wanted a divorce, she had wanted a new start in life, but as soon as she was faced with the very real prospect of losing Geoff she wasn't at all certain she was doing the right thing.

The next Sunday morning Anya followed Geoff when he left for lunch. She had wondered whether he would be meeting Fiona, maybe even having lunch at her parents, but he drove directly to his mother's house pulling into the drive as Anya parked on the road, out of sight. She wasn't sure why she was so suspicious, there was no reason why this should be any different from every other Sunday lunchtime. It was, she told herself, a family Sunday lunch just like every other week. She started the car and did a three point turn ready to return home when she saw a Jaguar she did not recognise turn into the drive with Fiona sitting in the back. She slammed on her brakes and cradled her head in her arms on the steering wheel. Fiona, with her parents, was invited to Kathleen's Sunday lunch. Anya bit her lip. It was all arranged. Kathleen had won. Geoff and Fiona were seeing each other. They were simply waiting for her, Anya, to be out of their way.

The next morning she phoned Tim at work.

"Does Geoff want a divorce?" She asked without preamble.

"Ask him not me." He was obviously annoyed to get the call.

"I'm asking you."

"Of course he doesn't." Tim didn't sound convincing.

"Then why is the sainted Fiona having Sunday lunch with the Philips family? Why are her parents there? Why is everyone there but me?"

"How do you know about that?"

"I followed him."

"You what?"

"I followed him. I parked the car at the end of the drive and watched everyone arrive for the cosy Sunday family lunch. How do you think that makes me feel?"

"It's Kathleen you know. Geoff's only doing what his mother wants him to do." Tim sounded almost apologetic.

"What? Divorce me and marry the sainted Fiona? Have lots of little Philipses? Keep the tight knit little group of snobs together free from outside infestation?"

"That's not exactly fair."

"You've given in haven't you? After all that rubbish about being my friend and ally against Kathleen you're really just the same as them. Margaret trapped you with her pregnancies and you've just given up haven't you? You've just given in for an easy life." He didn't reply for just long enough for Anya to realise she had hit home. She continued, letting her anger and frustration surface. "You promised me you'd help me when I needed it and now I need it. You've got to help me get out of this with a little dignity."

"Keep me out of this."

"So why doesn't he do it? I bet the families are all in agreement and the mothers are already planning wedding number two. Why doesn't he kick me out? Why doesn't he divorce me?" Tim didn't answer so Anya answered for him.

"I'll tell you why, it's because he still loves me. He doesn't want to do what his mother wants. He's holding out against them isn't he?"

Still Tim said nothing.

"What a fucking joke! I want a divorce and I'm more than willing to be the guilty party but he won't do it!"

In contrast to Anya's rising hysteria Tim's voice was calm, almost sad. "In time Kathleen always gets her way and she wants your nose rubbed in the dirt. She wants you humiliated, she will make sure as many men as she has evidence for will be named. She wants your reputation so destroyed you won't go near any of us again."

"She has evidence for?" Anya quoted back at Tim.

"She's had a private detective follow you for months."

Anya took that news in her stride even though she wondered what Kathleen would make of the reports detailing the following of Fiona. "But still Geoff doesn't want to do it?"

"Kathleen and Fiona will win in the end. You know that."

"Then make it easy for everyone. Be my single co-respondent. Sign the papers and everything will go through quickly and easily. No blood on the carpet."

"No Anya I won't do it. It would wreck my reputation and my family."

"So it's your reputation or mine?"

"You have nothing to lose. I have."

"That is so unfair. I'll name you anyway. I'll make sure you're on the list."

"If I hear you naming me I'll say you're delusional."

"That's hateful."

"I mean it Anya."

"So you'll leave me to the wolves?"

"Goodbye Anya."

"I can't believe you'd be so hateful. After all the promises you made."

"I made no promises to you Anya." And he put the phone down. She thought he almost sounded sad.

> Friday 23rd January 1976
>
> For months I've thought I'm unhappy, I've thought the only way out is to leave Geoff and make a life of my own and now it's about to happen I don't want it to. I look at him and I love him. But it's all too late now. I made myself read back through the last year's diaries. I can't possibly carry on like that. Can I? No.
>
> I started talking about it in a really reasonable way after we'd eaten. I said we needed to talk. He knew what it was about. I said I'd name Fiona as I'd seen them together. He laughed and said that was silly. They were just old friends. So I said I'd seen them last week, with all his friends from work. He said it was her birthday so he'd asked her up. And I said that was why she was at lunch with them on Sunday was it? He had the grace to look sheepish and I was trying to keep my cool. I said I was going to divorce him and name Fiona. He said couldn't we be civilised. He seemed quite sad when he said that he loved me, had always loved me, but he realised now he needed children more. I said no, he didn't, his mother did. I said I loved him too. This is so fucking stupid! We made love one last time. I said could we have an affair after he'd married her. He said he didn't think that would be a very good idea and we went to sleep in each other's arms.
>
> I woke up in the night so I got up and came in here to write it all down. I know I'll want to remember how sad I feel about it all. One day.

Anya was amazed at how quickly life could change once the decision was made. The next day she went into a letting agency to find a place to live. There were problems to be overcome, Anya had, as the girl in the agency pointed out with a singular lack of interest, no job and no regular income. It took some explanation of her circumstances and a down payment of six month's rent in advance, over and above the deposit of three month's rent, to secure her a home. She could move in in a week's time, subject to satisfactory references. She hadn't even seen the house, a two up two down cottage in a terrace of five in a tiny hamlet three miles from the town, but as she looked at the photograph she realised she knew the layout of the house without seeing it. It was identical to Tennyson Street.

> Tuesday 3rd February 1976
> I've just jumped off Beachy Head without a hang-glider, crossed the Rubicon and that bridge that's burned down behind me, and all the other metaphors, analogies or historical/hysterical references to having acted with no possibility of going back.
> I knew I shouldn't leave the family home. I phoned SB and he said it's the wrong thing to do but I couldn't stand it anymore. G was being so nice to me, helping me pack, pointing out stuff that was mine that I'd missed and all I could do was scream at him. He went off to stay with K while I moped around cleaning the house, tidying the garden, packing what little stuff I wanted to bring with me. I really didn't want to go but it's not down to me. I kept re-reading the diaries, trying to remember why I had hated living with Geoff so much but that didn't work. Hoist by my own petard etc etc. I almost suggested we stuck it out and tried to adopt but when I really thought about it I realised that would never work. K wouldn't accept the wrong genes.
> So here I am alone in a Tennyson Street look-alike cottage. I've never been alone before. Not really alone. There were those weeks in Hall after Mum died and a few weeks here and there but never alone like this.
> Monday shopping for all the things I need but didn't think to bring.
> Tuesday putting everything away, in its place. Wondering what G was doing. Thinking what I would be doing if I hadn't left. Wondering if G was wondering what I was doing. Oh Shit.

She stopped writing and looked around at the tiny living area that had been her home for just over a day. Would she ever get used to it? It had taken only one journey, in the car that Geoff had agreed she could keep, to transfer all her belongings. It had taken one visit to town to shop for kitchen essentials and she felt she had enough. The house was small but even so it seemed remarkably uncluttered.

She was about to turn back to her diary when she saw the light flashing on her telephone answering machine. She'd only told Geoff her number. She pressed the button to rewind the message to the beginning and the second button to replay.

'It's Kathleen Philips.'

Why did she bother to say that, Anya thought, the voice is unmistakable. Anya spoke out loud to the tape, her voice reverberating in the enclosed space of the small room. "Can't your precious son make his own phone calls anymore?"

'I understand you have left my son.' What subtleties were in that voice Anya wondered: relief? satisfaction? victory? 'You forgot to leave the rings. I'm sure it was only an oversight.'

"How could you say that! You so clearly don't believe it." Anya argued with the tape recorder.

'As you are aware those rings were only on loan to you as long as you were my son's wife. You will now return them.' Anya had intended to return the emerald to Geoff when the divorce was finalised, but she did not expect what followed. 'Do not forget that sapphire engagement ring my son gave you. Both are family pieces.'

"You lying bitch! That's not any fucking family piece. It's my ring, my mother's ring. Her brother gave it to her. What made you think he'd given it to me? You can fucking whistle."

Kathleen's voice continued, slow and deliberate. 'Geoffrey will require the rings to be returned immediately. He has found a suitable partner with whom to raise a family and he will be giving them to her.'

"You cow! Suitable! What's bloody suitable? No one will ever be bloody suitable enough! And 'raise a family'. Oh you do know how to hit below the belt don't you Mrs Kathleen fucking Philips." Anya was yelling at the tape. But Kathleen had not finished. She had paused simply for effect.

'You will return the rings to Atherton's offices by Friday. Is that clear?'

That was it. There was just a click to end the message.

Anya spread out her fingers and looked at the familiar rings. She waggled the emerald off her finger and the simple gold wedding band without a second thought. "You can have those you bitch." She spoke out loud. "You utter complete and absolute bitch. But not this one, no, not this one." She turned the sapphire ring round and round on her finger. She grasped her locket and thought of Dot. Dot would have known what to say, what to do, how to help her. As she held the engraved gold oval in her hand she wondered why she had never put Geoff's photo in it. Perhaps she had always known Kathleen would win.

The divorce has gone through remarkably quickly, Anya thought, as she took the large brown envelope from the postman, who smiled knowingly as he handed it over. Anya looked at the envelope, she had no need to open it. It was formal notification of her *Decree Absolute*. She was a free woman, whatever that might mean.

In the months since Anya's first visit to Stuart Benthall there had been periods when nothing seemed to be happening and periods of near constant phone calls as Stuart reported on and responded to the demands of Geoff's solicitor. Anya knew Kathleen was behind the extreme demands; that she should admit to infidelity with a number of men, that she should claim no maintenance and that she would move from the area. The terms were toned down only after her threat not to take the blame but to counter sue naming Fiona Shepherd. It was eventually agreed that one name would be acceptable as long as it wasn't Tim. Anya had found it ironic that, in the face of her supposed reckless infidelities, she had had difficulty in finding one single man who would admit an affair and who would sign the necessary papers. John, going through difficulties in his own marriage, had agreed 'for old time's sake' and so it was his name that had featured in the short paragraph printed in the bottom of page 7 of the local paper when the *Decree Nisi* was announced to the world. Anya wondered who read the legal notices and decided the women of the Golf Club Circle, like vultures, would pick everyone to pieces. She hoped John would never have cause to regret his generosity.

She had still not opened the envelope half an hour later when the phone rang.

"Anya Cave."

"Anya?" Geoff seemed tentative, almost guilty. "It's Geoff."

"I know. I can still remember your voice." She hadn't meant to sound so bitchy.

"Sorry. Look. I thought I'd phone to tell you, so you didn't see it in the papers first. I mean I thought you should know." He sounded very nervous.

"Know what?"

"I'm getting married."

"But Geoff the Absolute only came through this morning." Anya didn't know whether to feel surprised or hurt.

"I know. We waited until that came through before making the announcement."

"You waited?" Hurt won.

"Well I asked Fiona to marry me, well it was sort of agreed in April."

"April? The same April that you phoned to tell me how much you were missing me, and how much you really wanted us to get back together, and how little having a family could mean to you now you realised how much you loved me, the April you phoned to plead with me to stop the divorce proceedings and go back to you? That April?"

"Well. Yes."

"It's your mother isn't it?" Anger took over from hurt. "She got together with Fiona's mother and father who, of course, she had known since the year fucking dot and arranged it for you. Am I right?

Of course I'm right. That woman is lethal. Keep her away from Fiona when and if you marry her. Keep your mother away from her or if she's got the sense she was born with, which I doubt, your little Fiona will be divorcing you in double quick time. When that happens don't forget to get your bloody ring back!"

"Talking of rings…" Geoff's voice just stopped her from slamming the phone down. "Mother said you returned only the emerald and your wedding ring. She said you didn't return the sapphire you have always worn. She's convinced I gave it to you and therefore, since it must have been bought with family money, it should also have been returned. I told her it was your mother's, that I hadn't given it to you, but she just doesn't believe me. Will you tell me now? Who gave it to you?"

She spoke quietly. "It was my mother's. Why couldn't you ever have believed me?"

"Help me out Anya. If I don't give Mother a believable explanation she will just go on and on about it."

"It was my mum's."

"It was your mum's?" He sounded insultingly doubtful.

"Yes, my mum's. My father gave it to her."

"But… well…" He couldn't put into words the worries he had always had about the ring, worth several thousand pounds, coming from an otherwise penniless family.

"For fuck's sake Geoff I've told you over and over again. If you won't believe me then that's your problem. Goodbye, and good luck with Fiona, I suspect you're going to need rather a lot of it." She put the phone down knowing that Geoff would be listening to the cold phone tone.

She tried to work out her feelings. Was she angry that Geoff would not believe her about the ring, was she frustrated at his unwillingness to listen to her, or was she simply sad that that simple lack of trust was proof that he could never have forgotten the differences in their backgrounds.

Anya picked up her coffee mug and walked into the small garden. The day was hot already, in one way at least it was going to be a good summer. As she sat down she put her hand to her locket. Dot and Dr Hill had had so much faith in her and she had achieved only a failed marriage.

She wasn't proud of herself and she didn't think they would be either.

Chapter 10: Successes

Suburban London, 1976-1992

Resentment was an unfamiliar emotion for Anya. She had been used to feeling anger, exasperation and irritation in her years with Geoff, but resentment, persistent, all-consuming resentment, was something she did not know how to deal with.

Sunday 25th July 1976
Yesterday Fiona became Mrs Geoffrey Philips Junior the Second. This morning she'll be sitting in my garden. I worked hard clearing the channel between the ponds, creating a small waterfall which would feel so cool in this heat. Geoff will be sitting with her, listening to that waterfall, drinking wine from my fridge, drinking wine from a glass I used to drink from, held in a hand wearing my ring. Oh shut up Anya.
I liked the cottage. It had a garden, though nothing like as large as the one that is now Fiona's, and it had lovely views across the fields to the Downs. I could watch the sun rising and setting from that garden. I'd sit there thinking that things couldn't really be that bad if the world could look that beautiful. I'd hoped to be there for longer than six months but it wasn't to be. In the settlement G had to give me a lump sum and a small amount every month for five years or until I remarry (if sooner). Remarry? I doubt it. The only sensible thing to do was to buy somewhere and the cottage was not for sale so I ended up here. This miserable flat above a shop in a grotty parade of shops in the centre of what used to be a village but is now simply a bedroom for London was the only place I could afford to buy

outright. Five grand doesn't go far especially as I didn't want a mortgage even if there'd been anyone stupid enough to have given one to an unemployed (unemployable) single woman. But this flat is SO hot and SO depressing!

I've done a lot of thinking since I've been on my own. I'm trying to write but getting stuff anywhere near a publisher is horribly difficult. All those rejections are bloody depressing too. I'm beginning to realise I was in cloud cuckoo land thinking I could make any sort of living by writing. Perhaps it would have been different if I'd done it straight after University. Good degree. Good brain. Good prospects and look at me now! If I could go back to 1971 and have those years again I'd do things completely different. I'd have been an academic, I'd have a career, I would not allow myself to be seduced by Geoff and his middle-classiness. But then I'd be the same person so I'd make exactly the same mistakes again.

I've a horrible feeling I'll be writing a lot in my diary in the next few months. It's going to be so miserable. No garden, not even a balcony. No view, not even the sky unless I crook my neck. But I will get some decent furniture and I'll paint the walls and it'll be fine. It'll just take time to get used to it all.

Anya put her pen down and stared out of the window at a very different view from the ones she has been used to. Fiona would be in her garden, enjoying the sounds of her waterfall and the cool of the green shrubs she had planted. Anya had never talked to Geoff's new wife but ever since their first night together Fiona had been in the background. Just by waiting and being middle class Fiona had won.

Anya suspected Geoff's second marriage would be blighted, as his first had been, by his mother. Now Kathleen had established that she could dictate the direction of her son's life she would do so again if ever Fiona should step off the narrow path of Kathleen's expectations. Anya wondered why Fiona was marrying a man she had never shown any signs of caring for and immediately answered her own question: security, respectability and because their families expected it. They were the reasons Margaret had married Tim and Anya suspected the two marriages would be about as successful as the other.

> *I've got to get a job. Sitting in this bloody oven of a flat writing stuff nobody will publish is driving me to distraction. I look back at what I've written and I can't find one that might be worth publishing. Words used to come so easily, now I can hardly string two intelligent ones together. I've got to get some money so I'd better get a job. What? Work on CV. Focus on something then go for it. What though? I should have done a CertEd and then at least I could get a job teaching though I'd be crap at that too.*

She had chosen this flat, on the second floor above a rather run down looking estate agent in a small parade of shops, because the area had once been a village and, though it had been overrun by 1930s suburban housing, it still had a heart. It depressed her that all six shops in her block had two flats above and they were all identical to hers; eleven other flats occupied by people she would probably never talk to.

How she hated this place.
How she resented Fiona for being in hers.

> *Thursday 29th July 1976*
> *Drove to S and picked up the local paper. G & F married in a church, I suppose because his first wedding was in a register office, it didn't count. There was a picture. Fiona wore white. White! Geoff looked awkward in his morning suit. To all intents and purposes it's a first marriage. I've been whitewashed out of history.*

Anya carefully cut out the report and stuck it in her diary.

> *The marriage took place at St Luke's between Fiona Joan, beloved only*

> daughter of Mr and Mrs Richard Shepherd and Geoffrey Ian only son of the late Mr Geoffrey Philips and Mrs Kathleen Philips. The bride, given away by her proud father, wore a traditional dress trimmed with white lace. The bride was attended by Mrs Tim Cross, sister of the bridegroom and Miss Margaret Cross, niece of the bridegroom. The best man was Mr Tim Cross. The reception was held at the Town Golf Club.
>
> So Kathleen had taken over the wedding completely. And the reception at the Golf Club! Did Geoff remember Tim's reception? Did Fiona? Somehow I hope they did.

Anya looked carefully at the photograph. Geoff looked old, he was 26 but he was going bald and from the unflattering angle of the photograph he looked middle aged, he could almost have been the bride's father rather than the groom. Fiona was staring expressionless into the middle distance, almost as if she were looking regretfully at someone in the crowd of guests behind the photographer. Neither looked particularly happy. Kathleen, on the other hand, was smiling broadly. This was the wedding photograph she had always envisaged for her son. The wedding was the most important thing to Kathleen, she didn't care a fig about the marriage, Anya thought, as long as it produced a son.

"Move on. Put it behind you." She told herself as she closed her diary. But even as she spoke out loud to herself she knew she would never be able to do that. She had tried to persuade herself that getting their local paper every week so she could keep tabs on the Crosses and the Philipses was the best way to plan her revenge. But she knew it was because she couldn't bear to let them go.

> *Thursday 26th August very very late, probably Friday 27th already I woke up thinking about money. £100 a month from G for five years or until I remarry is enough to pay the bills but not enough to do anything with. I've really got to get up off my lazy bottom and earn some. It's nine months since I left and I'm no nearer finding anything to do with my life.*

On my walk this morning I was looking for inspiration. Each building offered an opportunity but nothing seemed vaguely interesting. I can't see myself working in the library or serving in a shop or serving behind the bar of the pub or tea in the tea shop. I could do any of those things, it's what I would have been doing if Dot hadn't intervened (interfered?) in my life but why should I? I can't have completely forgotten how to use my brain just because I haven't been expected to for years.

It was when I got back and was opening the front door that I realised, for all my qualifications, I really was quite stupid. I had never bothered to even look in the window of the estate agent by my front door. This morning I peered in through the glass door at a small room with two wooden desks and three four-drawer filing cabinets. I could make out a map on the wall with pins in. They must be the properties they had for sale. Everything was neat and tidy but it didn't have the look of a hive of activity. Perhaps this is something I can do. I'd have a lot to learn but it might be interesting. I ran up the stairs, rifled through the pile of newspapers and I've just spent the day and half the night reading everything I could find about the property market and making out my CV.

The next morning, dressed in her smartest blue suit, Anya walked into March and March Estate Agents.

"Good morning. Can I help you?" A lady who looked to be approaching retirement stood up from behind one of the brown desks.

"Is there a manager? I'm not here to look for a house, I was wondering if there might be a job available."

Anya found it difficult to read the woman's reaction, it seemed as if she was almost excited.

"I'll see if Mr March is free."

Anya thought that a good sign, Mr March must be one of the partners.

"Come through Miss …?" The woman paused, inviting Anya to complete the sentence.

"Cave, Anya Cave."

Anya was shown into a small, tidy office and was surprised at how young the man who stood with out-stretched hand was, and how good looking.

"Peter March." He held his hand out towards Anya. She took it and their first touch was a firm, business-like handshake.

"Anya Cave." She repeated her name. A trick, perhaps, but she felt it important her name registered.

"Do sit down Anya Cave. I understand you are looking for a job."

She immediately liked the humour in his voice and the gentleness in his eyes.

"Not just a job, a career." Anya thought this was a good answer. It implied commitment and ambition.

"Have you a CV?" He seemed uncertain of himself, as if interviewing her made him uncomfortable.

Anya pulled out a carefully type-written piece of paper.

He smiled as he took it from her. Quite an attractive smile she thought.

"I see why you are looking for work. I suppose all divorces are painful so I won't ask you about that, and I won't ask you about children, in fact I haven't a clue what to ask you. I'm hopeless at interviews. Jack always did this sort of thing."

"Jack?"

"My brother. There really were two Marches in 'March and March'. Until a few months ago when Jack …"

He hesitated and his expression changed quickly to one of such misery that Anya almost went round to his side of the desk to put comforting arms around him. "My brother died quite recently. So it's just me now but I just haven't been able to bring myself to change the name of the business." He had pulled himself together.

"I'm so sorry." She couldn't think of anything to say.

"No I'm the one who should apologise. Very unprofessional." He concentrated on the paper in his hands.

"First Class degree in History and a BPhil. Very impressive."

She took her cue from him and became business like. "But not very useful in getting any work outside teaching and I don't think I'd be very good at that."

"But no doubt the course was interesting."

"I enjoyed my time at university." Anya was pleased with her suitably ambiguous response.

He carried on reading. Anya thought he was trying to avoid catching her eye, putting off a time when he would have to ask her another question.

"Tell me more about the business." She said, hoping that talking about something he knew so well would help him feel less uncomfortable.

He looked at her with relief. She watched his face as he talked, it showed everything he felt. She wondered how this patently honest man could be a successful estate agent. "My father started it in the 30s, about the same age I am now, when all the woods were being cleared and the fields around the old village were being covered with rows and rows of houses. Stella, she showed you in, has worked here pretty much since the beginning. She knows everything there is to know about renting and selling houses in the area. She knows all the solicitors and knows how to get them to work at the speed our clients require, that's a very important skill but she's getting on a bit now and wants to retire. George, he's out at the moment, is getting on too but neither of them will abandon me until I've got things a bit more settled. Jack's death," Anya noticed how he spoke the words very deliberately, "Jack's death rather disturbed their plans."

"I've no qualifications in the business." Anya admitted when she realised Peter had no more to say. "Would I need to study? Take exams? That is if you gave me a job. I don't think I'm secretarial or Personal Assistant material. I'd want to do something more substantial."

"There's no need for qualifications to sell houses. I have none. You just need the personality to persuade people who want to sell their house that we can do the best job. Valuation is easy around here, most of the houses are identical. It's just personality. Some intelligence helps of course, and the ability to explain things to people, they can tell if you are pulling the wool over their eyes about anything. I know I shouldn't say it in these days of women's lib but being attractive, intelligent and female would do no harm whatsoever to your chances of success."

"Years ago that would probably have offended me but not now. I need something interesting to do. I've too many other things to worry about to question why I was given a job or why I was good at it." She tried to make light of it but the words were so obviously the truth that there were a few moments of silence during which Peter turned his attention to the CV again.

"You say here you do some writing?"

"Only short stories, articles for magazines and local newspapers, that sort of thing. I've never managed to get it to take off."

"But it shows you don't sit down and do nothing. Lots of people would do nothing if given half a chance, I don't think you're that sort of person."

"I don't think I am either."

"Well would you like to start on Monday? The salary won't be much I'm afraid but you'll get a good commission from any properties that you get on our books that sell and an even better commission if you do the selling. Stella and George will show you the ropes. I really think this might work. Mrs Cave."

"Miss. Cave is my maiden name, but please do call me Anya."

They both stood up to shake hands.

"I really think this will work Anya."

"I hope so Peter."

"It was a car crash." George explained to Anya as they had a drink in the pub around the corner to celebrate the end of her first week. "He was driving too fast. He always drove too fast."

"You sound as if you were very fond of him."

"I am, was. I'd known him since he was born. Everyone loved him, he was so outgoing, so generous, so like his father."

"Peter seems to find it difficult."

"He was always the quieter of the two. This really isn't what he wants to do with his life. Truth be told he'd rather be anything other than be an estate agent, rather do anything than have his own business. He does his best but he really does need someone to give him help and encouragement, someone his own age. Oh dear, I've said too much."

"Not at all. I like to understand what's behind people."

"You'll be good for him, for the business." George quickly corrected himself but Anya had heard enough from both him and from Stella to know that they were matchmaking.

"Do you mind if I make a few changes to these details?" Anya asked Stella tentatively on the first day of her second week at March and March.

"I know they do look rather dull, my dear, but there's not much you can say about a three bedroomed semi, the same as all the other three bedroomed semis in the road which is the same as the next road of identical three bedroomed semis. They seem to sell, though, whatever we do." Anya felt there was room for improvement even though she had been an estate agent for only five days and Stella had spent her entire working life in the business.

When she was alone in the office Anya worked her way through the filing cabinets, learning how the sales details were put together, what to look out for and how to work the wording as ambiguously as possible to hide any difficulties with a property. Her eye for detail led to corrections of errors which she pointed out with a tact she did not know she possessed. After shadowing Stella for a week, attending meetings, viewing houses, showing prospective buyers around properties, Anya felt this was something she could be interested in and do well. She spent Wednesday afternoons, when the agency was shut, having her hair styled and shopping for business suits and shoes with extremely high heels. She hadn't realised how long it was since she had worried about her appearance.

"Thank you for being on my side." She said as the four of them shared the bottle of champagne she had bought to celebrate the end of her first month at March and March.

> Tuesday 30th August 1977
> One year at M & M and I reckon it's been a pretty good one.
> I sold my ghastly flat last week for nearly twice what I paid for it. I know I made a few improvements but they were pretty insignificant and I've made over five grand profit. Peter said it was my money and I should invest it in another property as when we're married we'll live in his house. So I'm buying a two up two down terraced house handy for the station to let out and P said to keep the money for myself. He believes it's important I have my own money. Jack's wife never had any of her own and she would have divorced J if he hadn't died. I'm not going to argue.
> Why am I marrying Peter? I suppose if I'm honest I'd say because he's nothing like G. He's happy to have a joint bank account, allow me to have my own money, his mother's dead and he's no good in bed. He says he loves me and I say I love him but I don't think either of us is telling the truth. A marriage of convenience then, just like T & M and G & F.

When Peter had first taken her to his home she had opened the kitchen cupboards and drawers wondering how old the stained wooden spoons and assorted plates and dishes were. It was an old person's house, the wallpaper, the furniture, the pictures, the smell were all of old people.

"How long have you lived here?" She asked as gently as she could.

"Pretty much all my life."

"And on your own?"

"Since my mother died, that'd be about five years ago. Jack moved out when he got married but I stayed with my parents until they'd both gone."

"So this is still really your parents' home?"

"I suppose it is."

"Any objections to a re-vamp?"

"It's going to be your home too, so go ahead. Perhaps it is about time things were changed a bit."

As she lay under him as he made his version of love to her in what seemed still to be his parent's bedroom she was thinking that all the furniture had to go as well as the wallpaper, the curtains and the dreadful fringed green lampshade.

Saturday 8th October 1977

I'm in what used to be a spare room but is now my study. P said I should have somewhere where I can write and manage my own affairs away from the Agency. It's nice to have lots to do.

I've spent the week since the wedding buying curtains and better furniture and getting rid of the old stuff. Most importantly the new bed comes next week. P hasn't had much practice so he's very tentative. I'm not rushing him but it would be nice to enjoy that side of things again. It seems like a long time since G but it can't be more than 18 months.

P asked why I pick up a Courier from the newsagents every week. I'm not sure he believed that it was for the property pages.

For Anya her work took precedence over every other demand on her time, including writing in her diary which was again neglected. The conveyor belt of achievement and success that characterised so much of the 1980s swept her up and along and she did not think about slowing down. It seemed important to keep working because the work was there to be done and money was there to be made and there seemed to be no risk of failure.

Almost as soon as she had joined March and March the agency had become busier but she always told Peter that their success through the 1980s was nothing to do with her, simply the coincidence of the exploding property market in South East London. She and Peter worked hard and reaped the rewards of their efforts. Days began early, office hours were long, they ate out most nights and when they did get home, rarely in the light even in the longest days of June, Peter seemed happy enough to relax in front of the television while Anya would head to her study to manage her expanding personal property portfolio.

The terraced house by the station had been turned round quickly and, through a series of well-judged sales and purchases, had in ten years become an empire of twelve high value properties. Peter had advised her well in the early days but it hadn't been long before she was finding her own properties. She specialised in houses that needed work doing on them 'to make the most of my money' and to that end she employed a small firm of builders run by two brothers, one, improbably, confined to a wheelchair. They worked for her almost full time doing one property up then moving on to the next. It seemed that property values would never stop increasing and demand would never stop rising.

Peter admired his wife's energy, her skill at getting properties at less than the right price and selling them for more than they should really be worth but while his wife was getting more and more involved in the property world he was becoming less and less interested.

In the days when she was new to being a landlord she had gone out of her way to be fair because her mind was never far from Tennyson Street and she didn't want to be thought of by her tenants as she had thought of the Hodges. But as the years passed she began to see rents as returns on capital, something to be maximised. If the money were in a bank account it would be earning no more than 15%, she aimed to get far more than that from the properties. Her houses were there to give her the highest income possible and if people fell behind and couldn't pay they had to go elsewhere and be replaced by people for whom the rent was not a problem.

There was only one time in her week when she slowed down from her relentless chasing of success. Every Thursday she would pick up the Courier from the newsagent and take more time than was strictly necessary to read it.

In May 1979 she had seen the announcement of the birth of a

son to Geoffrey and Fiona Philips. They had called the boy, she thought unimaginatively but inevitably, Geoffrey. She noted that it had taken them long enough, it was three years since they had married, and Kathleen must have been getting very twitchy. But once started they moved quickly and just over a year later, in July 1980 there was the announcement of the birth of a daughter, Rosemary and in March 1982 another son, James. 'Kathleen's got what she wanted.' She thought wryly. 'She's got the Philips grandsons she wanted. Well I hope Geoff's happy.' She was surprised when she realised she meant it. Over the years she cut out all the announcements and stuck them in her diary, which was becoming more of a scrapbook than the record of her personal thoughts and feelings.

Through the summers she often found references to Tim in the sports pages. He had always been proud of his cricketing ability and that had obviously not changed. In the winters his exploits on the golf course merited an occasional mention, though, she realised he seemed to have given up rugby. In early 1983 Anya realised that references to Tim Cross began to occur more frequently. He featured on the letters page almost every week, writing about the state of the roads and pavements or the behaviour of children as they left the local school. He was leading up to that political career he had always planned on.

At the end of January 1985 she found no letter from Tim and carefully checked other pages. She realised why when she read the short article on page five.

> Tim Cross Denies Affair
> Information has been received by this newspaper relating to the behaviour of well-known local businessman Timothy Cross. We have received documents and photographs supporting allegations that Mr Cross has had a long standing relationship with his Personal Assistant, Mrs Gillian White. Mrs White has acknowledged the truth of the allegations. This newspaper understands that Tim Cross, who strenuously denies an affair,

has been asked to consider his position on the various committees of which he is a member.

Anya smiled as she read the report. This was the end of Tim's marriage. It had lasted nearly ten years, at least seven longer than she had expected.

She had a feeling that Gillian White was not going to be put aside easily. What had led her to go to the papers? A lover's tiff? Blackmail to make him leave Margaret and marry her? Whatever had been her motive she would undoubtedly be successful. She remembered Dave and John at the engagement party telling her how Tim's father had been thrown out of the Golf Club and the Rugby Club when he had been found out being unfaithful to Esme. She understood now, far better than she had then, what disgrace that would be.

She picked up the phone and dialled the number that had been at the bottom of all his articles.

"Tim Cross."

"You sound it Tim."

"What?"

"Cross."

"Who is this?"

"Anya."

"Ah." His voice didn't soften. "I suppose you've called to gloat."

"No, not really." She had hoped he would be pleased to hear from her but he didn't sound it. "I called to say hello, how are you, are you coping? We used to be friends Tim. Friends talk to each other at times like this, they give each other support and friendship, at least that's what I had always thought."

"I don't think there's anything you could say or do that would help." And the phone went dead.

As she looked at the receiver where Tim's voice had been just a few seconds earlier, she realised that she was as lonely and unhappy as it sounded Tim was now.

She and Peter never argued, that would require passion and involvement, but they bickered about the slightest thing at home or in the office. They slept in the same bed but hadn't touched each other, even accidentally, for a very long time. Whereas she had killed her first marriage with her inability to compromise she knew she was killing her second with neglect.

She had wanted Tim to suggest they meet somewhere and have meaningless but imaginative sex. Anya had sometimes wondered what would have happened if she and Tim got together. Children weren't important to him, he wouldn't have minded her forging her own career, he might even have encouraged her, and the sex would have been good. But she dismissed the idea, they would have tired of each other sooner rather than later. But there was, Anya thought as she stared at the silent telephone, something of unfinished business between them.

Four months later Anya read the notice of Tim's divorce and three weeks after that she cut out the short paragraph that noted his remarriage to Mrs Gillian White, who, the newspaper related, had been his secretary for more than five years. There was no photograph of the wedding. 'Out of the frying pan into the fire old chap,' Anya said to herself as she gummed the cutting into her diary.

Chapter 11: Reconciliations

Suburban London, 1987-1992

> *Tuesday 22nd September 1987*
> *I only asked him if I could go with him to see a property. Maybe it was my tone of voice, P always seems to hear an edge in it even when there isn't meant to be one, but he got all aggressive and accused me of thinking I didn't trust him to do it right on his own. I explained I'd been looking at a property round the corner and would like to see a comparison and he just yelled "You and your bloody empire." It was a horrible argument. I didn't think we cared enough to argue.*

Anya stopped writing and remembered breakfast that morning.

"You and your bloody empire." He was shocked at the unfamiliar anger in his voice.

"You've always encouraged me with my properties." She tried to sound reasonable.

"My mistake." Peter said under his breath.

"What did you say?"

He hadn't meant the morning to go this way, but once the floodgates of his built up frustrations were opened the flow was relentless. "You have to do everything don't you? I can't do anything right."

"That's ridiculous."

"You do all the paperwork because you don't trust me. There's nothing I do that you don't do better."

"That's not true."

"It is Anya." She had been surprised at the change of tone, now there was just sadness in his voice. "Ever since you walked into my office so confident and alluring you've made me feel pretty useless. It's you that's made the business a success. I would have sold out long ago if it had been only me. I've never been particularly interested in it, selling houses is such a parasitic way to make a living."

She hadn't answered immediately, there was just enough truth in what he had said about her not trusting him to do things well enough to make it difficult to reply. She hadn't had to because he continued relentlessly.

"I was ready to give it all up when you walked through that bloody door. I really wish you hadn't, my life would have been so much better."

She had tried to hide her surprise. "Your life would have been better?"

"It was a mistake."

"A mistake?"

"Yes, a mistake. I should have realised I only got involved with you because I didn't know what to do after Jack died."

"You married me on the rebound from the death of your brother?" Anya had difficulty believing that Peter had bottled up so much resentment for years.

"I was alone. My parents were dead, then Jack. I had no family. No-one."

"So that's it. Why can't you be honest? You want a family, you want children. You want more little Marches to carry on the family name."

"Of course I want a son, every man wants a son. Why has it never happened?

After Jack …"

"Ah Jack of revered memory. From all accounts he was an arrogant, drunken womanising shit."

"You never knew him."

"Thank goodness for small mercies."

"You should listen to yourself sometimes. You're so tied up in your life and making more bloody money you don't have a clue what's going on around you."

I knew we had never really loved each other, not the first-flush-of-youth-in-love kind of love but I thought we might have a fighting chance of making it work. I suppose we just worked too hard at the wrong thing. Perhaps sometime in the past ten years we should have realised that our marriage was more important than making more money. Or was it?

"What do you mean 'I don't have a clue'?"
"Has is ever occurred to you that I might be attractive to another woman?"
"Don't make me laugh."
"What would you do if I said I had a mistress?"
"I'd ask when you get the time to screw her."
"Mostly we meet at her house, when her children are at school."
"She's got children? You've got a mistress and she's got children? Yours?" Anya had begun to take what Peter was saying seriously.
"No, not mine, unfortunately, though I'd be proud to have been their father, we've been together…"
"Together?"
"We've been together for five years."
"How long?" Anya wasn't sure she could take any more of Peter's confessions.
"Just over five years. Her name is Jenny and she's a widow. She's got three children who call me Peter."
"You've met her children?"
"Of course, three boys. They're very nice. The eldest is…"
"I don't want to hear about your bloody mistress's bloody children."
"You were always too busy to have children weren't you? You never asked me you just made sure you wouldn't get pregnant."

I really, honestly, thought I'd told him when we first got together but I can't have done. He must have spent month after month waiting for me to give him good news, and month after month been disappointed. The man wanted a son and he never said a word.

"It wasn't like that…"

"Sit down and bloody listen because I want a divorce. Jenny and I want to get married. I can't imagine why I left it so long to tell you."

"You want a divorce? What about the business?"

"Bugger the business. We'll sell out to Wolfson's they've made me a very good offer."

"You've talked to them about it?"

"Of course."

"Without a word to me?"

"Why would I have to talk to you? It's my family's business."

"You condescending, smug, unfaithful bastard."

"Well I wouldn't have had to if we'd had children, if you'd had anything on your mind other than making more and more money from your wretched property developments and…"

"… and your family business which I carried on my shoulders for years…"

"Which I wanted to sell, and would have sold, years ago if I'd had any sense."

They sat in silence for a long time, each planning their next move. Peter swallowed hard before eventually asking "Will you give me a divorce?"

Anya knew exactly what she would do.

"No. I will not. Carry on fucking your bit on the side just don't expect me to give you a divorce. Ever. Sell the business by all means. I could do with the money. I reckon I'd get at least 30% and there's a nice row of cottages I've got my eye on."

She would have no objections to the sale of March and March to Wolfson's, it was a good idea as the boom in the property market couldn't last much longer. But she would not end the marriage.

"You have absolutely no grounds to divorce me and I will make damn sure you never have any. I will not leave you, I will not take a lover, I will be the perfect partner as far as anyone who is interested is concerned. You will have no grounds to divorce me and I don't consider your unfaithfulness sufficient to make me think our marriage has irretrievably broken down." Anya was aware that she had been in this situation before, though then the boot had been on the other foot.

"I'll leave you then."

"What and go and live with Jenny? What will that do for her reputation? And what about the children? How do you think they'd get on with their mother living in sin with a married man?"

"If I did I'll be able to divorce you after two years."

"I think you'll find it's five years if I don't agree. And I won't."

"You really are a selfish bitch."

"I am aren't I?"

> Friday 15th January 1988
> Three things to record
> Firstly M & M now trades as 'Wolfson's Estate Agency incorporating March and March' and I am half a million pounds richer.
>
> Second thing. A couple of weeks ago there was a letter in the Courier signed Tim Cross. There was an article about him, to go with his letter, and they described him as 'local businessman'. Perhaps he's trying to get back into public life. Two years were probably enough to get fed up with the secretary, perhaps even for the electorate and the golf club committee to forgive his indiscretions (they'd never forget). Why do I care?
>
> Third thing. Nearly four months now of the non-marriage. I'm completely friendly, I do as much in the house as I've always done. I sleep in our bed but if he chooses not to join me that's up to him. Peter spends a lot of time out of the house, but comes back every night. I suppose they've come to some arrangement whereby they keep the children cocooned from reality and wait for me to change my mind. Well I'm not going to.

With no job to do Anya found time hung heavily on her hands. Every week she went up to London to shop for expensive shoes and clothes she would never wear and eat extravagant, and unwanted, meals at fashionable restaurants.

She read a lot of novels and wondered whether to write one herself, she had enough material from her life for several, but somehow she never got round to it. She did buy a word processor and spent a month transferring her hand written diaries onto floppy disk.

As she typed up the diaries of 1968 she felt how lost and broken she had been then. She recognised the self-pity which she was feeling again. Now, as then, she felt that she had nothing to look forward to. As she worked through to the early 70s she wondered what her life would have been like if she had channelled that discontent more positively. She could have countered Kathleen's influence and she would have made a career for herself. She and Geoff could have made a good life together and she would have been with a man she loved and who loved her. She bitterly regretted giving up so easily.

> Saturday 6th May 1989
>
> Geoff's Geoff Jr Jr is 10 today. Rosemary is 8 and James is 7. There'll be a party which will probably be ruined by Grandma Kathleen and Aunty Margaret fussing around making them eat jelly and play pass the parcel or musical chairs. Geoff always said how much he had hated his birthday parties. I hope G's GJJ has a happier time.

Perhaps too many of her entries were self-pitying, perhaps far too many related to birthdays and anniversaries of people who were no longer part of her life.

> Tuesday 10th April 1990
>
> Geoff 40 today. 40! that means it'll be me soon. I wonder if Kathleen has allowed him to celebrate. It will of course be 40 years since Her Loss. A far more important anniversary than her only son's big 4 O. What a happy day that'll be!

She had made a mistake by rushing into divorcing Geoff because she had wanted to be free to start again before she was 30 and now, ten years later, her life was on hold because she wouldn't let Peter go. Was that a mistake too? She knew she was being vindictive, she knew she was being unreasonable. She just didn't know how to be anything else.

Women of her age were guiding their children through their teen years, supporting their husbands as they reached the peaks of their careers. She could do neither of these and she had no one to blame but herself.

Thursday 9th August 1990 Liverpool
40. And what have I got to show for it? A degree, two failed marriages and a great deal of money in the bank. Wonder if Geoff is remembering it's my birthday. He used to make such a fuss of it, lots of cards and presents. It seems so long ago.

Yesterday P said he'd be away for a few days. He's obviously forgotten it's my birthday. Since he won't be around I decided I'd risk leaving the house and come north so I booked a suite at The Adelphi and drove up. The room's much nicer than the one where I screwed that chap for twenty quid. That was 22 years ago, almost to the day. More than half my life. Where has all that time gone?

I got a taxi down to the ferry and watched as others walk around the deck as it crossed over to Woodside. Walked up to The Anchor, it was still there though it looks as if it has gone down market, if that were possible. There was a bunch of yobbos hanging around outside, probably the next generation of Longtons. The surgery was still there but no Dr Hill on the plaque so I went in. I should have expected it. It's nearly 20 years. But it was still hard to hear he died only last year. I should have come up to see him. I wonder if he ever thought of me. I wonder if he was disappointed in me. I expect he was. I am.

The few times Anya thought about what she was doing to herself, to Peter and the people he loved she was almost ashamed but as the months passed she became more determined not to give Peter any grounds on which to divorce her. If he'd really wanted to, he could just have upped and left and gone to live with his Jennifer. One day, she told herself, she would find she could do something with her life other than fuck up other people's.

> Sunday 26th August 1990
>
> I woke up wanting to see old places and old people so I drove first to the Golf Club. I calculated Tim would get away from his wife as early as possible on a Sunday to allow plenty of time in the bar before heading back home to change before Sunday lunch. I reckoned he'd be back in the clubhouse by 12 latest and I didn't want to miss him.
>
> There's a new extension but otherwise nothing much has changed. Unlike me. That carefree, super-sure girl I'd been has long gone. She'd been so confident she could do no wrong, so sure that anything and everything she did was allowable and anything and everything she wanted to do was possible. If I met that girl now I don't think I'd like her. I'm not sure if she met me she'd be very impressed. I've done nothing at all that she would have wanted me to have done. Except make a lot of money.
>
> Tim was wearing a pink jumper and crimson cord trousers, probably not the most flattering. Most surprising thing is he's gone grey. All that curly blond hair he had been so proud of has gone. If he'd been a punter coming through the door of March and March I would have said he was wealthy, he had that air about him. His car (blue Jag, personalised number plate TJC 2) shows he's doing well, despite no doubt having to pay enormous sums in maintenance to Margaret and private school fees for the children.
>
> I followed him as he drove out. He turned into a private road less than half a mile from the golf club (why hadn't he walked?). All the houses were six beds, at least, detached triple

garages, swimming pools, tennis courts, each one set in over an acre of some of the most expensive real estate in the county. I did a quick valuation, well into 7 figures. He turned into a drive where the electric gates parted as he approached.

She drove slowly passed the closing gates, catching a glimpse of red brick through the trees, and headed into the country towards the house that had been her home. She needed to know if Geoff still lived there; it was where she always pictured him.

She parked at the end of the lane so she could slowly walk past. There was a new concrete curb along the road edge, separating it from the grassy hedgerow, and one or two new builds in what had been gardens but it still felt like countryside. Her hedge had grown and no one, unless on horseback, could see into the garden so she walked through the open gate. There were no cars in the driveway and no sound of children playing from the garden.

The trees she had known had grown, bushes she had planted had reached maturity, the lawn was carefully tended and the green stripes showed it had been recently mown.

"Can I help you?" The voice made Anya jump. She turned and was relieved to see a middle-aged woman she didn't recognise.

"I'm so sorry to disturb you. I was unexpectedly in the area and thought I'd call on the off chance that an old friend still lived here."

"An old friend?" The woman sounded suspicious.

"Geoff Philips".

The woman showed no sign of recognising the name. "No one of that name lives here. Mind you we've only been here a few months and the people before us had only lived here a year or so."

"So you wouldn't have an address for the Philipses?"

"No. I don't."

"Thanks anyway, sorry to have bothered you."

Anya felt the woman watching her as she walked back down the lane. She wondered where they had moved to, they certainly wouldn't have left the area though she had seen no references to them in the local paper for some time. She drove towards the town, there was one place she knew they would be on any Sunday lunchtime.

She parked where she had done in January 1976 when she had seen Fiona and her parents arriving for Sunday lunch. She sat wishing she could transport herself back to the last time she had sat in a car outside this house. She would do things so differently. She wouldn't divorce Geoff. She would hang on, regardless of what he and his mother and sister could throw at him. She should have known Geoff loved her and she loved him. She should have had faith that they would have found a way through it all. She drove home resolved to get something of her life back.

> Monday 27th August, 1990
> Talked to P at breakfast. Explained I was going to go back to work on the properties. He seemed surprised, asking dryly if the money I got from the business hadn't been quite enough. I asked him why he had never moved out, we'd be nearly 3 years into the 5 by now. He said he would never leave his parents' home. It was the house he and his brother had grown up in, it held memories he liked to think of as well as ones he tried to forget. Bastard. I'd often wondered why he hadn't gone to Jennifer and left me to it. What is this power houses have over people?
> On Sunday I visited the houses that have mattered to me, one way or the other, since I came south and I wasn't happy in any of them. No, that's wrong. I probably was happy I just didn't know it at the time. Something has got to change.

Under different circumstances the first day of October 1992, would have been a day to celebrate but breakfast for Anya and Peter was the same cold affair it had been for years.

"Fifteen years Peter. I won't say Happy Anniversary."

"Best not."

Anya soon realised something was wrong. Peter wasn't turning the pages of his newspaper. Normally, by the time he finished his coffee, all the supplements would be put to one side and the paper would be folded to expose the crossword which he would have half finished.

"Is everything all right?"

She didn't expect a response.

"Is Jennifer ill?" Anya's false concern finally stimulated Peter to answer.

"No. She's not ill."

"Then what is it?"

"She's moved."

"Moved?"

"Yes. Moved. Gone back to Shropshire. It's where she was brought up. She said it was obvious I was never going to be free so she's gone. I would have married her. I would have done if only you had given me a divorce."

It horrified her when she realised tears were rolling down his cheeks. She had never seen him cry. It upset her more than she could have imagined.

"You must have known it was coming." She tried to sound sympathetic but knew that, after so many years of bickering, even had she succeeded he wouldn't have heard it for what it was.

"I suppose I did. I just didn't want to think she'd really go. You're always so busy you won't have noticed but I've hardly been out of the house for the four weeks since she left."

"A month?"

"A month in which time you've barely noticed me, so wrapped up in your own little world are you."

Anya realised he was right, she had long ago stopped wondering where he was and what he was doing. Perhaps she should have noticed more.

"How long have you known her?" Anya was genuinely interested. It hadn't seemed important to know anything about her husband's lover until now as his tears filled her with a guilt his words could never have effected.

"Do you really want to know?"

She thought for a few seconds and then spoke gently "I think I do."

"I met her in 1982, the 5th of June." Anya thought that odd, he rarely remembered dates. She did a quick calculation, for more than two thirds of their marriage he had wanted to be someone else. She almost apologised to him for the shocking waste of love and life. "You were out of the office that day and she came in wanting to sell up. Her husband had died leaving her with a house she couldn't afford and children in private schools. He had been something in the city and there had never been any shortage of money but they had never saved a penny. There was an enormous mortgage on the house and she was in a bit of a state." He paused, waiting for the sarcastic comments about 'poor little thing, cried on your shoulder did she?' but none came. He caught Anya's eye and was surprised to see real sympathy. "I helped out where I could, made sure the sale of the house went through smoothly, found her a smaller one at a good price, made sure that went through. Everything very professional but, well, we both knew it was going to be more than that."

Finally Anya spoke. "When did you first sleep with her?"

"Christmas Eve that year."

"Ten years ago."

He carried on as if she hadn't spoken. "The children were with their grand-parents and we had a few too many mulled wines. It just happened."

"She must have loved you very much to wait around all that time."

"We did fight it you know. It was a long time before we talked about getting together permanently. But we didn't want anyone to get hurt."

"Me?"

"Yes. You."

"And I was just too wrapped up in myself."

"It was obvious you weren't terribly interested in me."

"I'm sorry." She was surprised to find that she meant it.

"You and I haven't had a marriage for years but Jen wouldn't have me while I was still married and you were always going to make divorce difficult. One divorce is unfortunate but two seems careless." He spoke with dry irony.

They both thought how much of their lives had been wasted because doing nothing had been the easiest thing.

Peter regained his thoughts first. "And you had the Crosses and the Philipses."

She looked at him, surprised. "What do you know about them?"

"Not much. Just that you can't let them go. You were always checking the papers to see if there was anything about them. Jenny said I shouldn't worry about it…"

"You talked about this with Jenny?"

"Of course I did. She said you'd never go back to him."

"How the hell would she know?" Anya managed, with difficulty, to keep her anger at bay.

"We were both hoping you would."

There was an uneasy silence as Peter topped up their coffee, spilt some and Anya rushed to clear it up, it gave her time to calm down.

"You never loved me did you?" Peter asked in what Anya had always thought of as his 'little boy voice'. She found it rather pathetic but she was over her anger and said nothing. "I mean you married me because it suited you at the time, not because you loved me." Anya started to say something denying that what he said had any truth in it but Peter put his hand up to silence her. "You invested nothing in our relationship. It was the job you married, the business, the prospect of making something of yourself, or whatever other stupid reason there might be but you didn't marry me because you loved me did you? I didn't realise at first, it took a year or two but I did eventually."

Much of what Peter said was true. Anya just shrugged and put the mug to her lips.

She was unprepared for what Peter said next.

"We really should have seen a counsellor about not having children. We should have found out the reason, whether it was your fault or mine. If we'd had children we would have been a bit more cemented together. You know the worst thing is that in all these years you've never trusted me enough to talk about it. Every month in those first few years I thought you'd say something but you never did. It was as if you knew you weren't ever going to get pregnant."

"That's right." She spoke quietly. She could never have told him. She had never cared enough to tell him.

"Right?"

"I can't have children. I thought you knew. I thought I'd told you."

"How on earth would I know?" Peter spoke slowly, barely containing his inadequate anger.

"I thought I must have told you." She shrugged her shoulders.

"You didn't. I never gave up hoping. Why did you never tell me?"

"I thought I had." She repeated.

Eventually he broke the uncomfortable silence speaking with barely contained resentment. "Do you think you might explain to me now?"

She had long ago forgiven her mother, she understood why the sterilisation had had to be done but she would never forgive her father. Victor had had sex with his 15 year old sister ruining not only her life but her baby's and, Anya recognised, the lives of all the people she had allowed herself to get close to. She had never told anyone, not even Geoff, how could she tell Peter?

She spoke, in the end, without thinking, the sentence spoken before she realised what she said. "I was sterilised."

"Sterilised?" He seemed surprised, as though it was not the answer he expected.

"I was seven years old."

"Seven?" Peter was shocked.

"I didn't know until my mother died and I was reading through her papers. She'd kept all the forms. I've still got them in her silver trunk."

"It's unusual to sterilise someone so young isn't it?" He sounded concerned.

Anya sat turning her mother's ring round and round her finger. It was strange, she thought, to be having a civilised, sensible conversation with Peter for the first time in years and it was about the most fundamentally personal part of her.

"I understand exactly why it was done and, if I'd been my mother, I'd have done the same."

"Why?"

"I've never told anyone, not Geoff, not anyone."

"Perhaps you can trust me with the knowledge. Maybe our fifteen years together is worth something." He waited for her to say something, but when she didn't he gently prompted her. "Perhaps if you told someone it might not be such a burden." She looked up at him. He was a kind, understanding man. She had been so cruel to him.

"My mother was just 16 when I was born."

"So she was under age when you were conceived?" Peter was trying to help.

"Yes. She was raped."

"Oh. I understand now."

"No you don't. You couldn't possibly understand."

"She was raped, she was pregnant, she didn't trust men, she never wanted the same to happen to you."

"Being sterilised would not have stopped me being raped." Anya pointed out sensibly.

"I suppose not."

"It was who raped her that was the problem."

Peter began to get some inkling of the pain Anya felt and reached out across the kitchen table to take her hand.

"She was raped by her brother. She had me sterilised so I couldn't pass on all those bad genes." It all came out in a rush. She gripped Peter's hand and immediately forced a laugh. "God that was easy to say! After all this time it was so easy!"

"You're sure it as your brother?" Peter asked gently. "You're sure there could be no mistake?"

"Incestuous rape. That's what the piece of paper said. It had to be her brother."

"It could have been another male relative." Peter was being logical, trying to reduce the level of emotion.

"She didn't have any other brothers, at least I don't think so, there were no other birth certificates."

"There is one other option." Anya looked at Peter as she had never seen him before, he was in control, trying to help her through this painful conversation with understanding and tact. "It could have been her father."

It was a thought that had never occurred to her. Vincent had been the object of her hate for so long she couldn't put anyone else into that role.

"You say you have papers. Bring them down, let me look at them, we'll look at them together. You never know, as a dispassionate observer I may see something you haven't."

He was most interested in the grand parents. "You never met them? Never heard anything from them at all?"

"No. Mum never talked about them. They must have thrown her out as soon as they knew she was pregnant. It was 1949 it must have been the most shameful thing to have an unmarried mother in the family!"

Then she showed him the letters, the scraps of paper with her mother's writing on, the little box wrapped in brown paper that had contained her ring.

"I always thought that ring was a reminder of your time with Geoff."

"I'm so sorry Peter. I have never been very open with you have I?"

"You have sometimes been a little difficult to live with." He spoke with measured understatement and they turned their attention back to the letters. Peter picked up one.

"Listen to this one. 'Whatever happens to you Mel never forget you are worth more than any jewel. I'm so sorry I left when you needed me most. You know I will think of you forever, your loving brother, Vince.' They're hardly the words of a guilty man. Mel needed him and he left. Would Mel have needed him if he had raped her? And look at this. 'I'm sorry for everything. I just ran when I found out. I didn't know what else to do. It was me nicked the rent box there wasn't much in it but it got me here. Write to me. Tell me how you're getting on. Sorry for leaving you when you needed me. Your loving brother,

Vincent A Cave'. He feels guilty because he ran away leaving her to deal with everything on her own. These are the words of a man, a boy really, who abandoned his sister not one who raped her."

Anya sat listening to the words she had read once all those years before and which had sealed in her mind the guilt of her uncle/father. She picked up the letter that had hurt her most, that had led to her life of self-loathing.

"Can you understand how I felt when I read this? *'It's a girl. I've called it Anya because it's got to have a name and the woman in the bed next to me was reading a book by someone called Anya something. Perhaps it's too pretty a name for something that should never have existed. I should have got rid of it like you said.'* He told her to have an abortion, that would have been a back street one, nothing clean and clinical like today. I knew someone who couldn't face having one in the 60s because it was so dangerous and it would have been a lot worse for Mum. *'But you'd left and I was too scared to do it on my own. I will never forgive you for leaving. Now what can I do? Just put up with everything I suppose. It was alright for you, you could leave.'* She always hated me."

"Oh Anya." Peter reached out across the table and took his wife's hands in his. "You should never have taken so much of this to heart. She couldn't have meant it. She looked after you didn't she? She left her parents and she didn't abandon you or have you adopted as she could have done. She kept you and looked after you for the rest of her life."

"I'd never thought of that."

"And I suppose you'd never thought that any resentment she did feel might have made her into the person she was? She had no time to have fun, she had to live with what had happened to her. Had you never thought of that?"

Anya hadn't. She had never looked at her mother's life from any other point of view than her own.

"She must have been a clever woman, Anya, she had you for a daughter."

"I'm not a very nice person am I Peter?"

"You haven't been very nice to a lot of people but then I don't think you've been very kind to yourself either."

When Anya didn't reply and just sat looking at all the papers that had dictated so much of her thinking about herself and her life, Peter carried on talking in his calm, understanding voice, full of sadness. "There's another scenario that fits the facts. What if Mel and Vince's father had abused both of them? What if they had both wanted to leave but only Vince, young and fit, was in a position to make a new life for himself? Perhaps he felt guilty for the rest of his life, perhaps he's still alive and still feeling guilty."

Anya re-read Vince's letters from a different perspective. For 30 years Vince had been the hate figure in her life now she realised she might have jumped to the wrong conclusion. She should have talked about it years before.

"Thank you Peter. I'm so sorry."

"I'm sorry too Anya, if you hadn't been so angry about things we might have made a better fist of our time together." She noticed he hadn't said 'their marriage' as Peter busied himself with the coffee percolator.

The spell was broken and Anya changed the subject. "Would Jennifer have you back?"

"I told you, she's given up on me and moved back to her family."

"Would you move to Shropshire if she'd have you?"

"She'd only have me if I could marry her. She's made that clear and so have the boys. They're old enough to have their say in what their mother does."

"What if you were divorced?" She spoke softly.

"You'd give me a divorce?" Peter wasn't sure he'd heard her correctly.

"Yes." In the end it was so simple.

"But I couldn't drag Jenny's name into it."

"What if I gave you grounds and I'm the guilty party? Perhaps that would make up for some of what I've put you both through."

Peter reached over the table and took Anya's hands in his. "You'd do that?"

"Yes."

After five years of hanging on to a dead relationship, knowing she did not love and was not loved, it really was quite simple.

> *Friday 2nd October 1992*
> *P's phone call to his Jenny was a long one and then he left. He said he'd be in touch. 'Don't prove me wrong Anya, I've told her we can trust you.' I told him not to worry. It's the closest we've been in years. What could life have been like if we'd had that conversation years ago. Now I need grounds, incontrovertible, unarguable grounds for him to divorce me. It wouldn't be fair to target Geoff (children and maybe I care too much) so it has to be Tim (children nearly grown up and probably living with Margaret and it would serve him right). His ego will make him susceptible to flattery but just in case he's grown up at all I'll make myself irresistible. The Golf Club's New Year Ball will be nice and public.*

Anya was 42 years old and although she had looked after her appearance she knew she had some work to do if she was to seduce Tim. She was determined not to let Peter down.

A fortnight in an exclusive health farm helped but when she looked in her mirror she still saw a woman in her early middle age. She needed something to make her stand out from the crowd of middle aged women on the one day of the year when they would all be looking their best. She decided that nothing would be more flattering than an expensive mid-winter tan so she phoned a travel agent and booked three weeks in Barbados.

'Who knows?' She said aloud as she put the phone down. 'Perhaps I'll come across Vincent Albert Cave.'

As her driver waited at the gate house to be let into the lush tropical grounds of the exclusive resort she felt more relaxed than at any time she could remember. Divorcing Peter was liberating. She should, she told herself, have done it years before.

A few minutes later she sat on the balcony of her room drinking the welcoming bottle of champagne and reading the book that detailed all the services available to her. There were pages of massage and beauty treatments and there would still be plenty of time for the tan.

As she spent her days enjoying the attention of the well trained staff in the beauty salon, in the restaurant and at the beach bar, she occasionally thought about Vincent. But she only had a 40 year old PO Box address to go on. At the beginning of her holiday it seemed to her there was plenty of time to try to find him and then, towards the end, not enough.

On the day before she was due to fly back to England she stood in her room, naked in front of the full length mirror critically examining her reflection. Apart from the small areas that had been covered by her bikini her skin was a deep bronze. She put her hands underneath her breasts and pushed them up. With the right underwear and the right dress they could be the breasts of a far younger woman. She turned sideways on to the mirror to check her body in profile. Her stomach was flat, her bottom compact. She faced back to the mirror. Her legs looked good from the front, she turned in profile again, then turned her back on the mirror and looked over her shoulder. They would pass muster too.

'Tim' she mouthed seductively to the mirror 'you will not be able to say no.' She walked up to her reflection and pursed her lips. After three weeks of luxury the lines of tension around her eyes had disappeared, her neck had lost the hint of flabbiness. She could see no flaws.

She lay down on the bed pleased with the success of her holiday in the sun then she sat bolt upright.

"Shit!"

She thought back through the years of her marriage. How long had it been? She hadn't had sex with anyone for over ten years and then that had only been with Peter. She couldn't count on Tim taking the time to arouse her, if her plan worked there would be nothing in the way of foreplay. The implications of being so out of practice worried her, it would be uncomfortable, painful, perhaps even impossible.

"Shit!"

She dressed carefully in a blue linen skirt and white t-shirt and headed for reception to ask for a taxi. There were many men in the resort who would probably take kindly to her advances but she preferred to do her revision course where she was unknown.

Three hours later she was in a small hotel room apologising to the young American man who was lying on top of her. "Sorry. I'm a bit out of practice, it's been a while."

"No problem Ma'am."

And, despite an awkward start, it wasn't.

"Like riding a bicycle." She had laughed as he rolled off her. "Something you never forget how to do."

He was breathless. "You seem to have remembered quite a lot." The young American ran his finger down her back.

"Perhaps I need a little more practice, just to make sure I remember absolutely everything."

Chapter 12: Retribution

Kent, December 31st 1992

"I'm with the Philips party."

"What was the name again?" The elderly lady taking her ticket on the door appeared flustered as she peered uncertainly at the long list of names on the sheet of paper in front of her.

"Philips. Anya Philips. I'm a cousin of Mr Geoffrey Philips." She felt her explanation rather weak but the lady on the door gave up looking at the guest list as a large and noisy party arrived behind Anya.

"I'm afraid the rest of the Philips party isn't here yet but I'm sure someone will get you a drink while you're waiting. Ah Mr Cross! Just the person."

Anya had taken great care over her hair and her makeup and she was completely satisfied with the way she looked. Her deep tan and the shine in her hair were flatteringly youthful and her dress was perfect leaving little of her trim figure to the imagination. Her dressmaker had done a perfect job in replicating the dress she had worn on only one occasion over twenty-one years earlier. She knew she looked as beautiful as she had ever done as she turned expecting to begin her seduction of Tim. Instead she looked up into the admiring blue eyes of a man who looked just as Tim had done when they had first met on Charing Cross Station.

"Matthew Cross." He spoke with the confidence that only being his father's son could give him.

"Anya." She held out her hand. "I'm an old friend of your father's."

"Not so old I think." He said with some charm.

As Matthew held her hand a fraction longer than was necessary

Anya thought quickly. He had been born in September 1974, he was over 18, 'old enough' she thought as she rapidly adjusted her plans. Maybe it was being back in the Golf Club House, maybe it was wearing the replica of her mother's dress, but despite all her resolutions not to hurt people unnecessarily something of the old Anya was resurrected. 'Matthew then Tim, why not?'

"Can I get you a drink? I think there's champagne doing the rounds."

"Lovely." She resisted saying she hadn't seen him since he was a baby and how much like his father he was. "Then you must tell me about yourself. Are you at university?"

It didn't seem to occur to him to question why a woman who was old enough to be his mother was spending so much time with him, listening attentively as he talked about himself and his family. She seemed especially interested when he talked about his grand-mother Kathleen. 'She's a witch,' he had said with no humour or affection in his voice. 'She's all over Uncle Geoff's children, but she never seems so keen on Maggie and me.' 'That'll be because you aren't Philipses, you're Crosses' she had said sympathetically. He looked at her with renewed respect as it was clear she understood something of the dynamic of his family.

"Are your parents here?" Anya eventually asked.

"Yes. Dad's Captain this year so he's chatting everybody up. Would you like me to take you over to him?"

Anya was in two minds. She wanted to meet Tim, she wanted him to be disconcerted that she was here this evening, perhaps it would make him think, remember, worry, and that could only be a good thing, but perhaps now was not quite the time.

"Thank you Matthew, I would love to meet up with him later in the evening. Come on, let's have a dance. You can do traditional, hold onto your partner, dancing can't you?"

Tim was on edge. As Captain it had been his decisions that had set the tone for the evening. Every one of the tickets had been sold, at £100 each, to people who expected value for their money. Many guests would not arrive until later but as he heard the clock in the bar strike nine he was pleased to see the dance floor, if not yet crowded, then well occupied. He sipped at his champagne, hoping that the evening would be a success and reflect well on his captaincy. He always drank too much at events like this but this was his evening, he must not be drunk before most of the guests. It was his responsibility that they have a good time, only when that was assured would it be his turn. He caught sight of his wife across the room. She had put on weight since their marriage and the dress she had chosen to wear did not suit her. 'Mutton dressed as lamb and ugly lamb at that' he thought, 'God how I hate the woman but such is the result of having to lie in beds one has made.' He downed the champagne in his glass and signalled to the waiter for a top-up. Just one more couldn't hurt.

He smiled and waved at people as they arrived and hoped again that all would be well with the evening, the social high point of his year as Captain.

"Good evening Sir Christopher." Tim stood to shake hands with the club president, who also happened to be chairman of the local constituency party.

"Everything going well Cross?"

"It seems so, thus far at any rate."

"It had better Cross, people have long memories and it isn't as if you haven't blotted your copy book in the past is it?" He nudged Tim suggestively. "Well it seems your boy there has found himself a cracker for the evening. Not sure I recognise her. You must tell him to introduce me y'know?" Tim looked in the direction Sir Christopher was nodding and saw Matthew's back. He couldn't see the 'cracker' he was dancing with. "Seems a tad on the old side for the young buck but sometimes the older ones are the best if you know what I mean." Sir Christopher chuckled lasciviously. Tim wondered if Sir Christopher was getting his money's worth simply in champagne.

Tim tried to get a look at his son's partner but all he could see was a pair of well-manicured hands resting loosely on his son's shoulders. Tim's first instinct was to check for rings and the ring finger of her left hand was unadorned. He promised himself he would investigate by the end of the evening. If she was the cracker Sir Christopher had said she was, and with no man hanging around to be difficult, the time might be well spent. He turned his attention back to Sir Christopher, it was important the president knew he was on top of things.

Anya excused herself from Matthew's company after their dance and walked around the room. She knew people were watching her, perhaps wondering who she reminded them of.

"Anya? It is Anya isn't it?" Anya looked round to see who had tapped her on her arm.

"Esme! Yes, it is me I'm afraid."

"Don't be afraid dear girl. It is so wonderful to see you. And you haven't changed a bit!" Anya wondered if Esme wasn't a little the worse for wear even though it was still early. "Sit down my dear girl, talk to me. Tell me how you have got on since we last met, that must be a few years ago now. You know I always hoped you and my Tim would make a go of it, you were always a far more interesting person than Margaret and that awful woman Gillian. If she has any saving graces I've yet to see them."

"You shouldn't say such things!" Anya laughed. She had always liked Esme who, when she had escaped Kathleen, had shown a wicked liking for speaking her mind.

"Of course I should. If I don't I know of no one else who will. If only Timothy had had half your guts he wouldn't have ended up with such a complete drip of a girl. Both his wives have about as much personality as one single wet rag between them."

Anya stifled a giggle "But his children seem to have turned out well?"

"Ah you've met Matthew? Maggie isn't here tonight. But yes, Matthew is a sweetie. He's wicked you know. Somehow he's managed to inherit that spark that Tim used to have."

"Is Maggie as nice?"

"Oh no, not at all. Maggie is so like her mother and Kathleen. I know I shouldn't say that but really she's had every advantage and she's turned out to be a complete nonentity."

"Is Tim happy?" Anya managed to make herself sound concerned. For some reason she desperately wanted Esme's answer to be 'no'.

"Seven years they've been married now. He should never have allowed himself to be inveigled into it. He was doing extra-curricular activities with his secretary after work and I'm sure it was really only a bit of fun on his part, nothing serious at all. Then she blackmailed him into marrying her after the most acrimonious of divorces. Margaret was really unnecessarily vindictive. She took him to the cleaners, is that the phrase?"

"Oh dear." Anya tried to sound sympathetic, what Esme told her was much as she had imagined.

"Serve him right, my dear. He should never have allowed himself to get into that position. He should have married you. I always thought it." Anya wasn't sure what to say so she just smiled and said nothing. "She had forced him into a corner, you know? When Gillian wrote that letter to the paper she knew he'd have to marry her if he was ever going to bluff it out. You can't just have affairs all over the place, you know, not willy nilly." Esme giggled at her small joke. "She knew he'd have to make it look like they were in love, only then would the local party and the Golf Club Committee ever accept him back into the fold. Even so it's taken years."

"I suppose having a bit on the side is one thing but being caught out, and so publicly, is another." Anya suggested thinking that history may well be about to repeat itself.

"Absolutely. I knew you'd understand. You would have been so good for him, you would have brought out the best in him. You really would. Now, dear girl, tell me what you've been doing with yourself all this time. I have missed you!"

"My bet is that that vision of loveliness is The Unsuitable Anya."
"Who?"
Matthew was discussing his dance partner with three of his friends. "A couple of friends of my Dad's first told me about her years

ago. She screwed my Dad and yours and just about everybody else at his stag night."

"Well it was the 60s. They did that sort of thing then. Lucky buggers."

"70s. It was 1971."

"Same thing."

"They used to make bets apparently. Dad said at least £500 a go."

"Nothing more than a prostitute then."

"I don't think it was quite like that. It was Uncle Geoff who paid her, not the screwee. Explain that if you can."

They were drinking, enjoying themselves, aware that all the rather middle aged pompous men around them were their future. In 20 years they would be the Golf Club Committee and the stalwarts of the local Conservative Party, one of them would undoubtedly be the local Member of Parliament. They were aware they were by way of being apprentices, absorbing the customs and mores of their class; accepting unquestioningly the advantages given them by the circumstances of their birth.

"OK then."

"OK what?"

"I'll bet you five hundred quid."

Matthew looked at his friend Roger. "What?"

"I'll bet you five hundred quid that you don't screw her tonight."

"Who?" Matthew knew exactly what his friend was suggesting but he was playing for time, looking across the room and deciding whether it was a challenge he wanted to take on. He decided he wouldn't say no. From what he had heard of her he didn't think she would either.

"The unsuitable Anya of course."

Matthew looked at Roger, wondering whether he was really being serious. "You're on. But inflation has taken its toll so if Dad was worth five hundred quid to her then she's got to be worth at least a grand to me."

"What? Just like that? A thousand quid?"

"Start saving up old chap."

"You're really going to have a go? Here? Tonight?"

"Of course. If everything my dad said about her is true the money's as good as mine."

They solemnly shook hands on the deal. Matthew wasn't about to lose the bet and he wasn't going to waste any time. Five minutes later he had wrested Anya away from his grandmother, provided her with a full bottle of champagne and a glass and introduced her to his friends. She was surprised how well she got on with them. At first they were just as she expected boys of that age to be; coarse, confident and crude but the conversation became interesting when they started talking about property. It seemed that even at their age they were interested in making money the easy way.

"When do you think the upturn will come?" One young man asked seriously.

"Soon. A year, maybe two at most."

"Residential or Business?"

"Residential of course. More flexibility."

"I'd invest now, in fact I have." Anya answered the original question. "But let's not talk business, tonight's for other things. Let's dance Matthew."

She had no shortage of partners for most of the next hour as she danced with a succession of young men who all seemed to want the opportunity to hold her. She did not complain as it gave her the opportunity to see and be seen. Tim seemed to have disappeared but Geoff was there, sitting at a table next to Kathleen. She thought he had lost a lot of weight, he had always been lean but now he appeared almost gaunt. When she had last seen him his hairline had been receding but now he was almost completely bald making him appear not just middle-aged, but old. Sixteen years was a long time but she thought he did not look well. She could not see the Blessed Fiona at the Philips table, perhaps she was looking after the children, they couldn't be much older than 10 or 11, not old enough to be at such an event as this.

As she looked around she felt Matthew stop in mid step. She bumped into him and was worried she would lose her balance. They really were very high heels.

"Hello." A woman held her hand out to Anya to be shaken looking intently, almost aggressively, at her. "Matthew? Aren't you going to introduce me to your partner?"

"Aunt Fiona, this is Anya, Anya…" He was embarrassed that he didn't know her surname.

"Anya March. How do you do?" Anya was formal, looking down from her greater height at the second Mrs Geoff Philips.

Fiona was to the point. "Why are you here tonight? I've never seen you at the club before."

Anya answered slowly and politely, using the time to appraise Fiona. She decided she had not aged well. "I used to be a regular here, just social you understand, I'm no golfer! I moved away from the area years ago but I'm now thinking of moving back. That's why I'm here this evening. That's why you won't have seen me at the club before."

"Really?" Fiona sounded as disbelieving as her icily formal politeness allowed.

There was more of an undercurrent in Anya's reply. "If it's any of your business I have many old friends here. I do hope to meet some of them tonight. Don't you love renewing old acquaintances?"

Fiona ignored Anya's question. "I think my husband used to know someone called Anya."

"I seem to remember he was married to someone called Anya."

Fiona saw her opportunity. "He married when he was very young and impressionable. He's always said it was a dreadful mistake. He only married her because he felt sorry for her. She was very poor you know, but even being married to Geoff and having every advantage she was never anything other than working class. He divorced her as soon as it was legally possible." Anya had no time to respond as Fiona turned away then, glancing back over her shoulder, spoke to Matthew. "Take care, the woman's nothing more than an opportunistic tart."

"What on earth was all that about?" Matthew took hold of her arms and placed them on his shoulders, pulling her closer to him as they resumed their dance. She twirled his collar length hair around her fingers as they swayed together. Anya had decided now was the time to make her move.

"I think, perhaps, your question is something I should answer outside. We don't want anyone to overhear do we?"

He put his hand under her arm and led her through the open French windows wondering how many people had noticed. They wouldn't be missed in the time it would take to win his bet. He led her by the hand along paths between high bushes to a wooden hut.

"You've done this before."

"Oh yes many times." It was only after he had answered that he realised the implications of her question. "Done what?" he asked with faux innocence.

He kissed her and Anya was surprised at how much she enjoyed it. For his age he seemed unreasonably expert. She thought back just three days to the young American, there was a similarity in the way they both swiftly moved from kissing to more intimate contact. Then she thought back twenty one years to when she had been with this boy's father for the first time.

"Are you sure this is OK?" He asked politely as he ran his finger around the line of the deep cowl neck of her dress and began to ease the delicate fabric off her shoulder.

"Of course but let me. We mustn't ruin it." She elegantly stepped out of the dress and stood naked in front of him.

"Wow."

"Come on then Matt, I don't want to get cold." He didn't take his eyes off her as he undressed.

It was Anya's turn to be impressed as she saw that, where the father had had little to work with, the son was well endowed. She let him push her against the coats hanging on the wall and prepared to enjoy herself.

Ten minutes later, as they made their way back to the party, Anya felt remarkably calm. She had had the hors d'oeuvres and had now to prepare for the main course.

"Hello Anya." They had nearly reached the doors into the noise and warmth of the party when a man stepped out of the shadows.

"Matthew go inside. I can't believe you were stupid enough to risk being seen going back in together."

"Hello Tim."

"So you've managed to seduce my son."

"I don't think seduction is the word. He was very much the instigator; very willing, and I might add, very able. I wonder where he got that from, certainly not his father."

"You are a bitch. You always were."

"That's not what you used to say."

"No? I may not have said it but I always thought it. A bitch on heat."

He pushed his arms around her and pulled him roughly towards him. She could smell the alcohol on his breath but she didn't think it would matter that he was drunk.

"God you smell of sex." He pushed his mouth towards hers and his tongue into her mouth. She responded for a fraction of a second then pulled away.

"Was I a bitch to have sex with your son?"

"How was he?"

"Obviously not inexperienced."

"Good. I'm glad he is maintaining the Cross honour."

"He upheld that alright."

Tim pushed his mouth on hers again. This time she let him kiss her for longer, responding, tongue duelling with tongue as his passion rose. He remembered she was the only woman who had ever kissed him using her teeth.

She pushed his hand away from her breast. "No, Tim. You'll mark my dress."

"I remember it. I remembered it the moment I saw you."

"It's not the same dress. You may remember how you tore the original to shreds as we fucked under that tree. Three times wasn't it?"

"Four." He bent his head down towards her neck and kissed the soft skin. "I need you Anya."

She moved her head gently from side to side, aware she was teasing him further than was fair.

"I want you Anya, now." He took her arm and led her through a side door into the club house. The noise of the ball was muffled. "My office." he said. "It should be more comfortable than the professional's hut. I assume that's where Matt took you."

He took a key from his pocket and unlocked the door. He gestured for her to walk into the large room with a wide bow window, the sumptuous curtains drawn to ensure perfect privacy. She looked around the luxuriously furnished office with its leather three piece suite and old-fashioned, wooden desk, one wall lined with book shelves another covered with photographs of men she assumed were past Captains. The room exuded privilege.

"You've looked after yourself Anya, you look as gorgeous as ever."

"You look your age Tim. Sorry I can't be more flattering than that."

"Nice tan."

"I had three weeks in Barbados."

"You're doing well then? A rich ex-husband?"

She ignored the implication that she couldn't have made the money herself. "Getting by." She suspected that a woman having money was as attractive to him as a woman with a fit and attractive body or a woman skilled at love-making. "Getting by quite well, very well in fact."

"No wedding ring I see." That had been her stroke of genius, making sure she removed all rings from her fingers on her arrival in the sun. If he chose to assume that all married women would wear a wedding ring that was his mistake. He would never have made the same assumption with men.

"You'll remember the sapphire." She held her right hand out towards him, the fingers elegantly drooping, the ring sparkling. "It really was my mother's you know."

"It's a beautiful ring."

"I know."

"It's one of the first things I noticed about you when we were under the clock on Charing Cross Station. I thought you a dark horse, a beautiful dark horse ready for the riding." Tim poured scotch generously into two large glasses. "Here."

"Thanks. But won't your family be missing you?"

"No. I'd say we have enough time."

"Enough time for what Tim?" She asked provocatively. He sat down on the settee, patted the seat next to him and she obeyed. She sat back in the unexpectedly comfortable leather and watched him as he carefully removed his bow tie and undid the top buttons of his dress shirt. He didn't take his eyes off her as, in rather ungainly fashion, he prised off his slip-on patent leather shoes.

"We've all the time in the world." As he sipped his whisky Anya thought how unpleasant he seemed, how unattractive this dissipated, middle-aged, lecherous man was compared with the young man he had been.

"Anya?"

"Yes?"

"Why did you come here tonight?"

"I would have thought that was obvious."

"Matt? Me? Geoff? Anyone else?"

"Not Geoff. Matt was an unexpected bonus."

"Not another of your bets?"

"No. Tim. Not this time."

An hour later, just before the fireworks, songs and the celebrations to welcome 1993, they separately re-joined the party.

"Ah Tim. You've returned." Gillian sat, stiff backed, as her husband sat down opposite her. The way she was looking at him he knew he was in trouble. "I notice also that that Anya woman is back in the room, so intriguing that you should both have been missing at the same time, and for so long."

"Not odd at all my dear. She is an old friend. We had some catching up to do."

"I bet you did."

"What I mean is I wanted to find how she has been getting on since she moved away. She's done rather well actually."

"Oh I am pleased for her." His wife's dry sarcasm was something that had always irritated Tim.

"We're old friends, we've been talking. For Christ's sake Gill, don't make a scene, not tonight."

"A scene? Heaven forbid!" She gave him a look that told him she meant business. "Sir Christopher! Won't you join us?"

"Delighted as ever Gillian my dear."

He turned to Tim who was wondering if his tie was tied correctly, whether there was anything to show that just a few minutes before he had been on the floor of his office doing what he had fantasised for years of doing with Anya.

"Y'know it's such a shame about the cameras." Sir Christopher spoke in a conversational tone, as if commenting on the quality of the canapés or the familiarity of the tune the band was playing.

"Cameras?" Tim asked quietly, reacting just as they had expected him to.

Sir Christopher couldn't answer as the roar of the countdown denied all conversation. "Ten… Nine…" 'Cameras' Tim thought to himself, a shudder of dread rising from the back of his knees. "Six… Five…" 'What the hell did he mean about the cameras?' "Two… One…" Tim heard the strains of Auld Lang Seyn dying away, half-heartedly returning the 'Happy New Years' of the happy revellers who tapped him on the shoulder to shake his hand or kiss him on the cheek, as he waited for the axe to fall.

As soon as the hubbub had died away Sir Christopher continued as if there had been no interruption in their conversation. "Such a good idea, those new security cameras. They've been installed in all the main positions around the club. You signed the chitty."

"I did?" Tim looked at his wife and then at Sir Christopher. In those few moments he knew what they meant. He had forgotten. He had completely forgotten.

"You did. Security, you know, in case of burglaries. The cameras cover all the important places in the club house, the entrances, the car park, the safe in the secretary's office." Tim was slow to realise how much Sir Christopher was enjoying this. "And, of course, the valuable pictures on the walls of the Captain's Office."

Tim knew Sir Christopher had never liked him, had probably

voted against him for the captaincy. He was of the old school, play away by all means but never get caught and most of all never get caught with the secretary, those were his standards and Tim had failed to meet them.

"Ah."

"Yes, darling, Ah."

"You have been watching?"

"We have been watching. I must say I've learned quite a lot about my husband, Sir Christopher." Gill was talking in a tightly controlled voice. "He has a repertoire I have scarcely ever imagined let alone been lucky enough to experience."

"Who?" Tim could hardly finish his sentence.

"Oh just interested parties, close family."

Anyone watching Gillian would have thought she was making polite conversation but her husband knew she was absolutely aware she had him by the balls.

She had been waiting for Tim to be careless, to give her the grounds for the divorce she had planned since before they were married. She had expected it to take only a few months before she would have been able to divorce him but now she knew her waiting was over. Tim would have to give her a divorce and there could be absolutely no question that he was the guilty party. She looked forward to at least two thirds of his money, maybe more if she exaggerated the humiliation she was supposed to be feeling at this moment. She would have a million, perhaps a million and a half, a decent return for the seven years she had invested in being married to the shit.

"I've learned that a leopard does not change his spots, once a two-faced, deceitful, dishonest cad always a two-faced, deceitful, dishonest cad. Who was it that said if a man marries his mistress he creates a job vacancy? Well spot on. Don't imagine you can come home tonight but let me know where you're staying, my solicitor will need to know."

"Nice one Anya!" Matthew stood by Anya who was dancing with one of his friends. "My dance I think." He took Anya's arms from the shoulders of his friend and placed them around him. "Nice one. Son and father within an hour. I love it. You must tell me which one of us was the best."

"The better, Matthew, the better." Anya avoided answering the impossible but accurately anticipated question. "It's the better of two and the best of more. Since I have only been with the two of you tonight you should be asking me which of the two of you was the better, didn't they teach you anything at your undoubtedly expensive school?" Anya said with a twinkle in her eye.

"So there have only been the two of us tonight?"

"I'm afraid so. Though I have to say I've been tempted by one or two of your friends. Last time I was at a party here I had what the solicitors call 'intimate relations' with the groom, an usher, the boyfriend of one of the bridesmaids and also my future husband. Now that was a party. But I was young and fit then."

He pulled her towards him and grinned. "You're fun. I never liked step-mother Gillian, a sour faced, miserable treasure hunter. It looks like she'll get her divorce now, apparently there were security cameras in Dad's office. Everyone's talking about it."

"Cameras? Absolutely perfect." Anya couldn't have hoped for more.

"Now he'll get his divorce from that money-grabbing cow."

"She probably speaks highly of you too."

"I doubt it. But I think I understand now why they all speak so highly of you."

"They?"

"Uncle John and Uncle David. They introduced me to the legend of 'The Highly Unsuitable Girl' years ago."

Anya was remembering her times with John and David when she felt a gentle tap on her shoulder. She turned round to face Geoff.

"I think I deserve one dance at least."

Matthew relinquished his hold on Anya and, responding to his uncle's hint, left them to it.

"Hello Geoff."

"Hello Anya. May I have the pleasure of this dance?"

She had always loved it when Geoff played the old-fashioned romancer but he looked so tired she suggested they sit this one out and she let him lead her away from the dance floor to the bar which was surprisingly empty.

"Ah bar stools." Geoff smiled and Anya returned to smile at their shared memories.

Even if he had been a bit old-fashioned in his views on marriage that had hardly been his fault. He may have been a bit self-centred but he had also been the kindest most generous man she had known. He had been arrogant and selfish at times, but then all men had been in the 1960s and 1970s, that had been their upbringing whatever their class. And she had never found anyone since who could make her feel as he had done when making love. Their marriage had ended because of circumstances, not because she hadn't loved him or, she believed, because he hadn't loved her.

"How are you Geoff?" He knew she was asking after far more than his health.

"Oh. You know." She realised he wasn't going to tell her anything so she guessed quite a bit. He was disappointed with himself for giving in to his mother, he was disappointed with his marriage and what he had made of his life. He had missed her. These things she knew so she spoke for them both.

"I have missed you Geoff. You honestly haven't been far from my thoughts all these years. We were good for each other, we should have stuck to it shouldn't we?"

"If it weren't for the children I'd agree with you but they really have made it all worthwhile."

She watched his face as he told her of Geoffrey Junior, who he called Gezza, of Rosemary and of James. She realised how proud he was of them. He talked about how much he enjoyed talking to 10 years old Jimmy about computers, 'he can't believe they were around when I was at university all those years ago'; how good 13 year old Gezza was at cricket, 'looking forward to facing proper bowling now he's not at prep school any more'; how pretty 12 year old Rose could be 'at least when she smiles which isn't often enough'. "They're lovely children Anya, interesting, inquisitive and fair-minded. I'm so lucky to be their father."

They sat in comfortable silence for a few minutes before Geoff spoke rather tentatively. "I sometimes wonder what they would have been like if you had been their mother, not Fiona. We would have had wonderful children together."

"If only."

"Yes, Anya, my dear sweet beautiful Anya, if only." He lifted her hand, gently turned it over, and kissed her palm in a gesture she remembered so well and which always raised the fine hairs on the back of her neck. They sat, each with memories which overlapped so considerably, occasionally catching each other's eye and smiling. Eventually, though neither wanted the time to end, Geoff put his still half full glass down on the bar. "I must go but I can't tell you how wonderful it's been to see you."

She watched him walk back to the other three women in his life, his mother, his sister and his wife, and was overwhelmed with sadness. It was time to leave.

"Did you have a good evening?" Geoff asked his mother as he walked her to her taxi a few minutes later.

"Wonderful. Though I suspect Tim has had a bit of a setback to his budding political career."

"Tim? What's he been up to?"

"He was captured *in flagrante delicto* on the new security cameras. You know the ones Sir Christopher insisted should be installed around the club house."

"Yes? Oh dear. How unfortunate." Geoff sounded anything but sympathetic.

"It was great fun actually."

"You mean you watched? While Tim…"

"…had sex. Of course. Sir Christopher thought I might be interested. Oh don't be such a prude Geoffrey. Sometimes I wonder how on earth your father and I managed to produce you. Sometimes you are just so unbelievably boring."

He wanted to say he hadn't been boring or prudish when he had been with Anya and that it was only because of her prising them apart that he had changed. Instead he simply asked, rather surprised, "You watched Tim have sex?"

"Of course. The more witnesses the better Sir Christopher said. I watched with Gill and…"

"Gill? She watched her husband? That's obscene." As he said it he remembered the times in Liverpool when he had watched as Anya had had sex with other men.

Probably. But it wasn't just any other woman you know."

Geoff realised his mother wanted him to pursue Tim's partner's identity but he wasn't going to humour her. He knew who it would have been. He hoped his mother didn't see his smile.

"It'll mean another divorce but I suppose that's what the ghastly woman has been angling for ever since she married him."

"Before. She was a gold digger, only ever after his money."

"Still, although it will have undoubtedly cost him hundreds of thousands of pounds Tim did seem to enjoy this evening's experience."

Geoff helped his mother into the taxi. As he was about to close the door he spoke, as if as an afterthought. "Strange, I could have sworn I saw Anya here tonight."

"Anya?" His mother answered as if she was unsure to whom her son was referring. "Did you dear?" Geoff thought that sometimes butter wouldn't melt in her mouth. "So did I…" She left a dramatic pause before triumphantly completing the sentence "… on camera." Kathleen squeezed his arm. "Such an unsuitable girl. You were well rid of her."

"Oh Anya." He whispered, almost softly enough for his mother not to hear.

"And apparently she was intimate with Matthew in the professional's hut, or so at least three people have told me, including Esme."

Geoff wasn't listening to his mother. He was trying not to let her see his smile, she would never have understood. "Matt?" he asked, as he knew it would be expected of him.

"Oh yes. That girl would never do things by halves."

Geoffrey had no difficulty in believing what his mother was

saying. He said nothing. He could neither have hidden nor explained his feelings of joy.

"Tim? It's Geoff. Did she give you a phone number?" There was no need to explain who he was talking about.

"No. She did not."

Geoff didn't hear the anger in Tim's response. "Do you think she gave it to Matt?"

"I very much doubt it. I believe they were occupied with other things than exchanging phone numbers."

"How can we get in touch with her?"

"I have absolutely no idea."

"But we want to, contact her I mean, don't we?" Geoff still hadn't picked up on the coldness in Tim's tone.

"Of course we do but, I suspect, for very different reasons. She didn't come back to see you Geoff, she came to cause me trouble."

"And did she? Cause you trouble I mean?"

"You know she bloody did. She's cost me the best part of half a million. The bitch seduced me."

"Please don't call her a bitch Tim," Geoff spoke in what Tim thought was an annoyingly calm voice.

"I'll call her a bitch because that is what she was, a bitch on heat, she went to that party with the sole aim of screwing me."

"She probably had her reasons."

"They'd better be bloody good ones. Somehow I don't think they included love and respect for me."

"I don't think love or respect have ever dictated who she screwed."

"Well she's well and truly screwed me."

"Do you know where she lives?"

"No but no doubt Gillian's solicitors will be trying to find her as soon as they're back from this bloody holiday."

Geoff was smiling as he slowly replaced the receiver.

Chapter 13: Opportunities

Barbados, December 1993

"Have you everything you need?"

"I think so, thank you." Anya handed her empty champagne glass to the stewardess. It was her first trip on Concorde and she had already decided it was the only way to fly.

The captain's voice came over the intercom, the stewardess demonstrated the life jackets and the remarkably small plane taxied until it reached the end of the runway where it turned and accelerated at such a rate that Anya was forced back into the comfortable grey leather seat. The angle of the plane changed sharply and the engines were horribly noisy as they strained to lift the fully laden plane into the air. Anya dug her finger nails into the palms of her hands as she listened to the changing engine noises. It was only twenty minutes into the flight with the plane flying level that Anya could relax and enjoy the sheer luxury of being a passenger on the most prestigious plane in the world.

Barbados, again, just a few days under a year since her previous visit and in that time her life had changed beyond recognition.

The morning after the New Year ball Anya had phoned the number Peter had given her.

"I think you'll have grounds to divorce me." She said after they had politely wished each other a Happy New Year. All Peter said was 'Thank you. Was it Tim or Geoff?"

"Tim." She didn't tell him about Matt, perhaps he'd find out anyway. It wasn't that she was ashamed, it was simply that, with hindsight, she felt she had gone a too far.

A week later she read the reports in the newspaper and felt that the officers of the golf club must have called in a large number of favours to reduce the impact of the report. There were two pages of pictures of the contented, complacent, great and good of the area. She read the report carefully but there was no mention whatsoever of any misbehaviour. The day after she read the highly selective report in the newspaper she received a phone call from Stuart Benthall.

In the years since he had dealt with her divorce from Geoff she had put a great deal of work through his firm. He had always been grateful and credited her with making his career a success.

"I've had a letter from Eric Atherton asking if we are still in contact with you."

"Are you?"

"If you want us to be."

"Oh I think so. Somebody else's divorce this time, though mine will be hot on its heels."

"I'm so sorry to hear that."

"Don't be."

In early February she received the papers from Peter's family solicitor citing her adultery with Tim Cross on 31st December 1992 as the reason for the irreconcilable differences that would end their marriage. She drank half a bottle of champagne before signing where they had helpfully marked with a pencil cross and sending them back by return of post.

She and Peter spoke every week as they divided up those things they had accumulated in their sixteen years together. There was no argument about records and tapes, about the glasses, the plates or the furniture. 'Have what you want.' Peter had said, 'Jenny has most of what we need.' He could not realise how much that hurt but she said nothing. Even though they didn't love each other, and probably never had, she couldn't help feeling some sadness at what might have been. It occurred to her during one of their phone calls that she would probably never see him again.

She had decided, as she drove back from the Golf Club in the early hours of 1993, that if Tim should contact her she would say no to whatever he suggested so when she received the first phone call she put up with his anger in silence and just said 'No Tim, whatever you want the answer is no.' He phoned her frequently. Her answer was always the same and he became less and less patient with her.

"No Tim. I don't want to see you."

"You used me."

"What's it like the boot being on the other foot?"

She had thought that divorce and very public humiliation would break his insufferable self-confidence but that seemed undented. Perhaps, she thought, repeatedly denying him what he wanted would help burst the bubble of his ego. She knew he wanted her and she knew that through his life he had always got what he wanted. She was determined that, this time, he wouldn't.

The house that Anya had always thought of as Peter's parents' home was put on the market and, when it sold within days, she moved into one of her properties that was conveniently vacant. She spent time renovating, decorating, gardening but all the time looking to the future. She would get settled in her new house, and then, once the divorce was finalised, she could find something to do with the rest of her life. At 43 she wasn't too old to start again.

1994 would be the beginning of her new life and she had decided to say goodbye to the old one with Christmas in Barbados but she knew from the first evening it had been a mistake to return.

She nearly left at the end of the first week, getting as far as phoning American Express, but since no flights were available she stayed making the effort to enjoy the sun and the pampering of the always attentive staff. She found herself hating the false jollity of the Christmas period and welcomed in the New Year alone in her room, her mind never far from 'this time last year'. She found herself thinking not of Matt or Tim, but of Geoff, picturing him sitting at a table in the Golf Club with Kathleen and Fiona perhaps remembering the year before.

Thoughts of Vincent Albert Cave frequently crossed her mind and just as frequently she managed to ignore them. Maybe he still lived on the island but she persuaded herself that it was likely he had left years before, perhaps, he had only been here for a few months. She wouldn't know what to say to him even if she found him. 'Hello, I'm your niece. Your sister died years ago and for all those years I thought you had raped her and were my father. Did you? Are you? Or did your father rape her and abuse you and that's why you left?' No. She didn't want to find him because she wouldn't be able to ask the only questions that mattered.

After midnight on New Year's night she left her room and walked along the beach looking up at the crowded bars and restaurants. She returned through the bar, looking at her fellow guests objectively, they would all have fitted in with the Golf Club Crowd. She felt apart from them, she wasn't one of them and never could be.

After breakfast on the day before her flight she asked for a hire car. 'One of those childish cars with no roof and no doors, but automatic please'. The open-topped moke was probably more appropriate for people half her age but she felt it would help her recapture something of the optimism she had felt the year before.

"Thank you Pearson." She said to the concierge as ten minutes later he jumped out of the car and helped her negotiate the high sill into the driving seat. She turned the key, pushed the gear lever into drive and headed towards the open road.

She took the first turning off the main highway and headed into the centre of the island and entered another world. The roads were more pothole than tarmac; the vegetation, spreading over the road sides so she could reach out her hand and touch it, was lush and exotic. The tropical air buffeted her face and tangled her hair, she wished she had escaped earlier from the wealth and privilege that dominated West Coast life. As she passed through groups of houses too small to be called villages she waved at the men working on the road side or drinking in the rum shacks. She drove up steep inclines and down even steeper ones. She felt free and relaxed, the open car enabling her to talk to the people she passed, explaining more than once that no thank you, she didn't need directions, she wasn't lost, she was enjoying exploring their lovely island.

As she drove up a particularly steep and rutted hill, the ocean far below here to her right, she remembered it from a site-seeing tour she had taken the previous year. She knew it would be worth the effort to reach the top because she remembered the view and a magnificent avenue of ancient mahogany trees. When she reached the top she patted the steering well, elatedly congratulating the little car. She clambered inelegantly out and walked down the mahogany avenue.

The next day she would be back in England, cold and alone, but she had this one afternoon to soak up the exoticism, the beauty and the warmth of the island. She hadn't walked far when she saw a sign 'Abbey Open to the Public'. She turned down the drive to find not an abbey but a Dutch looking house. She could see the remains of a windmill and buildings with chimneys. It took her a few moments to realise it must have been a sugar plantation. She paid her entrance fee and walked around the ground floor imagining the differences between the lives of the people who had lived in these well-furnished and richly ornamented rooms and those of the people who had worked to earn them the money that made that life possible. She shrugged and tried to ignore the images that streamed through her overactive imagination of the system of slavery that had made estates such as this, and the island, what it was.

She stood for several minutes looking at a large map of the island hanging on a corridor wall. It was a while before she realised her head was tilted to one side as, on this map, north was to the left not at the top and without realising it she had moved to obtain the familiar triangular shape of the island.

"Things have changed a bit since then." An elderly gentleman was standing next to her.

"Indeed." She answered in a noncommittal manner. She wasn't sure she was in the mood for conversation but she gave him polite attention as he pointed out where the Abbey was on the island, the extent of the original plantation and various other landmarks.

"Let me show you this." He moved into the room that appeared to be a library and pointed to a large diagram of a family tree. "Many interesting people have lived in this house."

Anya felt the goose pimples rising on her arms and spreading down to her legs as she saw, many times through the generations, the name 'Cave'.

"So many called Cave." She commented tentatively, wondering where this conversation would lead.

"My name is Cave and that," he pointed to a name high up on the chart, "is my great great grandfather."

She held back from telling this old man her name, instead opting for a non-committal "It's a big family then?" Her attention was fierce she listened to him explaining the history of the house with a well-rehearsed and obviously frequently told tale of romantic intrigue, fortunes made and lost, murder and questionable lines of inheritance.

"I've taken far too much of your time Mrs…?" He said as his story came to its conclusion.

"Funnily enough my name is Cave." She said as lightly as she could.

"There are a great many of us around the world." He replied. "Where is it you come from?"

"Merseyside, in England. My grandfather was Albert Cave." She paused before adding tentatively "I have an uncle, Vincent Cave."

"We originally came from Somerset so I can't see there is a connection. But you mustn't let our lack of family connection stop you enjoying my home. Stay as long as you like."

She watched the old man walk back through the house, no doubt to give such a welcome to another visitor. She walked out into a courtyard and sat under a tree which seemed so old that Mr Cave's great great grandfather must have sat underneath it canopy.

She envied Mr Cave's sense of possession and belonging. She had never put down roots. In her mind she listed the places she had lived, counting on her fingers; Tennyson Street, Hall, the flat in Liverpool, The Beeches with Geoff, the cottage, the ghastly flat, Peter's parents' house and now another country cottage. She decided that she needed somewhere to call hers where she could happily live for the rest of her life.

It was some time before she walked back through the overgrown gardens and down the mahogany avenue awed by the fact that she had met the great great grandson of a man who would have walked under these trees when they were young, perhaps had even had them planted. She reached the car and sat for a long time, staring at the coast stretching into the distance far below her. She had no idea who her father was, let alone her great great grandfather. And there would never be another generation below her on any family tree.

Eventually she pulled herself together and started the car, driving back down the steep and rutted track she followed the road more or less in the direction she had come, but her mind wasn't on the route, her head was filled with the need to find a home that could mean as much to her as the Abbey meant to that old man.

She soon realised she had missed the turning back to the west coast and she had no idea where she was. She stopped the car and looked at the map. None of it made sense, none of the roads seemed to be where they ought to be. She drove off eventually reaching a small town which, in contrast to the tiny hamlets in the middle of the island, was deserted. She could recognise no names on the signpost at a junction so chose the wider of the roads. She was following the coast with steep, wooded hills to her right and the Atlantic to her left. It was rugged, wild and beautiful.

She parked under a clump of pine trees at a place where she could access the beach. It stretched north and south as far as she could see, and it was completely deserted. She understood why these beautiful sands were deserted when every scrap of sand on the west coast was covered in sun loungers as she watched the waves rolling in from the thousands of miles of Atlantic Ocean and relentlessly crashing over the low rocks at tide level. No one could swim in this sea so there would be no tourists, no hotels or resort developments. This wildness would remain. She loved it.

She watched the breakers crashing onto the rocks just off-shore, aware that the only noise was of wind and sea. Her optimism began to return; she would find somewhere to call home, something would happen to change her life and she would, one day, be settled and content. She walked slowly up the beach, she had no idea for how long or how far, she just knew that she was happy for the first time since she had boarded the flight three weeks before. It wasn't that she didn't enjoy the luxury that her money allowed it was just that she knew it could never be enough.

She turned back towards where she had parked the car and felt a moment's panic as she saw everything wreathed in a mist of spray. She had no idea where the car was, she had no idea how long it would take her to get back to it. The sun was sinking behind the hills and she knew it would be dark very quickly. For an instant she wished she was safely sitting in the bar at the hotel watching the sun going down, being served a second rum punch by the perfectly trained waiters and listening to the far gentler waves that lapped the sandy beaches of the Caribbean coast.

She was walking into the wind, shivering, not from cold for it was never cold on the island, but from anxiety. She followed her footsteps in the sand as the visibility grew worse in the gathering gloom of evening. Eventually she saw, with relief, her footprints leading from the road. Her knees folded and she found herself on the ground, sobbing.

'Stupid woman,' she eventually told herself, 'pull yourself together.' She stood up, dusted the sand from her legs and walked up the slight cliff to the car.

She swung herself over the rigid bodywork of the moke and settled into the driving seat trying to turn the headlights on. She fiddled with knobs and pressed switches up and down until light burst from the front of the car. "Stupid woman." She repeated, out loud. She couldn't drive back across the island, in the dark she would soon get lost in the maze of unlit roads with so many junctions and so few useful signposts. She would have to find somewhere to stay without having to drive too far.

She edged the car forward, driving carefully southwards. There was no other traffic, no cars, no vans, not even the pedestrians that crowded the roads of the other coast at dusk. Visibility was limited even with the headlights on full beam and she only just saw the sharp right turn in time. She felt as though she was driving in a tunnel, she had no sense of the angle at which she was climbing, only that the engine struggled. She was travelling so slowly she saw another bend in good time, "Lucky." She said to herself as it was a sharp bend and there appeared to be a steep drop to her left. She was still climbing. She was concentrating so hard on keeping to the road and avoiding the worst of the potholes that she let out an involuntary scream when what looked like two small children ran across the road in front of her. The car stalled as it skidded to a halt.

"Monkeys you stupid woman. Monkeys." She started the car again, offering a silent thank you to no one in particular when the engine caught.

"Stop it. Get a grip.' She realised she was talking aloud.

She followed the road as it turned to the left and climbed. She had no idea where she was heading but she finally saw lights ahead. It had seemed like an hour since she had climbed into the car but it could have been no more than five minutes.

She stopped by a roadside rum shack, ridiculously relieved to see signs of civilisation.

"You lost madam?" It was a polite enquiry from the man sipping beer from a brown bottle.

"I'm afraid so."

"It's a bit late to be on the road." His companion joined in the conversation.

"I think I need to find a hotel. Is there one nearby?"

"Lucky you find yourself here madam, very good places to stay in Bathsheba." Anya was just able to make out his words spoken in broad Bajun.

"Can you direct me?"

The first man stood up and gave what seemed to be complex directions and, since he spoke quickly, she caught barely half of them. She didn't even hear the name of the hotel. It was obvious, though, that she should turn off the road and head downhill again.

It was the steepest slope she had driven all day, steeper even than the one down from the mahogany avenue, she only just made the right turn at the bottom. She turned left at a T junction and the road then turned sharply to the right again. It was pitch black, her headlights barely showed her the road let alone what that road was passing through, she had no idea whether it was a town, a village or open country. Shapes loomed in the darkness, everything eerily out of focus in the spray mist. The road turned upwards again and then to the right. She could hear waves and surf crashing against rocks but she had no idea whether the noise was to her right, her left, behind her or ahead. She felt as though she had been driving round in a circle and wondered whether she would be pleased or embarrassed to come across the two men outside the rum shack.

The faded sign with an arrow pointing to the left and the single word 'Hotel' would have been very easy to miss. She turned the steering wheel and headed down an even narrower road, avoiding vast potholes wondering whether the place could still be in business. She pulled into the car park relieved that there were lights on and the hotel appeared to be open. She grabbed her handbag and climbed out of the car.

"I'm afraid I've got into a bit of a problem." Anya spoke to the woman behind the bar with as much dignity as she could muster, aware that she wore only shorts and a t-shirt and had no luggage.

The woman said something which Anya thought must be "You're lost." It didn't sound like a question.

"Not really. I think I know where I am it's just that I can't get back to my hotel tonight." She was determined not to admit how stupid she had been.

"Where are you staying?" Anya named the resort, aware that its name probably meant that her bill here would be doubled.

"You could get a cab if there was one. But there isn't one this side. I could phone your resort and they could send a car over but the phone not working."

"There must be a phone nearby."

"Mr Henderson, he got a phone. You could ask him. But he away."

Anya was wondering if the woman was being deliberately unhelpful when she added "Mr Henderson's man. He could drive you back."

Anya knew that that would have been the sensible thing to do, if allowing oneself to be driven by a stranger across the pitch dark island was in any way sensible. "How would he get back?"

"He'd manage."

If she allowed Mr Henderson's man to drive her back she could be back in her room in less than an hour, she could shower, dress for dinner, be back in her known world. It would have been the sensible thing to do. Anya looked around at the run down hotel and a thought was planted in her mind. Why would she want to do the sensible thing?

"Thank you for your suggestions but I just need to stay here tonight, if I may?"

The woman nodded. "You may." Then her tone softened. "You're lucky you found your way to Edna's Place."

"It certainly was more by luck than judgement." Anya responded to the woman's change of tone. "There were two men up on the main road, they tried to direct me here but I'm afraid I couldn't really understand what they said."

"It takes a few years to get used to the Bajan way of talking. I still have difficulty and I've been on the island for years."

"Are you Edna? You said this is called Edna's Place."

"Oh no dear, Edna died before the war but this was her hotel for so many years it will never be anything but 'Edna's Place'. It's officially 'Fishermen Rock' but no one local calls it that. You can call me Miriam."

The way she phrased it made Anya think that her name wasn't really Miriam she just liked to be called that.

"Anya Cave." She formally shook hands with the older woman.

"How do you do Anya Cave? Cave, that's a good Barbados name. Have you family on the island?"

She could have said 'I've never looked into it.' Or 'Maybe, do you happen to know a 57 year old man called Vincent Albert Cave?' But if she said that she would have so much more explaining to do. "Not that I know of." It seemed the simplest answer to give.

"Are you here with anyone?"

Anya was relieved the conversation had moved on.

"No. There's just me."

"I'll show you up to your room then."

Anya followed Miriam up a flight of dimly lit but wide stairs which would once have been elegant. The feeling that she was on 1930s film set was reinforced by the black and white prints of film stars that lined the walls of the corridor on the first floor. She recognised Humphrey Bogart and Lauren Bacall. They seemed absolutely at home.

"The best room in the house." Miriam opened a door and switched on a light.

"It's beautiful." Anya looked around the room taking in the quality of the furnishings, the generously sized bed, the large window covered by a mosquito screen. She could see out across a narrow balcony to the sea where the moon was just rising above the horizon to be reflected in the waves. "It's absolutely beautiful."

"Come down when you're ready."

"I've no other clothes."

"No problem. No other guests." Miriam's laugh was gentle as she closed the door behind her.

Anya stared out into the dark and watched the moon grow smaller as it climbed in the sky. Apart from its reflection on the wave tips everything was black. She listened to the surf, the waves alone broke the silence. There was no piped music, no falsetto laughter from a bar, no chattering of frogs, nothing. Pure, natural, peaceful, the contrast with where she had spent the past three weeks could not have been starker. She sat for more than an hour staring out at the dark sea, watching the moon's reflection move across the waves. England seemed a very long way away.

The dinner Miriam cooked was simple but excellent. A dish of the best soup she had tasted, 'spicy coconut' was the answer when she asked what it was, was followed by a simple plate of grilled fish with chips. But the fish was so fresh it must have been swimming in the ocean a few hours before and the chips tasted of potato.

"Thank you Miriam, that's the best meal I've had on the island."

"I should think so. You get fancy food over there but it won't be fresh and won't be cooked honestly."

Anya was relaxed after a whole bottle of wine and the excellent food.

"I don't mean to pry but why aren't you full? It's Christmas. Every hotel is packed."

"We were full last Christmas. But this year I didn't want guests." Anya, sensing a tragedy, waited for the woman to speak, or not, as she wished. Eventually Miriam began to talk. She told Anya how she and her husband Gary had moved from the north of England to the island in the 60s, how they had made a good living with a bar in the city.

"You had a bar in Bridgetown? I know this is a silly question but did you ever come across a man called Vincent Cave?"

"Lots of Caves but not a Vincent that I can remember, mind you we only knew nick names of the regulars and the non-regulars, well, we never knew their names at all. Why do you ask?"

"No reason. What happened to the bar?"

"We should have stayed there, we knew what we were about there, but we decided to try our hand at running a hotel. It seemed such a good idea at the time." Miriam spoke with so much regret Anya knew it could only have been a disastrous decision. "We sold the bar and put all our money into this place, we made it so nice. We knew about bars, we'd run a pub in Leeds for years, but we had no idea about hotels. We didn't listen when people said 'only do what you know'. We should have."

"But it's a lovely hotel." Anya hoped her words indicated the sympathy she was feeling. "What I've seen of it anyway."

"We thought we'd got everything right, nothing stinted, nothing second rate."

"Anyone can see that." Anya felt she needed to say something by way of sympathetic encouragement.

"We opened two years ago at Christmas. We had such fun, there was a good crowd of guests, everyone joined in. We had a great time. It's not the décor or the facilities that make a good hotel, it's the staff and the guests. Nice guests, guests who understand and are sympathetic, they are the ones that really make a good hotel."

Miriam stood up and walked to the bar, bringing back another bottle of wine.

"On the house." She filled the two glasses before continuing. "Then the bills started piling up. We'd been full but the place took more to run than even a full house of guests bought in. The building work and redecoration had taken all our savings. We had nothing to fall back on." She paused and Anya was shocked to hear the note of hysteria in Miriam's voice. "That's funny." Anya wondered why that was funny. Or sad. She realised Miriam had tears sliding down her cheeks. "He jumped, last spring. He didn't tell me what he was going to do he just went ahead and jumped. He couldn't stand the failure, the bills, the not having anything anymore. You haven't seen this place in the daylight have you? It's beautiful, so beautiful, but there's no beach, just rocks. Just rocks and sea. And it's quite a way down."

Anya wondered why Miriam was torturing herself in this way.

"I'm so sorry."

"Why would you be sorry? You didn't know him. You don't know me."

"No. But I don't have to know either of you to be able to sympathise do I?"

"I can't take any money." Miriam changed the subject, suddenly business like. "I have no licence. I'm not a hotel any more. You can only stay here tonight as my personal guest."

"Is there nothing I can do?"

"You can enjoy my food, you can sleep well in one of my rooms and you can take away good memories of this place."

When Anya woke the next morning her first thought was that she had slept through, normally she woke at least once in the night. The sky was a dark pink as the sun, still below the horizon, caught the clouds. The colour spread to fill her window and then become pale as the light became stronger. She quickly showered and dressed, venturing out of her room, down the stairs, past the table where she and Miriam had talked long into the night and shared more wine than she cared to remember, out through the open door into the garden. It was very quiet, last night's wind now died down, the sea quieter, the waves barely covering the rocks. She looked up at the roof and then down towards the rocks again, she shuddered, Gary must have been really desperate to jump.

She stood watching a lone fisherman dive into the sea and swim to his boat. After a few minutes the engine crackled into life and the boat headed out to sea. She felt a moment's jealousy of a life so simple, so free of complications. The thought that had first occurred the previous night was taking shape. She climbed back up the rough steps cut in the low coral stone cliff to the hotel patio where Miriam was laying a table with breakfast things.

"May I join you again?" Miriam seemed overly polite, perhaps she felt she had given too much of herself away the previous night.

"Please do. I'd like to talk."

"You sit down here and I'll bring coffee."

Anya sat and watched the fishing boat get smaller as it headed for the horizon. His existence wouldn't be as simple as she had imagined. The fisherman would have a woman or two in his life, children, money problems. Perhaps there was no such thing as a simple life.

"Coffee, juice, fruit salad and fresh bread, cold meats, a bit of smoked fish. Will that do?"

"Brilliant."

As they sat companionably together helping themselves to the varied array of good food Anya felt like she and Miriam were friends. It was a strange experience, she had never been friends with a woman before.

"Do you believe in Fate Miriam?"

"Fate?" Miriam asked blankly.

"You know that force that makes opportunity and inclination coincide in time and place to make life's decisions for you." Anya was quite pleased with her turn of phrase though she felt it must be a quotation from somewhere.

"I've never thought about it."

"I have and I think it was Fate that gave me the idea of hiring a car and driving to the abbey and to this coast, Fate made me spend too long walking along the beach, Fate led me to Edna's Place."

"That's a pretty busy Fate you had." Miriam was obviously wondering what it was that Anya Cave had in mind.

"I would like to buy your hotel."

Miriam frowned, she was not sure how she should react to what seemed like a silly suggestion.

"Although it doesn't look like it I'm quite well off."

Miriam gave no indication of her feelings, she wasn't sure what they were.

"I would get lawyers to sort out any problems, sort out all the licences, permits and stuff. You could stay on, I'd pay you a salary. Or we could be partners? Which would you prefer? Or Neither? I'm going too fast? I always go too fast. Sorry."

Miriam said nothing as she poured them both another cup of coffee.

"We'd get a proper valuation? You'd pay the proper rate?"

"Of course."

"I could stay here? Live here?"

"Run the place the way you want to."

"Get staff?"

"Whoever you want."

"And you'd pay me to do that?"

"Of course. If you wanted we could sort out a profit sharing deal."

"There'll be problems you know."

"Nothing a good lawyer can't sort out. I have great faith in lawyers."

"They're expensive."

"I have the resources."

"There's lots of debts, lots of money outstanding."

"I'll clear them."

"You've only seen the place for a few hours."

"I've seen all I need to see." Anya wouldn't tell Miriam that she had never had to look at any property twice before knowing it was a good buy.

"You sure about this?"

"Absolutely positive. Shall we finish breakfast? I'll drive us back to my hotel where I'll change, then we'll drive into the city and start the ball rolling. Willing seller and willing buyer, it shouldn't be too much of a problem.

Not many meetings in the city had been required for Anya and Miriam to agree a price which Anya thought too little and Miriam thought too much and as soon as the contracts were finalised Anya threw herself enthusiastically into learning about the hotel. She believed running a business would be much the same whatever and wherever it was but she soon appreciated how little she knew about the hospitality industry. Miriam answered her questions with a clarity and patience that made Anya think she should have been a teacher but every answer simply told Anya how much more she had to learn.

When the subject of the Cave family came up Miriam admitted to knowing many Caves, they were in all walks of life and in all professions on the island, but no Vincent Albert Cave. "I'll look into it one day," Anya said unconvincingly, "when I have more time."

Every evening, as she and Miriam shared a simple meal and a bottle of wine, she felt more strongly that she had found where she wanted to be and what she wanted to do. The more Anya got to know Miriam the more she liked and trusted her.

She never once wondered what Miriam thought of her.

Anya finally returned to England on the last Sunday of February. As Concorde banked sharply to the left and headed back across the Atlantic, she held onto her champagne and took a last look at the lights of the island.

She couldn't wait to be back.

Chapter 14: Reunions

Kent, March 1995

"Anya?"

"Who is this?" Anya had just returned from her latest trip to Fishermen Rock and she was concentrating on the mountain of post she had to deal with. Her assistant, Gemma, had ensured bills were paid, but there was still much she had to deal with after a month away in Barbados.

"Who is this?"

"David." The voice was vaguely familiar though she couldn't think of anyone named David who might be phoning her.

"David?"

"David George. I first met you on Charing Cross Station about 25 years ago. I know it was a long time ago but I had rather hoped you might remember me."

"Of course I remember you Dave." She should have recognised him. "How are you?"

"Old and respectable I'm afraid so I've become David."

"Do you still see John?"

"Not a lot, we all get together every now and again with the families, you know how it is."

"No David. I don't." Feeling cross with herself for being short she asked quickly, "Sorry David, I've just got off a long flight and I'm not thinking straight." That was true, she was always tired after the flight, now twice as long since Concorde no longer flew, and switching back to England from the Caribbean usually took her several days.

"That's OK. I think I understand though I'm not what you'd call a Yuppie Jetsetter myself."

"How's Tim? Do you still see him? Has he forgiven me for the Golf Club?" She hadn't meant to ask about Tim, it just somehow seemed safer than asking about Geoff.

"He's doing fine. You know Tim, he's been putting all his energy into making even more money to make up for the vast amount he had to pay Gillian. By the way, well done about that, we'd all been trying to get them apart for years. She really wasn't any good for him."

"So Esme said. Lovely as it is to hear from you David…"

"… why am I phoning you?"

"And how did you track me down. I didn't think anyone knew where I was."

"Well it wasn't difficult. I knew your maiden name, remember, and your date of birth and Anya Cave is not that usual a name."

"But why?"

"It's Geoff."

It was an answer Anya had not expected. "Geoff?" She felt the shivers of goose bumps course through her body, along her arms, even down her legs. She had a premonition of fear.

"He's ill."

"How ill?"

"Very."

"He was fine last year. He was fine at the Golf Club Ball." She was surprised to hear the panic in her voice.

"No he wasn't Anya, and that was over two years ago. He hadn't been feeling well for a long time but he didn't go to see a doctor until the autumn of '92. He was already having treatment at the time of your Ball and it was in and out of hospital all of '93. There came a point last year when he said the treatment had to stop. It was making him feel dreadful and he knew it was only postponing things. He knew the doctors weren't going to be able to stop the inevitable."

"The inevitable?"

"I'm afraid so."

"Oh God Dave. Let me sit down. I'm sorry. I've no right to be so upset."

"Perhaps you still care for him Anya? He certainly has never stopped caring about you."

"No?" Anya sounded sceptical but David's words only reinforced what she had felt when they had sat so comfortably together at the Golf Club bar. "What about Fiona?"

"She buggered off a year or so ago, as soon as it started being difficult for Geoff. She really was, is, a cow. They were never happy you know, she always did her best to make his life miserable. He told me she hated sex, she lay there frigid and immobile."

"Do I want to know this?"

"I think you need to."

"OK." Anya wondered why.

"You need to know she's gay, always has been apparently. She only went along with her mother's plan to marry Geoff for respectability and to have a child. She told him humans were like dogs, females should be bred at least once or their temperament was unsound. She said three litters was the optimum for dogs that's why she had three children."

"God that sounds awful!"

"She told Geoff that she had married him only to get her own back at him for taking her virginity all those years ago. She only let him make love, if that's what you could call it, when she wanted a child. Then, when it was obvious Geoff was ill, she gave up any pretence. She told him only women were worth caring about and buggered off with her girlfriend."

A multitude of scenes ran through Anya's head. She had always egged Geoff on, it was she who had made him break down the citadel that had been Fiona's virginity, it was her fault she had hated him so much. It was her fault he had had all those years in a loveless and hateful marriage. "He hadn't guessed?"

"He said it had never occurred to him. He just thought she was a little cold, but then he said anyone would seem cold after you."

Anya had no idea what to say so she resorted to platitudes. "How very sad, it must be incredibly difficult for the children."

"Very."

"Did Fiona know how ill Geoff was when she 'buggered off' as you put it?"

"Oh yes. She knew. It's probably what made her go. She wasn't about to look after Geoff on his sickbed. I don't think he was too upset, except for what it did to the children. You know how cruel kids can be and the fact that their mum went off with another woman made it particularly difficult for them at school."

"It's my fault Dave."

"It's not your fault. How could it be your fault?"

"Who was the woman?"

"One of her horsey friends. Geoff thought nothing of her spending so much time with her horses and other women with horses." David was choosing his words very carefully. "It never occurred to him that their friendship went a bit further than normal. Well it wouldn't would it?"

"Probably not."

"I have no idea why she couldn't hang on just a bit longer. They had a comfortable life together, her being married obviously wasn't ruining her other life and it is painfully obvious to all that Geoff doesn't have much longer."

"Perhaps she just got fed up with lying."

"I think she just was incapable of thinking about anyone but herself."

Anya knew the same could be said of her so she changed the subject abruptly, her voice harsher. "Would I be right in thinking you didn't go to all the trouble of finding me just to tell me Geoff is dying?"

"It's the children."

"What about the children?"

"They're not doing very well."

"How much do they know?"

"Pretty much everything, they're old enough to understand what's happening and that their dad isn't going to come out of hospital."

"I'm so sorry." It seemed a completely inadequate thing to say under the circumstances. She wished David would come to the point.

"I went to see him yesterday. He knows he won't be able to cope with, well, with organising things, for much longer. He asked me to find you."

"He asked you to find me?" She repeated, unsure of how that made her feel.

"He was worried I wouldn't be able to find you but I reassured him, we solicitors have our ways and means. He wants you to look after the children."

So that was it. "What?" Anya had heard him but was playing for time as some of the implications of his words sank in.

"When he's gone, he wants you to look after his children." David repeated the words he realised would mean so much."

"Me?" Anya was trying to take in what David was saying.

"It's an all-consuming worry for Geoff."

"What about Fiona? After all is said and done she is their mother."

"They were divorced before Christmas and she told me she wanted nothing to do with any of them as she they reminded her of what she called 'her false life'. She fought for custody in the court simply to hurt Geoff knowing that she would lose or, in case it looked like she was winning, she would withdraw at the last moment. It was horribly messy for Geoff and the kids, she just seemed to want to hurt everyone as much as possible." The tone of David's voice was so final Anya didn't press him.

"What about Margaret, or his mother, can't they look after the children?" As she spoke she realised the horror with which Geoff would view that scenario, he had spent so much of his life fighting his mother and elder sister. "Oh no, forget I said that, that couldn't possibly work."

"Can I come round? We can't talk about this over properly on the phone."

"Of course. Yes. Do." Anya was trying to take in what this phone call might do to her life.

"I'll bring my wife, if I may?"

"Of course, come to dinner, both of you. You obviously know the address. I'll see you both around seven."

"The eldest is another Geoffrey, though everybody calls him Gezza, he's nearly 16. That's him last year on his birthday." Linda and David were sitting in Anya's cosy drawing room, a photograph album on the table along with three wine glasses and a bottle. Linda pointed to a tall, rather self-conscious boy with glasses.

"He's not much like his father is he?" Anya looked at the photograph "He looks far too athletic."

"Fiona's genes I believe." Anya failed to read in Linda's tone what she thought of Fiona.

"And that's the daughter, Rose?" Anya pointed to a girl, also tall but standing in such a way as to give off the impression of sulkiness.

"That's Rosemary, Rose to everyone though she's trying to be Ros now. She thinks that's more grown up, she's 15 in July and full of it. She's gone a bit off the rails recently, she does exactly what she likes when she likes."

"Probably just like me at her age."

"I wondered whether you'd think that, you'd be far better at understanding her than her mother."

"Possibly."

"And this is the youngest." Linda pointed to another picture. A boy was sitting on his own, fondling the ears of a black labrador. "James, known as Jimmy, he's just 13. He's the sensitive one. Gezza is sporty and bossy, Rose is a rebel while James is a lovely boy, quiet and what we might once have called bookish but is now more 'computerish'. He works hard at school, reads a lot, enjoys working with computers which Geoff, of course, has loved. I think of the three James is coping least well with all this change, he bottles things up and takes everything to heart."

"You're fond of him."

"We're fond of them all. We have children of similar age, they come round and hang out together."

"When it suits them." David added.

"Even Rebellious Ros and Gorgeous Gezza?"

"We don't see as much of them as we do Jimmy," Linda's tone indicated disapproval of the elder siblings. "but then no one is very nice in their teens are they?"

"Surely Kathleen's clucking around her Geoffrey's brood." Anya wasn't afraid to let Linda know exactly what she felt about her ex-mother in law, though she had every reason to believe she would already know.

"She's been round at the house every day, she does her best but she's nearly 80 and has no idea how to cope with teenagers in the 1990s."

"She had no idea how to deal with teenagers in the '60s."

"They certainly don't like her very much and they take absolutely no notice of anything she tells them."

"She never did her very well with her own children, why should she do any better with Geoff's?"

"But what happens when Geoff's, well, when he's gone?" Anya didn't like euphemisms but she couldn't bring herself to say the words 'when Geoff's dead.'

"That's what he's scared about. He's accepted the fact that he hasn't got long to go and he's being very stoical about it. But he gets very agitated when he thinks of the children's future."

"Does Kathleen realise she won't be able to look after the children?"

"She thinks she's the only person who can but I think one day she will accept that she would be out of her depth."

"You mean that at the moment she thinks she will?"

"I'm afraid so. That's why Geoff asked me to call you."

Anya heard, but didn't take in fully, what David had said.

"But what about Margaret? Her children must be grown up and flown the nest by now?"

"Ah yes. Matthew and Maggie. Matt's in his final year at Durham and Maggie's teaching in Thailand of all places. We've never seen much of either of them."

"So why not Margaret? She must be ideal. The children must

know her, she must have the time on her hands." Anya pictured the prim, rather grim woman that she had watched at the Golf Club New Year Ball.

"Unfortunately she's her mother all over again. If you thought Kathleen was a control freak you should see Margaret as a mother. Nothing the children do is ever right. Ever. She criticises everyone and everything. She's not yet 50 yet she could be her mother's sister."

"But that's 50 going on 80." Linda joined in supporting of her husband's argument. "There was a family tea before Geoff went into hospital to which we were privileged to be invited, probably on Geoff's insistence. It was difficult to tell which was the mother and which the daughter, quite frightening really. Geoff's never liked her and he certainly wouldn't trust her to bring up his brood in the way he would want. Also, she drinks like a fish. Really, Anya, there are so many reasons why Margaret would be a disaster."

"So I'm the only one left?"

"Geoff asked me to talk to you. He says you're the best, the only, person he would trust to help them grow up without him. He told me 'she's the only one suitable'."

"Me? Suitable?"

"Ironic that isn't it."

Linda looked perplexed as Anya and David smiled at each other, aware that Geoff had carefully chosen his words. "He said you are the only person he could trust to bring them up as he would want them to be brought up."

"How's that?"

"With free spirits, confident, not afraid to be different, not afraid not to conform."

"Is that how he thinks of me?" She was touched.

"He always has. We talk about those early days sometimes. He told me how you'd fought against your upbringing to make something of yourself."

"I was lucky. I married money." She tried to laugh the compliment off.

"But you'd already made something of yourself before that."

"I was still considered a trifle unsuitable."

"Not by everyone."

"I've changed, you know, grown up. All that was many years ago and I'm a very different person now." She began to argue her case. She wasn't sure why she felt she had to.

"You didn't differ very much from everyone's expectations at the Golf Club." Linda was suddenly hostile. "I think I could just about understand Tim but why Matthew? Matthew was just a boy."

Anya bit back the response that he seemed a bit more than a boy at the time. He needed Linda to be on her side. "Tim and I have a long history."

"Have?" Linda asked pointedly.

"Had." Anya knew she should have spoken in the past tense. "You know I didn't want to come south when we graduated, Geoff rather tricked me into it, and I was very lonely. I needed a friend and Tim said he would help me in the seemingly permanent war with our mother-in-law. But he didn't, he left me to fight Kathleen alone because it was far more important to him to be acceptable to his clubs and associations. I don't think I've ever forgiven him.

"But why Matthew?"

"That was a mistake. I regretted it immediately afterwards. I should not have used him, even though he was actually the one that did the seducing."

"Are you really the sort of woman who can look after an adolescent boy? Gezza is not much younger than Matthew was."

Anya bit back the angry responses that immediately came to mind and spoke quietly and simply. "Matthew was a good two years older than Gezza is and probably a quantum leap more confident and experienced. He also had a bet with his friends, I believe Matthew won a great deal of money that night so it was hardly the seduction of an innocent. But honestly, if you don't think the relationship would be completely different were I to be in a position of responsibility, then I don't know why you're here."

"We're here because Geoff asked us to talk to you." Linda sounded defensive. "For some reason he trusts you."

"I think maybe you'll have to know me a bit better to understand that I do try to act appropriately according to the circumstances."

"I think perhaps I will." Linda still sounded as though she needed persuading.

"Please." It was suddenly very important to Anya that Linda trusted her. "You can't believe I'd act in the same way. You can't believe I'd seduce a boy in my care? Geoff's son? You can't believe I'd be that crass!"

"You know Geoff never stopped loving you."

Anya was surprised by the change in the tone of Linda's voice. "Really?"

"He said he wished he'd stood up against his mother and stuck by you. He said he should never have let himself be manipulated so much by his mother."

"He told you that?"

"Almost the exact words."

"And he really wants me to take on his children?" Anya didn't know whether to be scared out of her mind or flattered beyond belief. Her main emotion was one of sadness that it had come to this to bring her and Geoff back together.

"Will you come and talk about it with him? Will you consider it?"

"I'm really the only one?"

David sensed success.

"You are."

"However unsuitable?"

"Your word, nobody else's."

Anya looked from David to Linda and down at her hands. She did not know what she should do.

Since her purchase of Fishermen Rock fifteen months earlier Anya had split her time between England and Barbados. She still took pride in the successful running of her property business in England but she gained most satisfaction from the change of fortune of Edna's Place. Miriam was a skilled and efficient manager. She was used to dealing with the bookings, the hiring and training of staff, the ordering of supplies and had a brilliant manner with customers and Anya had soon understood that she should not interfere in the day to day running of the hotel because no-one could do that better than Miriam. Her own input was the wider picture. She had no lack of ambition or funds, so she had hired the best international hospitality marketing business in New York. As a result Fishermen Rock was becoming established as the fashionable destination of choice for the footballers, racing drivers, rock stars and actors who loved the idea of Barbados but who were put off by the formalities of some of the established resorts. But there was still a long way to go, she had plans for development and diversification, she had in her mind a detailed five year plan for herself and her businesses. For the first time in her life, as she had flown into Heathrow that morning, she had known where her life was heading.

Or so she had thought.

"Go and see him." David said gently. "No one will force you to take them on if it's wrong for you because if it's wrong for you it'll be wrong for them."

David and Linda had tried to prepare her for the shock of seeing Geoff. They had explained how ill he was, how he had changed, but no words could have prepared her. Involuntarily she sucked in air and grabbed David's arm for support. 'Oh God' she hoped she hadn't spoken out loud but she knew she must have done as Linda put her hand on Anya's other arm and squeezed hard.

Geoff lay, seemingly asleep, in the bed that occupied the centre of the room connected by a mass of wires to the machines around his bed that beeped and displayed numbers and graphs in different colours that made no sense to her. She stared at the almost unrecognisable face, there seemed to be nothing between the translucent flesh and his skull, his eyes sunken in over-sized sockets. His arms, resting on the covers, reminded her of the pictures of victims of concentration camps.

Her hand grasped at Dot's locket and she remembered that hospital visit, so long ago. She had liked Dot, Dot had been her friend and it had hurt her when she had seen her dying in hospital. But she had loved Geoff, probably had never stopped loving him. The hurt was so much greater. She knew, with a certainty that frightened her, that she should have trusted him enough to put his picture in that locket. Perhaps, after all, it wasn't too late.

"Hello Geoff old chap. I've brought someone to see you."

A surprisingly familiar voice answered David.

"You've found her."

"Hello Geoff."

Geoff opened his eyes and they smiled.

"Good to see you Anya."

She walked over and sat on the chair close to the bed, taking her hand in his. He returned the squeeze.

"Oh Geoff."

"Sorry I'm like this."

"Don't be daft."

"You'll have to do the talking." His words came in a rush and then he stopped, as if that had exhausted him.

"David and Linda say you want me to look after the children when…" Words failed her.

"When I'm dead." Geoff sounded very matter of fact. "You can say it. Will you?"

"Yes. I will." She had no idea what it would mean but seeing Geoff like this she knew she would have to try. Somehow she would rearrange her life.

"You know what it'll mean?"

"I haven't the foggiest idea but that's OK. You know I've always been a quick learner."

"Tell me about your life. What you've been up to for the past nineteen years."

"We'll be outside." David said quietly and Anya heard the door click shut.

"Tell me." Geoff repeated and squeezed her hand as he closed his eyes.

"Well, where do I start?" In a quiet and unexcited way Anya began to tell Geoff about her life. "It's been a long time since we've known much about each other hasn't it?"

She didn't wait for an answer as Geoff's eyes were closed but he squeezed her hand briefly so she knew to continue.

"After I left," she was amazed at how difficult it was to say the words, "I spent a shitty summer but then got a job. In an Estate Agents, would you believe it, me an estate agent? Anyway I eventually married the boss, Peter, but we're divorced."

"Was he nice?"

"Not as nice as you. But nice is such an inadequate word. He was kind, attentive at first but then he found someone else. We lived apart in the same house for years. Then we got divorced, that was the reason for the fiasco at the Golf Club Ball. I needed to give him very public grounds."

"Anyone else?"

"Not really. I live alone now. There's no one in my life."

"Sad." Geoff whispered.

"Not really. I could have got involved if I'd wanted to. I've changed you know Geoffers, I'm not the pushy grasping..."

"Sex-mad"

"...pushy, grasping, sex-mad, girl I used to be. I suppose I've grown up a bit. That mess a couple of New Years ago was my last stupidity. I really regret that, you know Geoff, I do regret making such a fool of Tim."

"He deserved it."

"Thanks, I hoped he would."

She was rewarded with a squeeze of her hand, though Geoff kept his eyes shut.

"What do you do?"

"I've got a bit of a property business, a range of really nice houses and flats that bring in a good income. I haven't had to worry about money for a while." She realised she sounded complacent but she meant only to comfort Geoff. "I bought a hotel in Barbados as well. I bought it on a whim, well not really a whim, more a desperate need to have something positive in my life. It's been doing really well and has been a very good investment. I'm ashamed to say how much profit it makes. I've been going over there three or four times a year, but if I can't go it'll run itself." If she was looking after the children that was something that she would have to give up. Perhaps they could go out once a year, for a holiday and she could pack everything into one visit.

"A business woman then."

"I was." She was already thinking that those times were past.

"I'll make arrangements." He had opened his eyes. "I'll get Dave to draw up something, make sure the children aren't…"

"Don't worry. I've done quite well for a scraggy tart from Liverpool." She tried to speak ironically but realised there was an unwelcome defensiveness in her voice. Geoff opened his eyes, looked at her tellingly, and closed them again.

They were quiet for a few moments and Anya thought maybe he had gone to sleep. His breathing was low and even, the pressure on her hand, slight as it had been, relaxed.

She found she was stroking his hand, gently, with the back of her fingers, keeping in time with his breathing. She spoke slowly, gently to him. Maybe he was asleep, perhaps he couldn't hear the words, but there was always the chance that he would gain comfort from the sound of a voice.

"Do you remember that first evening in the hall canteen? I'd been so lonely and all I was looking for was someone to latch on to. I was so lucky it was you, Geoff. So lucky. It wasn't all about sex was it? Even from that first time there was something more between us. Love? I think we were 'in love', from the beginning, but it took time to learn to love each other properly. I think I only realised that I loved you, rather than just being in love with you, the summer after I left you. Love is like happiness isn't it? You only know you've had it when it's gone."

She paused and looked at his shallow breathing thinking of the many times he had been breathless from the energy of their lovemaking.

"I have loved you for so long Geoff but the way I loved you has changed through the years. I think I was most in love with you before we came south. That's when it started to go wrong wasn't it? We had to work at it, dig deeper, forgive more. Perhaps that's where we went wrong. Neither of us could forgive the other for things we never even tried to talk about. Sometimes I loved you so much I couldn't imagine a life without you, at other times I loved you more when you weren't with me. Does that make any sort of sense? But whether I loved you or not, Geoff, I always liked you, always, and I hope I never blamed you. Your mother and sister were so determined to get their way. It wasn't your fault they wore you down."

There was no change in Geoff's breathing and she kept stroking his hand. There was no indication he was anything other than asleep. The only sound in the room, when she wasn't speaking, was the regular beep of the monitor. She couldn't bring herself to look at the line, imagining at any time it would stop its ups and downs and there would only be a flat line accompanied by a high pitched wail as the beeps stopped. Geoff turned his head slightly, but his eyes were still shut, his breathing still even, he seemed still to be asleep.

"I'm so sorry about Fiona. I shouldn't have egged you on to have your wicked way with her should I? But then how were either of us to know what she really wanted. I suppose she went along with her parents and your mother to give herself cover so she didn't have to explain what she was. They would never have understood. Perhaps she felt she had to get away from her parents so she could be free to be who she wanted to be. What I can't understand is her leaving you all now." Anya paused, she realised her talking about Fiona might upset Geoff, but he gave no sign of hearing her. "Your mother didn't care about your happiness at all. She just saw Fiona as good breeding stock to provide her with the grandchildren who would perpetuate her Geoffrey. I don't think she has ever really forgiven him for so obviously disliking her so much. And she didn't really care about Margaret either did she? How did Margaret cope with knowing her children weren't good enough because they had the wrong surname? We should have worked together more, you know Geoffers, we should have talked to each other more. We could have beaten her, we could have beaten them both."

Perhaps, Anya thought somewhat surreally, if she had had a flash forward all those years ago and could have seen herself now, sitting by Geoff's bedside, holding his hand in his last few days of life, she would have imagined they were still married, that none of the past 20 years had happened.

"But then, as you said, if we had stayed together you would never have had your kids and David and Linda say they are really nice. It was so obvious that you love them to bits and when you wake up you must tell me everything about them. I used to read the Courier to see if there was anything about you so I saw all the announcements. Isn't that silly? I was so pleased for you but so very, very jealous."

There was no response from Geoff, his breathing remained slow and even so she kept talking in her soft, expressive voice. "You know Geoff, when I realised I couldn't have children I thought it was the most liberating thing in the world. I was like any man and could have sex as much as I liked and I would never have to worry about Durex or coils or pills or anything. I felt so lucky. What did I know? It cost me you, well there were probably other factors involved there, but it was really the children thing wasn't it? Then it cost me Peter. I suppose that marriage was over well before he realised children were important to him. I was so jealous of Tim for having Maggie and Matthew, and so jealous of you with your brood. I kept getting the local paper, kept looking out for anything that related to you all. All those years I don't think I ever really let you go. It wasn't that I was worried about having no one to look after me in my fast approaching old age it was that I was worried that my years on this planet weren't marked in any way. OK, maybe a few properties would have my name on the deeds if anyone bothered to read them. OK, maybe some children existed because of what I've done to their parent's lives. But they weren't me, they weren't part of me. No part of me is going to remain on this planet after I'm gone and that has bothered me so very much. I do wish, more than anything in the whole wide world that I could have had your children. Life, for both of us, would have been so different. I'm so, so sorry."

She realised that her voice had risen and she looked up from Geoff's hand to his face to see if he was awake but he had not moved.

She watched the drip drip drip of the liquid as it flowed from the bottle into the tube and through the needle into his arm. She stroked Geoff's hand rhythmically as she thought about how different their lives could have been.

In a resolute but calm and low voice, she said things that should have been said years before.

"I never told you why I couldn't have children did I? I wonder why you never asked, I suppose it was one of those things that we just took for granted. I should have told you though, maybe it would have made a difference. I was sterilised when I was 7 years old because my mother had been raped by either her father or her brother, I don't know which. I've always felt like it was my fault, perhaps that's what made me so ashamed and so angry with the world. I should have told you years ago, it might have made everything different if you'd known."

She felt she had said too much, so she stopped talking and almost dozed off in the warmth of the room with the machine's hypnotic beeping.

It could have been seconds or minutes or an hour, she had no sense of time, when she felt his hand squeeze hers. She opened her eyes to see him looking intently at her. Then his eyes slowly closed and opened again, like a two eyed blink in slow motion. He closed his eyes again and Anya sat stroking his hand as the setting sun brightened the sky and then its absence darkened it.

"Anya?" It was a young man's voice, remarkably similar to that of the young Geoff.

She turned to see three children, standing by the door, Geoff's children. She wondered how long they had been there.

"Hi. He's asleep."

She wondered briefly how a room so full of people could still be so quiet.

"Hi Dad."

"Hi Kids."

"Have you been asleep Dad?" Rose asked, staring at Anya with a mixture of curiosity and hostility.

He looked deliberately at Anya "Not for one moment." and then, turning to his children, smiled.

"You're Anya." The older of the two boys held his hand out. Anya took it and was relieved to feel the firm handshake. It wasn't friendly, perhaps there was an element of suspicion in the way he looked at her as he shook her hand, but it was contact. "Uncle David said you'd be here. I'm Geoffrey the Third, known to all as Gezza."

"Hello Gezza. Yes, I'm Anya."

Geoff was still looking at Anya smiling almost imperceptibly.

"And you must be James." She turned to the younger boy who copied his elder brother and shook her hand firmly.

"Dad wants you to look after us." Rose's tone was not friendly, she was simply stating a fact.

"That's why I'm here. I've only known your Dad is … ill … since yesterday. It's a lot to take in." "You will though won't you?" James's voice was almost pleading. "Aunty Margaret's staying with us and it's absolutely awful."

Anya felt the weight of their stares, Gezza curious, Rose antagonistic and James desperate.

"We're just an excuse for her to control another chunk of the world." Rose spoke with obvious resentment. "Or try to."

"And she drinks. There's no gin left." James added.

"James." Geoff's admonition was so quiet they almost didn't hear it.

"It's true Dad." Gezza stood up for his young brother. "She drinks far more than Mum ever did and she's horrid. She's always saying how much better behaved her 'Matthew and Young Margaret' were when they were our age…"

"…and how we're all letting you down by not behaving as well as *they* did, and we're not." Rose looked as if she was about to cry, her bravado gone.

Anya caught the look in Geoff's eyes. She tried to understand something of the pain he must be feeling as he faced leaving his children to grow up without him.

"You really don't want your Aunt Margaret to look after you?"

She spoke calmly as if to adults. Any decision had to be made swiftly. Rosie was older than she had been when she had started to go off the rails. 'By her age,' Anya thought, 'I'd been having sex for nearly two years. What are the chances Rose is doing it? And what are her chances of getting pregnant if she has no reason not to and no guidance on how not to?' Gezza, nearly 16, was trying to be the strong one, old for his years, being forced to grow up too quickly. 'He's probably had to be' Anya reasoned 'feeling responsible for his siblings against a resentful, alcoholic, lesbian mother and a weakened, increasingly ill father'. James seemed the quiet one 'but quiet can so often mean vulnerable, sensitive and confused' he would need help to be brought out into the world. These children did not need Margaret to bring them up, and most certainly not Kathleen.

They needed her.

"We could look after ourselves." Gezza's tried to sound convincing, perhaps he realised this was a last stand against the devastating changes that were about to be made in their lives. Perhaps he had hoped that they could stay as they always had, just with no parents in the house.

"Gezza that's very noble of you, noble and brave, but you're suggesting taking responsibility for James and Rose without knowing what that might involve." Anya did not know either but she thought perhaps she had a little more of an idea than Gezza.

"I don't need looking after. I'm 16. I can look after myself."

"You will, but not yet." Geoff spoke quietly.

"So can I, I'm nearly 15." Rose added her unnaturally high pitched voice to the discussion. Anya wondered if she was finally realising what her father's dying was going to mean to their lives.

"Do you understand the sacrifices you would have to make Gezza?" Anya held Gezza's defiant eye, a defiance that Anya knew would only be a front to hold back fear. "You couldn't go to University, you couldn't do so many of the things you do now, the weekend sport, the hanging out with your friends." She was guessing, but she had lived in the town long enough to know what a boy of his age would be doing. "Those are the things you should be doing at 16.

Not checking that the bills have been paid and that your brother and sister have done their homework or have clean underwear."

They were the first parental responsibilities that came to her mind. She knew it was an inadequate list but it had the desired effect. Gezza turned away.

"Anya's right."

They all looked down at Geoff.

"But it's not up to us, it's up to the court."

Anya looked at Gezza's back, turned against her as he pretended to look out of the window, Rose was near to tears, she turned to James.

"James? Can you explain? Your dad's pretty tired."

Gezza turned around, he wasn't going to give up being the spokesman for his family. "When Mum left us she said she wanted a life for herself, we were holding her back from being the person she had always wanted to be." As he spoke Anya realised he was repeating, word for word, what their mother had said to them. She felt a wave of anger against the woman and made herself concentrate on what Gezza was saying. "At first the court said she had to have custody because Dad wasn't well enough. But she didn't want us, she was only fighting Dad to hurt him, and Uncle David managed to persuade the court that it would be wrong to give custody to someone who didn't want us. The magistrate didn't want to do it but she gave temporary custody to Dad. She said we had to come back when…"

"…when I'm dead." Geoff finished the sentence his son couldn't.

"Sorry, you're going to have to be a bit clearer." Anya was confused. "Does this mean you only need me until," she looked straight at Geoff knowing she had to be as strong as he was being, "until your Dad is dead? Then it's back to court?"

"But if we're got a stable home environment they'd look at it from the starting point of keeping us together." It seemed to Anya that James was also repeating a phrase he had heard others use.

"It's not going to be easy."

Anya tried to grasp the scale of what Geoff was asking her to do;

learn to be a parent, provide that 'stable home environment', help his children face up to their father's death, then convince the court to keep the family together whilst no doubt having to fight Margaret and Kathleen every step of the way.

And that would only be the beginning.

"Will you take them on Anya?" Geoff lifted his hand and reached out towards her. "I wasn't asleep." He was speaking very slowly and she could hardly make out what he was saying. "I heard every word. I'm sorry."

As she looked at him she realised there was something wrong, his eyes closed slowly, reluctantly and she realised there was no resistance in his hand, it was limp in hers.

"Rose," Anya said calmly "please go and get a nurse. I think your father needs some help.

They waited outside the room in silence as nurses walked in and out of the room pushing trolleys of equipment and men in white coats talked seriously, but inaudibly as they walked down the corridor without a word to the four anxious faces waiting for news.

"Is he OK?" James asked a nurse after half an hour. He was given a slight smile in reply that was probably supposed to be encouraging.

"He'll be OK won't he?" James asked Anya as if, as an adult, she would know the answer better than he.

"I think he was just a little faint. He must be very tired. It's been a very difficult day for him, sorting out the future of the three people he loves most in the world. And he does love you three, more than you could ever imagine." She put her arm around Rose, James sat next to her and slipped his arm through hers. "You should have heard him talking about you, he's so proud of you all." For a moment she was back in the golf club bar, champagne in hand, listening to Geoff talk about his children. If only she had known then what was to come. Things would have been different, she would have made them different.

The quiet corridor was disturbed by a shrill sound.

"What are you doing here?" Anya opened her eyes to see Margaret staring at her with undisguised hatred. She hadn't acknowledged the presence of the children and she ignored them.

"You!" She was almost screaming with anger, "I'm talking to you! What the hell are you doing here?"

Anya had no time to reply before another, also once familiar, voice joined in.

"Take your hands off those poor children." Kathleen tried to push Anya's arm off Rose's shoulder and pull James away from her. The strength and the violence of her actions surprised them all.

Anya knew that a bearing of dignity and restraint was the best answer to such open hostility. She did not answer, she simply tightened her hold on Rose and James and smiled at them in what she hoped was an encouraging way.

"I asked you a question. What are you doing here? Answer me!"

"She's here to see Dad." Gezza was the first to speak.

"I wasn't speaking to you young man. I was talking to that woman."

"Anya. Her name is Anya." James spoke very politely but they all heard the defiance in his voice.

"I know her name. I know exactly who she is. I want her to tell me what she's doing here."

"She has no right to be here, no right at all." Kathleen added her voice in support of her daughter.

"I told you." Gezza spoke with what Anya thought was admirable insolence. "She's here to see Dad. What's the problem with that? She was married to him."

"Was. Was. She was married to him. She hasn't been part of this family for a very long time. Thank God!" Anya remembered what James had said about Margaret's drinking and she thought perhaps she was drunk.

"Well Dad wants her to be part of the family now." Rose spoke up finding a voice as firm as her brother's.

"What could you possibly mean by that?" Kathleen was at her imperious best.

"She's going to marry Dad again." Gezza had made the decision.

Rose glanced at her brother, smiled and took up the theme, "Then she'll be our proper step-mother and she'll look after us, then you and the court can't do anything about it."

Anya hoped no one caught the look of sheer panic that she felt must show on her face. She was aware of, without actually hearing, the gasp of 'No!' from her ex- and soon-to-be-again sister-in-law.

"Well there's no reason why not and a lot of reasons why." As James spoke Anya heard a calm reason not shown by his siblings. Anya realised she was seeing their personalities in microcosm: Gezza the impetuous but protective one with the burden on his shoulders of being the eldest; Rose the emotional yet pragmatic one and James the thoughtful, logical peacemaker.

"Will you do it Anya?" Gezza asked her rather formally "Will you marry our Dad?"

"Don't you think we'd better ask him first?"

Ignoring them Kathleen walked towards Geoff's room. "We'll see about that." She opened the door just as the nurse was wheeling the trolley out smiling, oblivious to the drama that had been played out in the corridor. "He's better now, it was just a faint. You can go back in but don't get him too excited."

Anya noticed the subtlety of the re-arrangement as they filed into the room. Before they had all left she had been on one side of his bed with the children ranged against her amongst the drips and accoutrements of medical surveillance on the other. Now she sat in the chair she had left just a few minutes before with Gezza standing to her right and Rose and James to her left facing Kathleen and Margaret across the bed.

Anya took Geoff's hand, shocked again at the slightness of him.

"Geoff. For God's sake don't try to laugh but your children have just asked me to marry you."

"Good idea." He smiled, it was almost the smile of the Geoff of old.

"You think so?"

"I do." Still smiling, he closed his eyes.

Ten days later, the 8th April 1995, Anya was to become Mrs Geoff Philips for the second time.

Friday 7th April 1995

My last night as Anya Cave. Tomorrow it's Mrs Geoff Philips. Again. But for how long? The hospital won't let me stay more than a couple of hours at a time as he gets so tired. I know he likes me there, stroking his hand. I've told him about all the things he never asked before. I read pages from my diaries. 'I want to know you before it's too late' he said. How am I going to get through all this? What could we have been if we'd stayed together?

They're using more and more drugs, that means it won't be long. I must stop being self-pitying, I have no right to be when he isn't in the least.

When we left the hospital last Wednesday I drove the children home. They had to tell me the way as I had no idea where Geoff lived. I was horrified to see it was Kathleen's old house. The kids explained that Geoff moved into the house (after all it was his) when he married Fiona and the children have lived nowhere else. I won't move them what with all the other things happening in their lives but changes will occur. It'll help keep the children occupied. But living here will take some getting used to.

We hired a man and a van and moved and I moved in on April 1st. An agency is taking over the day to day running of the properties with Gemma keeping me informed as and when. Phoning Miriam to explain the change in circumstances wasn't easy. I said I'd get out as often as I could but it could not be as often as in the past. She said she understood but I'm not so sure she did, she sounded surprisingly down, almost angry, that I wasn't going to be out next month.

The children's schools don't break up until 12th but I've persuaded headmaster and headmistress to let them miss the last week so they can spend as much time as possible with their father. I was really nervous about visiting them but remembered just in time how nice Dot had been. Funny how life's experiences occasionally can come in useful.

Tomorrow I'll not only be wife but step-mother. How on earth will I cope? What on earth am I letting myself in for?

This might, just might, be the best thing I've ever done in my entire life.

The Registrar had been prepared for a solemn death-bed ceremony but quickly adapted to the atmosphere of laughter and hope that filled Geoff's room along with the flowers.

"Wow!" Geoff had said as Anya had walked into the room on Gezza's arm to the sound of The Beatles *All you Need is Love*. James had researched the music that would have been around when they had first got married and he had found he rather liked The Beatles, stoically ignoring his siblings' teasing for ignoring the superior claims of Blur, Oasis or Take That. Anya had thought carefully about what to wear and had discussed it in detail with Rose. She told her how their first wedding had been informal, how she had worn a denim skirt and cream t-shirt and wondered whether to do the same this time. Rose had been horrified. 'You must be really really glamorous.' So she had decided on the dress she had worn to the Golf Club Ball, she knew Geoff would get the joke. David and Linda acted as witnesses because neither Kathleen nor Margaret had replied to the invitations so carefully hand-written by Rose and James.

"Is that it?" Gezza asked when the registrar pronounced his father and Anya man and wife. "There's not a lot to it is there?"

"No need to make a fuss."

"We didn't the first time did we?"

Geoff and Anya found themselves telling the children about their first wedding and their life in Liverpool. Anya did most of the talking with Geoff prompting her, picking out the good times, ignoring the difficulties. The children had the sense not to ask what had gone wrong.

"Now it's time for you children to go." Anya handed an envelope to Gezza. Go downstairs and there should be a car waiting for you. When you're in the car open the envelope, it's our wedding present to you, your Dad's and mine."

"Not to mention that you want to be left alone." Gezza tried to laugh off his embarrassment.

"Enjoy yourselves. I'll see you at home by 9 tonight. No later. You have to do as I say now!"

As they shut the door behind them Geoff and Anya could hear their children's giggles.

"Where are they off to?"

"A stretch limo is taking them to the Hard Rock Café in Piccadilly."

"They'll be OK? Saturday afternoon?"

"Of course. The guy who runs it stays at my place in Barbados, he's going to look after them. A group I've never heard of but who are, apparently, something hot in the charts, will be sitting at the table next to them and will, casually, engage them in conversation. They'll be absolutely fine."

"That's some present."

"Your present too. Now, husband of mine, budge over."

Anya slowly took off her dress and slipped under the sheet next to her husband.

"The nurses?" Geoff did not want to be caught in bed with his wife.

"There's a 'Do not Disturb' sign on the door. At least I asked James to put it on the door as he seems to be pretty reliable."

"But Anya. I can't…"

"Of course you can't. But I can."

On the day after the wedding the children spent the time giving Anya and Geoff a thorough account of their afternoon in London. Anya made a mental note to offer the band a free stay at Fishermen Rock as Rose told them in awestruck tones how they had started talking to these lads on the table next to them and how they had joined them and, at the end of the meal taken them to the recording studio where they had seen the band work on their new album. Even Gezza had been impressed. Anya noticed tears in Geoff's eyes as all three children took turns to interrupt each other to add detail upon detail of their treat.

Every night Anya turned on her computer and wrote something in her diary. They were precious days, they were important, she would need to be able to relive them all her life. The end was going to come very quickly.

Monday 10th April 1995
Geoff's 45th. Invited Kathleen and Margaret to join us for a small party. I made the point, rather forcefully, that we would be celebrating on the correct day. Just this once G was having his proper birthday. It was all too much for G so after all that fuss we left after only a few minutes.

Some days were better than others. Some days Geoff wanted to talk and Anya would sit, holding his hand, listening as Geoff told her things about the children and their lives. She wanted to know everything he could tell her.

Friday 14th April
Good Friday. Very quiet in the hospital. Spend day with G. Kids with K. G having good day and he told me about his life with Fiona. He said I needed to know to understand some of the things the kids wouldn't want to do. If ever I meet the woman I won't be responsible for my actions. Before she left she told the children that their father had raped her when she was a virgin. How could she! What mother would say that to her children even if it were true! Times were so different then, and she'd led him on for years. G called her a prick teaser more times than I can remember. And then when it finally happened she made G feel so guilty. And then to tell that stupid story to the children! Words for once absolutely and utterly fail me.

Some days she would lie down on the bed next to him and hold him in her arms, carefully avoiding drips and tubes. It would have been funny, he said one day, if it weren't so sad.

Tuesday 18th
Doctor wanted to have a word. She was very nice. We've chatted briefly before, in the corridor or in G's room, but this time she wanted to see me in her office. She said he was getting weaker. Could we cut down on the visits so he could conserve his strength? I argued that surely time without his children would be just lying there waiting to die, not living. We agreed a compromise, me and one child at a time. More and more drugs are being forced into what's left of his body and each day he talks less and our visits are shorter.

The time spent at home seemed filled with the practicalities of living, cooking, eating, washing, ironing, cleaning. The children sometimes wanted to talk, sometimes they didn't. Anya felt the best thing was to let them do pretty much what they pleased as long as they were always home in time for dinner each evening when they all sat down together, as a family.

Sunday 23rd April
It won't be long now. I put the 'Do Not Disturb' notice on his door and lay on the bed with him. He knew I was there but said nothing. I tried to keep my breathing in time with his, as we had done when we first slept together. He lifted his hand and touched me on my breast. What he was trying to say?

The next day he was not aware she was in the room. She talked to the doctor and a few hours later she and the children, along with Kathleen and Margaret sat together silently waiting for the end.

Tuesday 25th April
He's gone. We sat all night, me holding one hand and Kathleen the other, the kids huddled together by the window. I couldn't help thinking, as we waited for my twice husband's

breathing to stop, that the tableau was a metaphor for his life. Poor love, torn between two strong women. Why had he chosen the wrong one? But then, maybe, in the end, he hadn't. I was right all those years ago, I searched for the words in the diary, 'wherever I went, whatever I did, I ended up with Geoff'.

We came home all together, even M & K, and sat in the lounge not knowing what to say or think or do. I wondered briefly what I would feel if one of these children, already the centre of my life, died before I did. How would I cope? It was Gezza who pulled us all together. 'Dad wouldn't want this.' He said. 'Let's put some music on and eat.' I made a supper that we all picked at while listening to the music tape James had compiled for the wedding. Such a two edged sword: the grief of loss and the guilt of thinking 'thank God it's over now we can get on with our lives'. An unsuitable thought? Surprisingly Kathleen handed over the Philips emerald ring. How she'd wangled it off Fiona I have no idea. Perhaps she did it with an imperious message on an answer phone.

The first week of her widowhood was the most difficult time Anya hoped she would ever have to live through. Gezza spent a great deal of time in the garden, Rose in her bedroom and James in the study on his computer. None of them seemed to worry about going out or the beginning of the summer term. She let the schools know they would be late back from holiday, they were very understanding.

She shopped, cooked, cleaned, washed and ironed. She was in touch with Kathleen and Margaret regarding the funeral arrangements, letting them make most of the running though they were appalled that, as Geoff's widow, it was she who had to sign all the paperwork and to whom the Funeral Directors turned for confirmation of instructions. 'Had Geoff known this would happen?' she had asked herself 'Probably' and she had smiled. She was not unreasonable in her dealings with Kathleen and Margaret, letting them discuss the date and time and details of the service with the vicar. She wanted nothing to do with that side of things. It wasn't Geoff lying in the hospital morgue, it wouldn't be Geoff disintegrating in that coffin underneath the soil a few feet above the coffin of the father he had never known.

Monday 1st May
Geoff why did you get me into this? I've got no experience, nothing to go on, I can't even think back to my childhood. The children are bereft without their Dad and are just going with the flow, doing what's asked of them, without any arguments. No doubt those are to come. The montage of photos for the wake was a good idea. Every evening we sit on the floor surrounded by photographs. It usually ends in tears. I can't think that's a bad thing. But sometimes there are laughs. There was one square photo from an Instamatic camera of you in a pink flowery kipper tie, purple shirt and brown flared trousers. I'm learning so much about them. I'm not pushing them about things like sharing out household chores. That'll wait till they're back at school, then I'll have to start getting them into some sort of routine. At the moment I'm just making sure there's food on the table at mealtimes (and they're there to eat it) with clean clothes on their backs.
I suppose it's a start.

Anya sat looking at, but not seeing, the words on screen.
Nothing in her life would ever be the same again.

Chapter 15: Responsibilities

Kent, March 1995

Anya occupied a front pew with the children, her children now. James held her hand tightly, as did Rose, Gezza sat slightly apart, as befitted the eldest child, but he wished he could be holding onto Anya as his brother and sister were. Kathleen occupied the front pew on the other side of the aisle. With her were Margaret, Maggie and Matthew. Anya knew Tim would be in the pew behind them but she made sure she never caught his eye. Anya was most relieved that there was no sign of Fiona, David had told her both of Geoff's remarriage and his death but she made no appearance at her ex-husband's funeral.

As Anya had feared with Margaret and Kathleen making the arrangements, the service was overlong and depressing; the contrast with the recent wedding could not have been sharper. The only slightly uplifting part of the service was David's eulogy. As he brought his memories to a conclusion he looked across at Anya.

"We all have our particular memories of Geoff, I have shared some of them with you but no-one has more than his beloved Anya."

She felt rather than heard the gasp of disapproval from Kathleen and Margaret but Anya was grateful to David for singling her out. Geoff's world, his friends, acquaintances and most of all his family, needed to know the new order of things.

"You should know that Anya and Geoff have loved each over nearly a quarter of a century. It has not been easy for either of them and they went their separate ways for a time, but theirs was a love that endured against all odds. In her hands now are the children who are Geoff's legacy. Anyone who knew Geoff knew how much he loved his children but they also know how much he loved Anya. He told me to tell you all that he has loved Anya more than was sensible since he was too young to know better. It was his particular joy in his last days that his children would be in her care for the rest of their lives and that she would be in theirs."

Many of the congregation seemed unaware that Geoff had married Anya again and there were some whisperings and disapproving looks as she, with the children, took precedence over Kathleen in the procession to the grave.

Gezza stood behind Anya, his hands on her shoulders, while she held on tight to Rose and James's hands as the time-honoured words of the funeral service were spoken and Geoff's coffin was lowered into the ground above the coffin of his father.

With eyes filled with tears Anya looked across the grave to Kathleen.

How must it feel to bury your son in the same grave as his father? Anya couldn't imagine the pain Kathleen was feeling and looked quickly away. She didn't want to meet Kathleen's glance now she was just beginning to understand the ties that bind a parent to a child. Her heart was breaking at the sound of their handfuls of soil and bunches of spring flowers from the garden hitting the wooden coffin. The four of them clung together as more earth was thrown over the coffin and the brass plaque with the words *Geoffrey Ian Philips, born 10 April 1950, died 25 April 1995* disappeared from view forever.

"All those years he was married to Fiona he always talked about you."

David handed Anya a glass of champagne. They were trying, against all the odds, to make the wake a celebration of Geoff's life.

"I think I realised that, towards the end. We did quite a lot of catching up you know.

"He understood about you and Tim."

"What about me and Tim?" She looked around the room and saw that Tim had not come back to the house.

"He understood the way you played against each other. How you were attracted to each other in a destructive sort of way. A love hate relationship he said. He never minded. He would never have divorced you if…"

"… if it hadn't been for his mother."

"He would have been happier if he'd hung onto you."

"But then he wouldn't have had the children."

"True, but would that really have mattered?"

Anya looked across the room at Geoff's children and she realised how much she already cared for them. "Oh yes, that would have mattered. Look at them, they're lovely children, they will be wonderful adults."

John handed them both a full glass, carefully removing the empties. "Gezza has just informed me that he wants to be called Geoffrey now."

Anya sipped her champagne. "I suppose we all have to grow up sooner or later, perhaps it takes times like these."

Wednesday 3rd May 1995

So that's it. The funeral's done with, the paperwork and public bit of death is over. All we've got to do now is live with it.

The children were brilliant, dignified and responsible. I don't think anyone told them what to do, I certainly didn't. They spent much of the wake showing photographs to people I must once have known but have forgotten. Most of the same people would have been in this house at T & M's party. 25 years ago, give or take. I reminded David and John about immovable objects and irresistible forces, I wanted to know who they thought would win, the battle is surely not over yet.

It's really odd but now Gezza is Geoffrey I see so much of the young Geoff in him. They aren't alike physically, but it's just the odd look, the occasional gesture. It's his 16th birthday at the weekend so we must do something then and then they'll be back to school next week. Somehow we will establish something like a version of normality.

The day after the funeral David phoned Anya.

"I'm so sorry Anya, but the court wants to review the children's situation now their father has died."

"They waste no time." Anya couldn't help the harshness in her voice "I'm sorry David, it's just that I think the Social Services and courts or whoever runs these things should let the children grieve, just for a few days at least."

"I suppose there are so many occasions when children are left uncared for, they have to be on the safe side."

"Possibly, but aren't they aware of the changed circumstances? I mean they do realise that the children have a step-mother now don't they?"

David couldn't give a direct answer to the direct question. "I need to draft your petition to them. We need to discuss everything and get all the paperwork spot on. I'm afraid I will have to be intrusive as they will want to know everything about your circumstances, even the reasons you re-married Geoff."

"You mean on his death-bed."

"We must act quickly, we need to be ready for whatever the court may throw at you. You will be formally adopting the children I presume?"

"Well. Yes. I suppose so. I hadn't thought about it. I haven't asked them."

"Can I come round? Go over all this face to face?"

"Can you make it Monday? The children go back to school on Tuesday and they must be involved, but they do need a bit of a recovery weekend. Also, in case you'd forgotten, it's Gezza's, I mean Geoffrey's, sixteenth birthday on Saturday. He doesn't want a fuss so we're just going to have a quiet day all together, though I suppose Kathleen and Margaret will have to be invited."

"It's all right," David interrupted an increasingly fraught Anya, "Monday will be fine."

"Sorry, I'm just trying to think of everything."

"Let me get this straight." David's voice allowed no doubt that there would be nothing about friendship in the meeting, he was the complete professional. He read the notes he had taken as he sat at the dining room table with Geoffrey and Anya on his right and James and Rose on his left. "You married Geoff for the first time in September 1971 having met at University. You were divorced in 1976 on the grounds of your adultery..."

"And my inability to bear children. Geoff's mother wanted grandchildren."

"Indeed, that may be so, but it is not a matter of legal record."

"Whereas my adultery is."

"I'm afraid so. The court won't be interested in details or motives, simply in the fact that you were the guilty party. Where was I? Ah yes. You married a second time, to Peter March in 1977 and that marriage ended in divorce in 1993. Again the reason was adultery and again you were the guilty party."

"It sounds awful doesn't it? But both times I wasn't the only one, Geoff was unfaithful to me almost as much as I was to him, it's just that we agreed for me to be the guilty one. The same happened with Peter. I was unfaithful to him once and he had a mistress for ten years. But it was kinder for me to be the guilty party as there were children involved on his side."

She wondered what the children made of the conversation as they sat around the table. She glanced over to them and, since they seemed neither surprised nor shocked, she reasoned they must already have known.

"Again, I'm afraid the court won't be interested in motives, simply matters of fact."

"I'm sure Peter would write a letter to explain why it was done that way, if that would help. We parted on reasonable terms."

"That might be useful. Do you know how we might contact him?" He scribbled the name and address as Anya told him.

"It's an easy address to remember." She explained as David seemed interested that she knew the address without checking. "But I'm not sure of the postcode. SY10 something."

"We can find that. Now let's look at your business life. You have built up a successful property development business and own a wide portfolio which brings in a good income. You also own a hotel in Barbados. You are financially independent and certainly did not marry Geoffrey for his money. Although your marriage invalidated your husband's previous will he did draw up another one the week after." David ignored Anya's frown of surprise. She had not thought there had been much time when Geoff was awake that she wasn't with him. "In that will he states clearly that his wish was for you to take responsibility for his children. He has left you this house on the condition that the children live here until they are 21 if they so wish. All his other assets, which I have to say are quite considerable, he has left to his children in equal parts, in trust till they are 21 with the income to go towards their education and general expenses."

"Equal parts?" Anya asked. "How times have changed. Wouldn't things have been different if Geoff's father had left his funds 'in equal parts' to his children."

"What do you mean?" Rose asked, perfectly reasonably and Anya spent a few minutes explaining that their grandfather had left nothing to his daughter. 'Just because she was a girl?' Rose's look of indignation made Anya smile. "No wonder Aunt Margaret has a bag of chips on her shoulder!"

David continued as solemnly as he could. "That, and your own not inconsiderable resources, will make you financially independent. You will have no call on the state to support you though you will of course qualify for allowances, as would any family."

"That must be a plus surely?"

"It will be one of several points the court will take into consideration."

"So we have good points, the money, and bad points, my unsuitable history."

"In a nutshell, yes. But we will do what we can to prove that you are an upstanding member of the community, a responsible person, perfectly suited to look after the children."

"Doesn't the fact that I am the children's step-mother count for anything?"

"I'm afraid not."

"How can we prove I'm an upstanding member of the community then? I've never been a member of this community or any other for that matter. I've been too busy."

"We will find witnesses to speak for you."

"We need character witnesses?" She was shocked and a little afraid. She had a feeling they might be difficult to find.

"Yes, we only need one or two responsible and respectable people who will vouch for your integrity."

"Even that might be difficult."

David hesitated a fraction too long. "I'm sure we will manage."

"Doesn't it mean anything that we want Anya to be our Mum?" Rose asked.

"It should." David paused, looking ominously thoughtful in Anya's view. "It should." He repeated "But it all depends on the magistrate. Some think that the children really aren't in any position to know what is best for them, even if they think they do. Some justices think that that is their job, some just don't like anyone else making the decision for them."

"Our magistrate?" Anya asked tentatively and was rewarded with a rueful shrug from David.

"Shouldn't the most important thing be what we want?" Geoffrey asked, sounding so like his father they all turned towards him. "They must listen to us."

"I will do my best to make them do that." David didn't sound overly confident.

The children left the room as he packed up his papers into his briefcase. He spoke gently, his friendly voice Anya had labelled it, as opposed to his formal, professional one. "Look Anya, I think there's something you need to know."

"What?"

"I've been talking to Tim. He's been taken back into the fold."

"You mean he's again a respectable member of the community?"

"Something like that."

"I haven't seen him since the funeral and he didn't stay long, in fact I felt he was avoiding me."

"You know he was ostracised after the debacle of the New Year Ball well now he's back on the golf club committee, I think they thought he'd suffered enough with his rather expensive divorce, either that or they all thought 'there but for fortune'. One of the other members of the committee is connected with the family court. I asked Tim if he would give you a personal reference. I thought his name might help."

"And?"

"He said no."

"You mean he didn't want to go out on a limb and support me."

David shook his head. Anya was not surprised.

With the children back at school some sort of domestic routine was established and Anya's began to settle into her new life. Kathleen and Margaret ignored her though they insisted the children visit them every week. The children didn't want to go but when Anya explained it would be held against her in court if it looked like she had prevented contact with their family they gave up their Sunday afternoons with a reasonable grace.

There were times when she thought the children were getting used to living without their father and they seemed to relax more, though she knew it would be a long time before they would stop looking back at what life used to be. Anya was proud of them but especially so of Geoffrey who needed no nagging to work for his GCSEs. Remembering how stressful her O levels had been she did what she could to encourage him and, when requested, she visited the school to talk to the headmaster. 'If only Dot could see me now' she had said to herself as she walked with the headmaster through the immaculately kept gardens of the expensive private school.

"If it weren't for bloody Social Services," she confided in Linda in one of their regular phone calls, "I could almost be happy."

Every week she spent the day being interviewed by the various agencies appointed by the court to identify whether or not she was a suitable person to look after her step-children. Anya soon understood that their preferred position was that the children should be returned to their mother, no one seemed to understand that Fiona wanted nothing to do with them.

David phoned Anya practically every day to keep her informed and give much needed support and finally he said the words she had been wanting to hear, but which filled her with dread.

"We've got the court date. It's next Thursday, we have one week to make sure we're as ready as we possibly can be."

"At least Geoffrey's exams will be over."

"It's only the preliminary hearing but things are at last moving."

> Thursday 22nd June 1995.
> Hateful day. Pompous woman magistrate (probably golf club member...) interviewed G at 2.30; R at 3; and J at 3.30 then the three of them together while I sat outside. It wasn't a proper court, just a room, more like an office really, with a big table piled high with very full files. David was with the children, Linda sat with me. She actually held my hand. Then they called me in and the children had gone. I panicked. They'd been taken to Fiona. I knew we'd lost. I over-reacted. I yelled I wanted to see my children. David told me to calm down. No decision had been taken. The kids were in the canteen having a coke with the girl from SS. SS – how appropriate! The magistrate asked me lots of questions mainly about why I'd married Geoff. I answered them, and cried. Anger and tears. The two things David had told me not to resort to. Bugger bugger bugger. Afterwards he and Linda said I'd done well but I know I haven't. I'm so sorry Geoff. I promised you I'd look after them and I'm doing my best but today my best just wasn't good enough.

'I've always been considered unsuitable.' She had told the children round the kitchen table that evening. 'It's something I've never worried about until now.' She had been touched to tears when they had all, including Geoffrey, got up and given her a hug.

Saturday July 15th 1995

David has at last scraped together the references. He found a business contact who's going to say how professional and honest and upstanding I am and Stuart Benthall is going to write one, though that's another business one, it's the personal ones that have been the problem. Peter's written a nice letter saying the marriage had broken down long before my adultery but I'm not so sure it will do the trick. David and Linda can't do anything, obviously, though they have been real friends through all this. John was brilliant and has written about how long he's known me and how I've always come out on top whatever life has thrown at me. I asked him to change the wording a bit! Didn't need Tim after all. If only I'd been one of those people who made friends. I've never had friends, not at school and not since. I've only ever had lovers, husbands and colleagues. I need friends now and I haven't got any. Why does that remind me of Mum?

'Swimming in porridge' was how Anya remembered the summer of 1995.

Whatever she did they wanted more, whatever she presented to them was never enough, another person needed to be asked, another agency needed to interview her. Then the important players went on holiday, all at different times, and it became obvious nothing was going to be resolved until the Autumn.

As long as their lives were being scrutinised the children did exactly as they were asked. They went out only with permission, they returned home by the allotted time, they didn't swear, at least not in front of anyone that mattered, and they weren't disobedient. Geoffrey did well in his GCSEs and looked forward to the Sixth form. There were lighter days when as a family they lazed around in the sun in the garden, when they argued over who was going to barbecue the sausages but everything they did was overshadowed by the impending court decision.

In the evening of the last Sunday before the schools went back, as Anya sat in the garden drinking wine with David, Linda and John, she broke down in tears. "All this would have been so much easier if I'd been respectable and conforming, if I'd ever made friends, if I hadn't been so bloody unsuitable."

"But if you had been suitable Geoff would never have fallen for you." Linda put her arm around Anya's shoulders and tried to comfort her. Her idea of Anya had changed completely since the spring. Then she had thought of Anya as a selfish man eater who did exactly as she wanted regardless of who might get hurt in the process. After the events of the spring and summer she saw an immensely strong woman who had never been dealt an entirely fair hand.

"He fell for Fiona." Anya didn't believe it was true but she was haunted by the idea of Geoff with the woman who could take the children away from her.

"No, no Anya, he never fell for Fiona. He fell for giving up arguing with his mother." David was embarrassed seeing Anya cry.

"Being a Highly Unsuitable Girl. That was your strongpoint, you played the role very well." He tried to cheer her up.

"It wasn't a role. I am unsuitable."

"Didn't you ever put some of it on?"

"I don't think so." Anya was mystified, she wiped her eyes with the tissue Linda had handed her. "I've only ever been me."

"We used to call you Hug." John broke the silence.

"What?"

"We used to call you Hug." He repeated.

"Hug?" Anya asked, bemused.

"Highly Unsuitable Girl. H. U. G. Hug. We've called you Hug ever since that day at Charing Cross. We knew Kathleen would hate you. We knew it would all end in grief…"

"Thanks John."

"Well, you know what I mean."

"Hug?" Anya looked at the men she had known now for 25 years, "You called me Hug? That's sweet."

Thursday 26th October 1995

The final court hearing is tomorrow. I haven't slept properly for days. I keep going over and over in my head the questions David has said I'll be asked and the answers I must give. But what about the ones I don't know are coming. How will I get them right? I MUST NOT let the children down. Everything has got to be right, my clothes, make-up, behaviour, voice, everything. What if I get any of it wrong? What if Fiona turns up at the last minute? What if Kathleen and Margaret argue successfully that I would be an unsuitable mother? What must it be like for the children? I can hear them all together whispering in James's room above me.

The court room was in a modern office block, an almost identical rectangular room to the one they had visited two months before. A similar large table was almost covered with buff coloured files that may or may not have been the same ones as before. This time they all sat around the table at the same time.

"We're here to do what's best for Geoffrey, Rosemary and James." The woman magistrate said. Anya nodded urgently. What would she do if the order went against her and the children were sent to Margaret, or to Fiona, or, worst of all, split up and put into care? They would be devastated. In the months since Geoff's death they had become her family, her children. She could not lose them.

There were so many people in the room, many that Anya recognised but others she didn't. She had known that Kathleen and Margaret would be there but it was still a shock to see them implacably resisting Geoff's wishes. The atmosphere was supposed to be informal, David had told her that, apart from calling the magistrate 'Your worship' there would be nothing of the criminal courtroom in the proceedings. Under other circumstances Anya might almost have said people were friendly. But too much was at stake.

Most of the questions David had schooled her to expect were asked and she answered as she had been tutored. She was nervous, her voice shook, she did not sound like the confident, independent, mature woman she had believed herself to be. She hoped that the magistrate understood her love for the children. She floundered, however, when asked what role the children's grand-mother and aunt would have in their upbringing, 'bearing in mind the history between you'.

Anya looked down the table to Kathleen and Margaret.

"Mrs Philips." Both Kathleen and Anya looked up. "Senior" The magistrate added. "Just why are you resisting the well documented wishes of your son that his wife should look after the children?"

"She is highly unsuitable."

"Unsuitable? In what way?"

"She has no morals. She is promiscuous northern slut who trapped my Geoffrey into marriage. She is not qualified to bring up children."

"That is harsh."

"She shows no respect for her betters. She is not of our class. You must understand from her broken marriages, she has led men astray, she has…"

"I think that is enough Mrs Philips. We have all the details of Mrs Anya Philips's previous," she hesitated, trying to find an appropriate word, "entanglements. She has been very open about them."

"And you Mrs Cross? What are your feelings on the matter of your brother's children?"

"They should be with me. I've brought up a family. I have a son and daughter who have done very well. I understand how to control teenagers. I would know how to keep my brother's children on the straight and narrow."

"Is there any indication that they might stray from that path?"

Anya tried to read the tone in the magistrate's voice but failed. She had been beginning to hope that she was on her side against Kathleen and Margaret but it was impossible to say.

"Mrs Fiona Philips has not attended?" The magistrate looked at her clerk, who shook her head. "Is there any correspondence?" The justice's clerk lifted a small sheet of paper from a file. "We have a note from Mrs Fiona Philips. She says she wishes only to forget her ex-husband and has no interest in his children."

The magistrate had been looking at Geoffrey and noted his lack of reaction at his mother's rejection. "You are the eldest child. I have spoken to you a number of times and believe you are old enough to know your own feelings on this. What do you think is best for yourself and your young brother and sister?"

There was a slight delay as Geoffrey scraped his chair back, stood up and straightened his jacket. No one else had stood to answer questions and Anya wondered if it was something David had suggested. "Your worship, I know that we want to stay together and I know what our father wanted. We want Anya to look after us. If she will?" He turned to her and she smiled encouragement, blinking hard to keep the tears in her eye from showing.

"Is that what you want Rosemary? James?"

Rose nodded silently. James carefully and clearly said 'Yes your worship'. Anya was so proud of them all.

"Mrs Kathleen Philips, Mrs Cross, you have put your feelings very forcefully to this court and also in your submissions which I will read again very carefully. Mrs Anya Philips, I will let you know my decision as soon as possible. I do have some understanding of the strain which you are under. You will recognize that the court's decision may take weeks, rather than days, as we have to be absolutely certain, for the children's sake, that the right decision is being made."

Four weeks later Anya and the children were having the full English breakfast that had become the habit on a Saturday morning. Geoffrey brought in the post and handed it to Anya, the letter from the court on the top.

"You open it Geoffrey. I don't think I can."

"*Dear Mrs Philips, In the matter of*" Geoffrey skimmed silently over the remainder of the letter before shouting "We won!".

Anya took the the short letter from him, read it and burst into tears.

"It's not that bad is it?" Geoffrey asked innocently.

"Of course not! It's absolutely bloody brilliant!"

When they had all hugged each other and once Anya and Rose's tears had been wiped away, when James and Geoffrey had cleared away the remnants of their breakfast things they sat around the table with fresh mugs of coffee.

"Well, what do we call you now?" James asked quietly.

For the past months Anya knew they had avoided calling her anything. She hadn't made an issue of it but she wasn't comfortable with them calling her 'Anya' and 'Mum' was out of the question.

"What is that name Uncle John calls you?" James asked sensibly.

"Huggy. It comes from Hug, H U G. Highly Unsuitable Girl. When they first met me they thought I was highly unsuitable for Kent society and the name stuck."

"Were you unsuitable?" Rose asked quietly. Anya wondered what impression she had of her step-adopted-mother after her character and history had been the subject of so much discussion through the summer.

"Probably. But all things are relative, unsuitable to your grandmother was highly suitable to other people."

"Dad?"

"I hope so."

"We'll call you Hug or Huggy then." Rose said firmly. "It sounds almost like Mum or Mummy but it's a lot nicer."

Thoughtfully, Anya folded the letter and put it carefully back in the envelope. Eventually she looked up to see three anxious faces staring at her. She smiled.

"So, children of mine, whose turn is it to do the washing up?"

Chapter 16: Explanations

Barbados, January 2002

Tuesday January 1st 2002
Another Year. Surely a time for looking forward but all I can do is think about the past. I'm overwhelmed with dread about the future. What am I going to do now the children have to all intents and purposes left home? What am I going to do for money? Why did I sleep with Tim last night?

I've sometimes wondered why we've seen so little of each other since Geoff died, after all we have some of the same friends, mix in similar circles, were once almost related. Even though we've spoken occasionally we've never had what you could call a conversation. Not once. Whether this has been by design or accident I have no idea, and if by design I have no idea either whether that was him or me.

2000 was a lovely year. James's 18th in March, then Geoffrey's 21st, James's A levels and the angst of getting him into the university of his choice (success!), Geoffrey's finals and graduation (that brought back so many memories we all had such a great time!), and Rose's 20th barbecue (we had to have a big party for her because the boys had each had one) then the weekend in Cornwall the children organised for my 50th then seeing G off for his year travelling, then J to Durham.

The years when they needed me have been such good years. They rebelled, of course they did, why wouldn't they? They were young. Life had dealt them rotten cards in some ways and it took me a while to persuade them that they had been dealt some pretty good ones as well. They have, more than any other family

I have seen, each other. When I think how different the three of them are as people I wonder how they are so close. They've fallen out and argued, and not spoken for weeks, but they've always gone back to each other. Overall, with the enormous exception of losing their parents, life hasn't been too hard on them. All three, I hope, are happy self-confident (but not arrogant), well-balanced and caring people.

It would have been much more difficult if we hadn't had money. I hope they've never taken that for granted. They have their trust funds to see them into adulthood and onto the property ladder when they want to settle down. I hope I've taught them to understand how lucky they are. But for the past three years Geoff's investments haven't brought in anything like enough. The house needed a new roof, the children needed cars, places to live at uni, we needed holidays. Interest rates went down and inflation went up so one by one my properties have had to go. I don't resent it in the least. What I do resent is the bad investment advice I was given and last year's crash. It looks as if all I've got left now is this house (after the children all pass 21) and Fishermen Rock.

Is that it? Have I anything to look forward to or am I on the run in to the end of my life? I'm 52 this year, that's older than Mum when she died and about the same age as Dot Hill. The children won't need me anymore, well maybe every now and again, but they won't fill my days as they have done. I'll have letters to write, perhaps a wedding to organise, maybe even grand-children to babysit in time. Is this how every woman feels, when her children leave home? I can't believe the years are going by so quickly.

It was Christmas that made me take stock. Rose and James came home but they really couldn't wait to get back to their friends. It would be the last one as a family, and even this one was without Geoffrey, though he did phone briefly from somewhere in India (I think) it was wonderful to hear from him but the line was really bad. Will there ever be another Christmas with all four of us together? I have just the smallest inkling of why Kathleen held on to her family Christmases. New Year's Eve loomed and although David and Linda invited me to their place I didn't really want to go. I wanted to do something to make me believe the best of my life wasn't all behind me. I told myself I've got to be positive so I found a restaurant that could squeeze one more person in at short notice. The only one was miles away but I decided it wasn't too great an extravagance, just this once, to get a cab each way. I spent a couple of days looking forward to dressing up, though my days of wearing heels higher than sensible and dresses tighter than necessary are long gone I felt I could still be pretty presentable for a woman my age. I looked forward to being someone I hadn't been for a long time, myself, instead of Geoffrey, Rose and Jim's mum. I needed to remind myself that Anya Philips still existed.

The restaurant was full and my table, being for one, was tucked out of the way but the staff were very nice, treating me with no less respect than others just because I was a woman alone on a night of large parties.

Excellent, well cooked food washed down with a half bottle of wine and one of champagne made me mellow. The New Year was being counted down and several tables got together to sing Auld Lang Syne rather self-consciously as it really wasn't that sort of restaurant. My taxi was due at 12.30 so I sat back with a coffee and liqueur enjoying some peace of mind because I'd made a decision over an excellent Beef Wellington. I'd spend at least the next three months in Barbados. Miriam has always been so cheerful and welcoming when we've been out for holidays and I could do with some TLC. Also, now it's my only source of income, I can get more involved even than I was when I first bought the place.

I was drinking my second cup of coffee when I noticed him sitting with two couples I didn't recognise. The table wasn't completely in view and I thought he must have changed seats, Surely I would have noticed if he'd been there for the past three hours. I looked away. I really, really, didn't want to catch his eye. But, I told myself, even if I did surely there was no problem in smiling, waving and mouthing 'Happy New Year' across the room. Could there? It was funny, as soon I didn't want to look in a particular direction in the room that was where my eyes wandered to. Why did the man upset my equilibrium so? After all this time.

I found myself staring at the table cloth. It must be nearly time for the taxi and I'd have to pass his table to get to the door. A simple 'Hello, Happy New Year' 'Sorry I've got to go. My taxi's here' and I would be gone. All would be well again.

Perhaps he would get up, go to the cloakroom, and I could pass unnoticed.

Why was it such an issue? Why was he such a problem? It must have been the atmosphere. Or the wine. Or the fact it was a New Year. Or my mood. Or something about wanting to recapture what was lost long ago.

As I walked towards the door I knew there was no way he wouldn't see me. He seemed surprised but also pleased and wished me a happy 2002 adding something about it not being possible that it could be worse than the year just gone. Then he asked me to join him. I couldn't, I said, a taxi is waiting. I'll get you home he had said. Join us. He sent a waiter outside to my taxi with a note to compensate the loss of fare. I thought that high-handed of him but then it was perfectly in character. The others at his table seemed genuine in the invitation so I'd joined them. They were nice people and I enjoyed the extension to my evening. I didn't ask how they knew him or why they were all spending New Year together and they didn't say. They left together, the four strangers, leaving us alone at the table.

I know I shouldn't have been taken in by him after all this time but somehow he seemed different, more interested in someone, something, anything, other than himself. Was he as embarrassed as I was? Was he nervous? I was. I have no idea why. Almost like a teenager on a first date. Don't be ridiculous I told myself as we finished our coffee and liqueurs, I have known this man for 30 years.

He took me home in his chauffeur-driven car. He had to have lost his licence somehow, drink driving probably, I was sure he hadn't had a chauffeur in 2000 when we had seen quite a lot of him. The driver talked without stopping as he drove, perhaps to keep himself awake. We sat on the back seat, luckily separated by the leather armrest. I spent the journey wondering what to do when we reached the house. Should I ask him in for coffee? Would he read more into that than there was? I would have loved to have had answers to some questions. Why had he abandoned me to Kathleen? Why hadn't he helped me adopt the children? Why had he been so distant every time we met? These things had bothered me because it had once seemed we had so much in common. It was as if we had never been attracted to each other. Perhaps it had only ever been sex.

When we arrived home he got out of the car with me. It was all so natural, it all seemed so uncomplicated. He gave me no answers because I didn't ask him any questions. We just went upstairs together. I'm out of practice I said, he said he'd be gentle and it was like riding a bike. I laughed remembering a young American 9 years before. A lifetime. So Tim and I made love (probably had sex is putting it more accurately). It was more comfortable than the Golf Club Captain's office floor, it was less urgent than those days in the hotel in Covent Garden, it was definitely more sophisticated than those times under the trees at his engagement party or on his stag night or on his wedding day.

Maybe we had both been trying to regain something of our youth and perhaps it meant nothing to either of us. Perhaps he had thought it was expected of him, perhaps I thought it was a good idea at the time, but I wish we hadn't.

Shit. I didn't even enjoy it.

As Anya flew into Bridgetown she was still trying to shake off the feeling of depression that had enveloped her since she had woken up three days earlier to see Tim asleep next to her, lying on his back snoring gently. It had been a most unattractive sight.

She had slipped out of the bed and taken some clothes into the bathroom to dress. She did not want him to see her naked, nor did she want the intimacy of having him watch her dress. She went downstairs and checked the answer machine. There were messages from all three children wishing her a Happy New Year. She went into the kitchen, leant against the kitchen table and sobbed. She waited for Tim to come downstairs dreading having to face him, wondering what she could possibly say. She was relieved when a few minutes later she heard the gentle opening and closing of the front door. He hadn't wanted to see her either.

The first day of 2002 had been a dreadful day, she hoped it wasn't an indication of what the year was to bring. She had tried to watch television but there had been nothing that could distract her. She had thought of phoning Miriam to discuss her plans but decided against it. It was New Year's Day, it was one of the busiest days of the year at Fishermen Rock with the traditional buffet lunch. She couldn't phone Geoffrey, she had no idea where he was, or Rose or James, not on January 1st when they would be recovering from their New Year celebrations so she sat at her computer, reading back over the past six years of her diary. That only depressed her more as they recounted the busy life of the house filled with voices and noise, with laughter and tears and arguments and loud music and love.

She tried to focus her thoughts as she wrote the diary of the previous day. Perhaps she was over-reacting, after all, all she had done was have non-committed sex with an old friend. It wasn't as if she had picked up a stranger. She would just try to forget the whole thing, if she forgot it then it would be as if it never had happened.

She looked out of the aircraft at the Caribbean Sea and the west coast of Barbados thinking, as she always did, how built up the island appeared to be from the air. Then the sea was directly beneath her as the aircraft banked sharply to the left in its rapid descent. She remembered the times when she had flown Concorde and how short and luxurious the flight had been then, but since the children had come into her life that had not really been an option. When she had made this flight with Geoffrey, Rose and James their excitement had been infectious and the time had passed quickly but this flight seemed to have gone on forever. She missed the children with a lurch in her chest that hurt. What were they all doing now? She had phoned Rose and James before she'd left home that morning and they'd just told her to enjoy herself but she hadn't heard from Geoffrey since his message at New Year. He hadn't said where he was or what he was doing, he just said he was OK and would be back in the UK in the Spring. She offered up a prayer to a God she didn't believe in that he was safe and happy.

As she walked down the aircraft steps into the heat of the late Barbados afternoon she tried to relax. She felt at home here, soon she would be sitting on the veranda sipping the welcoming rum punch and being seduced by the warmth of the breeze and of Miriam's enthusiasm.

She clambered inelegantly into the driving seat of the moke she had asked to be reserved for her. She had always liked the feeling of freedom that driving the open-topped and open sided car gave her, she hoped she would never be too old to drive one around the island. She slipped it into gear and drove away from the airport, turning right whilst the vast majority of the other traffic turned left towards the city and the crowded west coast.

It took her a moment to realise that, apart from Miriam's Toyota, there was only one other car in the hotel's car park. This was early January, the height of the season, the car park should be packed. She tried to think of a good reason for the absence of cars. Perhaps it was just that all the guests were out and about, but it was just coming up to sundown. The terrace should be crowded with groups of people enjoying rum punch and cocktails, yet she could see only one couple.

She wondered also why Miriam hadn't rushed out to greet her. She should have got the email the airline had sent from Heathrow and would have been expecting her. All the visits she had made with the children had begun with Miriam, arms outstretched, enthusiastically welcoming them back. Anya climbed out of the car slowly. She smiled absent-mindedly at the couple as she walked passed them into the bar acutely aware that there were no tables laid out for dinner, no staff, eager to serve, busying themselves behind the bar. Where was Dexter? He always had a drink waiting for her. Despite the heat Anya shuddered. Everything felt wrong.

Instead of bustling about urging the staff to be even more attentive to their guests, Miriam was sitting at a table at the far end of the restaurant with a man Anya did not recognise. He was not a guest. He was wearing a suit and tie. There were papers on the table and they were deep in conversation, neither looked up as Anya set about making a large jug of punch. She had to find out what was going on and perhaps the couple on the terrace could help her.

"Good evening, my name is Anya, would you like some rum punch? On the house. May I join you?" Seeing their perplexed expressions she added "I'm Anya Philips. I am the owner of Fishermen Rock."

In a short while she had a good picture of what was going on. 'The hotel had been crowded,' the couple told her 'over Christmas it had been full.' 'Yes. We've had a wonderful time.' 'A brilliant Christmas'. But then there had been an outbreak of food poisoning. Some officials had been called in by the doctor. The kitchen had been closed down. 'We're not staying here now, we just came to say goodbye to Miriam before we go back to the UK.'

"That's very good of you." Anya was trying to take in the scale of the problem Miriam was facing. Perhaps there had been other problems over the past few years that he had never known about. A rising tide of guilt engulfed her; how little she had been involved with the hotel, how many burdens she had put on Miriam, how little use she had been.

"You seem to be very fond of the hotel."

"Oh we are. We come every year for Christmas, have done for, what is it?" he asked his wife, "Five years now."

Anya and the children had always avoided Christmas and the New Year, not wanting to take up rooms that could otherwise be sold at the highest rate.

"Miriam has been brilliant. Every year she remembers exactly what we like and don't like. We get the rooms we ask for. She's brilliant, absolutely brilliant."

"We feel so sorry for her. She works so hard to give everyone a good time."

"She didn't need this."

"Will you tell me about the hotel?" Anya asked. "What's so great about it and what isn't? I've not been out here very much for the past six years, certainly not often enough, and I probably didn't look and listen enough when I was here, you see I had my children with me and had to make sure they had a great holiday." She had no idea why she felt the need to explain to the guests.

The couple painted Anya a picture of a hotel that hadn't had enough investment. She was astute enough to realise that guests didn't come back year after year because of the fabric of the hotel, they came because of the service and because of the personal attention Miriam gave them. It was seven years since the refurbishment and since then she had not invested enough, either in time or in money. She took a notebook from her handbag and, as the jug of rum punch was emptied, carefully noted all they told her of the improvements they would like to see at Fishermen Rock.

"Time, Miriam, there was never enough time."

Anya and Miriam sat on the terrace late into the night, the couple and the man from the Tourism Department long gone.

"I should have spent more time here."

"Yes. You should."

"But you never told me."

"You should have seen when you were here but you had your eyes shut."

"I was so involved for the first couple of years but then it was a question of priorities. You know when we started I had every intention of spending half the year out here, being part of everything. I didn't want to be an absentee landlord, a signature on cheques, a recipient of dividends. I really wanted to be involved."

"Then why weren't you?"

"You know why not, it was the children."

"And now?" Anya could hear Miriam's resentment.

"Now I'm here to help."

"But that's not why you came. You didn't know about all this. You came for a holiday, for your own reasons. And you should have known better than to turn up during the first week in January. If this had been a normal year we would have had no room. But, as you can see, this is not a normal year."

Anya knew Miriam was right but didn't want to admit it, she was feeling low enough as it was. "I didn't know there were problems because you didn't tell me."

"What would I tell you? I don't know what all the problems are yet, the list gets longer every day."

"Well it's obvious you've been shut down."

"You've been shut down." Miriam corrected with a steel of anger Anya had never heard from her before. "It's your name on all the paperwork. You're the one who will be prosecuted."

"We've been shut down." Anya conceded, reluctantly acknowledging to herself that Miriam was absolutely right. On the flight out she hadn't thought about what she could contribute, she had only pictured lazy days and long evenings sitting with Miriam on the terrace, surrounded by contented and high-paying guests. Anya had come to Fishermen Rock with no plan other than to enjoy a few weeks of luxury in the sun. As she sat in uncomfortable silence she remembered what she had written in her diary the night before:

'Wrong side of 50. Not broke but no longer well of. Capital: House but only when James hits 21, all others gone. Income: very small amount from what's left of investments, most must come from FR.'

Now she couldn't bank on any income from the hotel, instead it would cost a deal of money she didn't have to get it back on track.

"No. *You've* been shut down. I quit." Miriam's voice was as cold as Anya had ever heard it.

"But you can't!" Anya was horrified. "You are Edna's Place, you are Fishermen Rock. Guests come here because of you. You can't quit."

"I can and I do, with immediate effect."

"Let's talk about it tomorrow. Please, I'm tired. It was a long flight. It's been a long day, I'm too tired to talk about it tonight."

"You You You. Listen to yourself Anya. I'm tired too. I've carried this place the past six years and watched you take all the money out of it, never a penny put back. All your initial enthusiasm soon disappeared."

"Why didn't you say anything before? I've been over here every year. You could have said something, but you didn't so I could only assume that everything was going fine."

"You know where assumptions get you don't you?"

"You said nothing." Anya tried to answer calmly but she knew she sounded defensive.

"How could I talk to you when you were always running around with the children? You were only here long enough to get a tan and then back to the UK. If you'd been that interested you would have asked. You could have come out alone, you could have spoken on the phone about the business, you only ever called to see if there were rooms for you all."

Anya was surprised at how calm she felt in the face of such criticism. Perhaps it was because she recognised the justice in Miriam's complaints. She had made a decision when she took over the children, that they would be her life and Miriam was right, everything else had been unimportant.

"I'm sorry, I hadn't realised how thoughtless I've been but things will change now. Perhaps I should have tackled things differently it was just that the children, well, they have been everything. Perhaps I should have thought about you and the business more."

"Perhaps nothing. Of course you should have done."

"I can do now. I can help. I will help. But I can't do it without you."

"You'll have to. I mean it when I say I've had enough of this place."

"But please Miriam, please. I can't do it without you."

"You should have thought of that."

"But how am I to know what to do? I can't possibly sort it out on my own."

"Like I've had to sort everything out on my own for the past seven years?"

"But you knew where to start, I know nothing about running a hotel, nothing."

"Well you should have thought about that when you bought into it."

Since they had first met on that dark night in January 1994 Anya had thought she and Miriam were partners, friends even, but as she tried to persuade her to stay she realised that that had never been the case.

"Will you help me set off in the right direction? Spend a little time handing over? Go over the paperwork? Help me?" Anya softened her voice, trying to hide the panic that was rising within her.

"I'm going back to the UK as soon as I can get a flight. I'll find a pub somewhere to give me a part time job. I've got my pension, that'll do me. I don't need expensive clothes and fancy holidays." Anya took Miriam's comments as very personal criticism and tried not to be hurt by them.

"Give me a few days? Please?"

"Is it my fault if you're not suited to this business? Any business?"

"I'm not suited to business?" Anya was incredulous and began to feel a little angry. "I ran a business, as well you know, for many years in the UK. It was very successful. You can't say I'm unsuited to running a business. Valid criticism I will take but please, Miriam, don't say that."

"You may have worked hard years ago but you've got out of the habit. Now you'll never put in the hours it takes, you'll never find the energy to cope with all the administration at the end of a long day. We're not 9 to 5 here you know, nearer 5 in the morning to midnight.

Then there's dealing with the staff, and officialdom, the travel agents, and, of course, the clients. You have no idea how much is involved."

"Then give me at last some idea before you leave. Please. Then I'll know how unsuitable I am."

Anya wondered if Miriam could know how much that word had haunted her through her life.

When Anya woke up the next morning her initial thoughts were free from worry, she was warm, she was comfortable and the sun was rising. Then she remembered. She watched the sky lighten as the sun rose above the horizon trying not to think about the next seven days. In that time she had a great deal of work to do.

She had persuaded Miriam to stay one week. Miriam had known she held all the cards and Anya had had to give Miriam far more than she could afford to persuade her to stay even that amount of time. It could never be enough to learn all that she needed to know and it was a long time since she had had to learn so much that was completely new. And she had only seven days.

She made herself a cup of tea and found a new page in her notebook. She wrote the days of the week she had before Miriam left for the UK and she noted for each day the topic she wanted to cover. There were too many topics and too few days. Half an hour later she was downstairs at the computer copying her notes and adding a list of questions as they occurred to her, then carefully cutting and pasting them into some kind of order. She hoped to show Miriam that she may not know the answers but at least she knew what questions to ask.

As she made herself a coffee she wondered where Miriam was, surely she would be up and about by now. As she waited for the water to boil she glanced at the clock, it was past eight. She gazed through the window at the car park. It took her a few moments to realise that Miriam's car was not there. She had not kept her promise to stay. Anya's hand shook as she poured the hot water into a mug, wondering what she could possibly do. She walked back to the computer, sat down and stared at the questions on the screen.

The thought of selling the hotel came into her mind and would not go away. She would have to sell, but would anyone buy it in the state it was in? If she couldn't sell what else could she do with it? She couldn't afford to pay another Miriam even if she could find one. And as she looked again at the screen full of problems she knew she could not do it herself.

It was only as she faced up to the prospect of losing it that she realised how attached she was to the place. She walked out onto the terrace and looked out to sea. She thought of the houses she had lived in and owned. She had had eight homes and owned, at various times, twenty five different investment properties. Now, because of a combination of wanting to do the very best for the children, some ill-advised dealings in a stock market she didn't understand and disastrous world events over which no one had any control, she had only Fishermen Rock and, when James reached 21, their house in England.

She had hated the house in Kent when she had first seen it. She remembered standing outside the front door with Tim wondering what sort of people could live in a house like that. It had been Kathleen's house; formal, old-fashioned, darkly furnished. When she had moved in after Geoff's death it had been decorated and furnished to Fiona's taste. In the past seven years she and the children had made many changes and she had many happy memories of living there but, she recognised sadly, she had never chosen it, as she had chosen Fishermen Rock. It wasn't rational, she knew, as she had spent so little time here, but she felt more at home at Fishermen Rock than anywhere else.

She turned to look at the building and made herself notice how ravaged it had become since its extensive and expensive makeover. The paint of the window frames was peeling, the walls were discoloured, even the padlocks on the doors were brown with rust. She had to admit that the place looked neglected, almost abandoned. Anya had a vague memory of Miriam asking for some extra funds for redecoration a couple of years before but she hadn't wanted to spend the money. She hadn't seen the need.

She sat down by the pool, realising it, too, needed repair and a lick of paint. She wondered dispassionately whether crying would make it all seem better but decided that could achieve nothing so she made herself look around again. The gardens were unkempt, the trees needed lopping, the potholes in the car park needed filling, the walls, in part, needed rebuilding. Everything needed attention, everything was broken, dirty or out of date. She sat, her head in her hands, listening to the surf breaking wondering at the way properties had been so much of her life and yet she knew so little about taking care of them.

She was only pulled out of her slough of self-pity by the sound of a car engine as Miriam's Toyota pulled into the car park.

The week went far too quickly. The list of questions that needed answering seemed to grow each day as the more she knew the more she realised she needed to know.

Thursday 10th January 2002

Miriam's last day but two. I've got to make a decision. One thing is certain I can't keep both Fishermen Rock and the house in Kent and I can't sell up in the UK until next March when Jamie turns 21 and only then if the children don't object. But this place needs so much money spending on it soon if we're to get our licence back and not lose all this year's bookings. Loans, mortgages, all possible I suppose but I don't suppose I'm much of a bet with banks these days. Even if I managed to raise the money to invest in this place could I make it work? It would take everything I have to get the Fishermen back to its former glory and I've have to live out here. Miriam is right, everything is strange to me, but she's wrong to think I can't learn. I should know more than I do but that's history and not worth dwelling on. Every day, as I feel less and less confident about taking over the hotel I feel more and more convinced it's what I want to do. I'd live here, make new friends, get a life. I just wish Miriam wanted to be part of that and stay.

That evening Anya had sat with Miriam in the small office and had tried to persuade her, yet again, to stay but Miriam was determined. "You're wasting your words. It's time for me to go home."

"Why? Your life is here."

"I've been here for 20 years but it is time to go."

"But I promise things will be different." Anya was pleading. She so wanted to revive the hotel and she needed Miriam to do that.

"You say you left me to run this place because you had to look after your children. Well I've got children and grandchildren that I want to see something of and they're not so well off that they can afford to flit out here for holidays every year."

"I never knew that."

"There are a lot of things you haven't bothered to find out when you've been out here, about me and about your family."

"What do you mean 'about my family'?"

"You have never spent tried to track down your uncle have you?"

"What do you know about my uncle?"

Miriam didn't directly answer the question.

"On that first day you were here you said your mother's brother was Vincent Albert Cave and he used to live on the island. I would have thought you would have been interested to find him but no, you never bother about anyone but yourself."

Anya had thought about Vincent Cave from time to time but it had always seemed that there was something more important to do. There were never enough hours in the day or days in the week of her visits, but she knew lack of time was just an excuse. She had come to the conclusion that she was afraid to know the truth. She had even persuaded herself that it didn't matter, she was herself, who or what her father had been made no difference to that.

"I know a Vincent Cave."

Anya wasn't sure she had heard Miriam correctly, she had spoken so quietly. Anya said nothing, didn't want to pursue the conversation, there was so much on her plate, there were so many things to think about, she didn't want the complication of finding Vincent Cave. She stared out of the window towards sea, vaguely aware of the fisherman manoeuvring his small boat towards a buoy.

Miriam continued. "He came to the island when? 1965?"

"About then." Anya gave Miriam no encouragement but there was no stopping her. In a voice devoid of emotion Miriam told Anya everything she knew.

"A year after we re-opened there was a booking for lunch, a Mr and Mrs Cave. The moment he walked into the restaurant I saw the likeness. He was tall and willowy, a very attractive man for his age. He had long, tapering fingers, just like yours, and his hair, though mainly grey, still had flecks of dark brown. He had the look of you. As he came in regularly I found out more about him. He said he came from Liverpool, he never went back to the UK as he had no one who would welcome him there, his name was Vincent. I knew who he was and I encouraged him to talk. He would come during the week without his wife and family, we would sit on the veranda there talking about England and what it would be like to go back after so many years here on the island. He told me his history, how he had arrived on the island with nothing and had started out doing odd jobs earning enough to buy an old truck. He built up a successful business, his firm even did some of the work on Fishermen. His sons work with him and he is a happy man but there is something he worried about. Seven years ago he saw you and he saw your ring. He knew immediately who you were. He said it was a real shock, he had tried to forget his life before he came to the island but he saw you were well and happy and well off. But he was worried you had children. I said I'd talk to you, explain, you could meet but he didn't want you to know who he was. He made me promise to say nothing to you."

Anya didn't want to talk about Vincent. "If I can't persuade you to stay I'd better get some sleep. Tomorrow will be a busy day."

So Vincent had seen her, had known who she was and hadn't said a word. She must have seen him but not recognised any resemblance. Had anyone else? Had the children seen him and recognised something of her in this man? What did the fact that they were so alike mean? Could it just be that they were in the same family or would it mean more, could it mean that he was, after all, her father?

On Miriam's last night Anya insisted on cooking a meal and eating it together, just as they had on that first night.

"I'll do my very best you know." Anya said as they sat with the remnants of their second bottle of wine watching the whites of the waves reflecting the light of the moon.

"I know you will."

"And you haven't had second thoughts?" Anya asked hopefully.

"No. It's time to go. I should have gone when Gary died. I wanted to go then."

"And I stopped you."

"Yes. You stopped me then, but now you won't. I'm going back to Yorkshire."

"I won't say anything more, other than to wish you all the luck in the world and thank you again for all you have done to help me. I'm just so sorry I didn't realise at the time how much."

"Don't you want to know more about Vincent Cave?" Miriam asked when she realised Anya was not going to bring up the subject.

"Is there more to tell?"

"I thought you might ask some questions? Be curious? Want to know more about him?"

"Why would I want to do that?"

"Because he's your family."

"He's never been part of my family. He left England before I was born. He means nothing to me at all so why would I want to know anything about him?"

"Can I give you some advice?" Miriam asked in such a tone that told Anya she was going to give it whatever the reply. Anya said nothing and Miriam continued with barely a break. "Stop thinking that the world revolves around Anya Cave. You should look around you at all the wonderful people you never see because you focus on yourself all the time."

Anya thought that was a bit unfair in the light of her having dropped everything to look after the children but she had enough sense not to interrupt. She still hoped that, after a winter in England, Miriam would want to come back so she bit her lip.

"Anya Cave doesn't keep her eyes open. She only sees what she wants to see."

"I haven't been Anya Cave for a long time."

"You have always been Anya Cave." Miriam paused, perhaps waiting for Anya to say something in her defence. After a minute of silence broken only by the roar of the surf Miriam continued. "Look up Anya Cave. What do you see?"

Anya looked into the darkness of the sky. There was no light other than the candles flickering in their glass tubes on the table and the sky was alive with millions upon millions of white dots.

"Stars."

"So you are looking and you see stars."

"Yes. Of course I do." Anya struggled to hide her impatience, she wondered where Miriam was heading with this train of thought.

"Now tomorrow, you look up to the sky and what will you see?"

"Sky. Clouds."

"Where do you think the stars have gone?"

"They're still there. They haven't gone anywhere."

"You just don't see them because the light of the sun hides them."

"So?" Anya still didn't understand what Miriam was trying to say.

"Are the stars beautiful? Are they thought-provoking? Do they hint at untold worlds, life, civilisations far beyond what we can experience or imagine? Of course they do. We've sat out here many nights looking at the sky, made aware of the Earth's insignificance in the universe and our insignificance in our world's scheme of things. But then the sun comes out and we don't see the stars. We forget them, we forget they exist. For the hours of daylight we imagine we are the centre of the universe because there is nothing to remind us we are not."

"So?"

"Think what I am saying. You are the sun in your universe, you do not see the stars that are other people because of the brightness of your ego. Now imagine you are not so self-centred as to have this great sun of light preventing you from seeing what is really around you. You might even be a better person for it."

Anya felt hurt. She had given her life for the last six years to the children, she she had done everything she could for the children. She could take criticism but not when it was so unfair. "You are being so unfair Miriam, so very unfair. I have loved the children. I have done what I had to do for them. There is not one single grain of truth in what you say."

Miriam gave up arguing. "I've got a lot of packing to do and a long day tomorrow. Remember Anya, look for the stars that are the people who share this world with you, especially those that are nearest to you, your family. Don't just see them as they are in relation to you, they are themselves, and that may well be something you really don't allow them to be."

Anya stayed on the terrace after Miriam had left her. She didn't want to go to bed, she didn't want the next day to come. She tried to understand what it was that Miriam had been trying to say. Miriam couldn't really think she was that selfish. Perhaps it was just the wine talking on a starry night when both their lives were about to change.

Sunday 13th January 2002

Miriam left today and I'm on my own. The place is dark and quite eerie. Every creak of wood makes me think something dreadful is about to happen. I'm not going to sleep very well tonight, or for a while really...

I've been wondering about the children. Rosy and Jamey are at Uni but where is Geoffrey? He'll be somewhere in the world, growing more and more like his father every day. But what is he really doing? What is he really like? Do I really know him? And what about Rose, independent, determined to stand on her own two feet, determined to try things and make her own mistakes, what do I really know about my step-adopted-daughter that I hadn't guessed in those first few minutes of meeting her. Was she happy, had she ever been happy? Was Rose the kind of person to sit alone underneath the stars with a glass of wine? I don't know.

And I really, really should. Then there's Jimbo. Has he been my favourite? I've tried not to have one but he was always the most sensitive, the most dependent of the three, and the most determined not to show it.

Can I really do what I want to do ignoring what might be best for them? They may be grown up but they may still need me to be part of their lives even if I can no longer influence theirs. Could I really leave England and start my own life in Barbados just because it suits me?

I wish I could ask them what I should do, what they want me to do. They'd say I should do what I want to do, what I think is best for me. They would say it but a) would they mean it and b) who knows what the fuck is best anyway?

That evening Anya spent a long time holding a full glass of wine listening to the waves crashing against the rocks. She had thought of Miriam's Gary, he had been so desperate at the failure of this place that he had thrown himself from the roof to a painful and probably not instantaneous death on those rocks. What would she do if she sank all the money she had left into the hotel and it still failed? She looked to the stars and asked them, but they gave her no answer.

She didn't go to bed that night, she knew she wouldn't sleep, and she counted the hours through in bottles of wine.

She did not let herself think of Vincent Cave.

Chapter 17: Enlightenments

Barbados, March 2002

As the sun came up Anya walked down the steps into the pool trying not to see how much it needed repainting. She swum up and down several times, remembering the days when she had done the same, but when everything had been different. She lay on a lounger until the sun became too hot when she moved to the cool of the office to look through some papers. Not feeling she could face any of it she went back to the pool and swam two more lengths before settling under the shade of an umbrella. She remembered so many lazy days when she had lain down on the sun lounger after breakfast and not moved until Miriam rang the gong that told her, and their guests, that lunch was ready to be served. How could she have been so blind to what she should have been doing?

She should have been busy meeting people, drawing up schedules, raising finance, planning her future, but every day she found a reason not to do anything. All she achieved that first week was to arrange for the car hire company to take away her moke, she had the hotel's pick up now. She had no need to shop as there was sufficient food in the larder and the freezers and wine in the cellar to last some considerable time. She reasoned that she had paid for it so she could consume it. It would go to waste if she didn't eat it as no one else would be allowed to eat or drink at Fishermen Rock until the licences were renewed. If the licences were renewed.

Friday 18th January 2002

Miriam wanted to go home to England and start a new life after Gary killed himself, but I wanted her to stay so she stayed. Peter didn't want to carry on with March and March but I wandered in and made him stay in the business he hated.

It was my fault he carried on with it. Do I really make people do what they don't want to do? How many other people's lives have I fucked up? Well starting with Mum, probably quite a few.

The only person she saw after Miriam left was the post lady who arrived every afternoon on her motorbike leaving Anya with a sheaf of envelopes which she forced herself to open. They usually turned out to be bills or reminders, occasionally there were confirmations of bookings to which she wrote carefully worded replies of explanation. But she did little else.

On the Sunday after Miriam had left Anya was lying by the pool when she opened her eyes to find a man staring down at her.

"Good morning Dexter." She said recognising Miriam's deputy and the head barman. She sat up and drew her towel around her. "What can I do to help?"

"We need to know what your plans are." He said without preamble, his habitual respectful demeanour not in evidence. "We need to know what you going to do."

"I'm afraid I don't know yet." It was all the answer she could give.

"We haven't been paid."

She agreed to pay all the staff the month's money Dexter said they were owed and a further month in lieu of notice. He went with her into the office and they spent half an hour drawing up a list of people and how much each should have. "Tell me Dexter," She said as the list grew longer and longer, "why does such a small hotel need more than thirty staff?"

"I'm the main man, in charge of the restaurant and bar and Miss Miriam's deputy when she's not around, then we have chef and three under him, three shifts of table waiters and waitresses, two shifts of chamber maids, the kitchen staff, the gardeners, the pool team…'

"That's a lot of people."

"If you cut staff service suffers and we have always offered the highest standard of service."

Anya watched Dexter as he placed the carefully labelled brown envelopes full of cash in a plastic supermarket carrier bag. It was almost all the cash she had.

"Mrs Miriam said that the hotel will be closing."

"I don't know yet."

"If you do need staff you call on us first."

"I have no idea when or if I will be hiring again but I've everyone's address and of course I'll be in touch with you as soon as I know what's happening." She was determined to be business-like even though she was wearing a bikini with only a towel inadequately wrapped around her.

"You will call on me as soon as you know." Dexter was not to be fobbed off.

"Surely all the staff will find other jobs, they can't be dependent on me."

"There are no jobs this side." He had replied sadly. "We'd have to travel over to the west or the south. It'll cost in petrol. We all live local. Working on the west adds two hours to the day too. Women won't be home when schools out. Children will be left alone when they get into all sorts of trouble."

"Of course I'll let you know as soon as my decision has been made." As she watched him walk back up the road the knowledge of how her failure was affecting the lives of so many people depressed her still further.

She knew she would have to pull herself together and make the decision before too much more time passed. She sat on the terrace and watched the way the waves crashed, each one different, against the rocks. She knew she had to leave but she didn't know how to. As long as there was food in the fridge and wine in the cellar she could put off doing anything.

In the last week of January Anya sent postcards to Rose and James telling them she was still in Barbados and wasn't sure when she would get home, it certainly wouldn't be by Easter. It seemed a long time before she received a reply from Rose but it was probably only two weeks. The two page letter was chatty and Anya could find no hint that she was being missed. Two days later she received a letter from James telling her not to worry about him, he was fine. The feeling of not being needed overwhelmed her and she spent the evening drinking the last of the good wine left in stock. She looked to the stars, as she did every night, remembering what Miriam had said and trying to think how she could change herself for the better.

"Mrs Philips? Anya Philips?"

The polite, almost diffident, voice disturbed her as she leafed through the post. She looked up and saw a young man, perhaps in his late 20s, standing looking at her with what could only be interpreted as surprise.

"Yes?" She asked, implicitly asking the man for an introduction.

"My name is Kenneth Cave."

"Ah."

She looked at the young man trying to determine whether he would be her half-brother or her cousin, perhaps her nephew. Incestuous families, she decided, were very complicated.

"Look I realise this is difficult but I think we both know we're related don't we? My father asked me to come round to see if he could call on you."

The voice had the slight island twang but the accent was unmistakably that of a well-educated Englishman. It reminded her of the way Geoffrey spoke when he was trying to be extraordinarily polite to a stranger.

"He didn't want to come himself?"

The young man seemed uncertain. "He didn't want to be shown the door."

"Why would I do that?"

"Well you've been to the island many times and never made any effort to get in touch with us."

"True. But then I didn't know for certain he still lived here and besides, well, I've never met him and I didn't know what sort, well what sort of relationship, well, you know what I mean." Anya finished lamely. She could not find any of the right words and she knew she sounded feeble.

"Could he come round to see you?"

"Six? Tonight?" She didn't add the words she wanted to add 'let's get this over with'. Kenneth nodded and walked away without saying anything. She decided he must have felt as awkward as she did. She sat back in her chair feeling suddenly nervous. She was to meet Vincent Albert Cave in three hours' time, after all those years of wondering.

The first moments were easy, she welcomed him with an outstretched hand which he shook formally, she ushered him onto the patio and asked if he would like a glass of wine or prefer beer. He indicated wine would be fine so she opened a bottle and poured two glasses. It was when they sat down, on either side of the small table, that the silence began to be oppressive. She didn't want to look at him because she knew he was looking at her. Eventually he spoke.

"Is my sister, is Melanie still…" He broke off, apparently unable to finish the sentence.

"… alive?" Anya spoke with a confidence she did not feel. "No. She died a long time ago. 1970, August 1970."

"So young." It was a statement not a question but Anya answered anyway. He sounded very sad.

"She was 36."

"What…?"

"She had cancer." It seemed safer than saying she had committed suicide. She didn't know this man well enough to give up all her mother's secrets.

"That must have been difficult."

"It was."

"You were still very young."

"20. I was at University."

"That must have been difficult." He repeated. Perhaps he too was nervous.

Again there was a period of silence as they sipped their wine and tried to avoid each other's gaze.

"I wish I could have been there to help."

"Mum wasn't the sort to want help."

"No, she wasn't was she?"

Neither seemed to want to say anything in case it frightened the other away, they were like dogs, circling around each other, waiting to see if they were friends or foes.

It was Anya who blinked first. "Can I ask something and you will promise to answer truthfully?"

"You want to know who your father is."

"How did you know?"

"It would only be natural." He waited for Anya's response but when none came he continued. "How much do you know?"

"I know my mother was not married, that I am illegitimate."

"Did she ever marry?"

"No."

"Do you know anything about your father?"

Why wasn't he telling her straight out? Anya didn't understand why he was being so unhelpful.

"I know whoever he was he shouldn't have been with Mum."

"How long have you known that?"

"Since Mum died. I found out about you and the ring and the fact that my father was related to her and that, whoever he was, he had raped her."

"You think I'm your father?"

"You might be." She said guardedly.

"I am not." He was very definite.

"Then it was her dad?" Their conversation was low key, understated and punctuated by long gaps between questions and answers. Anya had avoided looking at Vincent until now. She was shocked to see suspicion and dislike in his eyes. She looked away before continuing. "I've lived with the knowledge it was either you or him for years. She never said anything. I thought it must have been you because of the letters she got from you and the ones she wrote to you and never posted, and the ring."

"Ah, the ring, it was that ring that made me know who you are."

"I always wear it." She twisted it around her finger self-consciously.

"If you want me to I will tell you about your family. There will be things you regret knowing and they will be impossible to forget, however hard you try."

Friday 8th March 2002
It's very late and I'm very tired.
Vincent has just left. His son Kenneth picked him up as we had had far too much to drink for him to drive. Vincent is not my father he is my uncle (my mother's brother) but he is also my half-brother (my father's son). That makes Kenneth both my half-nephew (my half-brother's son) and my cousin (my mother's brother's son).
Vincent told me so much, describing things in a detail I can't write down. I wish I'd taped our conversation. For the record then: Albert and Elizabeth Cave were married in the autumn of 1932. Albert was a lot older than Elizabeth, probably into his 30s whilst Elizabeth was still in her teens. At Easter 1933 they had a son, Vincent. E must have been pregnant when she married. Unmarried conceptions seem to run in the family – up to me that is. V believes that she would have done anything other than marry A if she had had a choice. In 1934 E had a daughter, Melanie. E had had a difficult time with V and had nearly died with M so the doctor said she must have no more children or it would kill her. There was no contraception, not for people of their class anyway, so she would have had to stop being a wife to A. But A couldn't forego his pleasures (V's phrase) so he brought girls back to the house and did what he had to do quite openly. They lived in a poor area near the docks and what men and women did together was part of life. There was no privacy, houses were small and many parents shared bedrooms, even beds, with their children, even when they slept in separate rooms walls were thin. Children knew what their parents did, Elizabeth knew what her husband was doing and so did Vincent and Melanie. It was just part of life.
V said the war had just started (he'd have been 5) when his

father started interfering with him (again V's phrase). Mum would have been a little older, maybe 7 or 8, when her father started doing things to her. Perhaps he couldn't get it any other way but with V and M.

I stopped V at this point in the story and asked why his mum didn't put a stop to it. He said she wasn't there. He didn't know whether she had died in one of the air raids or had left or why she had disappeared, she just wasn't there. I said she must have died because surely she wouldn't have left without her children. Perhaps he killed her when he was drunk V said matter-of-factly, as if it was quite a normal thing to think.

V knew what his father was doing was wrong but he had no way of stopping it. A's job in the shipyard meant he stayed at home when others went to war and V thought that made him feel inadequate. I said if he'd been in his 30s when he married E he might have been old enough to have been in the First War and perhaps something had happened there to make him who he was. V stared at me as if I was mad making excuses for his Dad.

V said whenever he tried to stop A getting at Mel he was beaten. After a bit she told him not to bother, she'd put up with it rather than see her brother knocked about. So M started sleeping in the same bed as her father and V had to listen to what was going on or go out and leave them to it.

I told V Mum had never told me anything about her parents or her childhood, now I understood why. I wish she'd talked to me, perhaps then we could have known each other better. I wondered if she had ever tried to talk and I'd ignored her, or argued or not heard the words she had spoken.

At the end of the war Mum's monthlies had started so she moved out of her Dad's bed. There was a succession of husbandless women looking for a home and whilst they were around A left his daughter alone, but when he lost his job he had no money to treat other women and V knew whatever he tried to do to protect his sister, it was inevitable he would go back to her. He raped her on her 15th birthday.

She didn't tell her brother until she could hide her condition no longer. V said he hit his father until he no longer felt any anger. He stole the rent money and left. He had had no choice, he said, but he had always felt guilty. 'I thought I'd killed him. If he survived he'd have made me leave. I couldn't have stayed. I couldn't have looked after her. Not her and a babe.'

V went to Liverpool, jumped a ship and ended up in Barbados. He wrote to his sister, she wrote to him. Their father died. Was it his beating that had killed him? He didn't know. Mel said she didn't care if it was. But he couldn't go back to England, just in case. He had to find a way of getting what money he could to Mel. He wasn't earning much but he saved and then he bought the ring. He sent it to her so she could sell it and use the money. He seemed angry when I told him she had never even opened the box.

Well that's it. It's no worse than I had imagined.

I wondered why V seemed to hate me so much, every time I caught his eye he was staring at me with thinly disguised dislike. It was as he was leaving he gave me the explanation. 'You have the look of him. You shouldn't have come to the island.'

Oh. I nearly forgot about the dress. I asked him if he knew anything about it. He'd sent it to her for her 21st birthday. He'd thought she would like something a glamorous. 'Did she ever wear it?' he asked. I said I didn't think so. I didn't say I had.

She saved the document and shut down the computer. For the whole evening she had been wrapped up in the past, in her mother's life, in Vincent's life. Now she had to concentrate on sorting out her own.

She was still in bed the next morning when the phone rang.

"Hello? Fishermen Rock? Can I speak to Miriam?"

Anya listened to the voice, so easily recognised, and she took a moment to compose herself before answering. "Hello Geoffrey, it's me."

"Anya?" Of course he had no idea she was on the island.

"Yes, darling, it's me."

"Are you really here in Barbados?"

"I am, darling."

"That's brilliant. We're in Bridgetown. We've just come in on a yacht from Grenada."

It took a few moments for Anya to understand that Geoffrey was only a few miles away. She wasn't alone. She could talk things over with him, today.

She tried to keep her voice light. "How long are you around?"

"We've signed off the boat. We thought we'd spend a few days on the island and then fly back to UK. I've been away long enough, it's time to face up to the real world now."

"Geoffrey, darling, you don't know how good it is to hear your voice. I'll come and pick you up. I can be at the harbour in less than an hour."

"We've got one or two things to do. Shall we say 11ish in the upstairs bar?"

"I'll be there. It's so good to hear your voice, you don't know how good."

"Are you OK Anya?"

She realised he hadn't called her Huggy. He will have grown up in his months travelling, he would never again be the Geoffrey she had known. Perhaps she had never really known him anyway.

"Geoffrey?" She tried to keep her voice steady.

"Yes?"

"Aren't I Huggy anymore?"

He paused before answering. She felt his embarrassment. "Sorry, Anya seems, well, somehow, more appropriate now."

She wondered what he meant by 'more appropriate now'? "That's OK darling."

It didn't matter, Geoffrey was on the island.

She had thought many times in the years since Geoff had died how much she had loved him and how wrong she had been to have divorced him. The waste of nearly twenty years when she could have been with him was the greatest mistake in her life of many mistakes. But whenever she wished she had never left him she was faced with the fact that, had they stayed together, the children they had both loved would never have been born.

The two hours she had to wait before she could reasonably leave for the city passed very slowly.

She saw him before he saw her and she stole those moments to look at him and wonder. He was taller, broader, and had filled out into his height. He was tanned, more muscled than she could have imagined. She thought he looked like so many of the other young men who made their living on the yachts around the Caribbean.

He was 21, a man, no longer the boy who she had held and comforted and supported through the past years. She had been prepared for him to be more like his father, but she was unprepared for the lurch of pain she felt when she saw him up close. This was Geoff, her Geoff, as he had been in those early years. But then it wasn't, this was her adopted step-son, grown up, transformed in his months away into a man so like the man his father had been.

Anya thought of Kathleen. She realised the pain Kathleen must have felt every day as she had seen her husband in his son.

"Geoffrey." She made her presence known by touching his arm and gently speaking his name.

"Hello Anya. You don't mind do you? You sounded a bit sad on the phone but Huggy seems a little, well, wrong now."

"Anya's fine." She said, wondering at his composure.

"Anya meet Lizzy and Lissa and that old reprobate is Joe."

"Hi Lizzy," she smiled at the bronzed dark haired, dark eyed girl she guessed was Geoffrey's girl.

"Hi Lissa and Joe" she smiled again at the two who seemed so wrapped up in their own company they weren't aware of anyone else.

"Don't mind them Anya, they've just met up again after over three weeks apart." Geoff put his arm almost absent-mindedly, but with easy possession, around Lizzy's shoulder.

Anya thought that Lizzy looked intelligent, her eyes were sharp and looked straight back at her with something akin to defiance. She tried not to think that that was exactly the look she had thrown back at Kathleen when they had first been introduced the evening before Tim and Margaret's engagement party.

She wondered what their relationship was, she was rather afraid of the answer. Was this how Kathleen had felt when Geoff had taken her home that first time? No girl was ever going to be good enough for their sons. At no time in her life had Anya understood her erstwhile mother-in-law so well. It wasn't jealousy, Anya told herself. It wasn't fear of not being loved any more. She knew what it wasn't but she could not find the words to describe what the feeling really was.

"Are you coming back to Fishermen Rock?" she asked, hoping her voice didn't betray just how much she wanted Geoffrey to say yes.

"If that's OK?" He replied but, with his arm around Lizzy and his eyes encompassing Joe and Lissa, Anya realised that all four would be returning with her. "We're not really dressed for it."

"No worries." Anya replied. She couldn't tell him yet.

"All of you are most welcome." It was best to make the offer, appear as if it was her idea. "You must all come up to Fishermen and you must all call me Anya."

'I am going to be nice. I am not going to do a Kathleen.' She told herself as they all walked to the pick-up.

Geoffrey sat with her in the front while the other three sat amongst the ropes, sacks and boxes in the back. The arrangement wasn't particularly chivalrous as Lizzy and Lissa had the least comfortable ride but, Geoffrey pointed out, it would give him some private time with his mother.

"Not a moke this time?" He asked, perhaps beginning to feel that things were not quite as they should be.

"No. I think you'll find a lot of things are different." Anya started to warn Geoff as she negotiated the narrow streets of the city out onto the airport road. "We're not actually open for business."

"Not open?" She heard his disbelief.

"No." She couldn't bring herself to explain everything yet. She knew she would have to soon but every second of his ignorance seemed to be precious. Once he knew she could hide no longer. Decisions would be cast in stone and actions would have to be taken.

It took a few moments for Geoffrey to digest this information. He had thought that Anya looked tired and drawn under the tan. "I'm looking forward to seeing Miriam." He ventured.

"You won't." Anya spoke unnecessarily sharply. "She's gone back to the UK."

"When's she back?"

"She's not coming back. She doesn't work for us anymore."

"Miriam's gone?" The disappointment in his voice struck Anya. All the children had been fond of Miriam and, she had thought, she of them.

"Yes. She's left."

He turned towards her but hoped she would keep her eyes on the busy road ahead. "What's going on?"

As they passed the airport and headed into the quiet roads of the south east Anya began to talk.

"I don't want to worry you but I suppose you'll have to know sooner or later. Things have changed a great deal in the world since you left on your trip, 9-11, the stock market crash. Well, without going into all the details, I'm broke."

"Broke?" His voice held disbelief and surprise in equal parts.

"Broke." She confirmed.

"How?"

"As with most people I suppose, spending too much, bad investments."

"But we've got money. Me and Rosie and Jim, we've got money we'll sort something out."

"Don't even think about it. I will not take any of your money." She had turned to face Geoffrey to show him how serious she was and just returned her attention to the road in time to swerve violently to avoid two children walking in the road. It took them both a few moments to recover.

"Sorry. But I'm serious Geoffrey. Your money is yours. It's what your father wanted."

"But what will you do?"

"I have no idea. I think I'm going to have to sell up here. It'll be a wrench but I don't see any other way. Maybe you can help when you understand something of the problem."

"Of course I'll try. Your problems are my problems."

"That's very gallant of you but really it isn't true. I've got to sort this mess out." Determined to lighten the mood she tapped him on the knee and changed the subject. "Now, tell me what you've been up to. Well a little of it anyway. I don't want all the no doubt extremely colourful details."

Anya tried to sound light and teasing, but she knew she wasn't succeeding.

Joe and Lissa stayed only the one night. They had another boat to ferry between islands and, as soon as they realised any stay at Fishermen Rock wasn't going to be as Geoffrey had described it, they brought their trip to St Lucia forward. "We can do it tomorrow, next week, next month it makes no difference." Joe had explained, "And it seems you need some time with Geoff and Lizzy." Anya thanked him for his understanding and wished them luck.

When Geoffrey decided to drive them back to the city leaving Anya with Lizzy it had been a calculated risk on his part.

"So you met Geoff in Mumbai?" Anya asked what she hoped was a leading question as she and Lizzy drank coffee on the terrace, as she and Miriam had done so many times.

"It was a complete chance." Lizzy spoke enthusiastically, in the accent Anya described to herself as 'posh middle class with just a touch of condescension'. "We were in Mumbai, that's Bombay, I was on my way to Goa. I was buying a railway ticket and Geoffrey was behind me in the queue. We queued for over 24 hours. That was quite quick really, I've heard of people waiting two or three days when it's coming up to a holiday period, and there always seem to be holiday periods in India." Anya tried to listen attentively but found herself wondering where all this was leading. Why had Geoffrey left them together? Wouldn't it have been more natural for Lizzy to see her sister off when they didn't know when they'd see each other again? "Anyway we got talking."

"As you do." Anya agreed with a smile "So where did you go? Goa or where Geoffrey was heading?"

"He wanted to go south too, he was heading for Trivandrum. Trivandrum is in Kerala near the southernmost tip of India. It's where you catch the plane to Colombo as there haven't been any ferries since 1982 because of the civil war in Sri Lanka. He had to go through Goa, it's about a third of the way between Mumbai and Trivandrum." Anya wondered why a simple question had ended up with a detailed explanation of places and recent history, perhaps Lizzy was nervous about something. "So we decided to travel together and got seats in the same compartment."

"That was when?"

"Last September. September 6th. I started queuing after lunch and we finally got our tickets on the 7th at tea time."

"You remember the date and times very precisely."

"Oh yes. Important ones."

"So what happened in Goa?" Anya regretted her question immediately. She had to assume that Geoffrey was his father's son in more ways than one and had slept with this attractive, if talkative, young woman within a very short time of knowing her.

"I was meeting up with Lissa and Joe in Goa so Geoffrey kind of tagged along." 'They were definitely sleeping together by then' Anya thought as Lizzy continued without pause. "Lissa's my twin sister, not identical, though a lot of people say we're very alike. I don't see it myself. Anyway we'd arranged to meet up months before. She's been with Joe for years and Joe's got this fantastic job. He ferries rich people's yachts around the world. He's so good at it that people even pay him to fly places to pick up boats and take them where they want them. He's been doing it for years."

"He doesn't look old enough to have been doing anything for years."

"He's 30. He comes from Lymington, you know on the south coast in Hampshire." Anya wondered why Lizzy thought that she was unable to grasp the most simple geography. She just managed to refrain from saying 'yes, dear, I do know where Lymington is' in what would undoubtedly have been a caustic tone reminiscent of Kathleen. She made herself continue to listen to Lizzy who she was determined to like, for Geoffrey's sake. "Joe sailed before he would walk. He started doing this ferrying around in the Med, the Mediterranean, in his gap year and kind of never gave up. Lissa and I have known him since we were kids."

Anya bit her tongue. She didn't want to sound old by saying that they were, to her, still kids. "Are you sailors too?"

"Oh yes. We come from St Mawes, you know, in Cornwall." Anya gritted her teeth, the assumption that everyone in the world is ignorant, especially if they happen to have grey hair, was a trait she had probably exhibited when she was Lizzy's age. "We've always been around boats."

"Did Geoffrey tell you his grandfather died in a yachting accident? His father was never allowed on boats after that." 'I didn't know he was interested' she added silently to herself.

"He said he'd always wanted to sail but couldn't as he lived miles from the sea but he started learning at University and he picked it all up very quickly. He's a natural really."

Anya felt she had failed Geoffrey in some way by not knowing he had wanted to sail and by not knowing more of what had interested him. He had never said a word about sailing at University. Miriam was right. She knew so little about her children.

"So where did you go from Goa?"

"We stayed in Goa longer than we'd planned because of the Twin Towers thing. Everything just stopped for days and Joe had just come in from Bahrain and Qatar and they're in the Middle East, you know, so the authorities were really suspicious. Especially as the boat he was to take on was registered in Abu Dhabi."

"Because that's in the Middle East as well?" Anya couldn't resist asking, hoping that Lizzy would see that she was teasing.

"Obviously." Lizzy showed no sign of humour as she continued. "Anyway, Joe eventually got clearance, it took a couple of weeks but we all hung around. I'd arranged to crew for him with whatever jobs he had for a few months and Geoffrey sort of just tagged along. The first job was to help get this fantastic boat down to Darwin, that's on the north coast of Australia."

"I know where Darwin is." Anya had failed to control the edge in her voice but Lizzy showed no sign of hearing it. Anya tried to give Lizzy the benefit of the doubt, surely this affectation of checking geography at every opportunity was because the girl was anxious about something.

"Well then we got up to Saigon."

Anya couldn't resist interjecting "Is that the Saigon in Viet Nam?" but Lizzy ignored her.

"That was brilliant. And then to Japan and then Hawaii."

"Joe really is a man in demand." Anya made no attempt to hide the sarcasm but Lizzy either didn't notice or ignored it.

"We hung around Hawaii for a bit as a job fell through then he got this job to take this fantastic gin palace of a boat from Vancouver to Grenada. All the way down the west coast of America, through the Panama Canal."

'That'll be the canal in Panama will it?' Anya thought but managed not to say.

"Geoffrey seems to have ditched all his plans to join up with you." Anya knew she was sounding as though she didn't understand how gap years worked, how people didn't make plans, how if they made plans they changed them for the smallest of reasons. And it seemed like his relationship with Lizzy wasn't 'the smallest of reasons'.

"We did talk about that. He just said he wanted to be with people he liked and he liked us. He said he'd always wanted to sail and he could do that with us so it seemed the right thing to do."

Anya didn't want to sound like a mother checking up but she couldn't help it. She needed to know more about this girl that Geoffrey was entangled with.

"And you. When this year is over, what are your plans?"

"We'll get back to the UK and then go down to see my parents in St Mawes."

"In Cornwall."

"And give them the news."

Aware that she probably didn't want to know the answer Anya asked "What news would that be then?"

"Didn't Geoffrey tell you? We got married in Hawaii."

Anya stopped playing the place game in her head and had to think before she answered. "You did what?"

"We got married in Hawaii…"

"I thought I'd heard you correctly."

"I thought Geoffrey must have told you. In the pickup. On the way here. He didn't?"

"No. He didn't."

"Oh shit."

"Yes young lady 'oh shit.'"

"I thought you hadn't said anything because you were so angry."

"He said nothing." Anya thought back to the drive back from the city. She hadn't given him any chance at all to talk about himself. She had only thought of her problems. 'Oh shit' she echoed silently to herself. She tried, but failed, to soften her voice. "Now tell me something about yourself. What sort of person are you that gets married without telling anyone?" She had a feeling she was sounding more like Kathleen than at any time in her life.

"Isn't that what you did? With Geoffrey's dad? He told me all about you."

"I doubt it."

"He told me how you married his dad when you were at uni and then again just before he died. It's so romantic."

"Geoffrey has no idea what he is talking about."

"But you got married without telling anyone. The first time that is."

"But that was different."

"How?"

Anya didn't like being put on the back foot. She should be the one asking the questions. She didn't like having to justify her actions of years ago to this girl. Her daughter-in-law. The daughter-on-law she had only just met.

"Geoffrey's father had money. He could support the two of us." Even to Anya it sounded weak. "And, as he has probably told you, I couldn't have children so there was no danger of a family coming along."

"We can both work and there's such a thing as the pill." Anya noted that she didn't mention Geoffrey's inheritance, perhaps he hadn't told her.

"But you're so young! You've got your careers to think about, you've got nowhere to live. It all seems very airy fairy to me, not well thought out at all."

"All the things we have to do we can do just as easily together as apart."

"But why get married? Why not just live together?" Anya knew she was beginning to sound desperate.

"Why did you marry Geoffrey's father? You were younger than he is now."

"That was different." Anya repeated unconvincingly.

"How?"

Anya knew it was an argument she could never win. Lizzy was right. They had done nothing she hadn't herself done.

She looked straight at Lizzy and shook her head in defeat. "Times were different then, no doubt you and I were in very different situations but we won't argue about it. Tell me about you. I want you to tell me, then I'll ask Geoffrey. Then I'll know whether to believe this is a mistake or not."

Lizzy told Anya of a privileged life, a happy family, a father and mother who had never been married to anyone else but each other; a stable background of boarding school, which Lizzy and Lissa had loved, long holidays spent mucking about in boats, travelling with their parents to compete all over Europe.

"But how would you describe yourself. What are you like?" Anya pressed Lizzy.

"I'm bright, clever, quick to learn, interested in everything and I love your son."

"That's what I wanted to hear."

"But loving him isn't enough. I like him, I find him interesting, intriguing, mysterious. Sometimes, when he turns in on himself and shuts everyone out, I want to comfort him, tell him everything will be alright. He hates to be in the wrong, hates, absolutely hates, being criticised even when it's completely justified, because he will already have criticised himself and he is his own worst critic. But when push comes to shove he's fiercely loyal and his own man."

Anya was impressed by Lizzy's reading of the man it was obvious they both loved.

"I don't think I could have put it better myself." She wasn't going to argue, or resist. Geoffrey and Lizzy had made their decision and she would have to live with it, make the best of it. Perhaps, even, grow to like the idea. She stood up, leant down to Lizzy and kissed her cheek. "You can switch fingers now." She would do everything with a good grace.

Lizzy carefully removed a ring from the fourth finger of her right hand and placed it on the fourth finger of her left.

Geoffrey drove in a few minutes later and Lizzy waved her left hand at him.

"So you know?" He asked Anya carefully.

"I do."

"And?"

"Well I can't say much can I? As Lizzy has very cleverly reminded me, your Dad and I did much the same thing, though I would have hoped you may have learned from our experience."

"People never learn from other people's experience. You've always said that. And this is definitely 'experience' not 'mistake.'"

"No. I'm the one still making mistakes, still not knowing where I'm going. You two seem set to face anything life throws at you together. And that's good. A trouble shared…"

"… is a trouble halved. My mother always says that too." Lizzy smiled. "We'll be OK Anya. Honestly."

"I really think you might."

It was agreed that Lizzy and Geoffrey would spend a week on the island before flying back to England though Anya saw little of them as Geoffrey showed his wife the island he knew so well. 'Well, it is their honeymoon' she told herself.

"It needs a lot of work." Geoffrey said on their last evening as they watched the sea as the sun went down behind them.

"There comes a point when shabby chic becomes just plain shabby." Lizzy pointed out, to Anya's mind rather unnecessarily.

"I don't think we ever aimed for shabby chic." Anya bit back.

Geoffrey knew he was in a difficult position, sandwiched between two strong women but he rather liked the way Lizzy was making Anya respond.

"I didn't mean that. What I meant was…"

"I think you did. Shabby Chic may be the fashion in St Mawes, Cornwall but it most certainly is not in the Caribbean."

"Please Anya. I really didn't mean to insult the place, or you, I wouldn't. I love it here. I really do."

Anya got such a filthy look from Geoffrey she decided she had probably gone too far. "It is beautiful isn't it? I fell in love with the place the first time I saw it. Have I ever told you, Geoffrey, how I came to buy Fishermen Rock in the first place?"

She had, on just about every visit they had made to the island, but he decided this was the olive branch and he must accept it.

"Of course you have Anya, but tell Lizzy. It's such a great story."

"I'd love to hear it." Lizzy took her cue from her husband and peace was restored as Anya recounted the events of that January day in 1994.

"I think I would have fallen in love with it too." Lizzy said as Anya came to the end of the story and was rewarded by a beaming smile from her mother-in-law.

"I'm sorry you two. Have I really been a bitch?"

"Yes." Geoffrey replied without qualification.

"It's just that I know I'm going to have to sell up and I really don't want to. It needs serious investment and I have nothing to invest."

As Lizzy put together a meal of cold meats and salad in the

kitchen Geoffrey opened another bottle of wine and filled the three glasses. "While Lizzy's not here tell me how bad everything really is."

"Apart from this dilapidated liability of a hotel and the house back in England I have enough to live on for a couple more months and then nothing. No income, no pension, just those two properties."

"Well the house must be worth a million or so? You could sell that." Geoffrey suggested sensibly.

"But I can't. Don't you remember the terms of your father's will? I have to keep the house until you three are 21 and James isn't 21 for another year. And in any case now isn't a very good time to be selling anything, the property market isn't exactly flourishing after what Lizzy rather brushed off as 'the twin towers thing'. Nothing is selling in the UK or here."

"What about all your other places?" Geoff had known she had run a property business and had had a number of houses she rented out but he had never known the details.

"They've gone, one by one, I'm afraid." Anya felt he deserved a totally honest answer to his unspoken question. "All of your father's money went to you children in trust. The income came to me for your expenses but it was never going to cover everything. It was so important you had everything you needed to hold your heads up with everyone at school and university. When your Dad died interest rates were a lot higher than they are now, stock market returns have dropped through the floor what with dot com booms and busts and then 9/11. His calculations were made at a very different time. For a while we've been existing on money from here." She looked around her at the shambles that had been her high-earning hotel. "I had no idea I was taking too much money out of this place. Miriam never told me."

Not for the first time Geoffrey was thankful for how much this woman, who looked so much older than he had remembered her, had done for him and Jim and Rose. His capital had been protected, his bank balance was so obscenely healthy that he had been able to take time out to travel the world. He hadn't worried about getting a job after his degree, as so many of his friends had. He had never had to think about money. It had always been his assumption that, as a family, they were rich, not just comfortably well off, but rich.

"We'll sort something out." He said, trying to comfort but unsure how.

"No need, the decision has made itself. The Fishermen Rock has to be sold even if I have to give it away for just enough to keep me until Jim's 21st. I've been a fool to think for one moment I could get it back to what it should be. I'll go back to England and hang on somehow until next year when I'll sell the house. Then I'll be comfortable. It's only a year or so."

Lizzy appeared balancing the three plates of food, to hear Anya talk of her decision.

"You can't sell this place!" Anya was surprised at the anguish in Lizzy's voice.

"Of course I don't want to sell but there really is no alternative."

"We'll take it over." Anya looked at Lizzy with amazement, then at Geoffrey to see if he had any idea what his wife was talking about.

"We've been talking about spending time here, working on the hotel, perhaps even sorting out something to do with sailing."

"We really think that it'd be fun making a go of it."

Their enthusiasm amazed Anya, she looked from one to the other as they explained their plans.

"It would be different, not the chic place it used to be…"

"More of a place for sailing."

"There's an awful lot on the other side of the island but not over here on the Atlantic coast."

Anya had to interject. "For very good reason, look at the wind, and the currents. No one in their right mind would rather sail here than on the benign Caribbean side."

"Exactly. We wouldn't go for the novice, only the extreme sailor, the one with experience who wants a real challenge. We could put money into the hotel. Help you run it. Work as a team."

Anya could not let them do it. "It's out of the question. It's too soon to tie yourselves down. And where would you be if the venture failed and you lost all your money? I won't have it."

Geoffrey had listened to Lizzy's ideas the night before and had been caught up in her enthusiasm. It would have been nice, he had agreed, to live in the sun but, although he would never admit it to his wife, he was relieved at Anya's veto.

"I won't get the best price but Fishermen Rock has to go."

She raised her glass, as if to toast the old place and drank the wine down in one. Geoffrey and Lizzy were leaving the next day. She would give herself one week to sort it all out before following them back to England.

She didn't drive straight back to the hotel after dropping them off at the airport, instead she drove through the city and up the west coast. She knew this would be the last chance she would have to see the island she could never get to know well enough. At the North Cape she sat for a long time watching the Atlantic rollers crashing into and over the sheer cliffs. She headed back down the east coast remembering the evening when she had first driven along those roads. She passed the Abbey and wondered why she had never followed up on the friendship of that Mr Cave. There were so many things she hadn't done, so many people she hadn't spent time with, when she had been content to sit in the sun and be served rum punch. 'What a waste.' She said to herself over and over as she neared home.

She was surprised to see a car in the car park as she drove down the steep approach.

"Good evening Anya."

"Good evening Vincent, and Kenneth." "Come on round and I'll get you a drink. We can talk better sitting down."

As she prepared a jug of iced punch Anya wondered why they had come over uninvited when she had heard nothing from them since that evening over two weeks before.

"Can we come straight to the point?" Anya was surprised that it was Kenneth who spoke.

"Of course."

"My father has been worried about you." Kenneth spoke as if

Vincent weren't sitting next to him. "We know the island as well as any and certainly…"

Vincent interrupted his son. "You have had visitors." His voice was brusque.

"Certainly it hasn't been a secret."

"Your son?"

"Yes, my elder son and his wife."

"You have three children, two sons and a daughter. We have seen them." He did not speak kindly.

Anya looked at her uncle-half-brother and saw the anger that should have been turned against their mutual father turned on her.

He could not know that she could not have children.

She bought time by talking brightly and confidently, lying by omission.

"You have just missed Geoffrey. He and his wife have been staying with me for a few days. They've just gone back to the UK this afternoon. Then there's Rose who's 21 and James who's just 20, they're both at university."

"And your husband?"

"He died."

"I'm sorry to hear that." There was no genuine feeling in Vincent's statement. He continued in his quiet, controlled, almost sinister manner. "But you should not have had children."

She remembered her mother's eyes when they had argued. Vincent's eyes, as he waited for her response, had the same darkness. The story of her life could sound so straightforward. She was 52 years old, She had married and had three children and then her husband had died. It had been a simple, normal life, similar in outline to countless millions of others. But she knew how misleading that simplification was and she didn't feel obliged to explain to these men, who, she was increasingly aware, were not on her side. Anya looked at him for what seemed a long time before answering. She decided, in the end, to be honest.

"I did not. They are my step-children. I am not their biological mother."

"We heard… your son… another generation… We thought…"

"Well you thought wrong. I have no idea why I feel I must explain but here goes. I married when I was young. It was his mistake to marry me as he discovered too late he wanted children I could not give him. We divorced. He remarried and the children were born. His wife left him. We met again. He was dying. We married. He died. I adopted the children and they have been mine for seven years."

"I needed to know." She nodded her understanding.

Kenneth had been silent through this exchange but now they had overcome the problem of Vincent's fear he got down to the real business of their visit.

"So what are you going to do now?"

"How do you mean?" Anya turned away from Vincent to his son.

"With Fishermen Rock. People are wondering. The men and women who worked here are wondering if they will ever get their jobs back, the fishermen are wondering if you will once again buy their catch."

"It hasn't been an easy decision."

"There are families that have had no income since you closed

"I'm sorry for that but it has not been easy…"

"I think it might be more difficult for them."

"I'm sorry about that."

"You have never thought about the people who have been dependent on Edna's place. They've meant nothing to you."

"I hope it opens again, but it will not be me that's running it. I will be selling."

"That is what people in the village have been thinking. That is why they came to me."

"They came to you?"

"They know of my relationship to you, no…" he pre-empted Anya's interruption, "nothing is a secret on this island, and they have asked me to find out what is happening here. Edna's Place is important to them, it is their employment, the market for their fish and produce, they have a right to know."

"I don't disagree with you. I promised Dexter I'd tell him as soon as a decision was made and that was only last night. I've hardly had time to put the things in process." Anya wondered why she felt so defensive. "It really isn't any of your business how I deal with the hotel."

"We think it is."

Anya looked at the two men, sitting on her terrace, drinking her punch, being so rude. She had no answer to their intimidation, she knew that in some ways they were right.

"I need some time, I have to speak to people. I have contacts in New York who may be interested, I must get in touch with them before advertising the sale."

Vincent had been sitting with his chin on his chest, his eyes closed, as his son had argued with Anya. He didn't move as he spoke. "You will sell to me."

"You?" It should not have been a surprise.

"Yes." He opened his eyes, looked at her directly. "Kenneth runs a place on the west coast and should not be making money for other people. You will sell to us."

"We have plans." Kenneth added with some enthusiasm.

"You have plans? Even though you couldn't know I'd sell?"

"We knew you would, eventually."

It was the way Victor spoke that made Anya suspicious. It was an easy jump in her imagination from the fact that they wanted to buy the hotel to their making it impossible for her to continue. It would have been easy enough for them to have caused her misfortune.

"Miriam was about to sell to us when you came along. We watched as, for a couple of years, you poured money and energy into the business. We looked elsewhere, but we always wanted Fishermen Rock and we knew you would be ready to sell, eventually."

Anya's mind was racing. They couldn't have introduced the food poisoning, they couldn't have informed to the authorities, they couldn't have engineered Miriam's restlessness. Could they?

"Why did you think that?" She spoke coldly looking back at Kenny, but it was Vincent who replied.

"I have known who you are for some years, almost since your

first arrival on the island. I was in the bar at that resort you stayed at. I saw the ring. I checked up on you. The barman said your name was Anya Cave."

"That was my second visit to the island." She corrected the error of fact as though it mattered that he had been wrong.

"Then we saw you driving around this part of the island in your silly tourist open top car." Kenny sounded as if what car she drove was important to their dignity. "And then we kept our ears to the ground, friends who ate here, the brothers of our maid who worked here, we visited regularly, yet even when you saw us you did not recognise us. We saw you neglecting the hotel, we saw you visiting with your spoilt little rich kid children. None of you had any thought for the people who worked so hard to provide you with all your privilege."

Anya was near to tears. "So you decided to force me into a position where I could do nothing but sell?"

"You were no good for the place. You weren't looking after it. You weren't looking after the people whose livelihoods depended on you. You never thought about them."

"We left it too long to bring things to a head." Vincent added his measured voice to counter Kenny's emotion.

"So you forced the hotel to close so you could buy it at a knock down price!"

"No." Vincent said quietly. "No. We have watched as you had taken everything this village and its good people had to offer and you have given nothing back."

"You knew who I was, you saw me, and you never said anything?"

Vincent looked at her long and hard over his glasses. "You are the past I have to forget but cannot. You are so like your father."

Anya gasped, how could she be like the violent, disgusting, Albert. "Your father too." She tried to retaliate.

"You use other people as much as he did. You will have used your body to gain power over other people, just as he did. You have all his bad genes in you."

"And you don't?"

A few minutes later, after she had watched their car drive up the steep slope out of the car park, Anya sat down and wept.

The unfairness of it all overwhelmed her, she felt powerless, manipulated, hard done by and helpless. They had won a battle she had never known she was in.

Perhaps they had deserved to win. So much of what they had said was true. She had been unable to show real commitment, she was self-obsessed, she had used her body to have power over others.

She looked up at the star filled sky and understood that she was so many things she should not have been.

Chapter 18: Conclusions

M25, March 2002

"Will Mrs Anya Philips please go to the Information desk. Mrs Anya Philips to the Information Desk."

Anya just about heard and understood the announcement. She looked around her to find the information desk and dragged her unwieldy case through the airport crowds.

"I'm Anya Philips. You paged me?"

"Ah Mrs Philips. Yes. This gentleman asked us to locate you."

Anya turned in the direction the man was indicating.

"Tim!" She wasn't sure she kept the relief out of her voice. As she had waited in the queue for immigration control she had been wondering if she could stretch to the extravagance of a taxi home, she wasn't sure she could face the train into London, the tube and then an over-crowded rush-hour train into Kent.

"Anya. You look wonderful as always."

"So gallant of you Tim but we both know I look dreadful. The plane was five hours late leaving and then took longer than it should, then the arrivals hall was packed and it's taken ages to get through customs and immigration. They seem to think everyone's a terrorist intent on wreaking death and destruction."

"Welcome to England." Tim spoke ironically. "Here, let me take your case."

"Well I have to admit I'm glad to see you. How did you know I was coming?"

"Geoffrey e-mailed, he said he was worried about you."

"Geoffrey e-mailed you?" Anya was surprised.

"When he left for his trip I made sure he had my e-mail address, it's far more sensible than a phone number."

"May I ask why?" That Anya was hurt showed in the coldness of her voice.

"Please don't be so suspicious Anya. It was so he could contact me in an emergency."

"He could contact me."

"But emails are so much easier and you weren't on-line when he left. Are you now? I didn't think so. Look Anya, I'll answer all your questions when we get to the car. The simplest answer to your original question is that Geoffrey said it would be a great favour if I met your flight so I did."

"Thank you Tim. I do appreciate it, it's just a bit of a surprise to find you seem to think it perfectly normal that you should be in touch with Geoffrey. What else did he say or write or whatever it is you do on e-mails?"

"Let's get to the car." As he took her arm and led her through the airport he was wondering whether the hour he would have her in the car as his captive audience would be enough for all the explanations that were necessary.

"I was more than happy to meet you, it'll give us an opportunity to talk." Tim turned to Anya who half smiled. She was relieved to be in the comfort of the car but she was not sure she was looking forward to hearing what Tim had to say.

He started with a compliment. "Geoffrey's a lovely young man, you did a brilliant job with him. Had Fiona hung around God knows what the children would have turned out like, spoilt oiks probably."

"Oh no, I don't think so, there was too much of Geoff in them for that."

"Fiona never let Geoff have any influence over them on the things that mattered. Take my word, they'd have been insufferable oiks."

"Well thank you very much for the compliment, it is much appreciated." Anya wondered where this was leading.

"Jim and Rose are exceptional too. Not just Geoffrey, though I know Geoffrey better of course."

"Why 'of course'?" she asked but Tim didn't answer so she continued, unsure where Tim was heading and wanting to delay wherever it was. "Has he told you he got married?" Anya continued.

"Yes, I've checked out Lizzy's family, very suitable I'd say."

Anya snatched a look at Tim but was unable to tell whether or not he was teasing her. "She's a nice girl but tell me Tim, how long have you had to check the family out? When did he tell you about Lizzy?"

Again Tim didn't answer her questions. "Well I wish them luck. They're going to need it, marrying so young I mean."

Again Anya snatched a look at Tim and decided he knew exactly what he was saying and that he was choosing his words very carefully. "Are you or are you not going to answer any one of my questions? How long have you known Geoffrey was married? How do you 'of course' know him better than the other two? And what did Geoffrey tell you this morning?"

"Well, last question first." Tim started slowly, "He emailed to ask me to meet you off this flight. He said you were worn out, that you were depressed about things and would I make sure you got home safely."

"Depressed?" Anya picked up on the one word she didn't like.

"Yes. And frankly I'm not surprised."

"Not surprised?"

"No. I've seen it coming for a while."

"You've seen it coming?"

"Anya, darling, will you stop repeating everything I say? Yes. I've seen it coming."

She didn't ask him to expand. She was uncomfortable with the idea that he had been keeping tabs on her children and she wasn't sure why he called her 'darling'. She hoped he would change the subject so she would have a chance for some of this to sink in. When he did she rather wished he hadn't.

"Can we talk about New Year's Day?"

"No. I don't think so. Will you answer my questions?"

"We must talk about New Year, in a way it'll allow me to get round to some answers for you."

She nodded with what she hoped was condescending grace.

"Have you ever wondered at the coincidence of our being in the same restaurant that night?" He asked eventually.

"Not really. I've tried not to think too much about any of it though now you come to mention it, it probably was a bit odd. *Of all the restaurants in all the towns in all the world and you had to choose that one...*"

"It was no coincidence."

"No?"

Anya tried to remember who would have known what restaurant she had decided on. She might have told David and Linda. She didn't think she had told them where she was spending the evening. She had told Geoffrey. He had called from, she tried to remember where. The thought occurred to her that he must have been married by then and he hadn't told her, perhaps he was going to but it had been a really bad line and their conversation had been cut short. He had asked what she was doing for New Year's Eve, she had told him she as going out on her own. She had probably told him the name of the restaurant.

"It was Geoffrey wasn't it? He told you."

"As I said, you have raised a lovely young man there."

"Tell me what's going on. He rang you?"

"He emailed me to wish me a happy New Year, I replied asking what you were doing and he replied telling me. Emails are, apparently, rather more reliable than long distance telephone lines."

"Did you know he was married?"

"I did. But before you get all shirty he made me promise not to tell you."

"When has a promise ever stopped you from doing something you wanted to do?" She asked tartly.

"He said it was something he really had to do face to face after you had met Lizzy. He said only then would you understand. He didn't want you to have time to brood and worry."

"Brood and worry?"

"His phrase. Well you would have done wouldn't you? You would have wanted him to get back to the UK, you would have wanted to know where he was and go out to meet him. Well he didn't want that. And I agreed. It was best you didn't know until he was able to tell you personally and to explain."

"They are obviously very fond of each other. But they're so young."

"About the same age you and Geoff were." Anya knew there was no arguing with that. "So don't do a Kathleen, be generous to them, believe in them and believe in what they believe in." Anya thought that was very wise of Tim but wasn't going to admit it to him.

"You haven't answered when this relationship with Geoffrey began and why he seems so happy to talk to you about such personal things."

"It started a long time ago."

"Are you going to tell me?"

"When you were going through all that trouble with the court and social services to get custody of the children…"

"Then?" Anya was incredulous.

"Geoffrey felt I wasn't helping you, he thought I should and he came round to my house one day to find out why. He was very adult about it, he simply wanted to know why I wouldn't help."

"Why wouldn't you?"

"I will explain Anya, but so much has to be said first, there is so much you need to understand."

The car lurched as they drove up the ramp onto the M25, switching lanes in the traffic and the road works. It was an excuse not to talk for a few seconds. Anya's mind raced. She was trying to find reasons why Geoffrey had said nothing about being in contact with Tim all these years. She was trying to find a reason that didn't make her feel he loved her less.

When the car had settled on a steady course again Tim gave her an explanation. "Don't worry about Geoffrey being in touch with me. Remember he was 16 when his father died, it's a really difficult age for any boy but it was an especially difficult time for Geoffrey. His mother had abandoned them under humiliating circumstances, his father was dying and suddenly this woman who he had never met but of whom he had heard scandalous things, appears and takes over the role of his parents. Of course he needed someone to talk to. He needed a man to talk to."

"But why you?"

"It would have to be me David or John. David was too involved with the legal side of things and perhaps he didn't think John knew you well enough. He knew I knew you better than most so he came to me. He needed a friend, Anya. It wasn't a slight on you, it didn't mean he didn't grow to love having you as a mother. Please think about how he felt then. The others were younger, able to respond more easily to the changes in their lives but Geoffrey needed a friendly father figure."

"You."

"Me."

Anya sat back and thought back to the conversation with Miriam. She had only ever thought about how she felt about her life with children. When had she thought, really thought, how they felt about their lives with her?

"I did it all wrong then? I didn't think enough about them?"

"I'm not saying that, no one could possibly say that. I think you just believed because you loved them they would love you in the same way. Life doesn't always work out like that."

Anya thought over Tim's words. She had spent her life worrying about who she loved, what she felt, how she thought about people. She had spent nothing like enough time looking at herself as others saw her.

"Am I really that selfish?" She asked rather tentatively after a long silence.

"Yes, I think you are."

"Miriam said that as well."

"Miriam?"

"The manager of Fishermen Rock."

"She said you were selfish?"

"Selfish, self-centred, and a lot of other things as well. Maybe you are both right. Maybe I've just gone through life just using and hurting people."

She thought of her mother, could she have done more for her? Should she have recognised that she was ill, lonely and frightened? She thought of Kathleen and Margaret and now, with her reaction to seeing Geoffrey with Lizzy, she realised something of what they would have felt when this highly unsuitable girl breezed into their lives and took over their son. And then she thought of the men she still thought of as boys, Tim, David and John. She had led them on, she had undoubtedly used them and she had never, not until now, wondered how they had felt. She had stolen years of Peter's life, and years of happiness from his new wife Jenny and her children. How much damage had she done to them? And how well did she really know the children who, for nearly seven years, she had been mother to? She had been so intent on doing the right thing, and being seen to do the right thing, she may have missed so many opportunities to get to know them as people. Had she ever worried about how they felt? Asked them about anything? Or had she always known best? She hadn't known that Geoffrey loved to sail, what else didn't she know about the children she had called 'hers'? How many other people had she hurt? How many other people's lives, wittingly or unwittingly, had she influenced for the worse? Matthew and Maggie, Tim's children who would have been humiliated by their father's humiliation, how many others? She began to feel as though all she had ever done was harm.

"I'm so sorry." She said, quietly and sincerely.

"You have absolutely nothing to be sorry for. Anya, you have always done what you thought was best at the time, often, though not always, for the right motives."

"But I never looked at anything from other people's points of view."

Tim didn't argue. He took hold of her hand and squeezed it. "That's not an easy thing to do, Anya, I don't think any of us do it particularly well." They sat for a while, Anya's hand under Tim's. She couldn't bring herself to hold his hand properly but she was pleased for the reassurance the contact gave her. Since Vincent and Kenneth's visit three days earlier she had been questioning so many things about herself. And now Tim was saying much the same thing. She was, and had always been, self-obsessed.

It was some while before Tim broke the silence. "I want to apologise for New Year's Night."

"There's no need, let's simply forget it ever happened."

"It wasn't supposed to happen like that Anya, really it wasn't. Nothing in our relationship has happened the way I wanted it to."

"What relationship?"

"Nothing has happened the way I wanted it to happen since the moment I first set eyes on you." Anya went to interrupt but Tim shook his head. "Listen. Please. Enough is enough. It's time for you to listen. We've got at least an hour until we get you home just listen."

Anya gently took her hand away and listened.

"It all began to go wrong under the clock that first evening. Geoff had wound us all up about meeting you after work. He had said you were the most beautiful girl he had ever met. He believed you would be able to hold your own against his mother and sister. He said you were clever, far cleverer than he was, and that you were beautiful. He also said that you were the most promiscuous girl he'd ever met. He didn't particularly like you screwing around with so many other men but accepted it because you always came back to him in the end."

"Which I did. Ironic that really."

"We were expecting, well I don't know really what we were expecting, at Charing Cross, I just know it wasn't anyone like you. The moment I first saw you, even before I knew you were you, if you see what I mean, I knew I shouldn't marry Margaret. I shouldn't marry anyone if I felt the kind of feeling I had for you that evening. It wasn't just lust, it was a recognition of a similar soul. I know that sounds ridiculous but it's the only way I can explain it. When you first looked at the clock I thought this wonderful person might be Anya, then you walked out of the station and I thought you couldn't be so I followed you. I had to know who you were. I have often wondered if it was love at first sight and have decided it was. You walked out onto the Strand, looking at shops, looking very lost and alone, you walked as far as the Savoy and then you turned back again."

Anya tried not to think of the word 'love'. "I remember that. I was scared. I wanted to go back home. I should have done and then everyone I've hurt would have had different lives. I wouldn't have ruined everything for everyone."

"Don't flatter yourself Anya, you didn't ruin anyone's life. Certainly you influenced them but you should know that people are sometimes strong enough to ruin their own lives or just too weak not to. I watched you walking back down the Strand towards Charing Cross and I knew you were going to be Anya. I knew there was going to be a good reason for me to know this beautiful girl. I knew that we were meant to be together. Sometime." Anya was surprised at the simple honesty in Tim's voice.

His tone became harsher as he continued. "I should never have married Margaret. I was far too young, far too immature to marry at all, especially to marry someone like Margaret with a mother like Kathleen. I should have been strong enough to say no. I should have been a lot of things I wasn't. Isn't it sad when you realise that too late?"

Tim looked at Anya's hand and turned it over. He raised the palm to his lips and kissed it. Anya did not resist.

"You were brilliant at the wedding, all my friends asked who you were and how I knew you and why wasn't I marrying you, even my mother. The moment I stepped out of the church, no it was earlier than that, the moment I woke up that morning, I knew I shouldn't go through with it. I knew, and I think Margaret did too, that the marriage was going to be a disaster."

"But you did go through with it."

"I shouldn't have but I did, I felt that I had no choice. There were so many reasons I had to go ahead with it, half the town was coming to the bloody wedding, mother would never have been able to face Kathleen, I would never have been able to face anyone. None of them seem like good reasons now but then? What choice did I have?"

"None I suppose, though if you really felt it was wrong…"

"I did. But I also knew I couldn't do anything about it against the combined force of my mother, Kathleen and Margaret. It was just all too much."

"I seem to remember you waited at least until the middle of the wedding reception before breaking your marriage vows."

"Anya that was not your fault. It was mine completely. I wanted you more than you can imagine I wanted you to be with me and I suspected you'd have a bet with Geoff. I wanted you to win. Was I a bet?"

"You were. I think that reception earned me more than a thousand pounds." Money had seemed so easily come by and so easily spent those days. She felt the contrast with her current situation sharply.

"Did you ever let me screw you other than for a bet?"

Anya wondered at the question. Did he want her to answer yes or no? Which would be the less hurtful response? She answered simply and truthfully. "Those three days in January in that hotel in Covent Garden." She saw the smile in his eyes and felt the pressure of his hand on hers.

"It seemed so strange that you felt you had to escape from Geoff, you always seemed so happy with him."

"Appearances can be deceptive." She wasn't sure he had heard her.

"I hated seeing you with him. It was so unfair. I thought at first that we had both married the wrong people, that you should have married me. But then I realised you and Geoff were happy, the glorious Anya happy with boring old Geoff! But you were."

"We were, at the beginning anyway. That first year was great. But then there was Kathleen."

"If you'd married me you wouldn't have had that cow of a mother-in-law on your back all the time. My mother always liked you, she stood up for you and had real rows with Kathleen about you."

"I didn't know that."

"How could you? Why would you?"

"I was happy with Geoff, we loved each other whatever it may have looked like from the outside. It was only later when Kathleen and Margaret began to put all that pressure on him that it all began to go wrong."

"I know. You were so happy with Geoff but I knew I never would be with Margaret. You know she tricked me into having the family so young?"

"I did wonder that Christmas. You weren't exactly acting the overjoyed expectant father."

"We'd agreed to wait for a couple of years and I'd hoped to be out of the marriage before children were involved, I could have left Margaret at the drop of a hat, but not children. Once Matt and Maggie came along I just had to sit back and watch you and Geoff being happy."

A suspicion began to form in Anya's mind. She looked at Tim to see whether there was guilt written on his face before saying anything.

"It was the only thing I could do."

"What was?"

"I had to split you up."

"You what?"

"I couldn't face seeing you with Geoff for what might have been a lifetime when I was tied to Margaret. She would never have divorced me unless really forced into a corner, Kathleen would never have stood for it. And there were 18 years or more until the children grew up. So you and Geoff had to be split apart. With Geoff married to Fiona he would be as miserable as I was, I wouldn't have to stare at happiness all the time."

Anya tried to comprehend the enormity of Tim's confession.

"So if you couldn't have me you were damned if Geoff would?"

"If I couldn't be happy you weren't going to be either, especially where I would be seeing you all the time. It wasn't that I wanted you to be unhappy, just that you should be happy out of my sight."

It was some time before Anya could bring herself to say anything. She eventually slowly withdrew her hand from under his. "What an incredibly awful thing to do."

"Probably."

"No probably about it."

"You made it easy though. Once you realised Geoff loved you and would even stand up against his mother for you, the challenge went. Your marriage would have ground to a halt of its own accord one day, I just brought that day forward."

Anya wondered if there was a grain of truth in what Tim said. Perhaps she and Geoff would have fallen out of love with each other when they were in a world of routine.

"You wore the chips on your shoulder like badges of honour. Do you realise how much time you spent bickering with Kathleen in those early days when we were all together on Sundays? You found fault in everything, had nasty little asides to Geoff which we could all hear, you put him in an impossible position. Geoff hated being torn between the wife he loved and his mother. It was so easy to suggest he left you at home. You really weren't very attractive at that time. I almost stopped loving you."

"Love?"

"Oh yes, Anya darling, I have always loved you."

She let the phrase hang in the air. The sound of the tyres on the concrete road surface seemed hypnotic as she gathered her thoughts.

"Let me make sure I understand you correctly. You wanted me and Geoff to split up. You drove wedges between us including excluding me from the family yet why, when I wanted to divorce Geoff, wouldn't you help me?"

"Wedges were easily driven Anya. I may have sown seeds of doubt in Geoff's mind but they would not have taken root if he had not, somewhere at the back of his mind, realised that you would leave one day."

"That doesn't answer why you wouldn't help me."

"I couldn't. I couldn't be seen to have anything to do with you. Since I was stuck with Margaret all I wanted to be was what the Golf Club wanted me to be, and the party. I was probably as arrogant and self-centred as you were."

She could not let that pass without interrupting. "You had no idea how lonely I was, how much I hated you, and Kathleen, everyone and everything." She was surprised at how all those feelings of frustration still hurt. "It's over 25 years ago and it still hurts that you all despised me, you all wanted rid of me. I was the 'Highly Unsuitable Girl'. I was always going to be a misfit, I would always be on the outside and it still hurts like hell." She realised she had tears in her eyes and wiped them away quickly. "I'm tired what with the journey, the delays, now all this reminiscing. Don't make anything of it."

While she made a big thing of finding her handbag and opening it, searching for a handkerchief and wiping the minute amounts of moisture from her eyes he spoke, as if to himself.

"I could never show you how much I loved you."

Anya rummaged in her handbag again. She needed time to think. All this history was leading somewhere, but she didn't know where.

"Anya. I was a shit then. Not even I would have liked me."

"What's changed? We're going through our lives, pulling them apart, trying to identify motives and make excuses for our actions when we were completely different people. What is that quote? *The past is a foreign country they do things differently there.*"

"L P Hartley, *The Go-Between* I think you'll find."

"Very erudite."

"Life has changed us Anya. I know you think I'm still the same Tim that you screwed at the Golf Club Ball but I'm not. And you're not the same person that went there with the sole aim of humiliating me."

"I didn't see it like that. Not really."

"Yes you did. Why else would you seduce Matt and me?"

"I seduced no one, you both wanted it without any persuasion on my part."

"You were too elegant, too beautiful, too available."

"I hated all of you that night. I hated what you all stood for, all that privilege, everyone being someone just because they were born to it rather than because they were good enough. Matthew's friends were swanning through life without a care, worrying only about who would be captain of the golf club or acceptable to the local committee for this that or the other. You, they, and your son, were all shits from another world."

"Were we really that bad? Are we?"

"Not as people. Not all of you. I just hated the way of life, the assumption that you were all better than everyone else. Geoff wasn't like that when I first met him but then, when we moved south, he absorbed it, he became what his mother had always wanted him to be. He fitted back into that life of privilege and money as if he'd never had those four years in Liverpool. He eased into his mother's view of what his life should be. It wasn't mine."

"So all this was about class?" Tim seemed genuinely perplexed.

"I suppose it is, was. If not about class what was it about? I had an attitude to life none of you could possibly understand because of who your parents were, and where and how you had been brought up. I may have had a good degree and been better educated than most of you but, as they say '*you can take the girl out of the terraced house but you can't take the terraced house out of the girl.*'"

"No one ever said that." Tim almost laughed.

"It's true though, you all saw me as Geoff's bit of rough. None of you could understand where I came from, what I had gone through. None of you wanted to know anything about who I really was."

"Now that's not fair. No one ever knows what other people go through even if they're from the same family or background."

Anya realised here was yet another example of her self-obsession. She spoke slowly and sadly. "I was probably so tied up with myself I never tried."

"We're different people, both of us, now." Tim reached down and took Anya's hand again. "Don't be so hard on yourself Anya."

Anya decided to change the subject away from herself and her shortcomings, it had been an uncomfortable few minutes. "In all these times you were Geoffrey's friend what did you talk about? And don't say 'man things.'"

"He talked about his girlfriends and cricket and sailing, about his worries about exams but mainly about his Dad. He loved to talk about Geoff. I remember he went through a phase of wanting to talk about Geoff and Fiona. He needed reassurance that his mother and father had, at some time, loved each other. I suppose they were all the things he felt he couldn't ask you."

"I suppose I should thank you. No, that's horrid. I do thank you. You're absolutely right. I couldn't have helped him with those things."

"We didn't speak all the time, and I'd always wait for him to contact me. I knew enough to know you were doing just fine."

"But you never helped me get custody. You didn't help when I was fighting the courts. You could have done but you didn't."

"I didn't because if I had done and it had all gone wrong you would have blamed me and I couldn't risk that."

"So you did nothing."

"You did it on your own."

"Only with a lot of help from David. But when I was respectable, you didn't talk to me, you more or less ignored me for years."

"I didn't think it was a good idea to get involved."

"You never came near us. Those years weren't easy but you never offered help. You hardly even talked to me. How could you be like that if you loved me?"

"I was always there for Geoffrey and for you, and the others, if you'd ever really needed it."

"How?"

Her aggression and disbelief stung him into an admission he had promised himself he would not make.

"Have you wondered how easily some of your properties sold? Oh yes. I know every single one of them has gone, the last one last September I seem to remember, very few properties sold that month."

"You?" Anya could hardly speak for the humiliation. He didn't answer, she took his silence for agreement.

"I've done what I could, I still own the cottages in Rye but the rest have been sold on. You wouldn't have thanked me would you? It was far better I did it in the background." Tim bit his tongue to stop adding more. This was not how he had planned the conversation.

It was some time before he broke the uncomfortable silence. "I was so jealous of you with your children."

"Jealous?" Anya was tired, she wanted to go to sleep not listen to Tim talking so seriously about such important things.

"I've been on my own for years."

"You'd never be on your own Tim. Never."

He looked at her meaningfully before answering sadly. "Well, Anya darling, there you are very wrong."

"You could have found someone. You're not bad looking for someone nearing 60, you're comfortably off despite the vast amounts of money you must have paid your ex-wives, you would be quite a catch." She tried to be light-hearted but knew she failed.

"Anya, would you believe me if I said there was really only one woman in the world I have ever wanted to be with?"

She couldn't answer him. She was tired. She was worried. She had gone back through the ups and downs of her life in the past hour and now she was having to face what was obviously a declaration of love from Tim, the man she had variously lusted after, disliked and even, at times, loathed.

"The children are grown up now, they're leaving home, you can have your life back. For seven years you've put your life on hold as you've looked after them. It didn't seem to matter to you that they weren't yours,"

"They are mine. I adopted them."

"You've got years ahead of you, Anya darling, you can't keep living your life through Geoff and his children. Look we're at Reigate Hill so I haven't got you long as a captive audience. I need to know something. And, honestly, if you tell me to piss off I will but I need to have asked and I need to have had a response."

"Well?"

"Well what?" He knew he was going about this all the wrong way.

"What do you need to ask?" She knew what was coming.

"I need to ask if you think we could make a match of it."

"God you sound like some Regency buck!"

"I mean a match. Not necessarily a marriage. We probably don't need to go through all that. What I mean to ask is do you think Mrs Anya Philips and Mr Tim Cross could link arms and face their future together? Equals. A match."

"You know the funny thing Tim?" Anya was suddenly relaxed,

smiling. "I have never lived with someone without marrying them. I lived with Geoff and married him, then Peter. I don't think it would go down well at the golf club if we weren't married so I think you should put your proposal as one of marriage. Then I might think about it."

"Would you? Think about it I mean?"

"Well, there's an awful lot to be said against it. I would have had sex with my step-son for a start."

"When was that? Ten years ago? He's a big boy now and he can cope with the disappointment of his old man winning."

"What about your daughter?"

"Maggie? She's been on at me for years to find someone to spend my latter years with so she doesn't have to worry about looking after me in my dotage. She gives me graphic descriptions of how she really does not want to get involved with clearing the house and finding a suitable care home."

"Is that what it has come down to Tim? We're both afraid of being alone as we get older and all we've got left is each other?"

"I can think of worse reasons for being together. But look what I'm offering Anya. Financial security for one, and don't say you don't think that is worth thinking about because I wouldn't believe you. Then there's respectability, a position in society? No don't look at me like that! It is not and can never be unimportant. And don't forget I love you and have loved you for 30 years. No one has loved you more or for longer. Marry me Anya. Please."

Anya looked out of the window as the sun set. She closed her eyes and saw herself standing in a food queue at university and seeing Geoff for the first time, standing under the clock at Charing Cross wondering what his friends would be like and then having fun flirting with them, challenging Kathleen at every turn throughout the years and losing Geoff to her, fighting for her own career and prosperity with and against Peter. She had been told by Miriam, by Vincent and Kenneth and now by Tim that others saw her very differently.

She still wore her unsuitableness as a badge of honour yet it was a very long time since she had been that unsuitable girl. All the years of her marriage to Peter had been in pursuit of money, comfort and respectability. As mother to Geoff's children she had made sure their life was as near as possible that of their father, and other children of his class. She had been absorbed into their privileged world. She valued the private school education, the skiing trips to Switzerland and the Concorde flights to luxury in Barbados. She had become one of them, indistinguishable from Kathleen or Esme, Margaret or Gill or Fiona or even Linda. Money had been her obsession even though she professed to despise people who felt that way.

"Can you drop me off at home, Tim? Give me a day to think things through?"

"Is that a 'no' then?"

"No, it's not a 'no', it's a 'please let me think about it.'"

She looked around her bedroom thinking if only the walls could tell their tales. She had first slept in it with Geoff on the weekend of Tim and Margaret's engagement party. Kathleen had last slept in this room on the night before her husband drowned. It had been Geoff's room throughout his childhood and then again after he had married Fiona. And for the last seven years it had been her own refuge, where she felt close to Geoff and could talk to him of the trials and tribulations of being mother to his children.

Anya sat on the side of her bed thinking about Tim's offer. It was certainly tempting. He knew her better than most people and yet he still professed to love her. He offered comfort, friendship and sex. She knew it was an offer any woman of her age should jump at. Everything he had said about what he had and hadn't done through the years rang true. For once she believed he had not been lying. He had cared about her, he had done what he thought was best most of the time. He had made mistakes. She had made mistakes. They had, perhaps, mistaken sexual attraction for something far more important. Perhaps.

She reached up and undid the clasp of locket she always wore around her neck. She opened it and looked into Geoff's fearless, happy eyes. When she had taken the photograph they had had their whole lives ahead of them. How little they had known. She put the chain back around her neck. Dot's locket would always remind her that she should have high expectations of herself and never accept second best. She held her hands out in front of her and looked at the rings that never left her fingers. There was Geoff's family emerald that she would have to give to Lizzy one day. 'Not yet' she spoke to Geoff as if he were in the room with her, 'not yet'. She wore two wedding rings, hers and Geoff's, together. She looked at her empty right hand where her mother's ring had been for so many years. She had taken it off as Vincent and Kenny had driven away after she had signed away Fishermen Rock. She would sell it, as her mother should have done. She looked down at her hands and clenched her fists.

Whatever she thought of Tim, however much she was tempted, she could not do it. He may have loved her for many years but she did not love him, and never had. She loved Geoff.

It was as simple as that.

She picked up the phone and dialled the number he had given her.

"Tim? Is that you? Tim, I'm touched, a little angry that you have been checking up on me all these years, but really touched, and flattered."

"It's a no then?"

"It's a no." She confirmed.

"May I ask why?" There was something in his voice other than regret.

"There are so many reasons."

"The children? Geoff?" Anya tried to find the right word to describe the tone in his voice.

"No, Tim, not them."

"Something wrong with me then?" Was it upset ego she heard?

"No Tim, you are a fabulous man in many ways. You must re-marry, you need to be married. But not to me."

"Then why?" He did seem to want to know her reasons, but it wasn't curiosity she heard.

"I would be so wrong for you."

"Unsuitable?"

Anya smiled. She realised that subtle tone was relief.

"Highly."

About the Author

Carolyn McCrae is the prize-winning author of *The Iniquities Trilogy*.

She was born in Cheshire in 1950. After a lifetime living and working in the south of England she has recently moved to rural Shropshire where she lives with her huband, Colin, and their ageing black cat.